MW01088538

By

Michaelbrent Collings

Written Insomnia Press
WrittenInsomnia.com
"Stories That Keep You Up All Night"

Sign up for Michaelbrent's Minions
<u>And get FREE books.</u>

Sign up for the no-spam newsletter
(affectionately known as Michaelbrent's Minions)
and **you'll get several books FREE**.
Details are at the end of this book.

DEDICATION

To...

anyone who ever believed they might do something great,
and then realized that belief was great in and of itself,

the genius who invented Diet Dr. Pepper, because that
person has probably saved my life several times over,

and to Laura, FTAAE.

Contents

prelude:
FALLEN

THE LAST FLIGHT OF AN ANGEL

From: POTUS <dpeters@secured.whitehouse.gov>
To: 'X' <xxx@secured.whitehouse.gov>
Sent: Thursday, May 29 3:32 PM
Subject: OUTBREAK

HOW THE HELL DID THIS HAPPEN? HOW AM I BEING PUT IN THE POSITION OF ORDERING A STRIKE ON US CITIZENS?

From: X <xxx@xxx.xxx>
To: Dicky <dpeters@secured.whitehouse.gov>
Sent: Thursday, May 29 3:32 PM
Subject: RE: OUTBREAK

Temper. Sometimes these things happen. Containment is the priority, not your poll numbers. Besides, when it comes out that you acted decisively and saved millions or billions of lives, you'll get reelected again, if not just made dictator-for-life.

From: POTUS <dpeters@secured.whitehouse.gov>
To: 'X' <xxx@secured.whitehouse.gov>
Sent: Thursday, May 29 3:40 PM
Subject: RE: RE: OUTBREAK

Wouldn't THAT be nice.

From: X <xxx@xxx.xxx>
To: Dicky <dpeters@secured.whitehouse.gov>
Sent: Thursday, May 29 3:40 PM
Subject: RE: RE: RE: OUTBREAK

;o)

***

Janice Kane was thirty years and two hips too late for this trip and didn't care in the slightest.

When the other three women she played pinochle with three days a week found out about her plans they went through a strange burst of emotions that Janice found difficult to understand until she realized that she was seeing the five stages of grief.

They laughed at first, thinking she was joking. They wouldn't accept she was serious. They just asked her to bid the next hand.

When they realized she *was* serious–she had actually missed spotting a full family in her hand, and she hadn't done *that* since she lost Frank in the accident–they turned strangely sullen. The rest of the game was almost silent until Sandy started muttering under her breath and then it was like a dam burst. Karen started cursing. That wasn't unusual, since Karen had a mouth that could have passed for a sewage processing center, but Janice had never been the target of the generous and creative curses that now issued.

Only Ethel didn't say anything. She just glared like Janice had run over her little Chihuahua on the road. Not that the thing needed a full-size car to kill it–a leaf tossed by a stiff breeze probably would have broken it in two.

After the anger they started bargaining. Offering her alternate trips, things to do around town that might be just as fun, even *thrown games*, for goodness sake. The last were offensive and simply strengthened Janice's resolve. She had refused to sit in the back of the bus before it was cool, she was hardly going to give up this dream for bragging rights around the coffee machine in the common room.

Seeing her unflagging intention to go, the others grew silent again. Not angry this time, but depressed. Karen switched from cursing to crying. The others sniffled.

This stage was the hardest to resist. But Janice thought about everything she had done. All the training. All the time.

She was a steel rod. Quite literally, in places.

Finally, by the end of the game, the girls accepted. They nodded. They blessed.

And Janice flew.

She had little trouble getting into the plane, but quite a bit getting into her seat. No surprise there: a pair of fused hips kept her from bending at the waist without extreme difficulty. Even in a first-class seat she barely had enough room to maneuver into place.

If I can't get into a damn seat how am I going to climb Kilimanjaro?

She folded her walker, handed it to the waiting flight attendant. He smiled at her and she smiled back. He was good looking, with wavy brown hair. A little chubby, which Janice liked. Frank had been chubby, which he hated, but she liked a man with something to grab onto.

She had trained for three years. Climbing everything she could get to, everything she could afford to train on while still hoarding enough money to make this final trip.

She wasn't insane. She didn't intend to climb all the way up. A woman with hinky hips didn't do that. Or at least she couldn't do that. But she wanted to climb partway. To look at the sun from the side of a sheer wall and know that she had pulled herself up by the strength of her arms like she had pulled herself through life by the strength of her will.

It had been a dream she shared with Frank. A long time ago. The memory had started to fade, and she needed to do this before it wiped itself clean away.

Kilimanjaro rested in Tanzania. Feet buried in earth, head rising above clouds. Just like Janice had always tried to be.

Her seat was luxurious. A single leather-covered chair that reclined to turn into more or less a bed. It had its own television with satellite and all the latest movies available. Janice didn't watch it. She watched the window, the clouds and the land that passed below her. They weren't even out of the United States yet, but she already felt like she was in a foreign land. A place that was strange and wonderful, like she had received a half-day passport to Heaven.

The only thing that kept it from being perfect was the ever-present throb in her hips.

That and the coughing.

Someone had a cold. She didn't know who it was, and was tempted to listen to one of the radio stations–also satellite-based–that would pipe in near-infinite choices of music. But that would mean she would miss out on the sounds of the trip: the near-subliminal whine of the engines, the soft voices of the crew as they offered free drinks (free!) and meals with expensive-sounding French names.

She dealt with the coughing. Into every life a little rain, etc.

She watched the clouds. Looking not for gremlins on the wings but for angels with wings of their own on her short trip through celestial realms.

Something fell. A sharp clatter of dishes that jarred its way into pleasant thoughts, cutting them as surely as the shards of broken glass might cut into flesh.

Then a scream.

Janice had heard screams like that before. She had seen a man beaten to death in front of her once. A pair of men who were afraid because some buildings fell down found another man who looked like the thing they had decided to fear and they killed him. He screamed like that.

The whine of the engines disappeared. The voices that had once been hushed out of respect for the paying customers now rose in wails of fear. The dishes that had already fallen crackled further as feet trod upon them.

Janice heard all this as she turned. Turned because she was terrified. Because she knew something horrible was happening and knew there was nowhere to run from it–not here, not in a steel tube passing through Heaven–and so knowledge would be infinitely preferable to ignorance. Perhaps a matter of survival.

She turned. She heard the sounds.

The screaming continued.

She realized the coughing had stopped.

A man stumbled up from his seat. He was bleeding. Not like he had been punched or kicked or even shot. More like he had somehow exploded. His skin hung in ragged strips from his body, and bone showed through in random places.

Some of the bone looked wrong. The wrong shape, the wrong size. Small spines seemed to have emerged from them.

One of the man's hands was gone. In its place, a blistering globule that seemed almost like a bubble of pus. Like he had rotted from within and now the rot was too great for his skin to contain.

"Whash…whash happening…?" he managed.

Then he slumped. His one hand and the ball of rot that had replaced the other flung forward. Another passenger in the middle aisle hadn't managed to get up. He looked like a businessman, middle-aged with CEO hair and a strong chin. He was pushing himself back as the dead man–

(Is *he dead? He has to be!*)

–fell forward and then managed to roll over the side of the luxury chair. Only his foot remained on the leather as he plummeted into the far aisle, colliding with the legs of one of the female flight attendants.

The dead man's hand touched the businessman's foot.

The businessman, who had looked strong and healthy only a moment before, immediately vomited up so much blood Janice wondered how he could still be alive.

The flight attendant against whom the businessman had fallen did the same a moment later.

More screams.

So much blood.

Janice had been wrong. There *were* worse things than ignorance. This was worse. So much worse.

People were coughing. Gagging. Blood everywhere.

Janice looked away.

She hadn't looked away when Frank died. Hadn't looked away when the doctors told her how bad her hips were going to be for the rest of her life.

Now she looked away.

Back out the window.

Back to the clouds

Back to Heaven.

She tried not to think about the obvious. Couldn't help it.

Disease. Has to be a disease.

And if it's this bad, then we're all dead. All dead before we even land.

As if to answer her thought with a worse one, the plane suddenly tilted wildly. The whine of the engines grew to a fever pitch, a scream that momentarily overshadowed the other screams in the plane.

She wondered what was happening in the locked cockpit. If there were men or women up there who were covered in blood and pus.

She kept looking out the window.

Please save us, Jesus.

The clouds were placid. They did not seem to notice the blood among them.

Then one of them *did* take notice. It moved. Just a puff, then it suddenly tore itself apart. It exploded upward and Janice wondered if this was an answer to her prayer.

Then she saw the cloud hadn't torn itself. It had been torn.

The missile struck the side of the plane and both exploded in a fireball that incinerated everything. Oddly, the only thing bigger than a basketball that made it to earth was a charred walker.

And Janice, in her last instant, chose to focus on the clouds that were once again constant and quiet.

Her hips did not hurt.

She smiled.

one:

AWAKENING

THINGS LOST AND UNREMEMBERED

From: POTUS <dpeters@secured.whitehouse.gov>
To: 'X' <xxx@secured.whitehouse.gov>
Sent: Friday, May 30 9:49 PM
Subject: Operation Falling Stars

Status report, please.

From: X <xxx@xxx.xxx>
To: Dicky <dpeters@secured.whitehouse.gov>
Sent: Friday, May 30 9:49 PM
Subject: RE: Operation Falling Stars

Why ask for things you already know? Your people are doing the best they can. But as you know, the ones they're after aren't the easiest to hunt. Or kill.

You should get some sleep. Running the world demands a well-rested soul.

***

He woke up and knew almost everything. But nothing important. Nothing that made him who he was.

A muffled beep bounced down a hallway and into his room, low but still loud enough to pound into his aching head. It slammed through his skull, then rattled around like a low-caliber bullet shot at long range, pulping his brain and making it hard to think. Still, he knew the sound instantly: a cardiac monitor. A moment later he could tell that it was beeping in time with his pulse.

He hadn't opened his eyes yet. Awake, but still in the dark.

He still didn't open them. Sometimes it was safer to pretend unconsciousness.

He didn't know how he knew that. But it was true. It was something he felt in every part of his body.

He sensed something taped to his right arm. Intravenous tubing, certainly. That and the cardiac monitor meant he was in a hospital. Not a question.

But why? And are the people caring for me friend or foe?

Again, a strange set of questions. Hospitals were not famous for being full of dangerous people. They were places of help and healing.

But again, he felt danger nearby. Like he had some kind of primal sensor embedded in his thoroughly aching head, a detector that was pinging louder and more painfully than the *beep...beep...beep* of the heart monitor.

Time to open his eyes.

He did, and saw nothing but light for a moment. Just a brilliant haze that burned through his eyes, through his brain, felt like it must be setting his body on fire. Tears streamed down his cheeks and he squinted until his eyelids were open to slits so slim that surely only single photons would be allowed through, one particle at a time like entrants to the most exclusive club.

After a while the pain and the bright light faded. He opened his eyes a bit more. Then a bit more.

There was a light directly above his head. Four fluorescent bars someone had left on. No wonder he could barely see. He looked away from the light and everything improved. His neck hurt when he looked away, but even that was an improvement and he wondered what idiot had turned a bright light on above a hospital bed.

Beside him was the cardiac monitor that was sending information to the annoying beep-machine down the hall. He recognized it: a Bionix B80 Multi-Parameter Vital Signs Monitor. A good multi-use monitor designed to be easily ported from room to room in a hospital environment.

Am I a doctor?

He tried to think of something else *doctory*. Drew a blank. And didn't know what that meant, if anything.

He didn't know a lot of things.

But knew a lot of others. He knew that the television playing a muted show in the corner of his room was a thirty-six-inch Sony flat screen. That the show itself had been running for six years and was due to be cancelled after this season. That the shelving unit was not as crappy as it looked, but was instead far crappier, made of particle board with a cheap laminate cover.

But he had no idea about…about….

Not yet. Focus on what you know. Focus on what you can control.

He was in a hospital. Nothing too nice, which meant he was either here because this was the level his insurance provided for or because he had been injured and taken in because of emergency medical treatment laws. He suspected the latter.

He looked down. His midsection was swathed in bandages. Many of them were stained–some the bright orange of Betadine, a pre-surgical scrub used to kill bacteria and microbes–

(*Another thing I know about….*)

–and some the dark black/brown of dried blood. The dark patches were centered in three areas. Two just above his diaphragm, one to the left of his sternum.

Knife wounds, he guessed. Maybe gunshots.

He realized that the guesswork had gone about far enough. Time to call someone.

There was a call button beside his head. He reached for it. Doing so hurt, but the hurt was manageable. Almost familiar, in fact. Like an old friend whose visits were never quite convenient. An old teacher come unexpectedly to call.

He was about to thumb the red button when a thought stopped him.

The mission.

The words crashed against him with the strength of a tsunami. He was glad he was laying down, because if he hadn't been he suspected he would have keeled right over.

The mission. Have to complete the mission.

He was frozen for a long moment. Maybe a few minutes, which was terribly short when you were doing something fun but when you were laying absolutely still in a hospital bed with your mind a blank it was a near-eternity.

What's the mission?

He didn't know. Just like he didn't know how he'd gotten here. Like he didn't know how he'd been hurt.

Like he didn't know his own name.

He moved his thumb away from the red button. Moved the call button back to the bed.

Don't call anyone yet. Get more intel.

He looked around for something that would tell him...anything. Not about his surroundings, but about himself.

13

The hospital bed was a Hill-Tomkin Surge-Assist Full Hospital bed set–another thing he inexplicably knew– and he also knew that this particular model had a sleeve on the foot where charts could be hung. Most hospitals used computers to keep records, but if he'd shown up on their doorstep bleeding–dying–maybe they wouldn't have had a chance to input anything before taking him into surgery. Maybe he'd have a chart.

He sat up. Expecting it to hurt. And right in his expectation. Still, he was able to push through the pain. A bigger problem was the monitors strapped to his neck and the wires that disappeared under his bandages. He didn't want them to pull out–doing so would send flatline signals to the computers at the nurses station down the hall, and he didn't want company just yet.

He looked at the cardiac monitor. Because it was a portable unit it had wheels on the base, and by tugging at it–and maybe popping a stitch or two under his bandages– he was able to yank it far enough along that he could lean the rest of the way to the base of the bed.

Fingers reached over the plastic lip. Blindly questing. And they found a bit of metal that didn't belong. He closed his grip and drew back a clipboard. His chart.

The first page was intake. The notations and letters all made sense to him, and again he wondered if he was a doctor or a medical professional.

No.

He knew that was wrong. He wasn't a doctor. Not a doctor, not an EMT, not a paramedic. Something else.

The first thing he saw was the entry in the name column. At first he thought he would find a clue to his identity, but when he deciphered the Sanskrit-like scrawl of whatever attending doctor had been at the ER he saw it said only "John Doe." The fact that he had no name was a strange depressant. Worse even than waking up grievously wounded in a hospital room. Like he could handle anything as long as he knew who was doing the handling.

He only allowed himself a moment's wallowing, then braced his mental shoulders.

Fine, I'll be John. As good a name as any.

The next letters that arrested his attention stood out large and black: "MULTIPPLE GSW." He wondered who it was that didn't know how to spell "multiple," but more than that was strangely relieved to know he had been shot. Not that he wanted to be shot, but at least he *knew*. That was something.

He scanned the rest of the chart.

Three gunshot wounds. Two above the diaphragm, one more to the left of his chest. Apparently he'd come to the hospital under his own locomotion, dragging himself into the ER before collapsing.

So I'm a fairly tough s.o.b.

He felt oddly proud of that fact.

He looked a bit further into the chart, past the original and hurried intake information. Surgical reports.

The bullets had not been recovered. Through-and-through shots that exited his back through large and ragged holes that required a tremendous amount of work to close. His blood type unknown, he had been supplied with four 500ml units of blood, type O negative.

The first part of that sentence chilled him. Another fun fact his brain supplied: four units of blood–about four pints–was the outside amount a human could lose and still survive.

What happened *to me?*

But the next thing he read not only chilled him, but made him feel like the world was playing a joke.

The bullets had passed through right lung and heart. The two that went through his lung had gone through at an angle that basically pulverized the oblique fissure and inferior lobe. The one that went through his heart cut a neat line through the inferior vena cava and right atrium.

Any one of those should have stopped him in his tracks. There was no way he could have gone anywhere, let alone walk into an ER.

No, don't play it down.

And he couldn't. It wasn't a fact of whether he could walk or not. Any of those wounds was not something that simply "laid a man low." He knew this the same way he knew the small details of his surroundings. He knew it the way he knew he had a mission to perform—even if he didn't know what that mission was.

No, these wounds were deadly. The shot through the heart, particularly. He should have died. Not slowly, either. Not after hours on an operating table. He should have died *instantly*. The heart should have just sputtered to a halt during the short time between upright and flat on his face.

But here he was.

So what was wrong?

Maybe it was Mr. Multipple. Perhaps the same person who had somehow gotten through four years of med school with a critical spelling deficiency had also faked his test results and didn't know one part of the heart from the other.

But no. In the first place, it was unlikely that the doctor who admitted him would have been the one to do the surgery and write up the post-op report. And in the second, anyone *that* incompetent would have killed John on the table.

If I hadn't already been dead, that is.

John couldn't feel his legs. And it had nothing to do with his injuries. Just a cold that was spreading from his extremities to his core. Like the death that had apparently already come for him once was now returning to finish the job.

He was so engaged in his thoughts that he failed to focus on the outside world. Didn't recognize the fact that the muffled sounds of life outside his room grew even more muffled. Almost still.

There are always sounds in a hospital. Not just the beeps and clicks of machines recording and in some cases regulating existence. No, there are laughs and cries, the whispered gossip and angry snips of any other place of business. Water cooler chit-chat exists independent of the water cooler.

The beeps and clicks were still there.

Everything else had quieted.

John noticed it, but only peripherally. The great majority of his mind bent to the task of unbending itself. Of straightening the maze that it had become.

Who am I?

How am I alive?

What is the mission the mission the mission the mission THE MISSION?

So much noise in his mind, a cacophonic counterpoint to the symphonic stop outside his room.

It was only when the door clicked that he jerked out of himself. He looked over, expecting to see a nurse enter.

But his body tensed at the same time. The silence outside the room finally penetrated the wall between John's subconscious and conscious.

He wondered how much more was beyond that wall. Suspected that it was a great deal.

Then he didn't have time to think about that.

The man who stepped in was dressed in jeans and a white t-shirt. He had a brown canvas jacket on, the kind of thing you might see worn by high school students, vacationing professionals, or geriatrics on their way to a bingo tournament.

The effect of the outfit was so nondescript that it sent John into an even higher state of alert. This was the outfit of someone who was trying very hard to fit in.

He wore a baseball cap. Gray, unmarked by team logos or the silly sayings that most people favored. Another sign that he didn't want to be seen or remembered. The bill would hide his face from security cameras, the rest of the bland outfit would hide his memory from any who happened to see him.

John saw him, though. Saw the eyes and knew they were the eyes of someone dangerous. Someone evil. They were so dark brown they were almost black. Even in the permanent shadow of the baseball cap they glittered as though lit from within.

The man took in the room in an instant. His eyes fell on John, and they widened so far John could see white all around the irises. The other man fell back a step, and John realized he was holding a gun.

The gun was a Russian MSS VUL. Just under two pounds, a seven-inch barrel. Not the most accurate gun in the world–only good to about twenty-five meters–and it only carried six rounds at a time. But it had a huge advantage: it was almost completely silent. The gun essentially sealed itself after every shot, preventing noise and smoke from escaping. The only sound it made was the hammer clicking.

It was a gun designed for assassination.

Now the man raised the gun and pointed it at John. The gun shook a bit, just a tremor. Not enough to stop the bullet from finding its mark, but enough to further betray the man's strong emotion.

Fear?

The man's voice quavered as he spoke. Definitely fear. But the gun still held true. Aimed at John's face.

"I don't understand," said the man. "I already killed you."

THE BODY ON THE FLOOR

From: POTUS <dpeters@secured.whitehouse.gov>
To: 'X' <xxx@secured.whitehouse.gov>
Sent: Friday, May 31 12:10 AM
Subject: Operation Falling Stars

I hear we got one.

From: X <xxx@xxx.xxx>
To: Dicky <dpeters@secured.whitehouse.gov>
Sent: Friday, May 31 12:10 AM
Subject: RE: Operation Falling Stars

How is it you heard that before I did?

From: POTUS <dpeters@secured.whitehouse.gov>
To: 'X' <xxx@secured.whitehouse.gov>
Sent: Friday, May 31 12:31 AM
Subject: RE: RE: Operation Falling Stars

They ARE my men, after all.

From: X <xxx@xxx.xxx>
To: Dicky <dpeters@secured.whitehouse.gov>
Sent: Friday, May 31 12:31 AM
Subject: RE: RE: RE: Operation Falling Stars

They need to report to me first unless you want to see this
all go to shit. And you need to answer my emails faster.

***

This is how you become a good nurse: you love your
patients, you put others' well-being above your own, you

work hard, and you get used to low pay and no sleep with a generous side-helping of being looked down on by doctors who work half as much for five times the money.

And yet Serafina Cruz wouldn't have changed it for the world–not even if offered a winning lottery ticket, a vacation home on the Riviera, and a chance to punch Doctor Hershel in the face.

Hershel was the worst of the doctors who made life hell for the nursing staff. He demanded respect, which meant he got as little as they could mete out without getting in trouble for obvious insubordination. He wasn't even a staff doctor, just a private practice guy who came around twice a week to check on his patients in between playing golf at the club and counting his money at the bank.

But those two days he was there, Hershel–aka Hershey The Squirt, a fitting nickname for someone so small, so irritating, and so very like a productive fart in quality and character–seemed to revel not in healing, but in causing as much disruption to everyone's schedules as possible. Especially Serafina's.

She knew why. She was petite, and pretty, and it had only taken The Squirt a week before he decided she'd be just the gal to polish his clubs for a while. Fortunately for her, it had only taken about an hour for her to decide he'd be just the kind of guy to make her life miserable, so she politely declined.

The Squirt had been making her pay ever since. She didn't know how he dug up so many patients with impacted bowels, but every single one was a "special case" that he "only trusted her to handle." Code for "dig out the poop with your bare hands, and think about your dating choices."

She dug, and thought. And considered herself luckier with every cubic foot of crap she got from the patients...and thus avoided from The Squirt.

Just as she considered herself lucky to be a nurse. In spite of all the blood, and tears, and–yes, it had to be said–the gallons of pee and cubic yards of poop, she loved the job. As she had always known she would, since the day she decided to change from looking after herself to looking after others. Since the day her mother died.

Had been murdered.

For a moment Serafina went to a different place. A place where she did not walk on cheap tile that smelled of astringent cleaning solutions with a faint undercurrent of blood and death, but instead on cheaper wood flooring that rotted away like the bodies strewn across it. She did not hear the breathy sighs of men and women clinging tenaciously to life–some doomed to failure–but the breathy sighs of men and women who had already given up and died and simply waited for their bodies to catch up to that fact.

"Onde está a minha filha?"

Serafina stopped walking. Motionless as she had been that day as words spoke through time.

"Onde está a minha filha?"

Where is my daughter?

Then: the struggle. The arms around her.

The blood.

Serafina forced herself to take a step. As though by moving her feet she might step out of the nightmare, step off the filthy flooring of her dream and into the squeaky tile of her reality. Passing from then to now, she went from a place ever cloaked in twilight to one where the lights burned always bright.

That was part of why she loved her work, she was astute enough to know that: the lights never went off in a hospital. They dimmed in a few places, out of respect for the sickest, the closest to death's door. But never did they completely extinguish.

Serafina could not stand the dark.

She kept stepping forward. And eventually she stepped out of the nightmare. Walked her way out of the past, out of the house where she had lost so much in muddled dreams.

"Onde está a minha filha?"

A last call, a final ghostly wail light as a last snowflake after a long winter.

Then she was alone in the hall.

Sound returned. The sighs of sleeping patients, barely heard through half-open doors. A few moaned in their sleep. The gentle beep of a few monitors, the *shhh-shhh-shhh* of oxygen being pumped into tents or directly into lungs too weak to do the job themselves.

Serafina was back to full speed. Walking a urine sample from the lab back up to the ICU. The sample had a STAT sticker on it, so it had to be hustled from the lab back up here, even though she knew perfectly well that the sample had nothing of import to it.

Hershel's doing, of course. In addition to making her deal with crap–literally–The Squirt delighted in making her travel up and down the seven floors between the ICU and the lab. If possible he would insist that she run the stairs, stating the results were "too time-critical to wait on the fickle nature of the elevators–which, when you think of it, are much like a woman in that way, don't you think?"

He was not simply a Squirt. He was a full-fledged jerk. The only thing that kept him from being an out-and-out dickhead was the fact that Serafina knew her mother would not approve of such language. Even mentally.

Sorry, mamãe.

She resisted the urge to cross herself. She went to church, but it made some of the other nurses uncomfortable to see her faith right there in the open. She didn't understand their discomfort, but respected it as best she could by keeping her faith as quiet as possible when she walked among them.

Serafina abruptly became aware that her steps had slowed.

That was unusual. She loved being a nurse, and even when she was doing a stupid job for The Squirt, she *moved*. She got things done. A tribute to her mother–always trying to make her proud of her daughter–and a way of making up for lost time. The only time she slowed down was when memory–*the* memory–occasionally intruded.

That wasn't happening now. Only her normal thoughts accompanied her, so what was wrong?

That's it, Serafina. It's just you and your thoughts.

She looked around and realized that was exactly it.

She was alone.

There were no nurses moving from room to room or gabbing with each other at the nurses station that stood nearby. The few doctors on rotation at this time of night were nowhere to be seen.

The hospital was a busy place. Contained chaos, hustle just barely under control. Especially recently, when so many sick and injured had been admitted it seemed like the whole city needed assistance. The doctors and nurses were all abuzz with it: a record, they all said. Serafina agreed.

So where *were* those gossiping, bitching, chatting, working, infuriating, wonderful members of the staff?

They could all be in patients' rooms at once, she supposed. This *was* the ICU. It was within the realm of possibility that several patients had required assistance at the same time, eating up everyone's attention.

But no. *Someone* would have stayed. *Someone* would be here at the–

Serafina had been moving slowly. Now she froze.

The nurses station was a high desk that ran a complete circle around the inside area of the ICU. There was a gate-like entrance at the back, but other than that it was a featureless expanse of white, broken only by file holders, pens, and a few other typical features of hospitals everywhere.

And this time, something more.

This time: a red handprint.

Blood.

Serafina felt something cold writhe through her stomach. A snake, frozen but somehow still alive and hungry that had long slumbered but was now awake and ready to feed on her courage and the sense of self she had nurtured over the last decade and more.

Blood.

She was no stranger to blood, of course. You couldn't be a nurse–especially not one assigned to the ICU–and not get used to the sight of blood.

But this wasn't blood on a patient. Not blood on a bed or even spurting from gunshot wounds as with the John Doe in room 753. No, this was blood that spoke of violence *now* and *here*. Violence not brought as a shadow of the past, but as a direct presence.

The fingers of the handprint reached forward. Fingers toward her, or at least toward the walkway that led to the patients' rooms beyond. Palm dropping off the back of the desktop. As though....

As though whoever bled had tried to pull herself up.

Serafina realized she had thought of the victim as a "her"–had automatically concluded that the injured person was one of her friends.

No. Not that.

But the handprint was small.

Hanging off the back of the desk.

There were other signs of violence as well, now that she was paying attention: a vertical file holder laying on its side, a cup of pencils spilled, a stapler upside down. Not much, though.

Whatever happened had been violent. Fast.

Serafina had to look. Didn't want to. Had to.

She leaned over the desk. She was short, and even on her tiptoes she could barely see over the stainless steel top of the desk and into the area beyond, the place that everyone jokingly called "the pit."

Still, see she could see enough. Enough and too much.

She saw Nancy first. Laying on her back with a neat hole between her eyes and a tiny dribble of blood that had run over the crest of her eyebrow and pooled in her right eye socket so it looked like she now wore a strange ruby monocle. So rich, so gauche.

Nancy, that doesn't go with your outfit at all!

Her thoughts spun. She turned away from her friend. But couldn't turn away from all of them.

Beside Nancy, half over her legs, lay Cristina. Facedown, but Serafina recognized the young woman from the Dominican Republic. Mostly from her clothing, since the back of her head was a tangled mass of blood and hair and bone and gray stuff.

Her brains. She was so smart, but now her brains are gone.

Doctor Gregson was there. The side of his face was missing. He had never been handsome, even though he smiled and the smile made him strangely beautiful. Now he was ugly in every way, because the side of his head was gone.

Doctor Marcus. She had been pregnant.

That was when Serafina turned away. She felt gorge rising up, felt herself on the verge of vomiting.

Choked it down.

She had seen violence like this before. Had seen–

(*men killing men hunting men willing to murder and men who* did *murder*)

–death like this and knew that whoever did this would kill her as well, if he–or she or they–was still around.

She grabbed the closest phone. It was behind the top of the desk, a cordless model with a range that would let her run to the elevators while she dialed 911 and then security.

She took two steps as she hit the "on" button.

It was dead.

She looked at the phone. The battery bar lit up, but the phone had no signal.

She resisted the urge to look at the phone's base. Knew what she would find: a cut cord.

Whoever had done this had been violent. Fast.

And careful.

Serafina didn't have a cell phone with her. There was nowhere to hold one effectively in her scrub pants. Even if there had been, the use of cells by nurses was viewed as unprofessional or rude, and ICU nurses in particular could not use them, since they might distract at critical moments.

She was cut off. Alone.

She felt her gorge rise again. And with it, her panic.

She turned around. The closest stairs were not by the elevators, but a few feet past the nurses station. She had no idea where the killer might be, but and even less confidence in her ability to deal with him.

She just wanted to get away.

She turned toward the stairs.

And saw the body on the floor.

It was Hershel. And suddenly Serafina knew she would never be able to think of him as The Squirt again. You could not malign the dead like that.

Even at this distance, and with the hall lights at half-power, even with the body stretched out so the feet were the only thing really visible to her, there could be no doubt. Hershel always wore those FiveFinger shoes favored by some runners, the ones that separated each toe into its own separate mini-sheath at the end of the shoe. He told everyone how comfortable they were, how great they were for running (even though Serafina doubted he had ever run in his life). Mostly he told everyone how expensive they were.

Serafina thought they looked ridiculous. Like he was in training to be some weird yuppie ninja.

They also made him easy to spot, splayed out in a pool of blood fifty feet away.

There was no doubt where he had been headed when hit, either: the John Doe. The entry of a strange man, unknown and shot three times, had raised the specter of media attention. Hershel jumped on that kind of thing. Maybe that was what the FiveFinger shoes were for.

Serafina realized she was running now.

But not toward the stairs. She had already passed them.

She was running toward Hershel.

No, not toward Hershel.

Toward John Doe's room.

A stranger showed up at the hospital. A man who had been visited by incredible violence. A man who should have died, by all accounts.

And violence had then come to call upon the hospital. They were connected. They had to be.

So why was she running toward his room?

The answer came with the question. Came almost *before* the question.

To see her friends dead had been horrible. Terrifying. But in a way they had been soldiers. They had been on the front lines of a battle against disease and death. And it was a battle that every nurse and doctor—every good one, at least—knew in their heart that they must lose. Serafina's friends had not just died, they had been killed in action, protecting those they had sworn to save though they knew such an oath could never be kept.

Soldiers died.

But the people in the rooms...they were innocent bystanders. Worse, they were people who came here for *sanctuary*.

Whoever had done this, whoever had killed the hospital staff, could have only one goal.

And Serafina, as the only soldier left, could not let him accomplish it.

This wasn't a conscious decision. If it had been, if she'd let herself think on any rational level, she probably would have turned and run. She knew instinctively where the assassin was. She knew what he was after. She knew she could likely escape if she just ran away from that place.

Her thoughts would require her to run away.

So she pushed thought away. She moved on instinct.

Because sometimes thought, *rationality*, were the enemy of what was right. Sometimes fools rush in where *only* angels tread.

She leaped over Hershel's body. She crossed herself, because no one would mind anymore. And because she would need whatever divine power she could glean from the action.

Words from her childhood came to her. Whispered by her mother when she was sick, when she was afraid.

She needed them now. They came to her in the language of her parents. Her father, dead before she could remember. Her mother, whose death she remembered all too well.

Pai Nosso, que estás no céu....

The Lord's Prayer was so beautiful in Portuguese.

She looked down at Hershel. He always wore a white lab coat. So proud of that. He was a doctor, and he never let anyone forget it. The lab coat was no longer white.

Santificado seja o Teu Nome....

Then over him. She landed in a puddle of blood. Almost slipped and wished madly that she had some FiveFinger shoes–good traction!

Venha o Teu Reino....

She was past him. Room 752 was at her right. Room 753 coming up on her left. John Doe's room.

Seja feita a Tua Vontade....

That was where the prayer stopped in her mind. *Thy Will be done.*

The ultimate in faith. Turning it over to God.

But of course, Serafina also believed that meant you did your part as well. You worked, and worked, and then left what was left to Heaven.

She hoped God planned on her living.

Room 753.

The door was open.

She ran into the room.

There was a man inside. Of course there was. John Doe was in there. He would be for a good long time, based on his wounds.

Only....

Only John was *sitting up.*

Impossible. He can't be.

But he was. He should have been out cold, still deep in a quasi-coma and then incapable of movement for days if not weeks.

But he was sitting up.

And there was another man, too. Dressed in a brown jacket and jeans and a ball cap and standing near the door, so near that Serafina almost bumped into him when she entered and he noticed her immediately of course because you notice when people run into a room while you're trying to kill someone and he definitely *was*.

The man with the jacket swung around and he was holding a gun that looked like the one James Bond used.

"How many goddam people do I have to *kill* today?" snarled the man.

He aimed the gun at her face.

THERE WILL BE OTHERS

From: POTUS <dpeters@secured.whitehouse.gov>
To: 'X' <xxx@secured.whitehouse.gov>
Sent: Saturday, June 1 1:02 AM
Subject: Operation Falling Stars

Conflicting reports.
Did we get him or not?

From: X <xxx@xxx.xxx>
To: Dicky <dpeters@secured.whitehouse.gov>
Sent: Saturday, June 1 1:02 AM
Subject: RE: Operation Falling Stars

Your idiot didn't follow instructions.

From: POTUS <dpeters@secured.whitehouse.gov>
To: 'X' <xxx@secured.whitehouse.gov>
Sent: Saturday, June 1 1:06 AM
Subject: RE: RE: Operation Falling Stars

What do you mean?

From: X <xxx@xxx.xxx>
To: Dicky <dpeters@secured.whitehouse.gov>
Sent: Saturday, June 1, 1:06 AM
Subject: RE: RE: RE: Operation Falling Stars

What part of "SHOOT HIM IN THE FACE" is hard to understand?

From: POTUS <dpeters@secured.whitehouse.gov>
To: 'X' <xxx@secured.whitehouse.gov>
Sent: Saturday, June 1 1:10 AM

Subject: RE: RE: RE: RE: Operation Falling Stars

I know him. He'll go back and finish.

***

When the killer appeared in his room, John experienced two emotions: confusion and despair.

Confusion because he didn't understand what the other man meant by "I already killed you once." John understood instantly that this was probably the man who had shot him, and understood that he was likely someone who did it professionally. He was a hitman, an assassin, a soldier. Someone whose life was death.

John knew this the same way he knew the man's gun inside and out, the same way he knew a hundred ways to break a person's arm.

Still, the killer's confusion didn't seem to come from John's survival. It seemed deeper than that. The man appeared...*unhinged*...on some fundamental level. Almost driven to the edge of madness. And the man's confusion seemed to leap to John like a virus leaping from one sick child at a playground to another.

The despair was a stranger feeling. Surprising. John knew he was going to die. And he felt regret not for the passing of his life, but only for the fact that the mission would go undone.

The mission will fail if I end here.

He still didn't know what the mission was. Only that it was critical. That it had to happen if....

What?

If the world was to survive.

He almost started in his bed. Would have done so if he hadn't been staring at the end of his existence.

The man shook his head. His gun was still twitching, micro-movements that wavered just enough to remind John how badly strung-out the guy was, but not enough to miss.

The man was a professional. He did not miss. And that, no doubt, was the source of his confusion.

As if hearing John's thoughts–and likely to reassure an ego bruised by apparent failure, the man said, "I don't miss. I don't *ever* miss." He shook his head again. Then grinned, his lips pulling back so tightly they almost disappeared against his teeth. "Doesn't matter. Won't happen again."

Someone ran into the room.

Of course the only person it could possibly be was one of the assassin's confederates. And of course it was no one of the sort.

It was a woman. She was petite, almost elfin, with fine dark features and eyes that would have been kind if they weren't ablaze with a mixture of rage and terror. She wore pink pants and a top that was decorated with rainbows and teddy bears and John decided he liked the shirt immensely.

The assassin swung around. The gun went from John to the newcomer. He felt no relief, though, only an increase of fear. He didn't want anyone else getting hurt on his account.

"How many goddam people do I have to *kill* today?" said the gunman.

The woman stopped short, jerking to a halt so fast that her feet almost went out from under her. One of her feet left a dark red smudge on the white tile floor. She had had to run through blood to get here.

She was terrified, but her anger won out for a moment. "Sorry to inconvenience you, *a-hole*," she spat.

The gunman growled. An animal sound that did not belong in a human throat. Appropriate, though, because it was obvious that this man had renounced humanity some time ago.

There was a small vase next to John's bed, with a pair of red daisies leaning out of the top. Nothing special, but he had an instant to wonder who had sent the flowers, to suspect for some reason that it was this very woman who had interrupted the killer's plans, before he grabbed the vase and flung it at his would-be attacker.

The glass vessel flew the ten feet between John and the killer and smashed against the man's head. The gunman pulled the trigger on the PSS at the same time. The gun coughed quietly and a bullet splintered the doorframe only a few inches from the nurse's head. She ducked away but didn't make a sound.

The killer lurched forward but was already retraining the gun on the nurse. Pulling the trigger.

The second bullet hit the other side of the doorframe. No vase this time: John's arm was the thing that knocked his arm out of line. He had flung himself out of his bed the instant after he flung the vase, following it as it flew across the room and hitting the killer only a moment after the glass shattered across the other man's head.

The killer spun around, facing John. The killer head-butted him. John managed to pull to the side fast enough to avoid having his nose shattered. Took the hit on the cheek. It hurt badly and his eyes watered, blinding him.

The killer drove the gun at him. John jammed his arm under the man's wrist as the gun went off once, twice, three times. The bullets sizzled by, passing so close to him that the noise as they split the air was louder than the click of the PSS firing.

The killer was already moving again. John barely made out the motion through the veil his tears had drawn over his vision. He slipped to the side and felt a thumb gouge against his temple.

Nearly blinded.

John stopped reacting.

He stomped down, planting his heel on the killer's foot and trying to crush the small bones and fibular nerve there. The killer grunted: even through his shoes John's hit had been painful.

At the same time John drove his knee into the other man's crotch. The killer swung sideways, prepared for such a move, but John was counting on that.

Fighting was a chess game. One played at a hundred times normal speed. While free-falling through a pitch-black elevator shaft.

As the killer shifted to the side, John drove his foot sideways. The assassin had to twist his leg slightly to move his hips away from John's attack on his groin, and now John's foot found its way into the slight curve inside the other man's knee. He pushed out and down. There was a loud pop.

The killer didn't scream. His eyes widened and he gasped, but even the pain he had to be feeling–a knee that now bent in a direction it had not been designed to go and that would probably never be the same after this–did not steal the fight from his soul.

He tried to use the gun again. Not to shoot John, but as a blunt weapon. He slammed the side of it at John's temple. A blow that could have fractured John's skull.

Most people instinctively jerk away from that kind of attack. John moved *toward* it. The gun bounced off the back of his head–an awkward angle that stole most of its power. It hurt, but the move transformed it from a crippling or even killing blow to an inconvenience.

John's face was next to the killer's. He ripped the other man's ear off with his teeth. Moving so fast that though blood flew in an arcing spray, none of it touched him.

Now the killer *did* scream. The pain gave the other man strength. He swung the gun again.

Again, John managed to be one step ahead in the chess game. Hoping for a quick checkmate, because he was getting tired.

The assassin brought the gun down in an arc. John dropped back, almost falling down. He caught the other man's hand but this time didn't try to stop it from moving. Instead he drove it around. Hoping he could move fast enough to avoid being shot as the gun crossed his body.

He was.

He used the other man's momentum. Drove the gun into the killer's chest.

Got his finger on the other man's trigger finger. Pulled it. Again. Again. Again.

The last pull was a dry click slightly different than the others had been. Empty.

The other man sagged.

John looked at his face. His eyes were open. Unseeing. Or perhaps seeing something that no living person could comprehend. Fires so bright and hot that they blinded and left one glassy and mindless.

John let the man fall.

The nurse was still standing just inside the doorway. Her mouth a perfect "O" of shock, surprise, terror.

"You okay?" he said.

She nodded. The mouth stayed round. He almost laughed. Didn't. He knew the urge was a reaction to the fight, to the death that had almost touched him and that had come to rest instead upon another.

He felt sad about what had just happened. He had had no choice. But still....

"We should...we should call the police," said the woman. Her voice started out tremulous. By the end she was speaking firmly. John glanced at her. She looked solid. Couldn't be more than five-foot-five, but he got the sense that she was strong. Sturdy as a mountain.

He shook his head. "Wait," he said.

She didn't move.

John rifled through the killer's pockets. He didn't touch the gun. It was useless anyway.

In an inside pocket of the man's jacket John found a wallet. He opened it. Looked through its contents.

The nurse spoke. "What's your name?"

"I don't know."

"You don't know?"

He shook his head. Taking out the cards in the wallet one at a time. Looking at them closely.

"How can you not–?" Her voice was trembling.

"What's *your* name?" John couldn't look at her. He needed to attend to what was in his hand. But he didn't

39

want her to get hysterical, either. Not with what was coming.

"Serafina."

"Pretty name. Spanish?"

"Portuguese."

"Well, Serafina, why don't you just call me John. That's what it said on my chart, and it's as good as anything."

"John…how did you do that?"

John glanced at the dead man below him. "I don't know that either."

"No, not the fighting. I mean…." He sensed her gesture at the bed. "You shouldn't be able to get out of the bed. Forget about fighting a murderer, you should still be fighting to *live*."

John shrugged. "I guess I heal fast."

She was silent a moment. He turned over the last card. Shuddered.

She stepped backward. No longer in the room. "I'm finding a phone. The police."

He stood. Moved toward her nearly as fast as he had run to the killer when he threatened Serafina. "You can't," he said. He grabbed her arm.

"Let go of me!" She tried to twist out of his grasp. Couldn't.

"Listen."

"Let *go* of me."

"Then listen."

"Not until you *let go!*"

"Please, listen." He spoke softly, pleadingly. Something in his voice must have convinced her. She stopped fighting. For a moment at least.

"What?" she said.

"We can't go to the cops," he said.

"Why not?"

Because I have a mission, he thought. Because I don't have *time* for that.

Out loud he said, "Because that'll probably get us killed."

Serafina's brow furrowed. "That's crazy."

He nodded. "I know." He jerked his chin behind him, at the killer. "He was a professional. And he's not alone."

"What do you mean?"

"I mean he's got someone helping him. Maybe lots of someones. And they're very powerful."

"What are you saying, that the cops might kill us?"

He shook his head. "I doubt it. But they'd definitely put us in a pair of isolated rooms until they could take our statements. And while they did that another killer would come and blow our brains out."

She laughed. "They don't let just *anyone* in those places, you know. It's not like they have a special go-to-the-front-of-the-line pass for killers…and…."

Her voice drifted away as he held up what he had taken from the killer's wallet. Just the front one, then he fanned them out for her to see them all.

"I assume we're in Los Angeles?" he said.

She nodded. The "O" mouth had returned.

The top card identified the killer as Los Angeles Police Department detective Sean Richards.

The one under that said he was FBI Special Agent Keith Jonas.

The next one: Secret Service.

NSA.

CIA.

"He had an entire bowl of alphabet soup in his wallet," said Serafina. This time John allowed himself to laugh. Just a quick chuckle, then he grew serious.

"They're real, too, near as I can tell. Which means either he's the biggest overachiever in history, or he's got someone who can pull some very serious government strings. Someone who can essentially get him anywhere he needs to be. Like–"

"Like an LAPD interrogation room." Serafina's dark face grew pale. She was, John realized, extremely beautiful, but now the beauty was shaded by terror that manifested in circles under her eyes and a tightness at the corners of her lips.

"Yeah," he said. "Like an interrogation room."

"How do you know all this?"

He shrugged and shook his head at the same time. The closest human beings have to a nonverbal way of expressing complete ignorance. "I don't know. But I knew how to kill that guy. And I knew to look for this," he said, fanning the cards again. "I won't make you go with me. But I'm leaving, and I think you'll be safer with me." He looked at the killer's body. "Because there will be others. There will be more."

Serafina grinned. Some of the color came back to her face and a wicked glitter illuminated her eyes. "You'll need pants."

John realized for the first time that bandages still swathed his chest. He wasn't wearing much else.

He tried to smile through his full-body blush–the blush that was all-too visible to Serafina.

Then the smile faded. "Let's find some fast," he said.

"Because I think we've only got a few minutes before more of them come."

TO JUDGE AND ATONE

From: POTUS <dpeters@secured.whitehouse.gov>
To: 'X' <xxx@secured.whitehouse.gov>
Sent: Friday, May 31 12:51 AM
Subject: Operation Falling Stars

I'm so sorry about the erroneous report. The back-up operatives are already on their way in.

From: X <xxx@xxx.xxx>
To: Dicky <dpeters@secured.whitehouse.gov>
Sent: Friday, May 31 12:51 AM
Subject: RE: Operation Falling Stars

I didn't know you had back-ups. Sigh.

I suppose it doesn't matter. Send them in if that will make you feel any better about the colossal screw-up you've lorded over so far. Not that you waited for my advice on this.

But don't think they're going to have any more luck than the first one did. Your men don't have the capability to deal with this one.

I think I'm going to have to outsource.

***

Not for the first time, Isaiah stared through a scope, centered the crosshairs on his target, and wished that he could simply deliver death and pain. Those were easy.

Messages were so much more difficult.

But he banished the thought as soon as it came. After all, he thought–and he heard his grandmother's voice say the words in his head–if it were easy then everyone would do it.

The sound of his grandmother's voice, even imagined, managed to wring a smile from him. She had been the one person he knew growing up who was, simply and genuinely, *good*.

Every Sunday she made cookies. Occasionally sugar cookies or snickerdoodles, but Gramma Bain's specialty was chocolate chip. The kind of cookies that were so gooey they *required* a handful of paper towels, and woe to anyone who dared eat them while wearing white.

She made them for everyone. All the kids in the neighborhood were free to stop by Sunday evening and have cookies until they ran out. The only thing they had to do in return was stick around for the evening scripture, which was never onerous. Gramma Bain usually read a short one, something from the Beatitudes or a single verse out of Proverbs.

"Just something to keep your souls as sweet as your teeth," she'd laugh.

Then she died, and childhood ended, and the bad times began.

Isaiah missed her. Every day. Sometimes he missed her so much he could *smell* those cookies. Mostly on days when Katherine was doing poorly or when he had to kill someone in a particularly ugly way. Because Gramma Bain had always been so good, and Isaiah knew that no matter how many people he killed, he'd never be as good. Would never see her again.

Because she was in Heaven, and he'd never get there.

The man in the cross-hairs picked up a tortilla chip and swiped it through the salsa on the table. The salsa looked good, even at this distance. Lumpy. Some people whipped the ingredients, turning them into slurry. In Isaiah's opinion, that no longer counted as "salsa." Salsa–*real* salsa–had to be lumpy so you knew you were eating real dip and not just a tomato milkshake.

The man abruptly spit out chip and salsa. He didn't do it elegantly or discretely. Gramma Bain had told Isaiah that if he *must* spit something out he should do it into his napkin, then fold the napkin and put it on his lap. He had never spit out any food at all, because he had never seen his grandmother do it. He wanted to be like her.

The man in the scope just spewed the food everywhere. He looked like he was trying out for a third-rate slapstick comedy. Until, that is, he stopped spitting his food and raised his arm so he could begin beating the woman who sat slightly behind him.

Isaiah had seen this before. He had watched the man do this over and over again during the course of the month. An imagined slight. A beating.

Often the beating would be followed by a rape. That it was his wife receiving what he termed his "lucky love" mattered nothing. It was still rape.

Isaiah would have shaken his head in disgust if he weren't looking through the sight.

But he *was* looking. And he'd seen enough.

He pulled the trigger.

The weapon he had chosen for this mission was an Alias CS5 loaded with .308 supersonic hollow cavity-ammunition. It was a very loud rifle, made louder by bullets that cracked as they broke the speed of sound.

Typically he didn't go for that sort of thing, but in this case it worked well.

The man was named Claude Ferrell. Every night he beat his wife, and raped her more often than not. He did this because he was a dog. He could do it without fear of being seen because he lived in the hills, in a place where the rich placed homes far enough apart that no one had to deal with the inconvenience of human interaction.

It was a place where loud sounds just made echoes and would be impossible to target. No one would even call the police.

Every night Claude beat his wife. Every seventh night he invited friends to play poker. They played together, and they watched Claude beat his wife when he felt like it. That was why Isaiah had chosen this night to move.

He never moved in less than three weeks. He always verified the truth of what was happening, always waited though it meant more pain for the innocent. He would not be duped.

But he had waited extra in this case. Had given Idella Ferrell four extra days of pain and abuse to get to this moment.

Poker night.

So Claude's hand went up.

And Isaiah pulled the trigger.

The boom was deafening, even through his ear protection. It ricocheted off the hills, bounced through his skull. But he didn't let that stop him. He just jumped to his feet and began moving.

The rifle went over Isaiah's shoulder, slung on a harness over his back. He had been laying at the end of

Claude's driveway, only fifty feet away from the window through which he had been looking, so by the time he stowed the rifle he was already at the window.

The glass had shattered. He kicked away what was left and stepped through. Pulling a KA-BAR from the sheath on his hip as he did so.

He could hear the screams. Smell the blood.

Claude hadn't even lowered his arm. The high-caliber bullet had hit the hand he had been about to use on his wife. It mushroomed as it was designed to do, and the man's arm suddenly ended in a ragged stump at the wrist.

Isaiah smiled behind his ski mask as he wondered what it looked like to the other men in the aborted poker game. Business as usual, just a bunch of buddies getting together for a bit of fun. Watching their ringleader knocking the old lady around, the way all of them did–Isaiah had verified that as well–and then....

And then an explosion.

Claude's hand blowing up.

Blood on the wall.

Screaming.

And a hulking form dressed all in black with a dark mask over his face crashes through what's left of the bay window.

Isaiah pulled a Mark XIX Desert Eagle off his other hip with his free hand. He aimed it at the men who hadn't been wounded.

"First one to move will die," he said. His voice came out strange, machinelike. There was a microphone sewn into the lining of his mask that altered his voice and completed the terrifying image he wanted to present. It lay along his throat, a strange analogue to the very different collar he usually wore. "Any man in here twitches I will shoot in the head."

They weren't his job. Only Claude was his job. But if they gave him an excuse, well....

Idella was staring blankly. She hadn't even moved when the explosion occurred. Isaiah hoped it wasn't too late for her. He knelt before her. Leaned in close enough that he hoped she could hear him over her husband's screaming.

He thumbed a switch that turned off the voice-altering hardware. "He'll never do this again," he whispered, words meant to give comfort and so meant only for Idella to hear.

He turned the collar back on and looked back at the other men. "Your tires are all slashed, the phone lines are dead, and there's a cell disruptor in the house. You can't get out in a car, you can't call for help. So sit tight. Anyone leaves and I shoot the rest of you and go hunting." He grinned, knowing they wouldn't see the smile but also knowing they would *sense* it. He lifted the Desert Eagle, knowing how huge the ten-inch barrel was; how much huger it would *seem*. "I'm very good at hunting."

He wasn't lying. About any of it.

He helped Idella to her feet. She moved like a doll, barely responsive.

Please be alive inside, Idella.

He led her down the hall, just out of sight of the front room. Let her sit against the wall.

Went back.

Claude was still screaming, though the screams were growing weaker as the blood pumped out of him. And the other men hadn't left.

Isaiah approached Claude. He grabbed the stump. That wrung a new set of screams out of the other man. "You won't be hitting anyone anymore, Claude." Claude gripped the edge of the poker table with his free hand.

Perfect.

Isaiah slammed the KA-BAR through the other man's remaining hand. Twisted it. More screams, more blood.

"No more hitting at all."

Someone retched. Isaiah didn't bother looking. Didn't bother checking to see if he was safe. These men beat their wives and families. They were cowards. He had nothing to fear from them.

"And I don't like the other things you do to your wife, Claude."

Claude's eyes, hazy with pain, suddenly cleared as Isaiah wrenched the knife out of his target's hand. Claude seemed to know what was coming.

"No, please," he whimpered.

"No fun to be the one saying that, is it?" said Isaiah.

He buried the knife again. Claude's scream was high and clear as a child.

Isaiah let the KA-BAR stay there, pinning Claude to the expensive leather chair he sat on week after week, master of all he surveyed, now king of nothing. He turned to the other men. They were pale, weeping, holding hands in font of eyes. A few of them sobbed so hard their cries devolved into choking coughs.

"He'll die," said Isaiah matter-of-factly. "And you'll watch it. When he's dead, then you can call the police. Tell them everything. Leave nothing out. And remember how it happened. How I knew everything. Remember that I knew

Claude was beating and raping his wife. Just like I know all of you pigs do the same thing." Another grin they couldn't see. He could feel the fires of Hell reaching for him, and didn't care.

"I expect each of you to leave your families. I expect each of you to leave them your money, and buy them the best counseling and never, *never* touch another person again. And if you do...." He yanked the KA-BAR out of Claude's groin. "I'll do much worse than this. Because you should really know better."

He stepped back through the window. Ruminating on how odd it was that the only person in the house who had dry eyes should be the only one who lived in constant fear and pain.

By the time he set foot outside, though, he realized that it wasn't odd at all. It was the way of the world: the innocent suffered silently and the guilty wept in anguish when their sins were shown–but they kept on sinning, and the innocent kept on suffering.

Isaiah hoped Idella's suffering would lessen. Claude was gone. Perhaps she would find some peace without him.

But he knew that was a fool's hope. And not his job. His job was not now–and never had been–to bring hope. Some of the people who hired him *thought* that was his job, but they were mistaken. Hope was beyond his grasp, now and forever. He had none for himself, so how could he bring it to others?

All he could hope to do was provide a measure of the one thing he completely expected to one day receive.

Judgment.

He walked past the line of cars that belonged to Claude's poker buddies. Shiny, late models all. Most of them cleaned not by professionals but by wives and children with purple ridges along arms, with deep bruises on backs, with tremors in their gazes.

Isaiah had meant what he said. The cars were out of commission. And they would not be able to call anyone for a few minutes yet. Not until after Claude was surely dead.

He had also meant what he had said about them leaving their families. He would be watching, and if any of them touched their children, their wives...*anyone*...he would end them.

Judgment. Usually it was a paid job for him. He couldn't afford to freelance. But occasionally he did make exceptions.

His own car was waiting a few feet down the road. An older Nissan he had stolen from a shopping center about fifteen miles away. It belonged to one of the people who restocked shelves at the Walmart there, and with luck he would have it back before anyone noticed it was even missing.

He would walk from the parking lot. Meet the client. Get paid.

The he would go home. Think about getting drunk, though he would not actually do so. He never allowed himself that escape. He did not deserve it. And the last time he *had* permitted himself to do so....

He winced.

He got in the car. He wasn't worried about fiber or hair samples. In the unlikely event police managed to track the car back to the Walmart, he knew the owner of this car also moonlighted as a small-time meth dealer and pimp. Lots of people drove in this car, for lots of reasons, none of them good.

Judgment, though incidental, would also come to him. Isaiah was very careful whom he implicated in his work.

He drove without incident. Obeying all rules of the road. Isaiah was a careful driver. Not only because it wouldn't do to be pulled over in a stolen car with the kind of weaponry he was carrying. He always drove carefully.

Always.

Along the way, at the various stoplights between judgment and payment, he stripped off his mask. Then the holsters and sheaths and straps that bound the various weapons to him–both the ones he had used and the ones he had not had to. They all went in the black duffel he had brought for this purpose.

He breathed easier once they were stowed. Even if stopped for some fluke, few cops would notice the bag, and he was confident of his ability to talk his way out of his lack of registration or insurance for this vehicle.

He was not worried about his outfit, either. Black clothing might arouse suspicion when worn by others, but not in his case. He buttoned his shirt. Added the final touches.

The Walmart parking lot was nearly empty. He got out, dropped the keys he had stolen on the seat. He had been wearing gloves for his entire mission, so no worry about prints.

He walked away.

He threw the duffel with his weapons in a Dumpster that was heavily used and emptied daily–would be emptied in two hours, in fact, so it was highly unlikely that anyone would notice the duffel or investigate its contents before it was taken to a landfill. And if they did, all the weapons were clean - no prints on them or the remaining ammo or the duffel itself. DNA evidence masked by the contents of the Dumpster–which was outside a free medical clinic and so had some old blankets, towels, a few things that, while not biohazardous, were crawling with hairs, skin, and other DNA that would drive even the most dedicated forensics officer to madness.

Then more walking.

Three miles to the final meet.

Three miles to the second part of the job.

Three miles to a small bit of atonement.

No. Never that.

There is no atonement for the damned.

FALLING DOWN

From: POTUS <dpeters@secured.whitehouse.gov>
To: 'X' <xxx@secured.whitehouse.gov>
Sent: Friday, May 31 12:52 AM
Subject: Operation Falling Stars

Just out of curiosity, if the back-ups *don't* succeed…who do you have in mind?

From: X <xxx@xxx.xxx>
To: Dicky <dpeters@secured.whitehouse.gov>
Sent: Friday, May 31 12:52 AM
Subject: RE: Operation Falling Stars

I have several interesting possibilities. People I've been trying to recruit for years. This might be the job that tips them into service.

Win-win, both for the country and for me personally.

As for names, it's probably better you don't know at this point. Plausible deniability and all that.

From: POTUS <dpeters@secured.whitehouse.gov>
To: 'X' <xxx@secured.whitehouse.gov>
Sent: Friday, May 31 12:57 AM
Subject: RE: RE: Operation Falling Stars

Will you at least give me status updates?

From: X <xxx@xxx.xxx>
To: Dicky <dpeters@secured.whitehouse.gov>
Sent: Friday, May 31 12:57 AM
Subject: RE: RE: RE: Operation Falling Stars

Don't whine, Mr. President. It doesn't become you.

***

Serafina was gone only moments. She came back holding jeans and a t-shirt.

"The guy who was wearing these came in with a gang-related knife wound. He's unconscious and handcuffed to his bed. I figured he wouldn't need these."

The t-shirt displayed the name of a popular band whose songs featured despair and a stated desire to travel to Heaven so they could do pleasant things like "rape angel babies."

John, again, wondered how he knew that while still remaining sketchy on his own personal details.

He did know he wasn't a fan of the shirt. Or of the bloodstain on the side of the jeans.

Serafina must have correctly interpreted the expression on his face, because she grimaced as he threw the clothes on. "I know. Not the classiest. But we had to cut your clothes off, and this is better than running around nude."

John nodded. "Thank you," he said. She went to one of the cabinets and took out a pair of shoes, sturdy cross-trainers that John didn't recognize at all but which she handed him and so he knew they must be his.

He was suddenly struck by how well she was taking this, and how quickly and resourcefully she had reacted.

"Thank you," he said again as he put on the shoes. He dragged the killer's body behind his hospital bed. It was still visible, but less so. It might buy them a few seconds if anyone looked in. And that might buy them life.

Seconds would count.

Serafina's gaze flicked to the corpse. Her lips pursed. "You're welcome," she said. "You sure you don't know what's going on?"

The mission.

"I know we have to get out of here." He looked at the bloodstain.

Serafina produced a red bandana. She wrapped it around his thigh. It mostly hid the bloodstain.

"Very tough. Very legit," she said.

"Thanks." He grabbed her hand. It was warm. Alive. "Let's go," he said.

They ran into the empty hall. John saw the dead man and knew what had happened. Saw the small red smear on the desk at the nurses station and didn't have to look into the area behind it to know what lay there. He didn't know the quantity, but the quality of mayhem was certain.

He didn't know how many more would come, but he felt in his bones that come they would.

He also felt...a *pull*. Like he was an iron filing being drawn by a magnet. A consistent tug in a particular direction as unwavering as the pole to a compass needle.

John needed to move. Not simply to escape, but to go. To achieve a goal, and find a thing.

He felt like a prophet or a shaman, driven by some force beyond himself. Something from his past that was striving desperately to pierce the forgetfulness that had drawn itself over his mind.

Move. Follow the mission.

They were at the elevators.

"Where do we go?" said Serafina.

"East," answered John. "We head east." He didn't know why he answered that way, but he knew it was the *only* way to go. The only way to safety, the only way to see this through.

It was the way of the mission.

The elevator seemed to take forever. He could hear the quiet dings coming from inside the shaft as it stopped at each floor. A placard on the side of the doors had the number seven: the floor they were on. Good to know.

John also realized he knew the number of exits nearby. Where the stairwells and fire extinguishers were. Several other items of tactical importance.

Am I a soldier?

He thought he was.

The elevator dinged. Louder this time. Steel panels slid apart, revealing a chamber wide enough to allow a pair of gurneys to slide in side by side.

John couldn't see how the two men inside had managed to squeeze in together. It was comparable to compressing Mount Rushmore into a shot glass, if Mount Rushmore had had only two faces. And those two faces wore Aviators and were carved of something even harder and more emotionless than stone.

He reacted instantly. By the time Thing Two had a chance to widen his eyes in surprise and say, "How did you–?" John had driven the hard ridge of his right hand into Thing One's throat.

It didn't matter how big or sturdy you were. A few places were always soft. Eyes. Groin. The Adam's apple.

Thing One gagged and his hands flew up. He pitched backward, slamming into the rear wall of the elevator.

John followed up with a kick at Thing Two's solar plexus.

Thing Two didn't block. It felt like John had just kicked the Rock of Gibraltar. He bounced back and Thing Two just grinned and reached into his jacket.

John leaped forward. No kick, he drove his entire body weight forward. Leaping at Thing Two, driving both his hands into the other man's arm, pinning it in his jacket. If Thing Two got a weapon into the mix, John was dead.

But Thing Two now had one free arm. John didn't. The huge man punched the side of John's head and everything exploded into a series of sparks and rainbows.

Someone screamed. Not John, not either of the killers.

Something flew past him. Thing Two screamed now. A thud.

The sparks cleared from John's eyes and he saw Serafina slumped against the side of the elevator, her eyes rolling independently of one another. Thing Two's face was bleeding in four long furrows. Serafina must have attacked him, clawed the bigger man's face and gotten knocked to the floor for her troubles.

Wow.

No wilting flower, this girl.

John still had a fight on his hands, but he used Thing Two's distraction to his benefit. He drove his right hand into the bigger man's jacket as well, finding the huge hand grasping the gun, half out of the holster hidden there.

John helped him along. Put his finger over the killer's and yanked.

The explosion was deafening. Thing Two's knees buckled suddenly as a bullet passed down through his hip, probably shattering it. His finger came off the gun and John yanked it out.

One more shot ended Thing Two.

He looked at Thing One, prepared to shoot him as well.

The remaining killer was on hands and knees, still gagging. John waited for him to either get up or collapse.

The man suddenly coughed. Coughed again.

Blood exploded from his mouth. Poured all over the steel diamond tread plate on the floor of the elevator. Another cough. More blood.

Serafina groaned. John glanced at her and saw her spot the blood. She stood hurriedly and moved away.

"What's that?" she said. "What'd you do?"

John shook his head. "I didn't do *that*."

He realized the doors had closed. They were heading down. He should push a button, should decide where to get off. But he couldn't look away from the bloody man at the back of the elevator.

The killer coughed one more time. More blood, and this time it didn't stop. It poured out of his mouth and nose in a fast-flowing river of gore. Thick and red, and then thick with bits of brown.

Then it was a black muck.

Thing One shuddered and fell face down in the pool of effluent.

The elevator dinged as a floor passed them by.

John wondered if more stone-faced men were waiting for them wherever they were headed.

Two dead men in the car, but he only had eyes for one of them.

What happened to him?

NEW BLOOD

From: X <xxx@xxx.xxx>
To: Dicky <dpeters@secured.whitehouse.gov>
Sent: Friday, May 31 1:45 AM
Subject: Operation Falling Stars

You wanted a status report. I've got someone who can fix at least part of our problem.

From: POTUS <dpeters@secured.whitehouse.gov>
To: 'X' <xxx@secured.whitehouse.gov>
Sent: Friday, May 31 1:52 AM
Subject: RE: Operation Falling Stars

I won't ask who. But that was fast.

From: X <xxx@xxx.xxx>
To: Dicky <dpeters@secured.whitehouse.gov>
Sent: Friday, May 31 1:52 AM
Subject: RE: RE: Operation Falling Stars

I've had my eye on him for a while now. And there's a certain irony to this situation that I find rather amusing.

***

In spy movies, a shadowy figure would sit at a bench. He would light a cigarette as a sign to a far-off someone who would give the "all clear" to another someone. The shadow-man's contact would approach and sit down and say something like "The rain is windy in Kiev." A dialogue would then begin.

In real life it was much simpler, much more banal.

Isaiah walked the three miles to the last part of the job. It was an all-night FedEx office in West Hollywood. No one would notice two men who briefly met to chat before one–Isaiah's client–went in to make copies.

Isaiah would walk away. His car–his real car–was parked another mile down the street.

Liam Donaldson drove up exactly when he was supposed to, which was exactly when Isaiah walked up. They met at the third space in the middle row. There was one other car there.

Liam was a short man with a few hairs that clung to his scalp with the tenacity of mountain climbers refusing to let go and fall to final doom. Still, he had a face that was usually open and smiling. Isaiah knew this because he had watched the man and seen the smiles.

He always watched his clients as well as his targets. Part of the service, though none of them realized it.

Liam had three children. He did not beat any of them. Nor did he hit his wife, Bea. They had been married for fifteen years and were as happy as anyone reasonably had a right to be in this fallen world.

Liam liked to golf, though he did not get to play as often as he wanted. He also enjoyed old movies and had a love of video games that made his children believe him to be the coolest dad in the world.

Liam owned a construction management firm that netted approximately thirty-two million dollars of business a year. He was doing very well for himself. That was how he had found Isaiah, and how he could afford him.

Liam was Idella's big brother.

He had noticed the change in his little sister, of course. And one didn't become a rich man in charge of a company that oversaw multi-million dollar construction projects by being stupid. He quickly figured out it was Claude who caused his sister's withdrawal, her transformation from vivacious woman to shell of a human.

He tried to get Idella to do something about it. To press charges, to leave her husband.

She refused.

In the last year, he grew concerned for her life. The police refused to help him. Their hands were tied by her refusal to cooperate and by Claude's good standing in the community and by the law. Justice–as so often was the case–failed to protect the weak or punish the wicked.

Liam found Isaiah.

Now he was waiting with a manila envelope in one hand, a pile of office papers in the other.

Isaiah appreciated that the smaller man neither fidgeted nor looked guilty or apprehensive. He had no qualms about what he had done.

Isaiah nodded. He took the envelope.

"Did he suffer much?" said Liam.

"Extremely."

"Did Idella see?"

"As little as possible. But you're going to get a call on your cell any minute, and you need to be prepared to sound horrified. And to help her for a long time."

"We've had an extra room ready for her for years."

"You may fall under suspicion."

Liam shrugged. "If I go to jail, that's the price. Worth it to save the life of a good woman, wouldn't you agree?" Then he squinted at Isaiah. "Maybe you wouldn't."

That cut Isaiah deeply. He tried not to show it. "Remember: you don't tell anyone about me. Ever."

Liam nodded. He took a few steps toward the FedEx.

Then he stopped and turned back. "It's probably a bad idea to pry into the life of a man like you, but I just can't resist."

Isaiah waited. He knew what was coming. It always did. At least, from the brave ones. And Liam was definitely a brave one. Hopefully that bravery could be found in his sister. It might save her.

Liam took a breath, then said, "So what's with the collar? You really a priest?"

Isaiah didn't touch the white collar that ran around his throat, but he was suddenly acutely aware of it. He always was, but more so when someone noticed or mentioned it. The sole thing he ever wore that wasn't black, whether on a job or off. Even when going to bed, he slept in black shorts and a black t-shirt.

The collar was the only bit of brightness on his person. There would never be anything more.

Liam was waiting for Isaiah's response. "Am I a priest?" It was hard to answer, no matter how many times he heard it. No matter how many times he asked himself. "Some say so. Others don't."

"What do you say?" said Liam.

"I say…probably. I'm just not sure for whom."

Liam nodded as though this made sense to him. Maybe it did. He walked toward the FedEx again.

"Liam?" The other man stopped. "Are you aware of the final ramification of our contract?"

Liam looked confused. "I…."

"You hired me to right a serious wrong. I did it."

"So?"

"So I hope *you* never commit such a wrong."

Isaiah let that sink in. Saw Liam grow a bit pale. Under the yellow lights of the parking lot, he suddenly looked jaundiced.

Then he smiled. "I guess that's fair, eh?"

Isaiah nodded. Liam walked away. Isaiah didn't think he'd have to see the man again. That made him as close to happy as he could be.

He walked out of the parking lot. Slower than he had walked to the FedEx, because he had no timetable now.

The street disappeared as he strolled. He no longer saw the sidewalk, the dark storefronts beside him. The occasional bench built directly into the sidewalk disappeared from his consciousness.

He only saw eyes.

They were blue. One bright and beautiful, the other clouded and sightless. One the source of what remained of his joy. The other the source of his eternal misery.

He wasn't sure which gave him which feeling, though.

He was less than a quarter-mile from his car when he came upon another night-walker. This wasn't unusual for West Hollywood. This was a place that catered to a class of people who enjoyed or even *gloried* in lifestyles so varied that said variation itself was their only categorization. So there were people who worked nine-to-five and went to sleep at decent hours, and others who believed the fun didn't even start until the stars were high in the sky.

The other pedestrian was an older man. Dressed in pink hot pants and a gold shirt that came to his belly button and screamed "IT'S RAINING MEN" across the front, it wasn't hard to figure out that he was a member of one of West Hollywood's most vocal and famous crowds. The city was the first one to have a majority of openly gay councilmembers, and was universally recognized as one of the most gay-friendly cities in the United States.

It was also the second city in the United States to change the term "pet owner" to "pet guardian" in its municipal codes. Isaiah did not mind or notice hot pants and gold shirts on sixty-five-year-olds, but he did think equating a schnauzer to a toddler was a bit silly.

The other man nodded as he passed. Isaiah nodded back, still lost in blue eyes that warmed him with happiness, then burned him with guilt.

He should have been more aware. Then again, he wasn't sure where the gun could have been hidden in those shorts.

The instant the older man passed, he felt the unmistakable poke of a gun barrel in his ribs. "Alley," said the man.

Isaiah complied. Going with an armed man into a dark place resulted in moving deeper into the spider's lair, but he wasn't worried. Privacy would be necessary for what came next.

It seemed it was to be a night of judgments.

They walked a few feet down the alley. The knife kept poking in his ribs. That was stupid. And a mistake that so many people made. What was the point of a ranged weapon if you were going to stand right next to the person, right in range of *their* weapons?

Isaiah stumbled. The obvious move that so many would have taken would be to twist, to try and disarm the would-be mugger with hands or arms. He didn't do that. He fell forward, his arms flailing in a convincing display of awkwardness.

"Get the f–"

The last word cut off. Isaiah's back foot, upraised as he fell forward, kept rising in a sudden kick that caught the older man's gun, knocking it up, and then continued upward and connected with his chin. A devastating blow.

The man slumped. Out.

Isaiah picked up the man's gun. A Sig P238, which explained why he hadn't spotted it. It was a small gun, specially designed for concealed carry, so it had probably been jammed in the back of the old man's shorts.

"Very clever," he muttered. He didn't like that the man had gotten the drop on him. Not because it was a shot to his pride, but because of what would have to come next.

He pointed the small gun at the man who was slumped against the wall.

"Don't."

The voice came from the far end of the alley. Deep and authoritative, the kind of voice that was used to being obeyed.

Isaiah's hand remained in place, gun still an extension of his arm, aimed directly at the unconscious man who had brought him here. But he swiveled his head toward the sound.

"We'd very much appreciate it if you didn't murder Agent Chambers," said the same voice.

Two things penetrated immediately. One was the "Agent" part of the sentence.

Not a mugger. And agents don't dress like that, so this was all a set-up.

The second thing that penetrated was that the man who spoke–a tall, painfully thin man in a dark gray suit– was not alone. He stood in the far end of the alley, aiming what looked like a 9mm Glock at Isaiah, and he was flanked by four others. All cut of similar cloth and bearing similar sidearms.

All a set-up. All to find me.

I'm done.

It was almost a relief.

He only hoped the blue eyes would someday both be bright.

He dropped the gun. The man who had spoken said, "Please come this way."

Isaiah did. He had no intention of fighting. Judgment had come for him at last.

And really, hadn't that always been the point? Hadn't that always been his goal?

He had crossed half the distance to the men when two of them split off and ran to the downed Agent Chambers. They gave him as wide a berth as possible when they passed. Their weapons were holstered. Clearly they knew him, and knew what he could do: they were worried he would incapacitate them, take their guns away, and kill the others.

He might have. He might have.

But did not.

They passed him without incident, and he heard them call for medical assistance. He did not look back.

Isaiah walked toward the other three. Two were typical agent-types. Brown hair, brown eyes, brown suits. Boring.

The tall, thin man was more distinguishable. Not only for his height and near-cadaverous build, but because of something only half-concealed in his eyes. An energy that he tried to hide but that kept slipping through. Isaiah didn't like the look, and didn't like the man.

The tall man put away his gun when Isaiah was about ten feet away. So did the other two men who remained.

Isaiah faltered at this point.

What's going on?

He had been ready to go to jail. To be put away for life or be put to death for the lives he had taken.

But that happened with handcuffs and flashing lights.

Now...neither.

"Come with me, please, sir."

Sir?

The agents turned their backs on him. They began walking.

Isaiah followed them. He didn't necessarily want to, he was simply so stunned that he had no choice but to do so. Dragged along by a riptide of shock, a current of incredulity so powerful that he would not be able to escape until it deposited him where it would.

The men walked him out of one alley and into another. The stores that Isaiah had been strolling in front of all backed up to a wide lane that was not quite a road. Cars could travel it if need be, but mostly it was used for the trash trucks to come through and empty the Dumpsters that the businesses filled like clockwork, twice a week.

A large black Ford SUV waited in the lane.

It was black and insectile, looking more like chitin and carapace than chrome and plastic and steel. The windows–even the front ones–were so darkly tinted that Isaiah could not see inside. Front window tinting of any kind was illegal in California, and he wondered for a moment how the vehicle got away with that without being pulled over every five minutes.

He wondered what the license plate said. Government?

The three agents who had accompanied him took up a semi-formation around the back door, and the tall, thin agent opened it.

A man stepped out.

The only word Isaiah had to describe him was *elegant*. He was tall, but not oddly so. Just enough that you would have to notice him in a crowd. Perhaps six-two.

His features were precise, as though he had not been born but rather designed by someone with an eye for symmetry and a flare for simple grace. A nose that was long and thin, a chin that tapered to a point that was fine without being weak. His hair was dark but graying at the temples, leading to an impression of agelessness–he could have been thirty or sixty. Isaiah genuinely couldn't tell.

His eyes were visible even in the darkness. Bright and glittering. Green and alive.

Isaiah thought those eyes were the most alert he had ever seen.

The man's suit was gray and exquisite. Not the kind you would get off a rack at Macy's or Nordstrom, but the kind of suit you traveled to a different continent to have tailored especially for you. The kind of suit that cost thousands of dollars just to *get* to...and was a bargain at that price. His tie was silk, ruby red. A matching handkerchief, folded to knife creases, stuck out of the breast pocket of his suit.

"Isaiah," said the man, "it's a pleasure to finally meet you."

Isaiah stepped back.

"Don't run," warned the cadaverous man who had brought him here. "We have agents ringing the area for a two block radius."

"Relax, Mr. Melville. Isaiah's not going to run." The elegant man looked at him. "Are you?"

Isaiah shook his head. And he wasn't. He had no intention of running. He had only stepped back because.... Why?

Because you were scared, Isaiah.

That was it. And not scared of death or imprisonment, either. When the elegant man spoke, a thrill of terror suddenly ran through Isaiah. This man, whoever he was, was dangerous. More than that.

Deadly.

Isaiah had met many men and women who were dangerous, and a few who were deadly. He had never feared them, because fear is just the mind's expression of concern that possessions–even abstract ones like love or family–may be lost. For someone like Isaiah, someone with no true possessions to speak of, fear was nearly impossible.

But when the man in this beautiful suit, this *exquisite* man spoke...Isaiah felt fear.

The man was smiling. Waiting as though he knew what Isaiah was thinking and willing to let him continue.

"Who are you?" Isaiah finally said.

The man laughed. A genuine, heartfelt laugh. "I don't think I'll tell you, my friend."

"Why not?"

"Because I'd rather not have you know my identity. After all, you're a dangerous man, Isaiah. And I'm not interested in dangerous men knowing too much about me. Still...." The man pursed his lips. "As we'll be working together very soon, you may call me Mr. Dominic."

Isaiah's blood sped up in his veins. "Working together?"

"Yes. You're going to take a job for me."

Isaiah shook his head. "I don't know—"

Dominic waved a hand. "Spare me, Isaiah. We both know that for the past seven years you have been a highly successful killer. Or do I have to go into the details of Donald Wilfred, Cary Wheeler, Don Begley?" He stopped for a moment. "I could go on. There are several dozen. Do I need to name them all?"

Isaiah shook his head. His blood thundered in his ears, and now he wasn't sure if it was fear or anger pushing his heart to beat like this. "If you know so much, then you know I don't take just any jobs."

"Yes, you're highly discerning." Dominic seemed to consider whether to laugh or not. He settled for a smile. "A persnickety hitman! Who would have thought?" The smile faded. "Still, I think you'll take this job. It's right up your alley. Takes care of good people, gets rid of bad, blah, blah, blah." Dominic shrugged and rolled his eyes dismissively.

Isaiah snorted. "I'd rather not." He held out his arms, wrists together and turned up. "I always knew this day would come. Let's just get it over with."

A shadow seemed to flit across Dominic's face, like a thundercloud inexplicably darkening a summer day. "I'm not accustomed to people refusing me."

"I'm not accustomed to caring about what people are accustomed to."

Dominic stared at him. He licked his lips. "We're not interested in arresting you. That's not the alternative here."

Isaiah realized the three agents had drawn away a bit. And their guns were out again.

He shrugged. "Fine. Get it over with."

Dominic looked confused for a moment, then understanding—or a dark mockery of it—washed over his features. "Oh, I *see*. Goodness, Isaiah, we're not going to shoot you! Heavens, that wouldn't be very cultured of us. Or helpful, for that matter. No, we aren't going to shoot you. Simply persuade you."

Dominic nodded. Someone inside the SUV kicked open the side door.

Before, when Dominic had exited, the vehicle had remained dark. Now the dome light shone and all was illuminated. The light even pushed through the front windows, allowing Isaiah to see the silhouettes of the two men who sat there. Two men who were aiming guns at him, waiting for him to move.

He wasn't interested in the front though.

He was interested in the back. In the man sitting in the back seat. In the person he was holding. A partially slumped form. Long red hair that should have been lustrous and lovely but instead hung lank and listless.

The head was turned toward him. A dark gag wrapped around the mouth. But the eyes were visible.

One bright blue. The other clouded. Joy and despair. Pleasure and pain.

Isaiah started to scream.

IDLE HANDS...

From: POTUS <dpeters@secured.whitehouse.gov>
To: 'X' <xxx@secured.whitehouse.gov>
Sent: Friday, May 31 2:52 AM
Subject: Two down

I've received word that several of the carriers have been terminated. Maybe containment will actually be possible.

Where are we with the one you're currently most concerned about? Is the new asset in play?

From: POTUS <dpeters@secured.whitehouse.gov>
To: 'X' <xxx@secured.whitehouse.gov>
Sent: Friday, May 31 3:03 AM
Subject: Status please

Answer, please. I can't sleep.

From: POTUS <dpeters@secured.whitehouse.gov>
To: 'X' <xxx@secured.whitehouse.gov>
Sent: Friday, May 31 3:18 AM
Subject: ANSWER DAMMIT DO YOU KNOW WHO YOU'RE TALKING TO [end msg]

From: POTUS <dpeters@secured.whitehouse.gov>
To: 'X' <xxx@secured.whitehouse.gov>
Sent: Friday, May 31 3:25 AM
Subject: Sorry

I'm very sorry. I'm tired. And scared. Please forgive me for the last message. I need your help. Contact me when you can.

Please.

***

Serafina's neck had transmuted from flesh and bone to something far stiffer and less helpful. Uneven ball bearings resting in a warped and rusted track.

She lay on the floor of the elevator and tried to look around, but it was hard. Sparks went off behind her eyes. She felt like....

Like she once had. Confused. Dazed.

Lost.

("Onde está a minha filha?")

A pair of blobs swam lazily across her field of view. One slowly came to rest. A mass of dark fabric that she finally saw as what it was: a body. Blood pooling next to it. Holes in the back of its dark suit.

Not his *dark suit.* Its *dark suit.*

The other blob took longer to stabilize. Serafina realized that wasn't because it was madly dancing, but because the ball bearings in her neck had slid off their track. Her head wouldn't stop bobbing around.

I must look like a deranged chicken.

She fought the urge to giggle.

The other blob finally stopped moving. It fell to earth like an angel that had suffered a sudden heart attack and plummeted from Heaven to Hell in a strange damning death.

The other thing was a body as well. Like the first it lay in a pool of blood. But unlike the first it had no visible wounds. And the blood it lay in was concentrated around its head. The blood itself looked strange. Dark and thick.

There was a third person leaning over the second. This one was alive. Familiar.

John Doe.

He saved me.

The memories rushed back into a mind still rattled. Confusion left, not so much as a function of time's healing as it was simply crowded out by a subconscious understanding that she didn't have time for leisurely recovery.

She stood and moved away from the bodies on the floor. As far as she could from the one laying in the weird, thick stuff around its head.

"What's that?" she said, gesturing at that body. "What'd you do?"

John shook his head. "I didn't do *that*."

"What's...?" She suddenly lost her voice. She licked her lips. Tried again. "What's going on?"

John was staring at the second body as well. He looked from it to her. "I don't know." He looked back at the body. The elevator dinged as it passed a floor.

"Where are we going?"

"I don't know."

He lifted the right hand of the dead man he was staring at. "You ever seen anything like this?" he asked.

The hand was covered in....

She shook her head. She had to repress a shudder. "What is that?" she said.

He shook his head as well. "Don't know. That's why I asked you." He smiled. Even tamping down horror and the nausea that she knew was a normal aftereffect of a concussion, she noticed that he had a nice smile. "You're the professional."

He helped her to her feet as the elevator dinged again.

"We have to get out of here. There are probably more of them."

She nodded. The ball bearings were loosening. Maybe if she was a very good girl and prayed extra hard she would actually get the bones in her neck back.

If I have time before someone kills me.

That catapulted her mind to the two dead men.

To the hand of the second man.

She glanced at it. She couldn't help it.

He lay in a muck of his own making. A muck that, like his hand, she had never seen before. But it wasn't as fascinating or fearful as the limb.

His right hand had become something else. The fingers had somehow fused into one single digit. It was covered in a shiny substance that reminded her of a rhinoceros horn. A huge fingernail where four fingers had once been.

The thumb had undergone a similar metamorphosis, becoming a curved claw with no fleshy base. It sprouted, whole and uninterrupted, from the man's palm.

The palm and hand had also changed. They had elongated slightly. Not so much that it would have been obvious unless your eye was already drawn to it because of the change to the fingers. But easily seen when you looked.

More conspicuous was the flesh itself. The skin.

As with the fingers, the skin had been replaced. No longer soft and pink, now there was only…what? Scales?

Yes, that was the best word. But not small scales like you would find on a snake or lizard. These were overlapping plates the size of Serafina's thumbnail. Mottled gray and green, the color of rot.

She looked away.

The elevator dinged again.

The doors opened.

John pushed her behind him.

Under any other circumstances she might have protested. She didn't see herself as some porcelain doll, to be put in a glass case for viewing only, no touching allowed.

Not that she allowed touching, either–at least, not without her permission.

She normally could take care of herself. After what had happened with her on the night her mother died, she had vowed that she would never be helpless again. She had kept that promise in innumerable ways.

But part of taking care of yourself was learning discretion. She had seen how John moved. She was a competent and careful person. *He* was actively dangerous. Standing in front of him would be like having a missile launcher on your keychain and insisting on keeping it in your purse while traveling through gang territory.

Or going to a crack house.

She tried to banish that thought. And, of course, failed. She always did.

The elevator doors were burnished steel. Slightly reflective, so it looked like you were staring at your own ghost if you looked at it long enough. She hoped that wasn't an omen.

The two ghosts disappeared as the doors slid aside.

She tensed, ready for more men who would attack. She heard John take a breath and let it out, a living weapon locked and loaded for the next fight.

No men in dark suits were waiting. Two old women. One had an oxygen tank in a small cart she held with a hand so delicate Serafina could almost see through it. The other was thick and sturdy-looking as a Midwest farm girl. Serafina recognized her as someone she had treated numerous times—a repeat cancer patient—though she couldn't remember her name.

Both women saw the bodies on the floor at once. The delicate one gave a little scream, then clapped a hand over her mouth as though the sound might be considered impolite.

The farm girl just tossed a concerned look at Serafina, then a challenging glare at John. "You save her?" she demanded.

"Yes, ma'am. And she saved me," said John.

"You have plans to hurt her later?"

"No, ma'am."

The fragile woman squeaked again. "Shut up, Mert," said the farm girl. "No chance Serafina's a bad guy." She looked at the dead men. "These the only ones?"

"Probably not," said John.

The farm girl moved out of the way, and maneuvered the fragile woman to the side as well. "You better get a move on then."

John nodded his thanks. Drew Serafina with him as he exited the elevator.

Farm girl grabbed her arm. "You trust him?" she said in a stage whisper.

Serafina looked at John. She didn't know him. He had saved her, and it was certain the men he had saved her from were violent and seemed to be up to no good. But that didn't mean *he* was on the up-and-up.

Still, he felt right.

She shrugged. "Time will tell."

The farm girl mulled that over for a split-second. "Good enough, I guess," she said. Then drew the fragile girl a bit farther away from John and Serafina. "Come on, Mert. Let's head to the staff kitchen. They keep all the good Jell-O there."

John pulled Serafina away.

Mert kept her hand over her mouth.

Farm girl winked at Serafina as they left. That made Serafina feel better.

She turned forward. John was pulling her along at a hurried but not ridiculous pace. The kind of motion that would not draw attention in most places. But here....

"You better let go of me."

"We have to move."

"I know. But people are going to wonder what a strange guy is doing hauling a nurse around. Plus unless you were listening while they carted you around in a coma I know my way around better than you do."

He glanced back. Smiled sheepishly, then let go of her. "Where to?"

"My car's–"

"No." He cut her off sharply. "They'll be on the lookout for your car soon, if they aren't already."

"Who *is* they?"

"Beats me. Don't want to find out, either."

"Okay, then how do we get away from them if we don't know who they even are?"

John snorted. "Makes for a tough game, huh." He looked around. "We shouldn't go out the front. Is there a fire escape?"

"No, but the stairs at each corner of the wards have fire doors that lead outside to the different roof levels, and the roofs have stairs leading to ground level."

John was quiet a moment. "We're on the second floor, right?" She didn't answer, sensing he wasn't really asking, just working over logistics in his mind. He looked at her. "Where's the ER?"

"Right under us."

"Good. Can you take us to the roof exit closest to the ER?"

"There's actually one that exits on the ground near the ER."

He shook his head. "They'll be watching ground exits."

"He do you even *know* that?" she demanded. Frustration welled up within her; terror not only of a hunted creature but of prey who did not understand its predator.

"Because it's what I would do." He looked almost surprised at that statement.

And that reminded her of something.

"Come here," she said. This time it was her turn to grab *him*.

"Where are we–?"

"Shut up."

She wasn't mad, and he smiled a bit, as though he knew she wasn't.

Not mad, but she had to know.

She looked into the rooms as they passed until they found one that was empty. She dragged John into it. Closed the door.

The room was an exam room. She gestured for him to hop up on the exam table. She didn't bother covering it with the tissue paper that was meant to provide a measure of sanitation. Infection was the least of their problems today.

"Take off your shirt," she said.

"We don't have time."

"We're making time. And I'm not telling you where to go until we do this."

"Do *what*?"

She crossed her arms. "Take off your shirt."

He pursed his lips. "You're scary when you're mad."

"You haven't *seen* me mad, buster."

He smiled. Took off his shirt. While he did she looked through the drawers built into the wall unit near the door. Found a pair of bandage scissors, some gauze rolls, some tape.

"What's that for?" John said when she turned around.

"We need to change your bandages before we do any more running."

It was a lie.

She had to know.

The bandages sheathed him from stomach to armpits. Stained red in several spots.

The blades of the scissors were bent at about a thirty degree angle, with a blunted edge so as to avoid the danger of cutting skin. They slipped easily between bandages and flesh at John's right clavicle. She cut down, making quick work of the gauze that encircled him.

She pulled it away, unveiling his wounds.

She gasped.

PACKET FULL OF POSIES

From: POTUS <dpeters@secured.whitehouse.gov>
To: 'X' <xxx@secured.whitehouse.gov>
Sent: Friday, May 31 2:59 AM
Subject: WTF

ONE CARRIER'S BODY STOLEN. WHAT OTHER ASSETS IN PLAY THAT YOU'RE NOT TELLING ME ABOUT?

From: X <xxx@xxx.xxx>
To: Dicky <dpeters@secured.whitehouse.gov>
Sent: Friday, May 31 2:59 AM
Subject: RE: [redacted]

This is an automatic message: I am away from my office right now, and busy with work that is more important than you are.

If this is Dicky, please take a moment and breathe. Remember who you are and what you stand for.

And get some sleep.

***

Isaiah stopped screaming. Dragged himself away from the sea of terror that threatened to drown him. A sea that was half crystal blue, half murky and dark. A sea that represented his great failure and his only chance at purpose.

Not redemption, never that. Just purpose. That was all he had left, and the best he could hope for.

He stepped forward, and sensed the guns of the three men outside the car inching forward.

If they had been pointed at him, that wouldn't have stopped his motion. He would have taken his chances. He would have attacked.

But they weren't pointed at him. They were pointed inside the black SUV. Into the open back door.

And there were guns in the SUV, too. Pointed at the same place. An agent in the back seat who held onto her, and dug a gun into the hollow point between neck and chin. The gun was a mirror of the Desert Eagle Isaiah had used earlier this evening.

A single pull of that trigger, and Katherine's head would be splashed all over the inside of the SUV.

What's left of her head.

Even in his terror, his guilt intruded.

Isaiah stopped moving. His hands wanted to rise, to go over his head in the universal gesture of surrender. He willed them to remain at his sides. Channeled terror and despair into rage.

"I'm going to kill you. All of you," he said. He looked at Katherine. "You okay, honey?"

She didn't answer. Of course. She was gagged.

But even if she hadn't been gagged, she wouldn't have spoken. She hadn't spoken for seven years.

She was beautiful. Even though her one eye was clouded and sightless, even though her muscles were weak and atrophied from seven years in which they had seen little use. Even though her lovely red hair had grown brittle over the long period of her disability.

Even with the one side of her skull deeply cratered, giving her head the appearance of a lopsided ball.

"Get the gag off her," demanded Isaiah.

Dominic shook his head. "I'm terribly sorry, but we really can't," said the elegant man. He adjusted a pair of cufflinks. In just about anyone else Isaiah would have suspected the gold to be fake, the huge rocks at their center to be cubic zirconia. Not these. They were real. Whoever this man was, he had the treasures of the world at his disposal. Beyond rich. Beyond powerful. "What if she screams?"

"She won't. She doesn't have control of her salivation. Shut her mouth like that and she could drown," said Isaiah.

"That would be tragic indeed," said Dominic. "Please pay attention." Isaiah didn't look away from Katherine. She was looking in his direction, but her eyes did not focus on his.

They never had. Not in the seven years. He suspected they never would.

"LOOK AT ME!"

The scream was so unexpected it jerked Isaiah's attention to Dominic without his volition. There was no choice involved–he was commanded, he obeyed.

Dominic grinned. "If she could die, then I suggest you listen. Because the gag doesn't come off until we are done in this place."

Isaiah's mouth curled into a snarl. "What do you want?"

"I want you to kill a man."

"No."

"You'll want this job."

"No, I won't."

"Yes. You will." Dominic gestured down the lane. There was nothing there but a black sedan. "That's your car now," he said. "It's registered to you, insured to you. Don't worry about tickets or accidents, though. You drive as fast as you need, anywhere you need. No officer of law enforcement will pull you over for any reason."

"How can you–?"

"There is a phone on the seat. Hold down the number one key and it will connect you to my people. They will provide you with anything–*anything*–you need to complete this mission." Dominic smiled. "Ask and ye shall receive, eh, Father?"

"I'm not–"

Dominic cut him off again. Apparently the man only had time for himself. "Under the phone is an envelope and a match. The envelope carries the particulars of your mission. Read it and then burn it and its contents. Do you understand?"

Isaiah nodded. He would do everything these men asked. Except the job. He was going to find them. Find Katherine. And then kill every single person involved in this nightmare.

Dominic last. And longest.

"I know you are thinking of vengeance," said Dominic. Isaiah almost started. Then reminded himself that such a thought would be fairly obvious. The man wasn't a mind reader, just following the natural logic of the moment. "Know this: the same resources we are providing you will be given to hiding Katherine. The moment I sense–the moment I even *believe*–you have abandoned the mission, I will issue orders to have her hands and feet cut off, her tongue and eyes burned out of her head, and then she will be raped to death. Do you understand?"

Isaiah couldn't answer for a moment. The threat had been delivered so matter-of-factly it almost didn't compute.

"She's...she's *fourteen*, for God's sake."

Dominic grinned. "My men have access to all sorts of deviants. Some of them *are* deviants." He let that sink in, and from the look in his eyes Isaiah suspected the one of the deviants was Dominic himself. "Do you understand?"

Isaiah nodded. He couldn't speak. His tongue felt like a block of petrified wood.

Dominic squinted. "I don't know if you believe me. If you believe I will do what I have said I will do."

"I believe you."

The squint didn't leave Dominic's face. "Well, suppose you don't. Suppose you decide alternative arrangements are in order. What then?" Isaiah didn't respond. It didn't seem like the other man was talking to him at this point.

Dominic shook his head. "No, I think we need to prove our seriousness to you. Our dedication to this mission, and the importance we attach to your attainment of the assignments we provide."

The elegant man nodded. At the motion the thin agent stepped forward and Isaiah couldn't stop a sharp yell from escaping. He clamped his mouth shut when the agent in the car, the one with the gun on Katherine, shoved it harder into the base of her jaw and the girl moaned under her gag.

Isaiah also realized that the thin agent wasn't moving toward the side of the SUV. Not toward Katherine. Thank God, not toward Katherine at all.

Instead, he moved to the trunk hatch of the vehicle. He popped it open and moved behind it, out of sight. The

SUV rocked a bit, then the agent came back, dragging something.

Isaiah gaped.

It was Idella Ferrell. The woman he had just gone through so much to save.

She was dead. Nude. Her body covered in cuts and bruises and stab wounds. And more. Worse. There was little doubt why she was nude, or that what her husband had done to her once upon a time paled in comparison to the manner of her death at the hands of these men. Probably the same man who had pulled her from the SUV, judging by his smile–as thin as the rest of him, twice as cold.

"Why...?" He couldn't even finish the thought. His mind blanked.

The thin agent returned to the trunk and dragged a new package to them. This one not dead. This one kicking spastically. Thrashing. And all the more awful for that fact.

"Nicholas?"

The old man was bound, trussed with so much rope he looked almost cartoonish. His white collar–the mirror of Isaiah's own, only it always seemed so much whiter, so much more earnest–was visible among the rough-woven loops that held him.

"Nicholas?" Isaiah said again.

The old man looked up. Tape wrapped around his face. Over his mouth, around the back of his head.

His eyes smiled. They always smiled.

The thin agent shot Nicholas in the back of the head. The bullet exploded through the front of his face. The old eyes no longer smiled.

The agent's too-thin face crinkled as he grinned.

Isaiah did not scream. It happened so fast that the scream was stolen by the violence, the surprise.

The disbelief.

Nicholas?

The priest wasn't dead. He *couldn't* be dead, so he *wasn't* dead. He would live forever. He had saved countless souls–had almost saved Isaiah's.

But his eyes no longer smiled.

The thin man dragged the body away. The trunk slammed. Another agent mopped up the blood and brain with a towel and Isaiah knew they had planned this before they caught him; that it was an inevitability. Whether he had presented himself as groveling or defiant, Idella would have been shown to him, both she and Nicholas would have died.

Because of me. I tried to save Idella and failed. Nicholas tried to save me *and he died instead.*

Isaiah dragged his eyes away from the spot where his near-savior and only remaining friend had died.

Dominic was smiling at him. Smiling an ample, sincere grin of simple joy.

"I hope we understand each other," he said.

Isaiah nodded. There was no more to be done.

Though no one made any movements or signals that Isaiah could see, another black SUV suddenly pulled into the lane and stopped behind the first one.

Dominic got back in the first vehicle. Sitting beside Katherine.

The tall agent who had led Isaiah here began to close the door. Dominic gestured for him to stop. He looked at Isaiah with a very serious expression.

"Isaiah, I know what you do. I know *why* you do it. And you have to believe me about two things: one is that I don't want to do this to Katherine. But I need you very focused on your assignment. The second thing is that the reason I need you focused is because the future of the entire world will depend on how well you do this job." He paused a moment, then continued, "You have been righting wrongs for years. This is the ultimate chance to do that."

The door closed. A moment later the remaining three agents piled into the other SUV and both vehicles pulled away and were gone in an instant.

Isaiah stared into nothing for a long time. The lane was dark, illuminated by spots of brightness where the occasional store had a light in the rear of their business. Bright and dark. Like night and day. Like the world itself.

Like the eyes of a little girl.

Something flashed.

The headlights of the car. His car.

It pulled him out of his stasis, the near-coma induced by the sight of Katherine and the threats Dominic had brought against her.

He turned to the car. Someone must be in it.

Someone could give him answers. Maybe an immediate lead on Dominic.

But when he threw open the door, there was no one inside.

The lights must have been activated remotely. Urging him to get a move on.

Which meant he wasn't alone. Dominic had people watching.

How long before he decided Isaiah wasn't going to help?

How long before he made good on his threat?

That he would was not in doubt. Isaiah had seen a good many vicious and ruthless men in his life, both before he began killing for pay and then after. He knew the look of a man willing to destroy another, willing to see a human soul crushed underfoot.

Dominic was such a man.

Isaiah glanced around the lane. Scanned the tops of the businesses, looking for someone with a sniper scope, someone watching.

No one. No one he could see, at least.

But he had to move.

He got in the car.

The interior was luxurious. The seats and other surfaces were hand-tailored leather. Trim looked like handcrafted wood with aluminum accents.

The engine was already on, but he barely heard it. The interior glowed gently, illuminated by hundreds of purple LED lights around the dash and center console and by the red dash display.

There was a huge display in the center of the dash: a system that carried GPS, Bluetooth connectivity, and a WiFi hotspot. Everything he could possibly need to stay connected on the move.

The phone and packet were on the passenger seat, just as Dominic had promised.

He opened the packet.

Inside were two pictures. One was of a woman. Information on the back. She was a nurse named Serafina Cruz. Not the primary target, though she was aiding him.

The other picture was an illustration. Hand-drawn in exquisite detail, but Isaiah wondered why the man had no photographs available. The name given was only "John," no last name.

Behind the illustration was a single stapled sheet.

Isaiah read. As he did he grew shaky.

There was a moment where he thought it wasn't true. That it *couldn't* be true. Things like this just didn't happen.

But what if it *was* happening?

The guys who grabbed me were government.

That was true. There was no other group that had the kind of resources and professionalism these guys had. Isaiah had made enemies over the years, but always anonymously. And even if any of his victims had been survived by vengeance-minded friends or family–doubtful, given their character and temperament–those types were likely to kill or torture. Not give him a job to find a person whose only picture consisted of a skilled pencil drawing.

So government.

And they wouldn't just do this to jerk him around.

So it was true.

Unless they are *jerking you around.*

Okay, yes, it was possible. But why?

No, the idea that this was just a big joke or a setup was unlikely. Isaiah was very good at his job. Maybe the best. He knew that. So it made sense that someone who needed the best would reach out to him.

And if what was in the packet was true, then the best was definitely needed.

He reached into the packet. One more item.

He pulled out the match. Leaned out of the car and struck it against the pavement. A moment later the photo, the illustration, the information pages, and the envelope itself were ash beside the car.

The paper flared brightly and disappeared. The words written on it flared brightly in Isaiah's mind, but they remained. Particularly key ones about the threat John represented.

...highly contagious...

...rogue asset...

...mortality rate exceeding 98%...

...adaptable, transformative...

...determination to destroy...

Isaiah was a killer.

And he was hunting a weapon.

FOUND OUT AND DISCOVERED

From: X <xxx@xxx.xxx>
To: Dicky <dpeters@secured.whitehouse.gov>
Sent: Friday, May 31 3:07 AM
Subject: New player on the field

Don't worry about answering this; I know you're asleep and no doubt very cute all curled up with your blankie in one arm and Patricia in the other (does the missus know about you and the Press Secretary?).

Nevertheless, be strong and take heart: I managed to acquire the asset I spoke of earlier. He is a true professional of outstanding achievement and I have no doubt that he will bring to pass outstanding results.

Sleep tight. Remember that Viagra and nitrates don't mix.

***

John didn't look down. He was too struck by Serafina's face, by her reaction to whatever she saw when she removed his bandages.

The bandages themselves pulled away with a vague tearing sensation that was not entirely unpleasant. A slight ripping accompanied it, the sound of fabric cleaving from fabric and dried blood cleaving from flesh.

"What?" he said. "What is it?"

Serafina didn't answer. She just said, "I wondered. I wondered how you could be fighting like that, running like that. How you could…," and then fell silent.

John looked down. He didn't see anything wrong. And with that, he understood what had terrified the nurse.

He looked up to see she now was peering at him. "You were shot," she said. "I changed the bandages myself. You almost died. You *should* have died."

He nodded. "Yeah," he answered. His throat was dry.

"So where are they? Where are the wounds?"

They looked down together.

His skin was unbroken. There were three scars over his chest and ribs. But they were gnarled and faded, nearly the same color as the surrounding skin. The color of scars long-healed, of wounds all but forgotten to time.

John lifted a trembling finger and touched one of them. The one on his chest. It was shaped like a brittle sea star, a creature closely related to a starfish that had a round central body and long arms it used to crawl across the sea floor.

Another random fact I seem to know. I'd kill at Jeopardy.

The legs of the sea star curled in on themselves as though the scar pre-dated the bullet, and the gunshot wound had caused it to pull in its legs in a final death throe.

Serafina reached out a hand and touched the spot as well. Their fingers came together for a moment and John felt as though the air had grown electric, like the ozone snap before a lightning storm. He didn't look up, acutely aware how beautiful Serafina was, how capable and strong, worried that the nurse might be looking back at him, just as worried she might not.

"What are you?" she said.

The question stung. "I'm just a man," he said.

She shook her head. "Men don't heal like this."

"Okay, so I'm a man-plus. Like you see on a Wheaties box. Or one of those sports drinks commercials."

She shook her head again. Pulled her hand away. John felt the loss acutely. But it brought him back to reality. He pulled his shirt back over his head.

"We should go," he said.

It was true, but he sensed he was fleeing this room as much as the possibility of further pursuit.

"What are you?"

He didn't like the question. Didn't like the implication that he might be something other than human.

He was a man. He bled, he had almost died.

But he also remembered the chart. The fact that the bullets had shattered his lung, had pulverized his heart. Mortal wounds survived.

And now healed.

He could not deny that there was something strange going on. But did that make him not a man?

No. He felt like a man. His heart pumped. His body was warm.

He had felt something when Serafina touched him; when their fingers came together.

That more than anything reassured him. Surely something not a man would fail to feel that.

He got off the table. He almost took Serafina's arm to lead her away as he had before. Stopped himself. She was looking at him with confusion, maybe fear. What if she shrank away from him?

He was surprised how much that mattered. How much even the possibility of that hurt.

He had no past. Nothing before the moment he woke up wounded–but strangely not–in a hospital bed. So how could he care about the future?

About *her*?

About the mission.

"Come on," he said. It was a request, not a command.

She nodded. They left the room. She led the way down the hall. Turned left, then through some double doors.

Serafina had been right not to let him hold her arm. She nodded to five different people on their short walk. Two nurses, one doctor, and a pair of patients all out for late-night walkabouts. They all waved and called to Serafina by name: apparently she was well-liked. John wasn't surprised.

The nurses and doctors said hello but did not stop what they were doing. They were all busy, all walking as fast as or faster than John and Serafina. Indeed, after the doctor waved to Serafina he got a page and after looking down he broke into a run and was gone. He bumped into a pair of people in his hurry, almost knocking them down. The pair appeared to be late-night visitors, though both wore hospital masks as though to protect others–or themselves–from contagious disease. One started screaming about lawsuits.

The doctor didn't seem to care. He kept running.

The hospital was a busy place, all around.

John wondered how long it would be before the bodies were discovered in the elevator. Even in the middle of the night it would have to be soon, and the higher-than-average levels of activity around here would shorten their window of safety. He increased his pace a bit.

At the next turn there was a door with a red sign indicating stairs with an emergency exit. Serafina took them in and led them to the right, up the stairs.

An echoing scream, like that of a ghost that has just discovered the reality of its forever-doom, wafted down to them.

John shared a look with Serafina. Someone had discovered the bodies.

They abandoned stealth and ran.

There were only a dozen or so stairs, then a landing, then another dozen. Even so, John felt the hairs on his neck prickle and begin to stand. Any confederates of the assassins would be alerted by now. They would have a general area to work with; would know where to concentrate.

He felt a noose tightening around them. One not merely of rope, but of barbed wire, vicious hooks that would gouge their way into flesh and never let go.

The next landing led to the third floor. Two doors: one to the hall, one that said EMERGENCY USE ONLY in thick red block letters.

Serafina looked at him. "This is going to set off alarms all over the hospital," she said.

"I think that ship has sailed."

She nodded, smiled a quick smile that lit up her face, then slammed into the crash bar on the door.

A pealing alarm shrieked out at them, but got quieter the instant they went through the door.

John realized he had failed to pick up any of the guns the men in the elevator might have held. They were still weaponless.

Careless.

I'd been out of a coma for all of ten minutes.

Still careless.

No help for it now.

The roof was ugly, industrial. Gravel crunched underfoot and hulking air conditioning units buzzed and hummed every few feet, a couple electrical boxes interspersed here and there. Pipes and conduit ran between all of them at shin height, converting the area to an obstacle course.

"That way," said Serafina, pointing to the right.

She was off before he could move, a colorful blur in the night. She hopped over the white-painted tubes that gridded the roof as though she had practiced for just this eventuality, and John admired how fleet she was.

The exterior stairwell was marked by a square sheet of steel that hung over the side of the roof. It was partially enclosed by a white railing at waist-height, and three steps led to it from the roof. Other steps disappeared down the side of the building, presumably emptying out near the parking lot area beside the ER.

That was excellent news.

John took the lead now. Serafina seemed to sense that he was in his element, falling back to let him go first.

The stairs clung to the side of the hospital wing, an easy incline with wide stairs that would be simple to navigate. Clearly whoever designed them had a real concern for the ability of sick people and those barely operating under their own strength to get out and get down.

John was operating under his own strength. A strength not only beyond what it should be but growing greater by the moment. He felt energized. Alive.

The stairs emptied about ten feet from the corner of the building. Just a quick run and a turn and they'd be in front of the building. John assumed the emergency room entrance would be nearby, and the obligatory parking lot in front of that.

They were almost down the stairs when a man rounded the corner of the building. The same dark suit. The same no-nonsense movement.

Another one.

He spotted them only a fraction of a moment after John spotted him. He had a gun in his hands. Raising it fast.

Not fast enough.

John threw himself down the stairs so fast the last treads were a blur under his feet. He grabbed the rails on either side at the last second, halting the inertia of his upper body just enough that his legs swung out from under him. Legs snapped forward with the kinetic energy of all his weight. One hundred eight-three pounds of muscle.

He knew that was his weight. Exactly.

His heels caught the man in the center of the face. A sharp crack, a duller crunch. The man crumpled.

His gun flew into the grass to the right. Another weapon lost, and John knew they didn't have time to look for it.

He spared a glance back. Serafina was still barreling down after him. She hadn't stopped running. Apparently she had either decided she had nothing to lose by continuing, or she had trusted that he would handle the gunman.

John turned forward and ran as well. He jumped over the gunman. The man was dead. John did not mind that. Not only had the man tried to kill him, but he thought it likely that he was….

Bad.

Yes, that was it.

He had to be *bad.*

Because John himself was *good.* And only bad men would try to kill a good one.

Only…only how did he know? He had no memory of himself.

What if *they* were good? What if *he* was the killer, and they only police or other men trying to stop him from whatever nefarious goal he had to reach?

No.

He couldn't accept that. He couldn't accept a view of himself as an evil person.

Besides. It gets in the way of what you have to do.

He tossed that thought aside for now. No time for it. Or he didn't want to think about it. Same thing, really.

No, it's not. And you know it.

They ran to the parking lot. John took Serafina to the third row of cars and hunched down so he was out of sight of the front entrance of the ER, which seemed busy for this time of night.

"What now?" whispered Serafina. The words came between gasps.

"We steal a car."

"You know how to hotwire one?"

John did. "Hopefully we won't need to. Most people at the ER are worried about whoever's sick. Not automobile security."

Serafina nodded and immediately grabbed the handle of the closest car door and pulled it. John let her, but stopped her before the next one. "We want an older model car, mid-eighties or before, not a classic, kind of dumpy. Either that or a BMW that's around five years old with a window cracked."

Serafina looked confused, but she nodded. Both of them peeked over the roof of the car they were hiding behind, looking around the lot. Serafina spotted something first. She grabbed John and hauled him down.

"Found one?" he asked.

She shook her head. "Not a car. Another one of *them*."

She poked a thumb in the direction she had been looking. John nudged his head over the top of the car they were hiding behind–a late-model Mercedes that looked like it probably belonged to a doctor–and looked.

Another suit, walking between the rows. He was murmuring into a walkie-talkie and frowning. Probably wondering why the guy at the stairwell wasn't answering.

John dropped back down to Serafina. "We don't have much time," he said.

"Will he spot us?"

"Not if we're careful." John led her away from the man and hoped Serafina didn't hear the words he left unsaid: *I hope.*

There were an unknown number of men around them. Probably a lot. Certainly more than John could handle if they descended on him and Serafina *en masse.*

They had to get out of here.

They found a BMW with its window open. Not far, just enough for John to get his fingers through.

"How does that help–oh." John answered Serafina with action. He rocked the window back and forth, careful not to rock the car enough to trigger any alarm but with determination and firmness. The window suddenly slid sideways and forward as it tumbled off the track that kept it seated in the power window mechanism. He shoved it down further, until he was able to get his upper body into the car.

He risked a quick peek to the front of the parking lot.

The man, the agent, the killer, whoever, had moved a row closer to them.

John leaned in and fumbled beside the driver seat.

"I get the older cars," whispered Serafina. "No car alarms, right?" John nodded. "Why the BMW?"

John found the switch he was looking for. Pulled it. The trunk popped open with the near-silence of excellent design embodied in a quality automobile.

It sounded like a gunshot in his ears.

He looked over the top of the car again. The suit hadn't noticed. Hadn't appeared to, at least.

He moved to the trunk. The left side had a panel designed for removal. He popped it open. Inside was a tool box. He opened it. Hoping for what they needed.

"BMWs tend to be owned by people who aren't interested in doing their own repairs. A lot of them never open the tool box. So a lot of them never know about a feature some BMWs have." He found it. Held it up with a smile.

It was a valet key. It couldn't open the trunk or the glove box. But it could open the doors and start the car. And if the owner hadn't activated the alarm, they could get out of here.

John circled to the driver side, Serafina to the other. He stuck the plastic key in the car door and held his breath.

Serafina was peering at him, only her eyes visible over the top of the car. "Moment of truth," she whispered.

He nodded. Turned the key.

No alarm.

He opened the door and got in, then leaned over and unlocked the passenger door for her. She was in almost instantly, buckling her seatbelt even before he managed to slip the key into the ignition. They worked silently, well-coordinated.

"We should take this show on the road," she whispered.

"The thieving nurse and the man with no name," he agreed.

"I was thinking more Beauty and the Bonkers."

He rolled his eyes. Started the car.

The lights came on automatically.

Illuminating the agent who stood right in front of them, pointing a loaded gun at John's face.

AND THE SIMPLE WILL BEWARE

From: POTUS <dpeters@secured.whitehouse.gov>
To: 'X' <xxx@secured.whitehouse.gov>
Sent: Friday, May 31 3:18 AM
Subject: Intnl Crisis

Russian minister called. The outbreak has been found in Asia. Managed to convince him to clamp down on media coverage. For now. He's a bastard but at least he's a bastard on our side.

I don't know what you're talking about. Patricia Radcliffe and I have nothing but a professional relationship.

From: X <xxx@xxx.xxx>
To: Dicky <dpeters@secured.whitehouse.gov>
Sent: Friday, May 31 3:18 AM
Subject: RE: Intnl Crisis

Bastards are the most helpful. Easy to understand. I have my own people in Russia as well. They'll lean on him and he'll do what's necessary.

I'm sure you and Patricia have nothing but professional interests. She gets paid about a quarter-million a year, doesn't she?

***

    Isaiah couldn't put down the paper he still held. His thoughts spun around, a whirlwind that picked out bits of past, present, and possible futures, presenting them in orders that seemed constructed to cause the most possible terror.

Nicholas dead.

A weapon loose.

Katherine captured.

A rogue soldier, made all the more dangerous for what he had stolen and intended to use.

Men with no qualms about killing and hurting others if it meant they could achieve their aims.

And Isaiah…Isaiah would go along with it.

Not because he was afraid. He was, and someday he *would* find every one of those men and kill them all. The skeletal agent. Dominic would be last…

…and would last the longest.

But for now he would be their pawn. He would not sell his soul to these devils–he had long ago done that deal with the real thing–but he was sure a sublease was in order.

And still he did not move.

Movement was important. Movement was action, and without action there could be no achievement. He had learned that as a young priest. Learning about faith had actually taught him that: had taught him that to pray was fine and dandy, but the Lord preferred a man who prayed five minutes and then worked the rest of the day to one who worked five minutes and then prayed the remainder.

God helped those who helped themselves.

And the same held true of the devil.

But there was action for its own sake and action for the sake of success. Isaiah preferred the latter. It was what made him good at his job. Not as a priest, but as a killer.

So he paused and thought.

After a moment he picked up the phone. Held down the "1."

A voice answered. A woman. "Yes, sir?"

"I need weapons."

"Check the trunk. Call back if you need anything else."

Click.

Not much for small talk.

That suited him. Isaiah wasn't, either.

He popped the trunk. Went to it.

Inside was a single syringe and some rubber tubing. He understood what it was, and why it was needed. He didn't trust the information in the envelope, not completely. But he also knew that it would be ridiculous for Dominic and his cronies to recruit him and kill him all in the same motion. And just as ridiculous for him not to take precautions against something as deadly as John.

No, not just John. The thing John is carrying around with him.

So he rolled up his sleeve and injected himself with what could only be a vaccine to the disease he was trying to stop. He knew how to administer it–part of killing was knowing how to heal.

Other than that the syringe and tubing, the trunk was empty.

Or at least seemed that way.

He felt around the corners. Nothing on the right, but on the left he felt a click and the carpet suddenly loosened. The floor panel lifted up. The trunk had a compartment built into the bottom, hidden unless you looked for it.

In the compartment: foam rubber molds that cradled enough weaponry to attack most small countries. A Steyr

AUG M203, an Atchisson Assault Shotgun, two Glock 34 handguns.

It even had two claymores and a line of grenades tucked like angry Christmas ornaments into the dark foam rubber.

That and the fact that the Steyr had the grenade-launcher modification, and the AAS had several box mags that looked to be loaded with FRAG-12 High-Explosive ammo made Isaiah feel a bit ridiculous.

Then it made him afraid. Because it drove home the probability that what the packet said was true. At least about the nameless man's skills and how hard it would be to kill him.

Isaiah picked up one of the Glocks. It was loaded. He tucked it in his belt. The larger items could stay back here until he needed them—no matter what Dominic had said about his legal immunities, Isaiah didn't feel like getting pulled over with an arsenal on his front seat.

And he didn't want to look at them. Didn't want to deal with the possibility—if not likelihood—that he was going to fail. Because then Katherine would die. Horribly.

She might well die anyway.

But his only chance to save her would be to do this thing. And so he *would* do it. To save her, to help her, he would kill who he had to kill.

He would kill the world, if necessary.

He got back in the car. The phone was blinking. There was a message on it: the name and address of a hospital he knew well. Under the address: **TARGET LOCATION.**

He started the car. Pealed out.

He drove over the small bits of blood that marked the defiling of a good woman and the murdering of his only friend. It was the fastest way to the main road.

Nicholas had been the only truly good man Isaiah had ever met. When Isaiah was doing his second stint in juvie–possession of drugs, assault, attempted robbery–Father Nicholas had been younger, but no less dedicated to righteous ideals. He worked every Wednesday at juvenile corrections. Not preaching, just...*being there*. Being someone–a first someone, for most of the boys–who wanted nothing, who offered nothing. Nothing but respect. And that was the only thing some of them needed.

"I'll not bother telling you you're a child of God," he always said. "You're a *person*. And people deserve respect. Simple as that."

Simple as that.

He always said that, and because he meant it many believed.

Isaiah got out of the gang. Not immediately, and not without struggle. But he did. He got out, and graduated high school–a bit older than most–and went on to college and later to follow his first and best teacher.

Father Nicholas insisted Isaiah call him simply Nicholas once Isaiah became a priest himself, though the other man would always be his senior in age, rank, and wisdom. "You're a brother, you're a fellow servant. Simple as that."

Simple as that.

They played cribbage together. Nicholas loved the game with a simple wooden board, jumping pegs to the tune of points accumulated by cards. A game part luck and part skill. The first time Isaiah saw the cribbage board, he thought it looked genuinely stupid. He quickly grew to love the game. Almost as quickly as he had grown to love the long talks while playing with Nicholas, and Nicholas himself.

Nicholas had seemed to save him. And genuinely *had* given him some good years. Some years of happiness.

Until Isaiah threw it all away.

Now, somehow, Nicholas had been called to judgment. Not for his own sins, but for the very fact of Isaiah's existence. For the original sin, the blight, that Isaiah represented in the sight of the Almighty.

He gritted his teeth. Pushed the car to go faster.

He had to avenge his friend.

He had to get Katherine back.

He had to save the *world*.

And so he would find and kill this nameless man.

Simple as that.

PRESENTING THE PAST

From: POTUS <dpeters@secured.whitehouse.gov>
To: 'X' <xxx@secured.whitehouse.gov>
Sent: Friday, May 31 3:25 AM
Subject: New methods

Wait, now we're supposed to BURN them as well?

First it was shoot them, then shoot them in the face, now burn them. What next, a stake in the heart? Silver bullets? Holy water?

From: X <xxx@xxx.xxx>
To: Dicky <dpeters@secured.whitehouse.gov>
Sent: Friday, May 31 3:25 AM
Subject: RE: New methods

Burning is the best method to insure the containment of the contagion. Don't be melodramatic. I can't see any need for holy water, now or ever.

***

Sometimes she sees the past, sometimes the present. Occasionally she thinks it possible that she is witnessing the future.

But it is (or was, or will have been) all fragmented, three separate vessels that once sat in a specific order until they were knocked off their shelf, shattered, then put back together. Only whoever had done the put-backing had mixed all the pieces. Today is tomorrow, tomorrow is yesterday, yesterday reaches fingers into today and turns all into a muddle in her mind.

She knows, sometimes, that she isn't *right*. That pieces of her have been lost. Never again to be found.

She very often hears fragments of a song, a woman's voice.

"Jesus loves me, this I know, for the bible tells me so...."

Then a bright light and a loud sound and nothing for a long time.

Often she sees a face when she hears the song. It is a woman, a lady with a face sometimes kind and sometimes harsh. She has blue eyes. She wears a gun under a flowing blouse that is soft and expensive.

Other times she sees another face. A black man with a smile that does not go all the way to his eyes. His eyes are always sad. The man is wreathed in sadness, carries it with him, uses it like a drug.

She has seen drugs before. Many many times.

Sometimes other faces swim into focus before her eyes. Then, now, now, then. Faces above white coats, faces kind of countenance, faces that seem bent on her destruction.

And now—yesterday? tomorrow?—another face pushes into her mind.

Usually the faces are mist. Ghosts. Only the woman and the black man have real substance. Though even if real she cannot tell if they are a reality of today or yesterday or some tomorrow still to come.

This new face is different. Different from the ghosts, different also from the woman and the black man. His face swims before her, and she feels strangely violated. As though his face has entered her thoughts by force. As though violence has just been done to her mind.

He is elegant. His hair is dark but gray flecks it along the temples. His eyes are jade green, rich and luxurious. They stare directly at her, and the girl stares back at him. This has never happened before. She has never been able to look directly at *any* of the faces. Perhaps that is why they all seem like ghosts.

The green eyes dance. They seem amused. She knows that they are amused by her. By her discomfort. Her confusion.

Her fear.

"You are the pretty one," he says. He has a gray suit on, and it seems to crawl over him. A trick of her mind, but the man seems suddenly as though he wears not wool or cotton or linen but rather a hard shell, an alien armor.

No one has ever called her pretty before. Not that she remembers. Not since the light and the noise and the change of everything. She should be pleased. But she is not. She is afraid.

The man runs a tongue over his lips. It is gray and fleshy. "Yes, very pretty."

There are others nearby. Men beside and in front of and behind her.

And this elegant man, this Other Man. She does not understand this. Is her mind unbreaking? Is she coming back to herself, to the She that was lost?

The man reaches up as though to touch her, but stops short. His hand stops in front of her cheek and he caresses the air. He looks as if he struggles not to jump on her. To rip and tear her flesh with his teeth, to kill and *consume* her.

She would shiver and shudder if she could. She cannot. Her body has lost that–and so many other–abilities.

The Other Man twitches, his eyes rolling back as though the urge to kill has turned to sublime ecstasy. His hand drops. "Not yet. Not yet, my flower. My innocent one. But soon." He looks at the other men. They are in a car, or perhaps a truck. It bounces as they travel to she knows not where. "Who wants a piece of her?"

"She's broken," says one of the ones in front. "I don't do broken. I break 'em, but after that…meh."

The others agree.

One voice speaks last. The voice of the man who sits behind her. "I'll play with her." The owner of the voice leans forward. He is thin. Bony. A grinning skull atop a to-thin neck. Again, the girl wishes she could shudder.

He touches her. His fingers scrape across the hollow of her throat. His skin is cold. "I like to play with the retards. They last longer. They scream louder."

The other men in the truck are quiet. The air has changed. They, too, are afraid. Of the Other Man, and the thin man.

The face of the black man suddenly appears in front of her. His eyes are sad, and she wonders if this is what he has always been so sad about. If, like her, he exists in past and present and future and has always seen this in store for her.

The man with the graying hair shakes his head. "Sometimes you astound me, Mr. Melville."

"In a good way, I hope, sir," says the thin man.

"Oh, the best."

"I'm so glad." The thin man touches her neck again and then disappears to the place he came from.

"Though I wouldn't use the word 'retard.' It rather lacks in style."

"I've never been stylish, sir."

"No, that's true."

The Other Man looks at her with those green eyes. They are so bright, even though the rest of the place they are in is dark. Like they are stars shining in a dark night. Only they are cold stars, bringing no hope.

"I can't wait to see what Mr. Melville does with you, my dear. He is an absolute prodigy."

Again his hand raises to her face. Again he does not touch her. His eyes glow with lust, hatred, murder. A thousand thoughts ugly and crude and naked for her to see.

Then one of her black moments must happen, because she blinks and the Other Man is gone. The others are still there and she wonders where they are taking her. She wonders if Mr. Melville is still with them but does not look behind her. Her body is not capable of that kind of movement, and even if she could make it move she does not think she would have the courage to do so.

She hears a whisper in her ear. The voice of the man no longer here. The Other.

"I look forward to your despair, my dear Katherine. And not even the shell you have created will protect you."

Inexplicably, her crippled body manages to shudder. She does not cry, but a tear escapes the one eye that still occasionally sees into reality.

HOLY ROLLER

From: X <xxx@xxx.xxx>
To: Dicky <dpeters@secured.whitehouse.gov>
Sent: Friday, May 31 3:35 AM
Subject: Update on current carrier

The new asset has accepted our assignment. He should arrive shortly.

The others on the scene are reporting decisive action and a fair amount of collateral damage.

This is going to be fun.

***

Serafina saw the man who appeared like a demon when they turned on the headlights, but she wasn't focused on him. Mostly she saw the gun in his hand.

She didn't like guns. She never had. Especially not since what happened to–

A hand slammed into the back of her head, jamming her forward in her seat.

"Down!" screamed John.

Her head went low as a shot tore the night apart. Glass showered her. Then the squeal of tires on asphalt, and a moment later a hollow thud that reminded her oddly of picking out ripe watermelons at the supermarket.

She looked up and saw the gunman splayed across the hood of the BMW. His arm was punched through a hole in the spider webs that had somehow replaced the front windshield, and his gun waved around in tight circles, pinned partially in place by John's hand as he tried simultaneously to keep the gunman from shooting either of them and to steer.

The car hit something–a parking curb?–and leaped into the air. The edges of the windshield ground audibly into the gunman's arm, and he shouted. Blood welled around his arm, but he didn't let go of the gun. He didn't fire, either. Waiting for a good shot.

Serafina shrank down into the leg space as much as she could. A tight fit, and she thanked Heaven for her tiny frame. Not so great when intimidating an uppity patient, but useful for this. She managed to flip herself around, and just as the gun was swinging to the side, in the instant before it hit pointed at John's face, she kicked up.

A crack. Not the deafening report of a gun, but the brittle stick sound of a compound fracture.

The gunman screamed, and finally let go of the gun. It fell to the space beside her.

The gunman fell off the car with a scream that ended as he hit the pavement and rolled away behind them.

Serafina righted herself–twice as awkward and difficult a process as dropping into the foot space in the first place had been–and then leaned down and picked up the gun. It felt like a dangerous animal in her hand. Warm from the killer's grip, lending it a sense of malignant life.

She handed it over to John.

He put it in his lap with a nod. "Thanks," he said. She didn't know if he was talking about the gun or the kick.

She nodded back. "Welcome."

They were weaving between lines of cars in the parking lot. About to leave the lot, then they could turn onto a side street, then onto a larger avenue.

Where then? She had no idea.

A flurry of gunfire shredded her thoughts. She ducked automatically. One of the bullets plunked through the seat between her and John and then buried itself in the in-dash CD player.

I hope the owner had insurance.

Did insurance companies even have policies for things like this? How would you make a claim for assassination-related firefights in a hospital parking lot?

The car swung into the hospital entrance. An ambulance was pulling in at the same time, and John got an angry blow of the horn for taking an overly wide turn. He didn't seem to care. Neither did Serafina.

They turned out of the parking lot, wound around the ambulance.

Five hundred feet to the larger avenue.

"Where now?" she asked.

His face tensed. She saw a muscle on his temple bounce as he clenched and unclenched his jaw. She rather expected he would tell her they had to go to ground, or that he had a secret safehouse or something like that.

He finally answered. "Lebanon."

"What?" The word didn't adequately express her shock, but she couldn't think of another one so she settled for repetition in lieu of creativity: "*What?*" Had she thrown in with the wrong side here? "What are you, a terrorist or something?"

His head snapped to the side, his eyes finding hers. "No. Not Lebanon in the middle-east. Lebanon, Kansas."

That surprised her more. "Lebanon, Kansas? There's a Lebanon in Kansas? What's in Kansas?"

John opened his mouth to answer. Or maybe to ask her to repeat her barrage of questions.

A car hit them.

Serafina flew to the side, slamming into John with bone-bruising force. Then she flew back the other direction, and only the side airbags kept her from ending up back at the hospital they had just left.

She bounced off *them*, felt the BMW still spinning on its center axis as something shoved them to the side and back at the same time. The world turned in front of her, the view partially obscured by the dash airbags, which had also deployed.

Still, she could see over them.

A black sedan had slammed into them. Her training took over and she automatically wondered how the other person was doing, if the driver had been intoxicated, a thousand questions that would need to be answered by the triage nurse at the ER.

The BMW continued sliding sideways. They turned completely around. The other car was now beside them, slightly in front, the BMW still being pushed, now backwards.

She saw the driver of the other car.

It was a big man, black and handsome. He didn't look dazed at all, didn't even look surprised. Maybe that was a function of his profession: he wore a Roman collar, the white strip clearly visible over the top of a black collaret.

A priest.

The priest pushed something forward. Dark. Familiar.

A gun.

A gun?

What the hell is a priest doing with a gun?

Shots fired. They were loud, so loud so loud so loud so loud! Serafina screamed and put her hands over her ears, then realized that she had not heard shots fired by the priest but by John. A tight clump of holes appeared in what remained of their windshield, a matching grouping in the safety glass of the black sedan.

The priest dove sideways and disappeared below the level of the dash.

Then John adjusted his aim downward and pulled the trigger again. Both dash airbags more or less disintegrated and he batted the tatters of his out of the way, giving himself free access to the wheel.

He cranked it to the side. The cars disengaged with a shriek of metal on metal. He accelerated past the black sedan.

She looked over. The other car's side windows were tinted. She couldn't see in.

Instinct screamed at her. She ducked. Saw John was doing the same.

Shots blew through the side window. Glass rained again.

Gonna have a tough time next time I wash my hair.

John stayed down, but their car didn't swerve. It remained steady as if a professional driver had been driving on an easy straightaway.

She heard the black sedan screech to a halt behind them. Knew it would be turning around.

She wondered what kind of priest took shooting lessons and courses in advanced stunt driving.

A holy roller. Hyuk.

She had become victim of the bad punchline to a deadly cosmic joke.

The BMW lurched slightly as the gears shifted and its speed increased. John lifted his head just enough to look through the gap between the top of the dash and the upper arc of the steering wheel.

Serafina stayed down. She edged over enough to see the side mirror. Headlights glowed behind them: the priest had spun the car around in record time and was already after them.

More shots. Too many. She wasn't a gun expert–she knew which end the bullet came out of, and that pulling the trigger while looking in the hole was a bad idea, but not a lot more–but she knew they did run out of bullets eventually.

The priest must be reloading. While simultaneously pulling his car into and then out of a mad spin and then accelerating after them.

She had wondered who John was and how he could be alive.

Now she wondered who this priest was and if they had any chance of staying that way.

John cranked the wheel to one side. The right wheels left the ground for a split second. She screamed, just a short yip, but was embarrassed for some reason.

"Sorry," he grunted.

"It's okay," she said. And that was a ridiculous exchange. In the middle of a life-and-death race down the

123

middle of a Los Angeles street, madmen trying to shoot them...but that's no reason to be rude!

They swerved again. John took turn after turn, trying to lose the black sedan.

Even in the predawn hours, the streets were littered with men and women who believed the sun was a buzzkill. One of them was an exception–a man ringing a bell and wearing a sandwich board that loudly proclaimed "The End Is NYE!" in handwritten letters.

Serafina hoped that wasn't an omen. Surely a guy preaching to people who didn't care a whit for his message– and one that was misspelled to boot–couldn't be right. And it couldn't apply to her, could it?

They passed a pair of transvestites, a group of college students, a man clutching his stomach in the classic pre-barf pose.

They turned, they turned.

The sedan kept following them.

Part of the problem was the people. Everyone they followed turned a head. Watching the mad flight in the middle of the night. The priest didn't really have to follow them, she realized. He could just follow the people who were staring down the road and be reasonably assured of finding them.

"Slow down," she said.

John snapped a glance at her. He kept his foot to the floorboards and screeched around another turn.

"Seriously, slow down."

"Don't worry, I won't crash."

"I know. But people are noticing us."

John looked around. Seemed to notice the pedestrians; to notice *their* notice.

He eased up as he hit the next corner. When he came off the turn he was going above the speed limit, but not ridiculously so.

No one looked.

He took the next turn.

The next.

Serafina looked behind them.

No black sedan.

John pulled the BMW to the side of the road.

"What are we doing?" Serafina looked around. She didn't recognize the area, but they sure weren't in Kansas, so she couldn't figure out why they had stopped here.

"Getting out. Come on."

He got out, leaving the engine running and the door open, then walked away.

She followed suit, though she closed her door. This wasn't a nice-looking part of the city.

"What's going on?"

John walked into an alley, cutting between two buildings and heading toward another street–a smaller one–on the other side. "The car probably has a GPS vehicle recovery system installed."

"Like a LoJack or something?"

"Or something." He smiled. "Whoever's after us has resources, we already established that. So we can assume they'll have noted the car's plate number, and they'll be scanning for it soon if they haven't already done so."

She nodded. "So you drove to a crap part of town and left the motor running hoping that someone would steal it and be a decoy."

He smiled at her. "Nice."

"No." She frowned. "What if they kill whoever takes the car?"

He sighed. "I sincerely hope that won't happen. But we have to move. And no matter what, we have to get to...."

He drifted off, and Serafina saw his eyes catch hold of something. He ran and she followed automatically, thinking they must be running for their lives again, at the same time aghast that her life could have shifted so radically that such a conclusion was the first thing to pop into her head.

But he wasn't running from something. Neither the men in suits nor the priest who she sensed was an even more dangerous threat.

No, he was running toward something. An old man.

The old man was stumbling, trying to catch his balance, failing. He careened into the side of a building, slamming his head into the wall, crying out but failing to stop his awkward, jittering fall.

John reached the man, then reached *for* him. His arms, which Serafina realized for the first time were well-muscled and strong, stretched for the stumbling man.

The other man screamed. Not in agony, but in rage. "Get away from me!" he shouted. He fell to his knees. Blood flowed from his temple.

He coughed. Blood surged from his mouth and nose, and Serafina stepped forward automatically to see what she could do to help.

He whipped around to face her and snarled like a wounded beast. Nothing remotely human about the sound. Blood from his nose wrapped around his mouth like gore on the muzzle of a feeding beast. His eyes glittered.

That wasn't what made Serafina step back, though.

It was his head.

The spot where he had pitched into the wall was shiny with blood. And something else. It looked like tiny spines lay in the lacerated flesh. For the barest fraction of an instant Serafina wondered what was in the concrete and how it had gotten so deeply embedded in his skin. Then she realized the spines hadn't been inserted there, but had erupted from that spot.

They were growing out of him.

The man snarled again. "Get. Away. *FROM. ME.*" He devolved into coughing. More blood spilled, thick and black.

It was dark so she couldn't be sure, but she thought she saw things crawling in the blood.

John took her hand.

They ran.

The night held them. The darkness held them fast.

interlude:
CORRUPTION

ON AXIS UNHINGED

From: POTUS <dpeters@secured.whitehouse.gov>
To: 'X' <xxx@secured.whitehouse.gov>
Sent: Friday, May 31 3:51 AM
Subject: Media Blackout

We had to scrub a hospital. An ENTIRE HOSPITAL. So far we've got the surrounding area sealed by an army unit, calling it a possible act of domestic terrorism. No one in or out, but it can't stay quiet. If nothing else, some search engine satellite is going to provide some nosey ten-year-old with closeups of the hospital and the dead people and the complete lack of any blast damage and then we're screwed.

Things are moving fast. I don't know how we're going to be able to stop this from getting out.

From: X <xxx@xxx.xxx>
To: Dicky <dpeters@secured.whitehouse.gov>
Sent: Friday, May 31 3:51 AM
Subject: RE: Media Blackout

Msg me the names of any journalists who are presenting problems. I'll have my associates visit them. They will comply with reasonable requests for cooperation, I'm quite sure.

***

Seymour hated his name. He hated his mother for giving him the stupid name. He hated the kids who had teased him about the name his entire life.

Most of all, he hated himself.

That was why he was in here again, in this stupid bar in this stupid neighborhood in this stupid city in this stupid world.

Nothing ever changed. Everyone bothered him, everyone made fun of him, he hated them all.

The bar was usually busy. Not full–it was too seedy a place for that–but busy. Always pervaded by quiet murmur, the sound of voices low and taut as men and women drank despair into oblivion.

Tonight, though, it was quiet. The only sound was the television in the corner over the bar, which was so low it was nearly muted. There was a news report on, the words "BREAKING NEWS!" screaming across the screen every ten seconds, a good-looking anchor that Seymour hated *because* he was good-looking speaking through an appropriately tense expression.

Seymour only heard every few words. "Hospital...cordoned off...no word yet...terrorism...."

Downer.

He turned the channel. It was only another news report, this one showing a bunch of people lined up outside a health clinic or an ER or something. Hospital staff were handing out blue face masks. A few people–mostly gruff-looking men–refused to wear them.

"Good for you," said Seymour. He held up his glass to toast the American Spirit. Finished off the booze inside– he was no longer sure what he was drinking, and no longer cared–then chucked the glass at the TV.

At this point he shouldn't have been able to hit the widest side of the universe, he was so utterly slammed. But somehow the glass made its way through the air and planted itself right in the center of the television. There was a single flash, a whiff of burnt electronics, then the set went dark.

Seymour laughed. This was fun.

He looked at the front door. Still sort of expecting someone else to come in, in spite of the fact that he'd flipped the "CLOSED" sign face out some hours ago.

No one came in. Just him. Just him and the bartender.

He looked over the bar. The bartender was still back there.

"You okay?"

The bartender didn't answer. His mouth was covered in duct tape. And the top of his head was gone, which probably didn't help much either.

"Well, you let me know if you get uncomfortable." Seymour giggled. "Don't want you to get a cramp or nothin'."

He hated everything. Everyone.

His boss at the plant apparently hated him back, and gave Seymour a beautiful pink present to seal that hatred. Not even two weeks' notice, just clear out your shit and get the hell off the premises.

Seymour brooded about that for a few hours. Made him feel pretty bad. He seemed to be catching cold, of course, and that made it all just that much worse.

And finally he did something about his anger. His hate.

He had a gun. Never shot it, barely knew how to use it. But he'd bought it in a fit of need, a fit of desire that approached lust. A craving to hold power in his hands.

It was easy to buy. He had no criminal record, not even a parking ticket. He got a gun and even a smile from the guy at the counter. Though of course the smile wasn't really for Seymour but for the commission. Still, it was a smile.

Today Seymour remembered the gun. He got it out of his closet, out of the box he had bought for it. He wrapped it in a pillow because he saw that in a movie once. Secured the whole thing with duct tape–the same roll he later used on the bartender.

He knew where his boss lived. Everyone did. The boss invited them over for Christmas parties. Seymour went once and stayed for five minutes before he realized that he had only been invited as a joke and everyone there was making fun of him behind his back.

Ding-dong.

The doorbell rang and the boss opened it and had time to look angry and then surprised and then scared and then his face fell apart.

The pillow wasn't a great silencer, no matter what the movies said. The boom was very loud, and hurt Seymour's ears. He liked it.

Seymour had hated his boss. He liked watching the man's face do what it did. Not just the death part, but the other part: the part where the man who had always held himself so far above Seymour suddenly realized that he *wasn't* above, he *wasn't* better, he wasn't…wasn't…

…anything.

That was when Seymour had his great epiphany: that we're all nothing. That his hatred came because everyone around him wasn't even worthy of his impotent loathing. He should either destroy them all or leave the world himself.

The boss's wife came to the door, screamed. The scream stopped when a bullet tore her vocal cords away and left her drowning in her own blood.

Seymour went through the house. There were a few other people, small forms hiding in places they thought he'd never look.

He didn't hate them. He didn't have to hate anymore. He was powerful. He was the *king*.

"Boom, boom, boom," he whispered. The bartender smiled behind the duct tape. Seymour knew he was smiling because he was, at last, a popular man. People smiled for popular men.

He coughed.

Damn cold.

He looked at the bartender's body. "You got any TheraFlu or something?"

The bartender did not answer. He had not spoken for hours, since the last patron of the bar left and the bartender tried to tell Seymour to leave as well and Seymour made his head fall apart.

Seymour hated him a bit for his refusal to help. He had to remind himself that he was beyond that now. He was beyond hating. He didn't have to hate anymore, he could simply kill and be happy.

Except for the damn cold.

He tried to reload his gun, but his hands kept trembling. His cough was getting worse.

The bar was dark, and Seymour suddenly wished he hadn't thrown the glass through the TV screen. The light from the boob tube would have been welcome. The darkness started to press on him.

His euphoria disappeared. He no longer felt like a king.

He coughed, and something splattered on the bar.

What…?

He coughed again. More splatter, and something splashed against his chest. He rubbed it blindly.

His legs went out from under him.

That was kind of expected, given the gallons of booze he'd probably drunk since last call. But this didn't feel like the beginning of an alcoholic blackout. It felt…different.

Seymour slumped to the floor beside the bar. He coughed on the way down, and fluid came out of his mouth. More of it flowed back into his throat as well, gagging him, drowning him on dry land.

He landed on his butt, hands limp at his sides, legs splayed in front of him. He felt like he'd broken his neck. Everything below his upper lip seemed numb.

Then it wasn't numb. It was on fire.

Seymour tried to scream. Tried to shriek. The pain was so bad he somehow overcame the paralysis that had clenched him in a numbing vise and managed to look down.

He shrieked even louder.

He was covered in blood. Not the blood of the people he'd killed tonight–he'd been very careful about that. No, it was his blood.

But that was all right. Or if not all right, then at least normal. Understandable. *Possible.*

The rest of what he saw, though….

No. No, no, no, nonononononono….

He was screaming the word in his mind. His mouth wasn't working the way he wanted it to. Wouldn't respond with anything but a raw, wretched shriek.

Nonononononono....

His arms at first appeared to be covered with yarn, maybe even rope. Thick, fibrous lengths that curled tightly over him like someone had knit the weirdest sweater ever and used Seymour as a display mannequin.

But then the fibers moved. They writhed, each independently. Not fibers, not yarn or thread or rope. They were worms or snakes. Seymour hated snakes. Hated them even more than he hated people.

Snakes. Yes, that's what they were, he saw them clearly now, each with the small, triangular head of a viper, ruby red eyes ablaze even in the darkness of the bar.

Then the snakes slithered away from one another, and he screamed even harder as he saw what lay beneath.

Him.

Yes, him, of course it was him. But the him he saw was also *them*. Also the snakes. Also the thing he loathed and feared. The snakes had sprouted directly from his body, each one rooted in his very flesh.

Seymour's screaming rose to an unbroken whistle, a trilling alarm with a chillingly fleshy tone. Then it dropped in tone and became a sibilant hiss. Terror on a new level gripped him as he wondered if his *face* was changing. What if snakes were growing from his head, his hair?

What was he becoming?

The vipers on his arms—and now on his legs, he saw—suddenly turned their faces down. They bit at the roots of their bodies, the flesh that was Seymour. Thousands of needle-teeth pierced him at the same instant. Thousands of bites injected venom that threw his body into paroxysms of pain.

He thought of his boss's face. How it had fallen away. He wondered what his face was doing right now.

His arms and legs were gone. They had disintegrated, become not four appendages but thousands of smaller ones. Tiny flagella that whipped back and forth and hissed angrily.

Seymour hissed as well. He tried to scream, but the hiss was all he could muster.

Something tinkled. The bell above the door to the bar.

Didn't I lock up?

It was his last rational thought.

Then he flopped on his belly and tried to crawl away, the gun forgotten, his vendetta against humanity forgotten. He only felt the thousands of snake-things that were his hands and feet and fingers and toes, gripping the floorboards with fang and tongue. Pulling him into deeper darkness.

"So you are the first," said a voice. Deep, powerful. The kind of voice to be feared. And obeyed. "You will do as my collector and keeper."

Seymour could not think, but he could feel. The voice scared him. He tried to run. Tried to crawl. Flight was all he wanted, to flee to the ends of the earth, to run from whoever had spoken, from the owner of that deep and powerful and awful voice.

Something came down on the back of his head. A heel. Strong, heavy. The weight of a world was on Seymour's neck. "You cannot run," said the voice.

Seymour hissed. The snakes on his body hissed. But he stopped crawling. He had no choice. He still hated–more than ever–but he was powerless to defy the voice.

He had to obey.

Something circled his neck. A collar. Metal, and cold. So cold it circled the spectrum and became hot and burned him terribly. Seymour tried to scream, found his voice had somehow been stolen away.

"Come," said the voice of the one who had captured him. The collar pulled, and Seymour had no choice but to follow. "We have many to find, and much to do."

two:
FLIGHT

UNEXPECTED ANSWERINGS

From: POTUS <dpeters@secured.whitehouse.gov>
To: 'X' <xxx@secured.whitehouse.gov>
Sent: Friday, May 31 5:15 AM
Subject:

The CDC is calling. What do I do?

From: X <xxx@xxx.xxx>
To: Dicky <dpeters@secured.whitehouse.gov>
Sent: Friday, May 31 5:15 AM
Subject:

Tell them nothing.

From: POTUS <dpeters@secured.whitehouse.gov>
To: 'X' <xxx@secured.whitehouse.gov>
Sent: Friday, May 31 5:16 AM
Subject:

How am I supposed to do that? They'll go public. They'll start conjecturing. And please for the love of GOD CAN I GET A PHONE NUMBER SO I CAN CALL YOU?

From: X <xxx@xxx.xxx>
To: Dicky <dpeters@secured.whitehouse.gov>
Sent: Friday, May 31 5:16 AM
Subject:

You are the *leader of the free world*. Grow a pair and tell them to wait a few hours.

***

John knew he could run for twenty-four minutes, full sprint, before he had to slow down. But he doubted Serafina could do the same. And even if she could, that kind of thing would leave them exhausted and vulnerable.

So they had to either go to ground or find another vehicle.

Going to ground was a bad call. Not just because the area they had just left would end up being tracked at some point. Even if there had been no one following them, John would have had to move. There was still the mission. Still…whatever waited for them in Kansas.

And what *would* that be?

He searched. Pushed back to the moment when he had awakened in the hospital, and then tried to pierce that darkness and see to the light that he hoped lay behind it.

He failed.

There was no way to look back. So he would have to push forward. Hoping that would illuminate not only future trails to travel, but past steps taken.

"Where do we go?" asked Serafina. "We gonna hide somewhere?"

"No."

"Kansas?"

"Yeah."

"What's there?"

"I really wish I knew."

She stopped walking. "No." She folded her arms. "You gotta give me more than this, John."

He stopped beside her. They still weren't out of the rotten part of the city they'd left the BMW in and he didn't want to leave her alone here, even though he was fairly sure she could take care of herself.

But it was more than that. He felt like he needed her to come with him. Like it wasn't just luck that had brought her to his hospital room–an event that undoubtedly saved him since it bought him a necessary moment to kill his would-be killer–but something deeper.

John didn't know a lot about himself. He didn't know who he really was, where he came from. He knew only where he needed to go.

And now...that he needed Serafina to come with him.

"I can't give you more," he finally said.

"I don't even know if you're on the right side here," she said. Her arms still crossed, her face stern. "What if I'm aiding a criminal?"

He shook his head. "You know you're not. Criminals shoot people in hospital rooms and attack them in stairwells and try to run them over in cars. We're running from the criminals, and if they're trying to kill me that means I'm a good guy, right?" He wondered if he sounded as plaintive as he thought he did, like he was trying to convince himself as much as her.

"What was the deal with that guy?" she said. The conversational shift was abrupt, but he knew exactly what she was talking about. The man who had fallen, the old man with the strange growth on the side of his head.

"I don't know."

"You don't know much, do you?"

"Hardly anything."

Serafina's eyes went distant. "There were some people admitted to the hospital with a cough like that today, but they didn't go crazy or pound their heads into walls or start turning into hedgehogs." She shuddered.

John considered asking her if the hospital was always as busy as they had seen it while leaving. He doubted it. Even large hospitals in big cities slowed down a bit at night, barring some large-scale disaster.

Serafina came to the same conclusion. "Everyone seemed kinda nuts when we were leaving, though." Another shake of the head. "I've got to call the hospital. I need to find out if they–"

"No." John didn't need to hear the rest of the sentence. "If these people are as powerful and dedicated as I'm worried they are, then they'll have your friends' cell phones monitored, they'll track you."

"Then I won't call their cells. I'll call the main switchboard and get transferred to the fifth floor nurses desk. That's the infectious disease ward, and I want to know if there's anything happening. Besides...."

She was quiet. She looked down. One hand dropped to her side, though the other clutched her arm. All her toughness dropped away and suddenly she looked like a little child, innocent and lost and very scared.

"What is it?" said John. He wanted to hug her. Not as a sexual advance, though there was no denying how attractive she was, but because the pain in her heart was so apparent it begged for help and healing.

Serafina looked up at him. Her eyes glimmered. "The people in the ICU. The nurses, the doctors. The man you killed, he...."

Her breath hitched, she stopped talking. John felt like weaving on his feet. How could he have been so stupid? Of course the first hitman had killed the staff up there, just as he had tried to kill John and Serafina.

And Serafina was well-liked, and had no doubt liked the others well in return. The people murdered had been her friends.

John had moved like a soldier. Thinking of evasion, survival, the attainment of his mission. He had missed the fact that there was a soul in pain traveling at his side.

"I'm so sorry," he whispered.

"I just need to know what's happening."

He nodded.

And realized they were not alone.

Four men stood nearby. Spread in a loose circle around them.

That they were predators was obvious. Even without the knives they held loosely in hands obviously accustomed to violence. All of them were well-muscled, dressed in tight shirts and tank tops that showcased their physiques and the gang tattoos that curled around their thick arms and chests and listed numbers and names–some sacred, some profane, all made dark in the context of ink signaling spilt blood. Four men, but only one soul, one corruption between them.

No, strike that. John realized that not all of them were the same. One–a thick-armed, thicker-necked kid whom John saw was probably only sixteen or so–shifted slightly. Had eyes that darted under veiled lids. Signs of fear, signs that he didn't want to be here.

"What have we got here?" said one of the men. Not the largest, not the toughest-looking. But he was the leader. The alpha. The one that would give the orders, and be first to feed on whatever kind of blood and flesh these animals sought.

John looked at the one who still had a chance. The boy who could still be a man; who could still choose to walk in the sun instead of slinking in the dark.

"You don't have to do this," he said.

"Who said you could talk?" said one of the other gangbangers.

John kept his eyes on the kid. The kid looked away. Looked back. Looked away. Back again.

"Please," John said. Begging. The others laughed at the anguish in his voice, not realizing he wasn't begging for Serafina or for himself. He was begging for a boy on the cusp of being a man. A man, or something twisted. A thing that looked like a man, but never could be.

"Yeah, you ask pretty we might let you go," said the leader. He touched his knife to his lips as though thinking. "'Course, it'll cost you." He looked at Serafina. John felt the nurse back behind him.

"You don't have to do this," repeated John. He never looked at the others. Only at the boy.

Was I ever that young?

He knew he must have been. Once, a long time ago, before he became a soldier, a killer, whatever he was.

"Please."

The last plea.

"I ain't waiting no more."

The gangbanger who spoke lunged at Serafina. Then the others joined in.

Not the kid. Not the boy. He trembled as though wanting to jump in. But he didn't move.

John was glad.

He took the others down. Took them apart.

He didn't kill them. He heard Serafina scream, but didn't know if it was fear or the fact that he shoved her away from a knife, then down on her butt so another blade passed over her head.

He broke an arm at the elbow. The arm would never be strong again.

He broke a wrist, crushed the small bones of the hand under his foot. No more knives for that man.

The last gang member–the leader–ended up in an arm lock, screaming as John put pain on shoulder, elbow, and wrist all at once.

"How, how, *how*?" he shrieked.

John nodded to the boy. Thick neck, thick arms. A boy who could live, who could do much good if he walked away. Not just from here, not just from this moment, but from the choices he had been on the verge of making.

"Go home," he said.

The boy did.

He left his knife behind.

The gang leader was still screaming. So were the other two, writhing in pain around crushed bones and mangled joints. But the leader screamed the loudest, in spite of his lack of injury.

"How?" he kept shouting, as though unsure how his tiny kingdom could have ended.

He coughed.

He vomited blood.

A moment later, so did one of the gangbangers writhing on the ground. He began to choke.

John couldn't spare more than a glance for him. He was too busy looking at the leader.

145

The man was writhing in his grasp. But it was no longer merely like he was in pain. He suddenly felt....

John had to search for a word, a concept. Some way of making sense of what was happening. He half expected to feel scales or spines under his fingers. Neither appeared. Instead his fingers suddenly sank deep into rubbery flesh. The arm–once rigid where he was pressing in a direction joints were not meant to go–sagged. Not slackening. It was as though the bones inside were melting.

The once-leader, once-king, slumped. John let go of him. He fell face down on the pavement and his body didn't crack with broken bone. It hit with a splat, and then spread out like a puddle of thick mud. The man's scream bubbled.

Serafina was on her feet. Tugging at John. Pulling him away.

"What, what, what?"

John realized *he* was the one saying the words now.

He let Serafina pull him.

They both ran.

When they stopped they began looking for a phone so Serafina could make a call. John didn't know if she still wanted to as much. He thought so–she was not someone who would let her care for others be sidetracked by something as unimportant as an impossible transformation in a slum–but maybe she was just searching for a way to get her mind off what had just happened. He knew he was.

There was some spare change in his pockets. Not much, but enough to make a phone call. Finding the phone turned out to be the hard part. In the era of mobile communications there were fewer and fewer public phone booths. And the first ones they found had the receivers yanked off them, just steel cords dangling like alien tentacles in the cool night.

They finally found one, though. John handed Serafina the change and she clinked the coins into the slot. They clunked into the bowels of the machine, each making a sound that was solid and strangely reassuring. In a digital era so much had to be taken on faith: you dialed a number and there was only silence until the voice answered. You sent an email saw only the words you typed until a response magically appeared. There was something comforting about putting an actual coin in an actual slot and hearing actual gears and levers moving, followed by an audible dial tone.

Serafina dialed a number. She waited, clearly listening as the hospital automated switchboard ran through its opening statements and options. Then she dialed a number, then another.

"Can I speak to the fifth floor nurses station in Infectious Diseases, please?" she said. "This is Nurse Cruz, I heard things are a little crazy tonight and I wanted to check if they needed any extra hands." She nodded, then said, "Thanks, I'll wait."

John looked at the phone. It had a volume control on the side of the handset. He motioned to Serafina and when he had her attention he pointed at it, making an "up" motion with his hand. She looked confused, then understood and nodded.

She pushed the button several times, turning up the handset volume until it was loud enough John could easily hear the hospital hold music.

The music cut off. A voice whispered out. It was a pleasant voice, articulate and elegant, but for some reason it put John instantly on edge, more so than he already was.

"Miss Cruz?"

"Yes, who is this?"

"Miss Cruz, I presume you know how very much trouble you are in. The man you are with is a fugitive, and you are looking at a very long time in jail if you continue helping him."

Serafina looked at John. He felt like screaming, *Don't believe him!* but knew that wouldn't accomplish anything.

"Who is this?" she repeated. She didn't look away from John, and he got the feeling she was taking his measure.

There was a pause. Then the voice said, "You may call me Mr. Dominic, Miss Cruz."

"Well, Dominic, you want to tell me why half a dozen of my friends are dead?"

"You should ask your companion."

"I did. He doesn't know."

"He doesn't? Interesting." The voice drew the last word out–*iiiiinnn-teresting*–and the elongated syllables felt like probes digging around in John's mind. "And you believe him, do you? That's charming."

"My belief isn't the point. The point is what happened to my friends."

"Ah, a woman who wants to *know*. Knowledge can be dangerous, don't you think?"

"Better than stumbling along blindly."

"Quite so. You're a woman after my own heart, Miss Cruz."

John started to tremble. He didn't know why. Every word that this *Dominic* spoke pounded a new spike through his heart. He felt like he was dying a bit inside. Couldn't figure out why. He felt something strange. Not hatred–not exactly–but a deep discord. Like Dominic represented something John could not stand to even be around.

He knows me.

And I know him.

The realizations rang through him with crystalline tones. Truth. He had known this Dominic before, though he sensed somehow that Dominic was not the man's real name.

What is his name?

Not important.

"Why did you send them after me, Dominic?" he snarled into the phone.

There was a long pause. When Dominic spoke again he had lost a bit of his polish. "So you are there. Good to have the confirmation. You'll never get where you're going. Either of you."

And then John knew. This wasn't a conversation for fun. Dominic abhorred him, hated him with a hate so deep and black it could swallow a thousand suns in its depths. So for Dominic to talk to John at all meant that there was something else going on. A reason for the conversation.

John yanked the receiver out of Serafina's grasp and slammed it down in the cradle.

"John!" Serafina was furious. "I didn't find out *anything*."

"And you never would have. Dominic just wanted you talking so he could get to us."

"What, like tracing the call?"

John started moving away from the phone. Then running. Serafina followed after only a moment. "Traces aren't like in the movies," he said as they ran. "They happen instantly, and they happen whether you hang up or not. They knew where you were the second you said your name. He just wanted to confirm that *I* was with you...and keep us on the line as long as possible."

"For what?"

He didn't answer. Afraid that if he told her what he feared she would try to do something about it, try to save people. That wouldn't save anyone and would only get her killed as well.

"For *what*?"

Again, John didn't answer. But this time it was because the explosion knocked them both off their feet. There was a rushing wind, a high-pitched whistle, then a distant shriek, then the phone booth–now half a block behind them–disappeared in a ball of flame that engulfed much of the apartment building it had stood against.

John sat up. The first ball of flame snuffed out, extinguished by its own sound and fury, but a moment later a second one erupted.

A third of the apartment building was gone.

"What? What?" Serafina struggled to sit up as well. Her forehead was bleeding.

"Missile strike," said John.

Serafina saw what had happened. She let out a small whimper.

A series of cracks rippled through the predawn air. Then louder creaks, then booms that were louder still.

Screams sliced bright tears in the darkness.

The apartment building tilted. Began to fall.

Right toward John and Serafina.

MEN AT WORK

From: POTUS <dpeters@secured.whitehouse.gov>
To: 'X' <xxx@secured.whitehouse.gov>
Sent: Friday, May 31 5:21 AM
Subject:

I'm okay, right? I mean, I'm not...

You know what I mean.

From: X <xxx@xxx.xxx>
To: Dicky <dpeters@secured.whitehouse.gov>
Sent: Friday, May 31 5:21 AM
Subject:

Your yellow streak is showing.

<sigh>

You're fine. I already told you. The vaccine will protect you and your family. My people just haven't been able to mass-produce it yet. The only way to stop the spread is to stop the carriers.

***

Isaiah had been shocked.

Not just at the speed at which the other car recovered from a surprise hit on the side, an impact that should have left both driver and passenger bruised, concussed, dazed and ineffectual. Not just that.

No, it was the return fire. The fact that the other car—a nice vehicle, a few years old, nothing special, had then erupted in gunfire that sent him diving for the floorboards.

Isaiah couldn't remember the last time he had to *react*. He was a planner, and his plans *always* went perfectly. His chess games were not merely five or six moves ahead of his opponents, they were planned out to an inevitable—and usually rapid—checkmate.

Not this time. This time his opponents—John and the Cruz woman—had managed to not only surprise him but to actually take one of his pieces off the board. Only a pawn, but still....

The car sputtered, shuddered. It was a fine piece of work, the crash had damaged it. Or maybe one of the bullets that came at him had punched a hole in something in the engine. In that case he should be grateful it hadn't pounded its way through to him.

Either way, the result was the same: the car was still moving, but he didn't want to count on it.

He picked up the cell phone and dialed.

A new voice answered, different than the first one he had spoken to. A woman, but a different one than before. "Yes, Isaiah?" she said. She sounded attentive and nice. He pictured a slightly overweight woman, forty-five. Making cookies.

She was probably hard-eyed, mean, cooking up assassination plans while she stabbed puppies.

"I need a new car. Same outfitting, same armaments."

She was silent for thirty seconds. Long enough he worried he had lost the call.

"Take your next left, proceed two blocks, then park and wait. Take your phone with you when you leave the car."

The call terminated.

Isaiah did as he was told. He waited less than five minutes. Another car pulled up and parked in front of him. It was a gray car, same make and model as the one Isaiah was sitting in now. A single man got out of the other car, another man dressed like an agent of any of a hundred branches of the government. He left the gray car, walked to the one Isaiah sat in, and opened Isaiah's door.

The agent–Isaiah was already thinking of all of them simply as "agents"–gestured for him to go to the gray car, whose engine was still idling. Isaiah did so, and before he had even gotten in the agent had gotten in his old ride and pulled away.

The engine of the first car sounded even worse outside the soundproofed cabin. Isaiah was glad he had abandoned it.

Katherine couldn't afford for him to sputter his way through this mission. She had *never* been able to afford his failure. But now least of all.

I'll come for you.

He got in the gray car. Put the car in gear and pondered his next move. Normally he would suspect that his prey, this John and Serafina, would proceed half-panicked. Hurried and thinking less-than-clearly.

But in this case? Would a man who righted a T-boned car, emptied a flurry of bullets into the offending vehicle, and then sped away in a straight line be likely to panic? A man with John's training and his dedication to a singular purpose?

Not likely.

Still, hope sprang eternal.

The words came to him, and with them the rest of the poem; words he not only heard, but heard in Nicholas' familiar scratchy voice:

"Hope springs eternal in the human breast; Man never is, but always to be blessed: The soul, uneasy and confined from home, Rests and expatiates in a life to come. Alexander Pope, Isaiah. 'An Essay on Man.' Fine piece of literature in which the poet recognizes that philosophy is but a tool that can at best be used to vindicate the ways of God to man, and not the ways of man to God."

Isaiah realized he was crying. He was also driving aimlessly. Neither would help Nicholas, who was dead, or Katherine, who was not.

More words came to him, again in Nicholas' voice: "Let the dead bury their own dead."

He didn't know what had been done with Nicholas' body. When he hunted down all the men responsible for his death, he would be sure to find out. He himself was dead, spiritually, emotionally, so there was none better to see to the final disposition of his old teacher, his original Father.

To business. He thought of where to start. The only thing he had to go on was where *he* would go in their position.

Assumption: the man was a pro.

Assumption: the car they had taken likely had GPS recovery capability.

Conclusion: they would ditch the car.

New question: where?

That was harder.

Based on the original direction they had been heading when they left the scene of the fight, Isaiah would conclude they had been heading toward Hollywood, maybe turning onto the 405 or veering toward the Valley. The Grapevine was a possibility, but that freeway led to the north and there was nothing there. Emptiness bore a certain appeal, but the problem with empty areas was that people tended to remember single vehicles passing by. Especially with a beautiful woman inside.

No. The city.

Isaiah turned toward the West Hollywood area. Beginning the next move in the chess game.

The phone rang.

A new voice. Male.

"They were just at this location."

The voice reeled off an address. Isaiah was irritated to have to turn around. They hadn't headed north, but south toward San Pedro. There was no way he could guess that, of course, but it still irritated him that he had missed that little bit. And as soon as he knew they had headed toward Compton he understood why, as well: they were going to not only ditch the car, but leave it open for someone else to steal. A merry goose chase for him and anyone else keying in on the GPS to find them.

Smart. Damn smart.

The address wasn't far. They hadn't had long to flee.

He got there quickly, but before he arrived he was already seeing something strange. The address was in the middle of a group of buildings, tenements that had been erected for the ostensible purpose of providing quality low income housing for people who needed such assistance. In reality it was a slum, run by unethical landlords–sometimes corporate, sometimes corporeal—with halls that boasted hot running urine, private knifings, and permanent vacancies in the lower floors due to the bullets that flew in on a semi-regular basis as a result of the neighborhood drive-bys.

Isaiah had come here often, to give what help he could, back when he had cared. Before he died in the crash and was resurrected as a man with no soul.

The buildings had a strange light above them. A flickering yellow and orange and red. Like the tenants—most of the good ones highly religious folk—had gathered on the roof for their own day of Pentecost.

He drove closer. Close enough to see.

"Good...."

He had no end for his sentence. No curse, no prayer seemed adequate.

One of the tenements had fallen into another. The first was just *gone*. Pulverized, nothing more than a giant heap of cheap rubble, cheap plaster, cheap metal.

The second had tilted dangerously, and a steady stream of dazed and bloody men and women were making their way out of the front door and the windows on the first floor.

Other people, mostly men with tank tops that revealed the dark gang tats on arms and chests and necks, were running *into* the building. Emerging carrying women and babies and men too old and frail to make the long walk down stairs from upper floors.

A hideous creaking screamed at the dawn. The people assembled near the tilted apartment shrieked and ran away.

The gang members, once-rivals and now fellow-workers trying save those they had cared nothing for only minutes ago, did not leave. They kept running in empty-handed, running out holding the injured, the terrified.

One of them came out, a young man who looked scared even though he had arms thick enough to crush trees and a neck broad enough to pull semi-trucks if you put a yoke around it. The kid was holding a baby in one arm, a screaming child in the other. Isaiah heard the child's screams even in his car: "Mama she died, mama she died, when's momma gonna wake up, mama she *diiiiiied!*"

Before, thinking of Nicholas, he had wept. Now his eyes were dry. He had no tears for this: it was too much. Too grand a horror for tears.

He stopped the car. Intending to get out, to help.

Then realized that if he did, he would lose time. And lost time would mean he might lose Katherine.

Isaiah paused.

What would a man do?

No, that didn't matter. He wasn't a man anymore. Hadn't been for seven years. Almost eight, in fact.

Has it been so long?

Then the choice was taken from him.

The second building fell.

"Mama she died, mama she *diii—*"

And then a crash, and a billow of smoke, and the scream was gone. The gang member with his thick arms and thicker neck was gone. They were all gone.

The phone on the seat rang.

Isaiah picked it up. Not because he felt like he needed to, not even because he felt like that was what he *should* do. He wasn't thinking. His mind was locked in a place with a young man and a boy and a baby.

But the phone rang, and his body knew that a ringing phone must be answered. His body knew to lift the device to his ear.

"Isaiah, we have a lead on them."

"I...I don't...." He swallowed. "There's a lot going on right now."

There was a click on the line, and a new voice broke in. Dominic. "We know, Isaiah. Who do you think did this?"

Isaiah stared at the phone. Like it was a snake, whispering evil to him. Like it might bite him. He had to force it back to his ear. "What?" he whispered.

"You heard me." Dominic sighed. "We've underestimated this guy. We knew he was dedicated to...well, to what we already told you. But we didn't know he had resources like this."

"*Resources*?" Isaiah couldn't tear his eyes off the dust that was settling around the area. His car was just outside the radius, but he could see into the cloud of flame and ash and make out the new pile of debris.

Gang-bangers were already heading back. Pulling huge pieces of cement and concrete away, working together if the pieces were too large. Isaiah saw three of them—each with tattoos marking them as lieutenants in rival gangs—hauling one huge piece of rebar and concrete off something that was moving. A person buried alive.

They reached into the tomb and brought forth the man who had nearly been dead. He was wrapped in cheap wallpaper and they peeled it off him.

"Resources," Isaiah said again. "How could one guy do this?"

"He's like you," said Dominic. "He's a planner. Near as we can tell, he had this area seeded with explosives weeks ago. Led us in here hoping to stop us from following him." The voice on the other end of the line was silent for a moment, then said, "He got three of ours."

"I'm sorry."

"Me, too." Then the voice added, "But a traffic camera caught two people with their descriptions in a dark Toyota Camry, 1988 model, heading east on Rosecrans."

Isaiah was silent, his eyes still roving over the massive destruction.

How could John have done this?

Then he caught sight of some people. Not the ones crawling over the rubble like ants over a fallen anthill. These were at the outskirts. Men and women who had watched but not entered the fray to help.

Many were curled on the ground. Writhing in agony that had nothing to do with the destruction around them. Others were coughing, thick rivers of blood and spit cascading from noses and mouths.

One of the downed people, what looked like an old woman, began to shiver. Isaiah looked away. He didn't want to see what came next, to her or to the others around her.

…highly contagious…

…rogue asset…

…mortality rate exceeding 98%…

…adaptable, transformative…

…determination to destroy…

This was proof. John *had* done this.

He hadn't minded getting rid of the information packet on John. The page they gave him was spare, not much information. Easy to memorize. But enough.

The man was a soldier. SpecOps. One of several men who had been given an experimental vaccine that had been designed to immunize them. Not against smallpox or anthrax or malaria.

Against *everything*.

The vaccine was a cutting-edge man-made bacteria that was actually modeled after some cancers. Like them, it bound itself to the cells of a host. Like them it hid from outside detection. Like them it was capable of changing.

But instead of creating tumors and malignancy, these cancers had been designed to attack all viruses and bacteria and anything else deemed harmful to the human body. From the common cold to HIV to the deadliest poisons, the bacteria would scrub the body clean. Keep it healthy.

It would wipe out disease.

Not only were the military applications immeasurable, but the real-world ones were staggering. How long could a person live without disease, without infection? Hundreds of years? Thousands?

Forever?

But the vaccinations hadn't worked the way they were supposed to. Instead of creating virtually invincible super-soldiers, they drove the men insane. All of them broke out of the facility where the experiments were being conducted. All of them were on the move.

And, worst of all, all of them were carrying something that turned out to be not merely highly adaptable, but highly *contagious*.

The secondary infections weren't anything like what was predicted. The bacteria had mutated. No one knew what else it was doing to John and the others. But when if ventured into the outside world, it caused blood to explode out of its victims. Some in seconds, some minutes, some hours.

And worse than the blood was what came after. The changes.

Some just died. The lucky ones.

Some just died. But some...*changed*.

John didn't just kill with weapons and with his hands and feet. He killed with every breath.

He had to be stopped. Before he ended the world.

A voice intruded into Isaiah's thoughts. It was a welcome interruption.

"Did you hear me?" Dominic said over the phone. "He was spotted on Rosecrans."

"I know the place." Isaiah watched the three men who were yanking huge pieces of concrete and rebar away from the pile of debris that had once been a stack of homes. Had they come in contact with John? How long before they were curled in pain and drowning in blood...or worse?

They pulled another person from the rubble. This one did not move. The three gang members walked the body reverently to the side of the road. One of them took his shirt off and draped it over the body. All three lowered their heads for a moment, two of them crossed themselves.

Then they went back to work.

Isaiah put his car into gear.

He would go into work as well.

"Isaiah? You there?"

"Gotta go. Gotta kill someone."

He turned off the phone and sped away.

He would find them.

He would kill them.

He would still kill the men who had taken Katherine.

But first…John and Serafina.

FACELESS THINGS

From: POTUS <dpeters@secured.whitehouse.gov>
To: 'X' <xxx@secured.whitehouse.gov>
Sent: Friday, May 31 5:41 AM
Subject: message from the President

This is President Peters' personal secretary. I finally prevailed upon him to sleep as he has been up for over 48 hours straight.

Before agreeing to rest he instructed me to send a message to this email address. I am to say I have never seen this email address before, and will never utilize it again. I am instructed to inform you he is asleep. I am instructed to request that you call him or email him with any updates. I am instructed to thank you for your time and consideration.

From: X <xxx@xxx.xxx>
To: Dicky <dpeters@secured.whitehouse.gov>
Sent: Friday, May 31 5:41 AM
Subject: RE: message from the President

This is another personal secretary. As one professional to another, tell your boss never, EVER to let anyone else use this email address again or it will be shut down permanently. I will not pass on your message as a professional courtesy.

PS "Before I prevailed upon him to sleep" makes you sound like an elitist twat with an enormous stick up your puckered sphincter. You may wish to consider rectifying such remiss linguistics before they culminate in a serious depreciation of your personal reputation.

***

In and out, up and down. Past is present, present is past, all wrapped up in the future with a neat little Mobius strip of a bow.

Sometimes she remembers her name. Not now. Right now she is trying to remember who the men are.

One beside her, two in front.

Something behind, something she does not want to see.

They are driving a car.

And then, abruptly, she is in another car. The woman with the face that changes from gentle and loving to hard and cruel, moment to moment, is in the front. A man is with her. She thinks she should know the man but she never quite remembers him.

The woman sings a song. The woman sings *the* song.

"Jesus loves me, this I know, for the bible tells me so...."

She laughs and turns and looks back and her eyes are kind but also strange. Dreamy and dark.

The man in the front laughs, too.

Then the woman's dark eyes turn white and wide. Then noise and thunder.

The black man's face appears. Black and red and white and black again.

Funny clothes, funny clothes. Funny clothes and a funny nose.

The words are hers, but she can never quite understand them. Nor can she understand the words the black man speaks as he leans over her with blood streaming from a flattened nose and tears streaming from gleaming eyes.

165

Then all is darkness and she is back in the car with the men again. She has wet herself several times, but they do not seem to mind that. They just drive, drive, drive.

One of them keeps mentioning, "The killer priest sonofabitch," and the others agree that it is best to keep moving until "they can take care of him, too."

She starts to notice something: they all have black faces. Not like the black man, not like the man whose face figures so prominently in her present/past/future. He has a black face of emotion and life and even a strange kind of light.

No, these are *dark* faces. They seem hard to see, like their heads sit in the middle of small thunderheads, the kind she sees sometimes when the black man takes her outside on walks, though of course she does not walk, but rides.

He takes me on walks.

She never knew that, or at least never realized that before.

And the realization that she never realized that before is also a revelation.

One of the men leans into her sight. He is the blackest of them, the darkest of them: the thin one who sits behind her. She cannot see his face now, only his eyes. Those eyes stare at her, rove over her.

"I can't wait," he says. "You're gonna be so much fun to play with."

He touches her. She barely feels it. She is glad.

She notices that the others lean away from the man who came from behind. As though his darkness frightens them.

One of the men in the front seat coughs.

The others all swivel to face him. They seem frightened.

"Just a cold," he says. "I had it already." But he sounds frightened, too. He coughs again.

Another person coughs. And now she is back in the other car. Still hearing coughing. The man in the front seat. His head is twisted around so she can see it.

His face is gone.

Glass has peeled off the skin, the nose, even the eyelids. One eye is gone, the other roves around sightlessly in its socket. That single eye and a bloody mouth are the only features on a red sea of muscle and blood.

She screams, though she is never sure if the scream comes from her mouth or exists only in her mind.

This is why she never remembers the man's face: because he has no face to remember. Something stole it.

An accident?

Another cough. The man in the front seat. Not of the car with the man and woman, but of the car with the dark men, for her present/past/future has taken her there once again.

"Just a cold," says the man in front. "I've had it for days–"

One of the other men shoots him in the head. They kick him out the door.

The car keeps rolling, rolling, rolling.

Moving like her memories, through a night that never seems to end. Past and present, present and past. Haunted at every turn by faceless men who wear only darkness, who see from within and who frighten her.

She whispers from within her own darkness. No sound comes from her. Her lips do not even move.

167

Jesus loves me, this I know....

BLINDING LIGHT

From: POTUS <dpeters@secured.whitehouse.gov>
To: 'X' <xxx@secured.whitehouse.gov>
Sent: Friday, May 31 5:35 AM
Subject: WH outbreak

Several of the staffers are coughing.

From: X <xxx@xxx.xxx>
To: Dicky <dpeters@secured.whitehouse.gov>
Sent: Friday, May 31 5:35 AM
Subject: RE: WH outbreak

Bully for them. Colds are still around, you know.

BTW: permitting your secretary to use this email was uncalled for and against the terms of our agreements. You realize you have to make a choice? It's between foregoing my company and foregoing hers.

From: POTUS <dpeters@secured.whitehouse.gov>
To: 'X' <xxx@secured.whitehouse.gov>
Sent: Friday, May 31 5:37 AM
Subject: RE: RE: WH outbreak

I will have someone see to it. She'll be gone as soon as I can make appropriate arrangements. Do you have someone I can use?

From: X <xxx@xxx.xxx>
To: Dicky <dpeters@secured.whitehouse.gov>
Sent: Friday, May 31 5:37 AM
Subject: RE: RE: RE: WH outbreak

You screwed up. You fix it. You have 24 hours to kill her or you will never hear from me again.

***

All those people.

Pai Nosso, que estás no céu....

The words of the Lord's Prayer, begun in the Portuguese of Serafina's mother and her mother's mother, the prayer that had always comforted her, failed this time to give her comfort or any hope. Instead of hearing the words continue as they should, she heard others.

Pai Nosso, onde você está?

Our Father, where are you?

A good question. She had always had faith; had never had a problem believing in something higher than she. She went to church, she prayed, and in doing these things she felt comfort even in the face of the death she saw every day.

But maybe that was because there was a sense that such deaths were appropriate. After all, a hospital was a temple to death, or at the very least an oracle where people discovered their fates. If the tests came back negative: good fortune and long life. If the MRI found a mass: the Heavens had frowned.

It was all part of a plan, at least in her head.

But what she had just seen...

There was no plan to that. At least, no plan she wanted any part of.

Father, where are you?

"You okay?"

Streetlights flashed by outside her window. Every third or fourth one was out. The sun was coming up and photocells were shutting down the lamps.

"You all right?" John repeated.

"No," she said. She didn't turn to look at him. Stared at the lights blinking off outside.

He sighed. "Me neither."

Now she looked at him. She didn't want to, but something inside, perhaps the same thing that had compelled her to be a nurse in the first place, made her do it.

He was driving straight. His eyes were focused perfectly.

But his hands clenched so tightly on the wheel she thought she heard it creak. His body was so rigid she could have bounced quarters off his muscles.

"I'm sorry," she said.

He laughed. "Shouldn't I be the one saying that?"

"Probably."

She turned back to the window. All the streetlights were off now. The dawn hadn't quite come yet. Which was good. She had driven down this street enough times to know that if you went down it when the sun came up, all it did was blind you. No pleasant morning rays, just painful shafts of light that turned driving into an act of…

…faith.

Just like going to work every day.

Just like taking a breath.

Just like sitting here, beside a virtual stranger in whom she had chosen to put her life and future.

Everything was faith. And that wasn't what she wanted right now.

She cursed under her breath.

"What now?" she said. Still looking at the dark streetlights, staring down at her like empty eyes. She thought of the many dead she had seen in her life. Too many.

"Now…we keep going east."

"Why? What the hell is east?"

"Something important."

He sounded uneasy. She turned on him again. Angry this time. "How can you say that? You don't even remember your name, John. So how do you know what's waiting for us beyond what you can see? Maybe all you're gonna find when you get over the next hill is *another goddam hill*. You ever think of that?"

He grimaced. "Didn't peg you for that type."

She folded her arms. "What type?"

"The type that would say something like that." He reached out and touched her. At first her body clenched and she thought she might be stuck in a car with a bigger, badder version of Doctor Hershel, sans FiveFinger Shoes.

But he wasn't going for a cheap feel. He pulled something from under her shirt. The tiny cross her mother had given her, a long time ago. The day she died.

Serafina knew John was referring not to her anger but to the fact she had taken the Lord's name in vain. She was suddenly ashamed that she had said such a thing—certainly her parents would not have approved—and in the next instant she was laughing.

Men were trying to kill her.

She was on a fantasy quest to who-knew-where.

Buildings were falling down all around her.

But she was worried about breaking the fourth commandment (or was it the fifth?).

Sure, that made sense.

A moment later, John started laughing as well. She wondered what *he* was laughing at. She suspected he was laughing with her; that he knew exactly why she was laughing so hard and that he thought it funny as well.

She laughed harder. So did he.

He patted her shoulder. Nothing sexual, but a purely friendly pat. A gesture that said, "It's all right, *we're* all right, we'll get through this.

"Have faith."

Have faith.

She kept laughing.

The dark lights passed outside.

The sun crested the horizon.

She would be blind in a moment.

John would keep driving into a sun that made sight all but impossible.

The laughter grew as the light came into the car. Serafina felt like everything might be all right. Like she might make it through this and maybe even find out what "this" actually was.

John stopped laughing. Not a slow petering-out like you did when gripped by near-hysteria. One moment he was in the throes of deep belly laughs that nearly doubled him over to the point that Serafina wondered if it would be best for them to pull over for a moment. Then, abruptly, all she could hear was her own laughter.

She stopped as well. Now the only sound was the wind rushing past weathered windows that had ceased fully sealing sometime in the early parts of the new millennium, the *click-clack-click* of a motor tumbling through its last days.

John had stolen this car because it was available. He had just tried doors until one opened, then looked for keys. She thought he had the best luck she'd ever seen until he told her that even in big cities about one in three people left their cars unlocked, and a huge percentage of them left a spare key in the glove box, under the seat, tucked in the visor.

She wondered how he knew that. Soldier? Assassin? Mobile locksmith?

Regardless, they were in an old Toyota, the air fairly slapping them as it passed by, the motor laboring to pull them up any hill steeper than two degrees.

And John was looking in the rearview mirror and not laughing at all.

Serafina's stomach sank. She looked over her left shoulder.

A car was behind them. Far back, blocks away. But coming up fast.

She didn't doubt who was inside. Sometimes faith brought hope and action, an ability to keep moving even when common sense demanded that you simply sit down and die.

Sometimes it brought a deadening certainty that a killer with a priest's habit was following you. A knowledge that the car you were in had no way of leaving him behind. Nor could they hope to ditch their pursuer in a series of turns: they were on a straightaway, a part of the street that had no side streets or intersections for a while. Just small storefronts built right against one another in a nearly unbroken line.

John spoke quietly. "You buckled up?"

She nodded. She didn't know why he cared. It wasn't like this car was going to get much faster than forty miles per hour. She could practically *run* faster.

"We can't outrun him," she said.

"I know."

As if in agreement, the engine coughed.

Serafina looked over her shoulder. The sedan was closer. Within a block. "Should I get out and push?"

"I wouldn't."

"Why?"

"You might want to face forward. And keep your hands and arms inside the ride at all times."

She did. She saw John's face as she swung back to forward position. His jaw was clenched. His arms were flexed, though there was a slight bend in his elbows, like he didn't want to lock them out.

She had a sudden inspiration. A horrible thought.

He's going to kill us.

And at that moment, John swerved off the street. Hard right. A huge bounce over the curb.

Straight into the face of a building.

Serafina screamed. Her hands went over her face.

"Pray," said John.

She did. In spite of her moments-old confusion and anger at God, she reverted to habit and whispered a quick entreaty. It actually helped–she realized that John wasn't trying to kill them. Why would he tell her to pray if he was trying to kill them?

Unless he was saying "Pray for our souls" or something like that.

All this went through her mind in an instant. The tiny eternity between the slam of front and rear tires over the curb and the impact.

Glass crashed. Wood crunched.

Something else shrieked. Brick collapsed.

Her body slammed forward. The seatbelt cut across her chest and stomach. It felt like it sliced her in half.

Then something creaked and thunked. A door?

A hand grabbed her arm. There was a click and the seatbelt slid off her.

"Come on." John pulled her out of the car through his side.

She looked around, coughing in the dust.

They were in some kind of restaurant. A little mom-and-pop place with round tables (kindling), cheap seats (bits and pieces), vinyl tablecloths (ripped and torn).

"What did you do?"

John started dragging her through the debris. "We couldn't outrun him." He jerked a thumb back toward the front of the restaurant. "We've blocked him off and there's no other way through. He'll have to find a way around and that'll buy us some time. Worst comes to worst he gets through on foot and at least we're even."

Serafina looked at the front of what had until recently been a restaurant. And understood.

The car was halfway through the front of the place. It had slammed through a window that she now saw spanned just the width of the car. On either side: reinforced concrete. The priest would have a tough time pulling a similar stunt. Even if he could bash his own vehicle through those concrete spans, there was no room in the restaurant for another car to get all the way through.

Not only that, but John had only jammed their car partway in. He had somehow spun a bit as well, so the old Toyota lay at a slight angle. The motion had caused most of the building roof to collapse, dropping it on the car's roof so there was no way to get through between the top of the car and the debris. And this building, like most in the area, was built in a solid line without gaps between the others. There was no way through to the other side for blocks.

John had pounded a door right through the wall, then sealed it behind them with several tons of glass, wood, and steel.

They were in the back of the restaurant. The kitchen. And looking around Serafina was glad she'd never eaten here. Several rats and more than several roaches, frightened by the collapse of their home, streamed across the floor. She figured that would probably warrant a downgrade by the health inspector.

Someone should close this place.

She almost giggled.

John was looking around. Looking for a way out.

Now it was Serafina's turn to lead. She had worked in a place like this while getting through nursing school. The back door tended to be by the freezer.

Sure enough, there was an emergency door with a crash bar right by the freezer, across from a unisex bathroom that looked like it hadn't been cleaned since sometime right after chamber pots went out of vogue.

Serafina actually paused. The door had "EMERGENCY EXIT ONLY–ALARM WILL SOUND" written on it, and she thought for a moment, What if the priest hears it? He'll know where we are.

Then she realized how ridiculous that was.

She hit the door with her shoulder.

The crash bar depressed, the door opened. Apparently the owners of this place believed in fire and safety protocols about as much as hygiene, because there was no alarm.

They exploded into an alley that ran behind the buildings that lined this part of the street and the buildings that lined the street that paralleled it. Serafina looked up and down the alley. She figured they would steal another car.

But John didn't move in any direction she expected. And she realized that, whatever she thought he had done when he crashed them through the restaurant, she had only figured it out in part.

John had a plan–maybe one he intended all along, maybe one he had just come up with.

Regardless, she didn't know what it was.

She just hoped it was a good one.

SMALL STEPS

From: POTUS <dpeters@secured.whitehouse.gov>
To: 'X' <xxx@secured.whitehouse.gov>
Sent: Friday, May 31 5:37 AM
Subject: CHINA FLASH

Just leaked that there are several men in China who are apparently carriers. HOW MANY ARE THERE?

From: X <xxx@xxx.xxx>
To: Dicky <dpeters@secured.whitehouse.gov>
Sent: Friday, May 31 5:37 AM
Subject: RE: CHINA FLASH

Will investigate.

From: POTUS <dpeters@secured.whitehouse.gov>
To: 'X' <xxx@secured.whitehouse.gov>
Sent: Friday, May 31 5:38 AM
Subject: RE: RE: CHINA FLASH

Wait you don't KNOW? Good CHRIST. This could end us all.

From: X <xxx@xxx.xxx>
To: Dicky <dpeters@secured.whitehouse.gov>
Sent: Friday, May 31 5:37 AM
Subject: RE: RE: RE: CHINA FLASH

Repeat: Will investigate. Let's worry about our own neck of the woods first.

***

Every moment felt heavy. Like the world's gravity was increasing, bearing down on John's shoulders more and more. A large part of him wanted to sit down and just wait for the priest. It seemed that whatever happened, the last rites he offered would be something quite spectacular.

Only…what about his mission?

What about Serafina?

And what would he say for his final confession? What does a man with no past say when given a chance to offer up his sin?

All this moved him along. Pushed him to action.

Serafina followed. Which was at once both a reason to keep moving and a reason to bow his shoulders a bit lower.

The building beside the restaurant looked like it had actually attempted some kind of outward appeasement of safety regulations. A fire escape clung to the back of the building, walking up to a second-floor back window.

John didn't care about the second floor. He had no intention of going in the building. He was interested in the ladder that went to the roof.

He ran up the ladder. Moving quickly but as quietly as possible. Serafina was a cat, her footsteps silent. He marveled at this for a moment, then realized it was only the same competence she had shown at everything else. She had no training, but she was tough and smart and enduring.

He went up the stairs, then the ladder. She followed without question. The weight on his shoulders grew.

On the roof, he bowed over. There was only a small ridge around the edge of the roof, perhaps a foot tall. He gestured for Serafina to get down as well, then he crawled on elbows and belly to the front of the roof. Peered over.

The car that had followed them had just parked at the curb. The priest jumped out. If he looked up, they were in trouble.

John trusted that he wouldn't. People rarely did.

Another bit of trivia. Another tidbit of knowledge useful only in very limited set of circumstances.

Serafina pulled at his sleeve. John looked at her. She shrugged her shoulders: "Why are we here? What are we going to do?" the gesture said.

He held up a finger. Wait.

He looked back down. The priest shouldn't be able to get through. He should give up and go around, looking for a way through the rubble. When he did that, John and Serafina could get down and run through a building on the opposite side of the street. They'd know which way the priest had headed and could steal some wheels and go the opposite direction on a street he had no idea they were even on.

The priest, though, had other plans. Other resources they didn't know about.

He spent a few seconds examining the blockage that John had created, then apparently came to the desired conclusion: impassable.

He went back to his car. Leaned in. But didn't drive away. Instead the trunk popped open and he walked to the back of the car.

He disappeared behind the trunk, and when he emerged he was carrying an assault rifle. John didn't understand what he was going to do with it for a moment:

shoot at the sky in frustration? Save them some trouble and blow his head off?

The priest did neither. He aimed at the rubble of the restaurant. And that was when John saw the extra tube hanging like a squat stinger under the main barrel, and he understood.

He dropped behind the shallow protection offered by the edge of the roof. Yanked Serafina down as well.

There was the deafening pound of the underbarrel grenade launcher and the even more deafening sound of a high-explosive round blasting apart concrete and wood and plaster. Bits of a building rained down on them. A few cut John's cheek. Blood flowed.

"Holy–" began Serafina. John clapped a hand over her mouth and glanced over the roof. Then he was tempted to say the same thing. The only thing that stopped him was the idea that he would look ridiculous slapping his hand over his *own* mouth.

There was no way through. So the priest had created a way *over*. Marching up steps he had created by blasting holes in the rubble.

Faster and more efficient. And truly amazing. The more so because most HE rounds armed only after a minimum of fourteen meters. The priest had stood just outside that zone, risking death or maiming by the blast blowback and the shrapnel thrown up by the explosion.

John leaned over. The black-frocked man was already halfway up, then three-quarters of the way. Truly dedicated.

Desperate?

The thought flew in and out of his mind. What could push a man to take this risk?

Regardless, his plans had to change. Quickly. The priest would get to the top in moments. Drop down the back. Scan up and down. He'd see the cars, see nothing moving. He'd also see the fire escape and check it out as a matter of course.

The priest climbed to the top. Dropped down.

John and Serafina had only one move.

"Come on."

He grabbed her hand and scrambled to the edge of the roof. He jumped into the rubble of the restaurant, lost his footing, and rolled head-over-heels the rest of the way down. He hit the back of the still half-buried Toyota with an "oof" and then hit the harder sidewalk with a "*uhhh*" that slammed the wind out of him.

Serafina came tumbling down a moment later. Luckily for her, he cushioned her fall. He wasn't sure how glad *he* was about that.

She got off him, bruised and bleeding from a multitude of lacerations she'd won on the way down. She helped him up. Seemed to already know what they were to do.

She headed to the priest's car. Was halfway in the passenger side before he managed to fully get to his feet.

He slammed the trunk shut, then ran around the car and got in the driver side.

The car was still running.

Thank Heaven for small miracles.

"Won't they be able to track it?" said Serafina.

"Probably. But right now I just want to get away from this guy."

He didn't ask who she thought "they" might be. Immediate survival first. Interesting questions later.

He slammed his door. Then slammed the accelerator down so hard he wouldn't be surprised if both pedal and foot pounded right through the chassis and hit the street below.

It didn't happen. Instead the car leaped forward so powerfully that if they hadn't enjoyed the benefit of the leather headrests, both John and Serafina probably would have suffered whiplash.

He risked a smile. They were away, and the priest had no wheels. He had no doubt the man would get new transportation–probably quickly–but for now they were ahead. And every turn of the wheels took them farther away.

"How did he find us?"

John's smile disappeared. "Good question." It wasn't like their mysterious hunters could have known which way they would flee, could have planted a tracking device on the Toyota. Nor did that car have GPS–it barely had a motor in anything but the strictest sense.

So how…?

"The traffic cameras," he finally said.

"No," she answered. "That would mean they completely owned the government. Like, *all* of it."

"Yeah."

"And they'd need some kind of facial recognition software that could just pick us out as we drove past."

"Yeah."

"And that program would have to be loaded into every government-tapped camera in the area. Maybe the country."

John paused a second, but finally said, "Yeah."

The air seemed cold. It had nothing to do with the perfectly-functioning air conditioning.

He looked at Serafina. She looked so stricken, so terrified, that he longed to hold her. To hug her and whisper it would be all right. To be friend and father and lover all at once. But he could do none of those things. He had to drive.

So he looked away.

Glanced in the rearview mirror.

The rubble was still behind them. A few people were on the street. Folks whose curiosity had finally outweighed their terror to the point they came out of hiding to see what was going on in their tiny part of the universe.

And a figure. Standing atop a roof that John knew.

John saw the figure. Far back, but not *too* far. Not for a driven, desperate man more skilled than should be possible.

John twisted the wheel. Serafina screamed as her head whipped sideways.

It didn't matter.

It was almost a whisper. A strangely soft sound, like a mother cooing. But that was a lie. It was Death come to call.

The priest launched the explosive round from what had to be the very edge of the maximum firing range. A place where aim was supposed to be impossible. Just a shot and a prayer and blind luck.

But John knew that whatever luck there was in the world, the priest would have it. That and maybe more. Because he was a man of God, wasn't he?

The explosion slammed into the pavement right behind them. John had an instant to appreciate that fact: a direct hit would have ended them, without fail.

Then something bucked in the back of the car. He realized the priest had pulled his weapon from the trunk. Realized he had failed to look inside the compartment before shutting it.

Wondered what else was back there.

The wheel whipped back and forth in his hands.

Then the caged beast that the trunk had held burst free. There was a flash of yellow and orange.

John hadn't buckled his seatbelt. Normally unlike him, but this one time he was glad.

He was going to die.

He flung himself across Serafina.

He was going to die.

She was warm under him.

He was going to die.

Perhaps she wouldn't.

That would be enough.

NINE LIVES

From: POTUS <dpeters@secured.whitehouse.gov>
To: 'X' <xxx@secured.whitehouse.gov>
Sent: Friday, May 31 5:40 AM
Subject: Germany

The *Bundeswehr* is going crazy. Any reason why a "defensive" military force looks like they're preparing to invade everyone in Europe at the same time?

***

Isaiah felt like a cat.

Cats could climb trees like nobody's business. Straight up, no problem. Coming down, though, they more or less sucked. Their claws hooked down and in, which meant they could capture prey, could grind their way into bark and yank themselves up vertical surfaces. But that curvature, the same curvature that made them efficient predators and enabled them to go so many places that other animals couldn't, worked against them on descent.

Isaiah was a big guy, and climbing up the roof of the building he had pounded to pieces hadn't been a problem. His mass grounded him, his feet dug in and held fast.

Coming down, though, he stumbled and constantly felt on the verge of falling.

Like a cat.

He'd had a cat when he was young. Before it all went to crap, before he ended up in juvie and then met Nicholas and life came together for a few blissful years of serving others and late-night cribbage games. Before the short good years, the longer bookends of the bad, he'd had a cat.

Isaiah's cat was always getting caught in trees. Always needing him to get it down. One time he couldn't. He asked his father for help.

His father got the cat down by shooting it.

Cats had nine lives, but either that cat had already used his other eight or he didn't want to risk them on the psychopath who had wasted one of them because Isaiah never saw it again.

That was the last time Isaiah had a pet.

He was a cat now. He wondered if he was going to end up shot. Probably. And that would be no more than he deserved.

That blue eye–that one beautiful blue eye. They'd both be blue if it hadn't been for me.

No. He didn't have time for pity. Not for himself, not for others. He could save her, to the extent salvation could be had. His was long gone, but even in her twilight damnation, the limbo in which he had placed her, he had to believe *she* had a chance. He had to believe that maybe he could save Katherine.

But he absolutely couldn't do that if she was dead.

Dominic was probably going to kill her. Isaiah knew that. But he also knew that right now his only chance was to find and kill John and Serafina.

Besides, he had seen the people sickened in their wake. The men who had threatened Katherine might actually be working for the good of the world. Might believe their threats were necessary–and might be right in that belief. Sometimes the end did justify the means.

That was his motto, his creed. He could hardly blame others for sharing it. Was he not a priest, if only a fallen one?

He made it off the roof, and neither fell nor was shot by the ghost of a father who pushed him into the beginnings of a life he cursed every day.

The car he had shot sat several blocks away, a dark shape in the middle of a bright halo of flame. Isaiah ran to it, covering the distance quickly and easily. Once he would have panted to run a tenth of that distance. Ironic that his damnation had brought better physical conditioning than anything he had ever enjoyed previously. The temple of his body had grown strong even as the spirit within rotted in its own corruption.

A bystander called out to him. An elderly man who apparently still believed in the old ways enough to trust that a man with a white collar could give answers. "Father, what's going–?" The old man broke off when he saw still-smoking Steyr assault rifle in Isaiah's hands. He crossed himself and backed away. But he didn't go back inside the building he had come from.

"Are you here to help?" he said in a quavering voice.

"Yes," said Isaiah. He hoped it was true. And he saw no reason to frighten an old man even more.

The phone he had been given had a camera function–they all did now–and he was going to take a picture of the charred bodies, send it, and demand Katherine's release.

Then the world would be safe.

Then his penance could continue.

Then...the real hunt would begin. The men who had taken Katherine would die. Justice would come for them, as it came for all.

He arrived at the car.

A burning skeleton. Too hot to get near.

But he could get close enough to see.

The passenger door was open. The car was empty.

He stared at it in shock. Not sure how long before he swiveled around, looking for the dead man and woman who had somehow left the explosion and subsequent inferno.

They were nowhere. Not in the car. Not in the street.

Gone.

He dug the phone out of his pocket. Thumbed the "1."

As before, a voice he had never heard answered. Male this time. Isaiah wondered how many people monitored this line.

"Yes?" said the voice.

"I need a new car."

The voice sighed. "*Another* one?"

GOOD FATHERS

From: POTUS <dpeters@secured.whitehouse.gov>
To: 'X' <xxx@secured.whitehouse.gov>
Sent: Friday, May 31 5:45 AM
Subject: France

And more good news: not only has Germany gone insane, but a source inside the French Directorate-General just informed us that France is mobilizing the *ENTIRE* Gendarmerie and has its AF doing flybys so close to the German border that they could toss water balloons into Berlin.

Okay, we couldn't keep this secret forever, but this isn't a first response to a possible external epidemic. They're acting like their neighbors all turned into Nazis overnight.

I NEED ANSWERS. CNN is going to run with this, which means Fox already knows about it and there's no way we can contain it. My head is going on a platter and if it does I swear to God I'll find a way to take you down with me.

From: X <xxx@xxx.xxx>
To: Dicky <dpeters@secured.whitehouse.gov>
Sent: Friday, May 31 5:45 AM
Subject: RE: FRANCE

Interesting choice of words. I like the water balloons image. Did you come up with that yourself, or is it going to be in your speech when you hold a press conference later today?

I'll email you some suggestions for your speech. You know I always come through on things like that.

But I'd rethink the threats. They are counterproductive and just make you seem like a schoolyard bully. Being a bully is fine until you come up against a bigger bully.

***

Melville was his only name.

He had had another name—once, a long time ago, before he had been found. Then his old name was taken from him, and another was given. Melville.

He barely remembered his old name, and that was fine. He liked his new name. It suited him.

Along with his old name, his old identity, his old family, everything he had once had and once been, had been stripped from him. Some had been simply taken, others he had had to give up himself.

It had been harder than he had thought it would be. The part where he shot his mother in the face had been the hardest part. Satisfying—he had always hated the old bitch—but hard just the same.

He had wanted to do it slower. More *personally*.

But Mr. Dominic had given him much more than he once had. Had taken a man whose only aspiration was to kill his parents in a way that left him comfortably set for life off the combination of the money they had and the insurance their deaths would bring, and had turned that man into…

…Melville.

And Melville was a much, *much* better thing to be.

As Melville, he was a ranking member of every branch of the armed forces, a senior agent in the NSA, FBI, CIA. He was the entire government, save only the Congress—a bunch of weak old men and women, hobbled by special interests to the point of being powerless–and the President.

Melville had no desire to be the President. It would be a huge step down.

All thanks to Mr. Dominic. The only man before whom Melville would ever bend his knee again, and that wasn't too hard on him since Mr. Dominic gave him the run of an entire world in return.

Melville could shoot a woman in Times Square in broad daylight if he wanted to, and no one would ever punish him for it. He would never even be *found*.

For a while, he had done exactly that sort of thing. That, and much better. Mr. Dominic hadn't minded; indeed, he had seemed to approve of it to some degree. "Working it out of his system," he called it.

Melville decided then that he loved the other man. Not in the way that he loved the men and women and children who screamed for him, or even in the subtler, cooler way that he loved the dead ones he sometimes kept in his home. No, this was a deeper, more sure love. A love that would never depart, just as Mr. Dominic would never leave him.

Mr. Dominic was his everything, and Melville was determined to live up to that great blessing and even greater responsibility.

Sometimes it was hard. Sometimes Mr. Dominic told him *not* to kill. But usually Mr. Dominic's orders were easy and even fun, like when he told Melville what he would "have" to do to the retard who drooled and pissed her way through the trip they were taking.

Drool and piss did not bother Melville. They were *exciting*.

He sat in the back of the SUV, in the third row. The three other agents who were left after they had shot one and pushed him out of the car kept glancing back at Melville. He made them nervous. That was fine. They thought he sat back here out of deference to their feelings, but it wasn't that.

The dead bodies were back here. The priest he had shot and the woman he had so sweetly defiled before stabbing and slashing over and over until she died.

She hadn't screamed, hadn't so much as whimpered. That made him sad.

Still, he liked to be near the dead.

And he liked to look at Katherine.

Mr. Dominic said they had to keep moving. He was fairly certain the priest/killer–Isaiah–would toe the line as long as they had the girl, but why take chances? And Mr. Dominic always knew. He was *wise*.

The car abruptly shuddered to a stop. Melville looked away from Katherine, ready to scream at the driver for disobeying Mr. Dominic's orders. The only time they were supposed to stop was when they needed gas.

The scream died on his lips, and the anger died in his heart.

Mr. Dominic was standing outside the car. He had a smile on his face. He always smiled. Even and especially when things were going wrong. The smiles were exactly the same, so you could never tell by looking at him whether he was genuinely happy or about to punish you.

It was another thing that Melville loved about him. He could not emulate it: he wore his emotions on his sleeve and the sharp edges of his many knives.

"How the hell did he find us?" whispered one of the agents. Another shrugged.

Melville knew the answer, though he did not say it: Mr. Dominic can find anything he wants. He found *me*.

Mr. Dominic looked elegant as always, even standing on the side of a deserted Los Angeles street. He elevated whatever place he graced with his presence.

He crooked a finger at Melville.

"Pop the trunk," said Melville.

The driver did. Melville clambered out. He enjoyed the sensation of crawling over the dead. It made him shudder, and he decided to bring these two home.

As soon as he was out the trunk closed behind him. Mr. Dominic waved at the SUV, motioning for it to move off. It pulled away and turned a corner and was gone and with it went the lovely dead. Melville felt sad.

But he was happier when Mr. Dominic spoke those magic words: "I have a special job for you, Mr. Melville."

Mr. Dominic always called him "Mr." It made Melville feel special. Like his mentor thought of him as a valued colleague; an equal.

"Yes, sir?"

"I am a bit worried that Isaiah isn't fully committed to what we're doing."

Melville frowned. "Doesn't he understand the stakes?" The priest had to have read the dossiers. He had to *know*. It wasn't just about his stupid bitch, it was about the *world*. If he failed, millions could die. *Billions* could die.

That would seriously impact Melville's lifestyle.

"I think he does," said Mr. Dominic. "But perhaps he doesn't fully believe what we've told him, or perhaps he just lacks ability. Regardless, talent or conviction, I've concluded that he could use–"

"An *assistant*?" Melville couldn't keep his lips from curling. All his work, his loyalty, and he was going from following in the footsteps of the great to giving support to the stupid?

"Good heavens, no!" shouted Mr. Dominic. He waved his hands in front of him, appeasement incarnate. Melville felt his blood cool immediately. "I don't want you to assist him. I need you to *babysit* him. Keep him on track. Make sure he's moving forward. And if the opportunity comes for you to blow a hole in the heads of our John and his lovely girlfriend, why, so much the better."

"What about in the priest's face?" Melville tried not to grumble. He failed entirely.

Mr. Dominic, once again, did not take offense. He never got mad, never corrected, never chastised. He was like the perfect father. "Once our two little carriers are dead…." He waved his hands again, a completely different meaning this time. "I think it would be absolutely *lovely* if our priest actually met God." He leaned in close to Melville. "And you could take him home with you. He looks like he would be a lovely one. Highly pleasurable."

Melville licked his lips.

A car pulled up. An agent got out. The idea of killing Isaiah was so *exciting*. He just couldn't wait.

Literally.

He looked at Mr. Dominic. His good father nodded.

Melville turned to the agent. "Standard outfitting," the man had a chance to say. Then Melville shot him and had the joy of seeing the man's face fall to pieces.

How do you like that, Daddy?

Mr. Dominic laughed. It was a beautiful laugh.

"I do love you," he said.

Melville beamed. Mr. Dominic was proud, and that made him happy.

He got in the car. The dashboard GPS was active, a dot showing his destination.

He drove away. He didn't worry about the agent's body or about how Mr. Dominic would get away from the area. Mr. Dominic would manage. Mr. Dominic would take care of it. He would take care of *Melville*.

He always did.

RUNNING BLIND

From: POTUS <dpeters@secured.whitehouse.gov>
To: 'X' <xxx@secured.whitehouse.gov>
Sent: Friday, May 31 5:52 AM
Subject:

This may be the first time since it was invented that a man in my position isn't answering. I'm just staring at the telephone and watching it ring.

From: X <xxx@xxx.xxx>
To: Dicky <dpeters@secured.whitehouse.gov>
Sent: Friday, May 31 5:52 AM
Subject:

See attached speech.

Let the phone ring a while. It will cement the idea that you are the granter of wishes, and that supplicants must wait on your mercy. It is never the other way around, and never has been. Besides, couldn't you use a bit of a rest.

Answer emails from me, of course. But other than that, take a break.

:o)

<Address.docx>

***

Serafina ached all over. She felt like she had been hit by a car, then whoever was driving had stopped, backed up, sat on her face and torso for a while, then pealed out and taken every inch of flesh from her body, right down to the bone.

But it wasn't that pain that woke her, it was the *bouncing*.

She groaned. Then, because no one came to her aid and the bouncing did not stop, she groaned again.

Nothing changed, so she took the ultimate action: she opened her eyes.

Blinding light speared through her head, scrambled her brains, bounced around her skull. She almost switched from a dignified groan to a classy scream. Managed to bite it back and slam her eyes shut.

The bouncing kept on bouncing. It was even and relentless. Someone was torturing her.

She cracked her eyes open. One at a time, just a slit. The spears that had nearly destroyed what was left of her body were only arrows this time. Painful but manageable. She managed to open her eyes a bit more, and with the pain came memory.

Driving with John. Fleeing the priest.

And then....

The rest of it drove her eyes the rest of the way open. Never mind the last bits of agony the light brought with it.

The light. The sound.

The explosion.

The bouncing continued, and Serafina finally realized what it was. Arms and legs dangled, head hung loosely. Only her trunk was supported, held aloft by a pair of arms so strong they felt like nothing she had ever experienced.

The light finally faded, drawing closer and closer to something until she could finally see a familiar form at the center of it.

John.

He was running. Running with her in his arms.

She dragged her head and upper chest a bit higher, wrapping her arms around his neck without thinking. She expected him to say something. "Hey," or "You're awake." He didn't.

She looked around. They were on a city street, but she didn't recognize it. Then they passed an intersection– deserted at this time of day, and John ran right through it without stopping, bounce bounce bounce–and she saw they were on San Vincente and Lime.

She wasn't sure, but she thought that was almost a mile southeast of where they had been. Maybe more.

How...?

She finally looked at John. Saw the reason he hadn't said anything. His face was blank. He looked less like the man she had known than like an exceptionally realistic machine. Like someone had taken the best wax museum replica ever created and packed it with state-of-the-art electronics hung over a titanium frame.

His eyes stared straight ahead. They saw nothing, they were somewhere far away, if they were anywhere at all.

"John?"

He didn't react. Just kept running. East. He had wanted to go to Kansas, which was that general direction. She wondered if that was where they were headed now. If whatever had happened in the car had shut him down to the point that all that remained was that directive. Go east, go east, go east.

"John?" she said again. Louder. Still nothing.

She shook him. Hard to do at this angle. And feeling the rock hard muscles that had clenched around her like a protective shell, she realized he was unlikely to feel the motion.

"JOHN!"

She was getting nowhere.

She kissed him.

Serafina did it without thinking. She realized as she did it that she had wanted to on some level for quite some time. He was strong, smart, brave. Aside from the fact that he had no apparent job he was quite the catch.

There was also the whole "meeting him meant sudden death" thing, but every relationship had its challenges.

Regardless, she kissed him, feeling both ridiculous for trying this reversal of the Sleeping Beauty motif, and delicious for allowing herself this flight into fancy. She would kiss him, he would wake. He couldn't sweep him into his arms—she was already there—but he could declare his undying affection and they would beat the bad guys and live happily ever after.

Failing that, they could go for coffee and see where it led.

The deliciousness quickly disappeared, the ridiculousness remained. The kiss was not returned. His lips were slack under hers. He was sweaty and drooling a bit and it was wholly unpleasant.

He was not Sleeping Beauty, and she apparently had a long way to go before she completed Charm 101.

Bounce, bounce, bounce.

The ridiculous feeling persisted, and grew. She soon felt not merely ridiculous, but embarrassed. Then *mortified*.

If her friends could see her now.

But most of *them* were dead.

Serafina punched John in the mouth.

She thought about doing so even less than she thought about the kiss. One moment she was irritated, the next moment mad, the third her small fist was planted firmly in the (terrible) kisser of the man who had both ruined and saved her life.

That did it.

John blinked. His mouth, which had been bouncing open and shut like the bones had been removed, suddenly firmed. He shook his head.

"What's going on?"

He stopped. And dropped her.

Both happened so abruptly she was utterly unprepared, and if she had it to do over she might have rethought the punch. She hit the ground and rolled painfully, every knot and bruise in her body screaming in protest.

"Serafina!" John shouted, and before she had finished rolling he already had his arms around her again. He pulled her to her feet and for a moment on the way up he was cradling her against him. She felt like staying there forever, like this might be the only–the last–safe place on the planet.

"What happened?" she said. "We were in the car. It...." She couldn't finish the sentence. Her mind shied away from the end.

John looked down at her. Tall and sure usually, not even armed men or falling buildings or people coughing their lives away before half-transforming into something else had fazed him for more than a second. Now he looked lost.

"We blew up," he said.

The words were almost painful to hear. The street was empty–strangely so, she reflected–and his voice sounded hollow. The voice of a ghost, foretelling a doom, or perhaps recounting one already passed.

Serafina shook her head. "That's not possible."

"I know." John looked around, still getting his bearings. He glanced up, and she suspected he was somehow figuring out their longitude and latitude by the sun's position. "But it's what happened. I remember a grenade hitting the street right behind us, then the car sliding around, then...boom." He made a nova with his hands, fingers drawn together then exploding outward. He didn't look at her when he did it.

"Then how'd we end up here?" she said, challenging him even though what he said was exactly in line with her own memories. Because what he said made no *sense*.

Just like a man who showed up at a hospital grievously wounded...and hours later bore only old traces of injuries.

Just like a nurse whose only problems had been paying off some student loans and dealing with a pig of a doctor who managed to quietly sexually harass her without actually running afoul of hospital policy...and now was on the run from persons unknown, but who had so much power they could start a small war in the middle of a city without batting an eye.

Just like men who were healthy one moment...and then vomited blood and grew scales and spines and died so suddenly it seemed a nightmare.

No, none of this made sense. But lack of sense didn't mean lack of truth. Sometimes the only thing that could be counted on in a fallen world was that things *wouldn't* make sense.

"I don't know how we ended up here," said John. He was still looking around. "But I think we were given a bit of a grace period, and we shouldn't waste it."

He held out a hand. She knew she could turn away. Could refuse to go with him. He wouldn't make her come along on his "mission," whatever that was.

But how long would she last alone? The men who were after them weren't likely to just let her walk away at this point.

Besides, there was something in her that cried out that she was part of this now. She had to come. Had to see this through.

She took his hand.

They ran.

NEARLY A COWARD

From: POTUS <dpeters@secured.whitehouse.gov>
To: FLOTUS <bpeters@secured.whitehouse.gov>
Sent: Friday, May 31 5:55 AM
Subject: Itinerary

I know it's early, and you're asleep. When you wake up go to the camp. Not THE camp, I'm talking about OUR camp. The one we used to go to before all this. Don't call the kids– it's the "right" thing to do, but you and I both know they're a pair of ungrateful assholes riding our backs until we die. I know that's not a great thing to say. I guess all this is actually bringing out my honest side. Who knew.

Do not alert anyone. Not the media, not your personal assistant, not even your hairdresser–hard as that will be. Just tell whoever's assigned to your personal detail today and leave. Pack a bag with MINIMUM supplies. Like a pair of jeans and a t-shirt. You look great in that, even though I know you don't believe it.

I know you don't understand. I know I haven't been a great husband. Please trust me, just this once. Watch the tube later today and you'll get a bit of an idea. I'll try to call you if I can.

I love you. First time I've said it without having to screw up first, but I think it might actually be true.

***

Isaiah expected a car. He expected an agent.

He did *not* expect the cadaverous man who had killed Nicholas, who had, he suspected, been the one to both kill and savage Idella Ferrell.

Isaiah was holding the Steyr. It still had a full mag. He felt his hands swing the weapon halfway to firing position as the other man got out of the sedan.

The other man grinned at him. "I wouldn't," he said. "Not if you want to see the little bitch again."

That was enough to bring the weapon *all* the way to firing position.

The other man seemed to realize he'd made a mistake. He blanched. Just the tiniest motion, but it was enough to tell Isaiah something instantly. The man was evil, sure, that had never been in doubt. Only an evil person could kill someone as good as Nicholas, only a *truly* evil person could be a part of what had happened to Idella.

But that look. That instant...it was enough to tell Isaiah that this man was a coward. The same as most evil men, he would swagger and strut as long as the power lay with him. But when things changed, he would crumble.

I'll use that. I'll see you cower the way Idella did. I'll show you the difference between the way you die and the way Nicholas did.

"Kill me and she's dead," said the man. He held up a phone. "I have to call in every hour. If I don't, they cut her to pieces."

Isaiah didn't lower the weapon. "I won't kill you," he said. But the tone of his voice left no doubt that there were many things worse than dying. And he knew them all.

Again, the thin man grew a bit unsure. "Don't," he said. "I swear, they'll–"

Isaiah lowered the weapon. He approached the other man. The agent was taller, but Isaiah was bulkier. Oddly, he also felt for the first time in years like his frock and collar really mattered. Like he was a true servant of Good facing down a slave of evil. His collar almost burned as he said, "I'm not going to kill you. But don't ever call her that again. Don't speak her name, don't even refer to her. You're not worthy to do so."

He stared at the thin man. Pressing against him with all the force of will he possessed.

The thin man almost wilted. If he had, Isaiah would have possessed him. Would have owned him, could have pushed him any direction he wished.

Somehow, the man found a spine. He straightened. Shoved Isaiah. The push wasn't hard enough to actually move him, but it said that he wouldn't be cowed. "Don't threaten me," he snarled. Spit flecked his chin. "Do you know who I work for? What Dominic will see happens to that little retard of yours if you even *breathe* on me?"

Now it was Isaiah's turn to fall back. The agent seemed changed. A different person had stepped into his skin, and now he was in charge.

"I'll make sure she dies in agony. What happened to the Ferrell bitch will be *nothing*, you hear me? *NOTHING!*" He laughed, a horrible laugh that made Isaiah feel like vomiting. "She'll be one of my special girls," whispered the man. "So cold, so compliant."

Isaiah didn't know what that meant. He didn't want to. He had seen so much evil in his life. His father, the gangs. The people who had confessed to him, the others he had brought out of their torment. The ones to whom he had brought justice.

And, of course, his own evil.

(*One eye clear, the other eye clouded.*)

But now, staring at this man, he realized that what he had seen was only the surface film on a deep lake whose corruption ran to profundities he would never understand.

There was evil, and there was Evil.

He was seeing the latter.

The agent smiled at Isaiah. "Call me Melville," he said.

Isaiah was confused. "Why should I–?"

Melville giggled. Less horrible than the laugh a moment ago, but the madness in the sound still made Isaiah feel like his blood was trying to escape through his throat. "Because we'll be *working* together, Mr. Sillypants."

Isaiah shook his head. "I work alone."

"I know, I know. But Mr. Dominic thought you could use some backup." He waved a hand in front of him. "I won't get in the way, I promise. You could say I'm here in a strictly advisory capacity. A consultant, you know? So you get all the benefits of my expertise and you don't even have to spring for insurance benefits." He clapped Isaiah on the shoulder. Isaiah felt like taking a shower. He doubted it would help the deeply unclean feeling the touch gave him. "Best of all possible worlds, right, friend?"

Melville grinned, and the teeth he showed off were slightly stained, slightly crooked. He moved to the passenger side.

"Come on," he said. He got in.

Isaiah got in as well. What else could he do?

"Where are we going?"

"That's an excellent question," said Melville. "We don't know exactly–not yet. But they're going to head east."

"How do you know?"

Melville shrugged. "Mr. Dominic told me so."

"And he's always right?"

Melville smiled that stained smile. "You can take it to the bank. And bet your life on it." The smile disappeared. "Now drive, asshole. Time's a-wastin'."

interlude:
SAVAGED

EARS UNHEARING

From: POTUS <dpeters@secured.whitehouse.gov>
To: Karen Valdez <kvaldez@secured.whitehouse.gov>
Sent: Friday, May 31 7:02 AM
Subject: Itinerary

Karen, dammit, you tell my wife to get her ass up here and/or start answering my calls or I WILL HOLD YOU PERSONALLY RESPONSIBLE. I don't care that you're "her" assistant, if you think you can keep yourself from reprisals from a guy who sits in my chair, you are sadly mistaken.

Please, please, PLEASE. I just need her to listen to me for five minutes. I know she's still pissed at me over the last incident, but this is important. Tell her she never has to listen to me again, but she HAS TO LISTEN TO ME ON THIS.

***

Sometimes life gives you lemons. And contrary to popular opinion and motivational posters all over the world, the proper response is *not* to make lemonade. All that did was fill your hands so you couldn't fight back when the inevitable sucker punch came, and only five-year-olds made any money selling the stuff. No percentage, a marked decrease in your ability to defend and attack. No, lemonade was a total gyp and in Rena Thomsen's experience when life gave you lemons the only reasonable course was the following:

1. Kick Life in the nutsack. If necessary, follow up with an eye-gouge.

2. While Life is down, rifle through its pockets.

3. Take anything in said pockets.

4. Regardless of what is in said pockets, take the lemons that started the whole kerfuffle and shove them up Life's ass.

She was involved in something like this last when it all came apart.

She was supposed to meet up with Chance. That wasn't his name, but she didn't care. All she cared about was the fact that he sold dope–a wide variety of the stuff, from 'shrooms to E to weed, even the more serious junk like crack and heroin–and the more important fact that she had finally figured out his deposit schedule.

She'd been buying from him for almost a month. Small amounts of ecstasy mostly, which was totally believable when you looked at her. Spiky hair that had been dyed in alternating strips of fire-engine red and sapphire blue, a dozen earrings on each side, a nose ring, fashionably ripped clothes. She practically *screamed* "screw me senseless at a rave."

She had no intention of either going to a rave or of having sex in the near future. She hated raves, and sex wasn't something she'd ever enjoyed.

But she did like money. And since she *didn't* like working, she preferred to steal it wherever possible.

Chance was Oriental–Chinese or Jap or some kinda gook, they all looked the same to her. Hunky in a Bruce Lee way if you were into that. She knew that today he'd be loaded with cash from his rounds, and this would likely be his last stop before he dropped off a percentage to the local gangs that let him operate in this neighborhood, then off to do whatever he did with the rest of it. Probably sound investments in low-risk bonds and a 401(k).

Right.

She looked around. She always met Chance in an alley just off a fairly busy street, which was another reason he wouldn't be expecting her to jack his bankroll. Too much possibility of someone coming by.

But the thing was that Rena had a gun, and she didn't mind wasting someone if it meant a payday. So she'd ask nicely and if Chance didn't answer right the first time, blammo. If someone else happened by, it'd just be a twofer.

All good. Just one more kick to the balls of Life.

Besides, she didn't think there was much chance of anyone spotting her. The streets were coated with a thick early morning fog, and that seemed to have encouraged even the crazy people who liked to jog before work to stay indoors. The street outside the alley was utterly deserted.

It was almost creepy, in fact. Rena didn't like to read, but she was all about a good movie. Scary ones were her favorites. Not ghost movies–those were too slow and they didn't usually have blood or anything–but she liked the ones with dudes who rammed pitchforks through people or other dudes who used weed whackers to whack fornicating teens to pieces. Lotsa guts.

But those crazy killers…they always came out of mist like this. A storm, a blizzard, the fog. The truly deranged seemed to favor crappy weather.

The lights in the alley–a few low-wattage bulbs that barely managed to illuminate the space in the night–

flickered and went dark. They must be on timers, keyed to turn off in the morning.

Only it wasn't morning. Not really. The fog was too thick. Not morning, or twilight, or day or night or anything else. It was just...*gray*. Like the world had turned into a nothing, was disintegrating, and the first things to fall apart were sun and moon and the sky itself.

Rena suddenly felt like she was all alone. Not in the alley, but in the universe.

How did you kick Life in the balls if Life had ceased to be?

"What's up, beautiful?"

Rena nearly jumped out of her earrings. She had been facing into the fog, half expecting something to lurch out of her like one of those zombies that chewed your face off and then had sex with your eyeball holes, and Chance had come up behind her.

He was already reaching into a pocket of the huge black coat he always wore.

Rena reached into her pocket as well. Not to get the fifty bucks she usually paid him, but to grab her gun. She pulled it out and didn't bother asking Chance for his cash. She just pulled the trigger and then pulled it again.

Dude had it coming. He'd scared her.

Rena went through Chance's pockets efficiently. She'd done this before, both on bodies horizontal and those still upright. She was an old hand.

She found his bankroll quickly. Pocketed it. Counting would come later.

She went for the drugs next. She wasn't a dealer, but there was always someone willing to buy in bulk for a discount. A fast buck could always be made.

She smiled and felt her confidence returning. Once again, foot had found groin. Lemons were going up Life's butt. All was well with the world.

A sound stopped her.

Her hand was still in Chance's jacket. She had his sweaty wad of money in her pocket. Worst of all, the gun that had wasted him was on her person. If it was the cops there was no way she could talk her way out of it.

But that wasn't what made her freeze. The sound wasn't footsteps coming closer or even other people trying to steal her hard-earned take.

The noise was low and bubbling. It rolled through the alley. It sounded a bit like the chainsaws that featured in so many of Rena's favorite movies, but wetter and quieter. As though the machine had already bitten through a hundred bodies and now was idling, saturated with blood and gristle and waiting to slash through its next unlucky victim.

It was coming from the mouth of the alley.

Rena looked toward the street. The fog swirled, turning around and into itself like a thousand tiny tornados had taken up residence just outside the alley. It was dark out there. Darker than it should have been, even in a fog as thick as this. There should have been *some* light. Some nimbus projected by the sun above.

The growling, grumbling sound continued. It got louder, and it sounded more and more like a machine designed to rend and destroy flesh. And more than that, it sounded like it could tear apart a soul, like it could pull sanity itself to pieces.

She backed away. Toward the other end of the alley. She realized she had pulled out her gun again.

Step after step. Never taking her eyes off the side of the alley the sound was coming from.

The fog started to drift *into* the alley. It curled in like a living thing, reaching wraith-fingers toward her, fog tentacles that grasped and grappled for her ankles and legs.

She moved faster. The sound grew louder.

It was coming from behind her as well.

She spun.

The sound wasn't the only thing that had encircled her: the fog had come into the alley behind her as well. She was trapped between two collapsing walls of disintegration. Two lines of nothing that held only....

What?

"Who's there?" she shouted. She was happy that there was no quaver in her voice. She was a tough bitch. People who kicked Life in the balls were always tough bitches. "I will shoot your ass."

She cocked the gun so whoever–

(*whatever*)

–it was would know she meant business.

The growling just got louder. Coming from in front of her. Now behind. She realized it wasn't two distinct sounds, but only one, moving in a circle. Only it moved faster than was possible. No way it could get behind her, in front of her, behind her. Not *that* fast. *Nothing* moved that fast.

Rena tried to follow the sound; spun until she was dizzy. And the dizziness was not caused merely by her turning but also by the sense that Life was, at last, about to kick back. That she had never really gotten the best of it, but that it had simply been waiting for this moment.

Something came from the fog.

Rena expected a man. A giant, perhaps, maybe wearing some sort of sports paraphernalia, certainly holding a grim and terrible weapon capable of the most intimate mayhem.

A man did emerge. Neither huge nor outfitted with the latest Sports Authority accoutrements. He held no weapon. Only a chain.

The chain led to a collar.

The collar was around the neck of a thing that Rena had never seen. But it was somehow familiar. She had never looked upon something like it before, but in that moment she knew it. Then her mind ran to madness like a child to its mother.

She fired her gun, pulled the trigger over and over and over until it was empty.

The thing at the end of the chain grunted as the bullets hit it. It did not fall. Its eyes narrowed in a strangely human expression. Rage.

The man who held the chain looked at Rena sadly.

He let the chain play out. Slacken.

The thing crouched.

Leaped.

Rena screamed.

She kept screaming for a long time.

***

Jack's name wasn't really Jack, it was Jim. But as his last name was Jones, and "Jim Jones" was a name with some of the worst possible connotations, he had started going by Jack over thirty years ago. He also avoided Kool-Aid, though that was because he was diabetic and he could never be sure if he was getting the artificially sweetened stuff or the original kind that would send him into insulin shock faster than a hummingbird's heartbeat.

Jack Jones' character was as far from that of his more infamous namesake as could be. He was quiet, not particularly charismatic. He never got religion, especially not the kind that called people to unthinking acts of devotion, and, except for the two times he went to bury his children in other states, he had never left the city in which he was born.

The greatest distinction between Jack and Jim, however, was easy and simple: Jack Jones was a kind man. He had no need to control others. He was happy enough to exist in the background, just doing his job—whatever it was—and seeing that those around him were as happy and comfortable as life allowed.

He was alone. That was another difference. He'd never been surrounded by thousands or hundreds or even *dozens* of adherents. But he'd had a family. Two kids—a boy and a girl—and a wife who clearly didn't understand how far out of his league she really was when she said yes and then stayed married to him until colon cancer stole her away from him thirty-two years later.

The kids died right after, which made some sense: Jack wanted to follow Evie as well, and given the chance he would have. But he didn't believe in suicide, and no one was so kind as to provide him a pathway to amble after his sweetheart. Only the kids got to go, courtesy of a pair of burglars who busted into Jack's house while they were over checking on him.

Ironic that he was on his way over to *their* houses. Didn't find out what happened until he came back, grinning like an idiot because he'd found out from his kids' respective roommates that both had decided to surprise him.

And they were gone. Son shot in the head, daughter beaten to death with a trophy Jack got for not missing a day of work in three straight years.

He kept on. He still didn't believe in suicide, though he certainly thought about it more. But Evie would not have approved.

Jack survived, and did his best to live. Two different things, and sometimes the gap between them seemed as deep and wide as the one between Heaven and Hell.

He was active with his local Shriners group. He played bingo twice a month at the local community center. There was a group of cute kids that lived across the street from him and he took them all to the dollar theater whenever there was an animated movie playing.

He survived. He lived. He waited to die. It was all okay with him.

Most mornings Jack was up well before dawn. He still had the same bed frame he had brought Evie into on their wedding night, and still slept on the same side of the bed. But even half of a half-empty bed seemed too big. It felt like it wanted to swallow him sometimes. And though he wanted to see Evie, Jack did not want to be eaten by furniture. That would make for an embarrassing obituary.

So he rolled out of bed on many mornings and walked the neighborhood. He always took a trash bag so he could gather up stray bits of litter in the area. There was lots of trash, and more every day. People didn't care much for keeping the world clean.

Maybe they just didn't care about anything. That worried him.

It was foggy today, and quiet. That was all right, though. Jack liked quiet. Quiet brought the sounds of the dead. Not ghosts, but memories. The cries of new babies, the whispers of love-making. Long-gone, but always present in an old man who counted the days until he would be old no more, and would find out if there was something beyond or if he had hoped for reunions in vain.

He heard the sounds of hospital equipment sometimes. The drip-drip of fluids, the weak rasps of his wife as she took her last breaths. And those were all right, too. He held her hand when she went, and though she was too weak to hold his hand back he knew she felt him there and knew that mattered. Not many people managed to be in love like he had. Falling in love: easy. Making love last was…not a job, no, never that. But a calling. And he felt he had fulfilled it.

Another sound suddenly intruded. Not as pleasant as the gurgles of swaddled infants or the sighs of a passionate wife. It was deep, resonant. It made Jack feel sick. He didn't know what it was, but knew instinctively that it belonged to something that you did not mess with.

He turned to go back. Even in the darkness cast by the fog, he knew he could find his way home.

The scream stopped him.

A woman's scream.

He turned around again, a jerky Hokey-Pokey that would have made Evie laugh if she had seen it.

Help me out here, Evie.

He knew he'd need whatever help he could get. Didn't know how, but knew it just the same.

He ran toward the scream.

The sidewalk slapped beneath his orthopedic shoes, the breath slammed in and out of lungs far too old to do this kind of thing. But he didn't turn back. A woman was *screaming*. He wondered if this was the sound his daughter had made, and wondered if she would be alive if someone had run to her.

He rounded a corner. Into an alley.

A woman was there. The fog didn't allow Jack to see much, but he could see a huddled form. Streaks of red and blue hair, a dark outfit with rips all over it. Probably fashionable, though to him it looked like she was going for some "street-walker-who-barely-made-it-out-of-a-scissors-factory" look.

A moment later he saw what she was screaming at.

He wanted to scream, too. But couldn't. Something held his tongue fast. Not just mentally, but physically. Some kind of invisible clamp had rammed its way between his lips, cranked open his jaw, and tightened around every noise-making muscle he had.

Help me, Evie.

The thing in the alley was low, sleek-looking. The rumble that came from it was dangerous.

The woman was still screaming.

Jack took another step. Not sure what he was going to do–not sure what he *could* do. He wasn't a hero. He was just a man, just someone who did the best he could, and God knew that was so often less than was needed in this world.

The woman had a gun. She started shooting. The sound felt like it ruptured Jack's eardrums, and he saw the thing beyond her jerk as the bullets hit it. But....

No blood. No blood, where's the blood?

The thing stepped toward her. It glided on feet that seemed somewhere between claws and tendrils, something that was neither plant nor animal but an aberrant half-thing that defied classification. Its legs shifted, and Jack realized that what he had taken for fur was in fact a sort of spiny mass, like porcupine quills, only rougher and with tips that glistened venomously. Then he blinked as the quills writhed and eyes glinted along their lengths. Now the quills looked like snakes.

Then they shifted again, and were spines. Snakes, spines, snakes, spines. One, then the other, and somehow both at once.

He fell to his knees.

The woman was no longer shooting. But she was still screaming.

The thing stopped moving. There was a long chain around its neck. What passed for its neck. What Jack *assumed* was its neck, because he had not the strength to look at its face. If he did, he feared he would lose himself utterly in the nightmare he had stumbled into. And what good would it be to come to Evie if he was a shambling wreck of a spirit? Could even a ghost go insane?

The chain was thick, drooping slightly and disappearing into the mist. Jack couldn't see what it was attached to on the other end. He got a vague sense of *something*. An almost-glimpse in the shifting fog that swallowed this place. But not enough. Or perhaps too much.

The thing that was plant and animal and everything and nothing but certainly madness, yes, *certainly* that, looked back. Into the mist at whatever restrained it.

The chain fell slack.

The beast turned to the woman.

She was still screaming.

And then her screams reached a fevered pitch as the thing leaped on her.

Jack wanted to run to her. Wanted to save her. To do something. He hadn't saved Evie. Hadn't saved his daughter or his son. No hero, just a man, and a failure at most things he did.

He stayed where he was. All he could do was play witness to death, and then follow that death with his own.

The woman's screams grew louder. He wouldn't have thought that possible. Would have thought she would have to shred herself to pieces to get that kind of volume from her mouth.

The beast was savaging her. Moving so fast and so violently that Jack couldn't really tell what was happening. He only saw blood, only smelled the sick thickness of voided bladder and bowels.

Shouldn't she be dead? How is she alive?

The thing snarled and snapped. Jack tried to keep his eyes away from the thing's face. He mostly succeeded.

Finally it moved away. The woman was still screaming.

How...?

She was nothing. Just a patch of blood and flesh, the barest bits of a body otherwise consumed by a nightmare. But those bits were shrieking, shrieking. No mouth he could see, no lungs he could find. But sound, sound, sound. Sound that rammed pistons through his brain, that drove him to his knees.

He tried to remember how to pray.

The bits of flesh on the blood-spattered asphalt suddenly writhed. Not much of them, but they drew together, pulling into a thick rope of muscle and viscera–

(*that still screamed still screamed still screamed!*)

–that writhed back and forth like a worm cut in half. The beast stepped forward again. It leaned down. Jack felt sudden relief. It would feed. Consume the rest. The woman could die. The screaming could end.

But the beast did not feed. It stepped one of those claw/vine feet forward, and touched the screaming cord of muscle that should be dead and somehow was not.

The line of muscle twisted around the beast's paw. It climbed up the paw, then the leg, then threaded into the quills and….

Jack shook his head. He almost slapped himself.

The woman–what was left of her–disappeared. The ropy knot of bloody gristle writhed and flopped among the quills, then was just gone.

The thing, the best, shuddered. It hunched over, and then it grew before Jack's eyes. As though it had taken what was left of the woman and made her flesh its own. It looked stronger, larger, more frightening.

And suddenly Jack he saw her–the woman, what was left of her–again. He didn't know how he could tell it was her, but he knew. The eye-rimmed quills that rode the beast had increased by one. It might have been his imagination, but he thought one of them actually swiveled to….

No. Crazy. It's crazy. You've gone insane, old man. Mad as a Jim. Finally drunk the Kool-Aid.

But it was true. One of the things was looking at him. And it was her. It was the woman in the alley. Changed to a spiny thing, a part of a monster. He knew it in his bones, knew it the same way he'd always known Evie loved him and he loved her.

The beast–not the thing that had been a woman, but the thing that had taken her into itself, and was now so massive it barely fit into the alley–looked at him. Jack saw its face for the first time.

Unlike the woman, Jack did not scream. His breath was stolen away.

He was already on his knees.

But he abruptly remembered how to pray.

three:
PASSAGE

OPTIONS EXHAUSTED

From: POTUS <dpeters@secured.whitehouse.gov>
To: G Etheridge <getheridge@detail.secretservice.gov>
Sent: Friday, May 31 7:18 AM
Subject: Mrs. Peters

Gill,
I've attached a map. It's encrypted, ask Jerry in IT for a Key27 USB and use the decrypt to get the map location. If it seems like I'm being paranoid it's because I am. You'll understand why in a few hours.

The map is to a remote location, and before you bother responding, yes, I know this is not protocol.

I need you to fetch my wife. Take her to the location. She is going to resist. Take her anyway.

Gill, this is important: if you have to knock her over the head and smuggle her nearly dead body out in the trunk of your own personal car, DO IT. This is highest priority to me. The recent Russia problems, the upcoming summit, even the dimwits from the ACLU that I'm supposed to have lunch with later today—they're all cancelled as of 0900 hours. The only things on my plate are a single issue the whole world's about to become aware of followed by BURYING YOUR ASS IF YOU DON'T DO THIS.

<vxys8394*x.2^pt>

From: POTUS <dpeters@secured.whitehouse.gov>
To: 'X' <xxx@secured.whitehouse.gov>
Sent: Friday, May 31 8:22 AM
Subject: NK

Getting prepped and I got a call from that Jenna bitch from Fox. Normally I wouldn't talk to her if I was drowning in my own feces and she was the only one around I could call for help, but my secretary put her through and said it was urgent.

Holy hell.

Jenna has a source in NK. ***The country's gone dark***. Not just avoiding contact with the outside world, nothing new about that, it's GONE. As though they all shut the doors, went into the cellar and shot themselves.

My people get briefed every ten minutes, and the sat flyovers happen every twenty minutes or so. Which means this occurred in a period of ten minutes.

How? This is related to the carriers, right? But how?

Please, I need some answers.

Jenna said she hadn't shared this with anyone yet—wanted to get a full-on exclusive with me. She's in some deep hole under the building, gagged and with very loyal people watching her who are under orders not to talk to her, let her eat, let her drink, or allow her bathroom breaks. But if she found this out someone else will. And when that happens we are looking at a cataclysm. A few people can disappear *in* a country and no one will miss them. An *entire* country disappears and it's a different story.

PS The meteorological reports are starting to scare people. Do you have any idea about the fog that's apparently starting to roll in everywhere? It was making the intel people nervous because it's impeding sat functions, but now it's everywhere. Forget the intel groups, it's scaring *me*.

From: X <xxx@xxx.xxx>
To: Dicky <dpeters@secured.whitehouse.gov>
Sent: Friday, May 31 8:22 AM
Subject: RE: NK

Push up the timetable. Go on your 10 am press con and give the speech I prepped for you to give later tonight. Don't worry about NK. Trust me on this, no one will worry about them.

From: POTUS <dpeters@secured.whitehouse.gov>
To: 'X' <xxx@secured.whitehouse.gov>
Sent: Friday, May 31 8:23 AM
Subject: RE: RE: NK

TRUST you? You?

And what about the fog?

From: X <xxx@xxx.xxx>
To: Dicky <dpeters@secured.whitehouse.gov>
Sent: Friday, May 31 8:22 AM
Subject: RE: RE: RE: NK

The fog will take care of itself.

And I know we have an unusual relationship, but have I ever steered you wrong?

***

John couldn't remember being this tired.

That wasn't exactly fair, he knew. Considering that he couldn't remember any specifics beyond a few hours ago, from a technical standpoint he couldn't remember ever being this happy, this sad, this excited, or this bored.

Everything was new. He had been born only the night before. But a strange birth. Every birth was one of blood and pain, but few involved so much death and none so many bullets.

He looked at Serafina. She was driving, as she had been since Los Angeles. He had gotten behind the wheel when they first "borrowed" the Honda a few blocks from where he found himself after being lovingly socked in the face (she had assured him it was, indeed, just a bit of tough love) by Serafina. But she reminded him that they likely had been spotted last time because of a traffic cam. That meant they were better off staying on smaller roads in bad parts of town, and unless his sieve-like memory had managed to catch an up-to-date map of Los Angeles, that meant she was better qualified to drive/navigate.

He moved out of the way instantly. He didn't know much about himself, but knew that it was better to accept a good idea than to insist on sitting in the driver seat.

She led them easily out of the city, taking them through a series of roads that were mostly potholes held together by crumbling strands of asphalt. Chain link fences separated the houses on either side of them, both from the roads and from each other. Bars on the windows were the norm, and pockmarks from stray drive-by bullets were not unusual, a strange sort of acne that cropped up here and there on the faces of the neighborhoods they passed.

A fog rolled in as they rolled on. It thickened quickly, strangely, and soon the houses were only dim trolls that lurked on either side of them, the streetlights cyclopean eyes that were friendly or forbidding depending on their color.

The fog was eerie, frightening. John didn't remember ever seeing something like this–of course he didn't–but even without memory he could tell it was wrong. Could tell by the absolute silence it brought, by the complete lack of traffic that was unusual if not impossible in a city this size.

Could tell by the way Serafina drove, body tense and shallow breaths pulsing in and out of her. Afraid.

The fog helped them in one thing, at least: even without Serafina's driving, after an hour or so the fog was so thick that John doubted any camera could have caught them even if they were standing within six feet of its unblinking aperture.

Serafina reached for the radio at one point. Her fingers stopped an inch away from the power button. They curled in on themselves, then drew back. John felt himself relax. He didn't want to hear whatever was playing.

Or, perhaps, whatever wasn't. The fog made him feel like they were alone in the world. And if she turned on the radio and found only static? What then?

They pushed east. Not directly east, but northeast.

"You know where we're going?" John asked when they were well out of city limits.

He didn't really worry about Serafina's ability to get them closer to his goal. He just needed to talk. To remind himself that, whatever existed beyond the mixt outside it, life accompanied him within the car.

"I know where Kansas is, more or less," said Serafina. "I think the easiest way to get there is through Nevada, and that means we take the I-15."

"You go to Vegas a lot?"

"I strip on weekends."

"Really?"

"I have to pay off student loans."

She delivered her lines with such a straight face that John might have believed her if it weren't for the small fact that there was no way he could ever picture someone with as much self-respect as she had dancing for men who would see her only as a physical fantasy and not the much greater reality she represented.

He smiled. "I used to do that," he said.

"Strip?"

"Sure."

"Ugh. You were fired, I assume."

"First night out."

"I can only imagine."

"Please don't."

She laughed. The first music in a night that had alternated between silence and screams.

She looked at the dashboard. "We're about half full."

He nodded. "We're in a 1992 Honda Civic. Four cylinders, two point two liters. Feels like it's fairly well maintained, so probably gets around twenty-two miles to the gallon. Eleven point nine gallon tank." He ran a quick calculation in his mind. "That means we can get about one hundred and thirty miles before we have to stop and find new transportation. Maybe a bit more if we drive on fumes."

Serafina shook her head. "How do you know all that?"

John shrugged. "I don't know."

She glanced at him. "What's the average air speed of a Boeing 747?"

John smiled. He opened his mouth. Closed it again. "I.... Huh. Beats me."

She laughed again. "Can't know everything, I guess. Just cars? What's the tank size on that BMW we stole?"

John's eyebrows came together. "I don't know."

Serafina glanced at him again. Longer this time. "Really?" He nodded. "You knew enough about it to steal it, you know everything about *this* car, but you don't know…." She was silent.

The car moved along, the wind hissing past the windows, the tires whispering over the road that was better-paved now that they had left Los Angeles. The eponymous angels of the city apparently couldn't be bothered with road maintenance.

"What's the capital of the United States?" she asked.

John thought.

She didn't wait long for him to answer–for him to *fail*. "The capital of California?"

Still nothing.

She drew a breath. "How many inches in a foot?"

John just looked at her.

She drove. She shook her head again. Not like she didn't understand, but like she suddenly *did*, and couldn't bring herself to believe the information. Head and heart at odds, and she couldn't decide which side to prefer.

"I know this is weird, but it's almost like…like you know anything you need."

John's turn to shake his head. "I think we just demonstrated that isn't true."

"No, you *do* know it all. But you can only access it when you *really* need it, or maybe when it's something you're right next to, or both. You know all about specific cars when it will help you accomplish something, you know all about stealing specific models when that information comes in handy. But if you think about it everything you've known has been something right there with you, something helpful in that particular instant. Even your name–"

"Which I don't know."

"*Exactly*. You don't need to know it. What good does it do you in surviving the moment? So it's gone. Stripped away somehow. You're like a RAM computer. Everything's there, but not at the surface. The information has to be requested through the right code interface–in this case, by a survival need–before it's accessible."

John thought about what she had said. About the things he knew, the many things he didn't.

"Maybe you're right." His lips curled up, not quite a smile. "But what does it mean?"

"Beats me. I got us this far, you can't expect me to do everything." She smiled, and hers was full and real. "Besides, you're the genius–sometimes–you figure it out."

Then the smile dropped off her face. "John?" She leaned toward him. Grabbed his shoulder. "You okay?"

He didn't understand what she was talking about. Then realized that he couldn't see over the dash. He was leaning forward at an angle so steep he was in danger of falling over. He tried to stop his slide and just managed to convert forward momentum to sideways motion. "Whatsh…?" His voice was slurring. He felt drunk. "Whatsh going…?"

Serafina struggled to hold him up as he slumped, but he was too heavy. All she could do was guide him sideways.

His head fell against her shoulder. Slid down and ended up in her lap. "John?" she said. "John? *JOHN!*"

Her voice turned into more and more of a caricature of itself with every repetition of his name. Got farther and farther away. It fell into a deep hole, but unlike most holes this one was not dark and frightening, but glowed with a light so bright it burned.

John followed the voice. Fell into the light.

One moment he was in the car.

One moment he was leaning against Serafina.

One moment he was in her lap. Vaguely aware of her crying his name, her palm cool on his forehead.

Then he was in another place.

The brightness of the hole surrounded him. Obscured almost everything. He could only see bits and pieces.

Sitting with several other men. He tried to look at them but couldn't. He faced forward, his neck stiffened by discipline, by the inevitable replay of a past that could not be altered.

There was another man at the front of the group. Speaking softly to them. And though John could neither hear the words nor see the man's face, he knew that this was the moment.

This was the mission.

He and the other men received their orders. They nodded. They stood.

They left. The man at the front of the room nodded sadly at them as they went out a door on the right.

The light took John to another place.

He was alone now. Alone, in a place that he knew but could not see. Given a job to do, a job that he would finish no matter the cost.

But what was the job?

He still couldn't remember.

He wandered.

The world was changing, he knew that. It wasn't just the fog, either. There were people dying. Coughing up blood, spines and scales appearing on flesh that had once been smooth and unmarked.

And why?

Because of me.

Perhaps. But that wasn't the mission, was it? Was the mission to destroy life, or to save it?

He didn't know. But he felt like…like….

The light took him away. And this time it did not let take him anywhere new. It was simply all there was, all *he* was.

John ceased to worry, ceased to think.

Ceased to be.

MISTAKEN IMPRESSIONS

From: POTUS <dpeters@secured.whitehouse.gov>
To: 'X' <xxx@secured.whitehouse.gov>
Sent: Friday, May 31 10:35 AM
Subject: Press

You were right. I didn't have to worry about how my speech would go over. There was no one *at* the press conference. A few staffers showed up, but no press reps. Not even Al Tenets, and he's made a career of following me around and giving me a hard time.

I don't

I don't

Shit

I keep thinking about the Constitution. Which is ironic, given some of the things I've done.

The first line and the first Amendment.

The first line begins: We the people.

The first amendment covers freedom of Religion, Speech, Assembly, Petition. Press.

If there's no more press to be free, can we be a country?

Certainly if there is no more "we," there can be no more country.

From: X <xxx@xxx.xxx>

To: Dicky <dpeters@secured.whitehouse.gov>
Sent: Friday, May 31 10:35 AM
Subject: RE: Press

Don't kid yourself. This is far from over, and giving up now is not an option. There are still many millions of people counting on you. Just because Tenet didn't show up doesn't mean the broadcast waves are down. Just because the seats weren't filled in the press room doesn't mean you don't have a country.

We have to move faster, more decisively. We can save this country, Mr. President.

***

John wouldn't wake up. She shook him for a while, but he was completely unresponsive.

She pulled off to the side of the road. Tried not to think about the fog that wept into the car. Ran a quick check. His pulse was strong if a bit more rapid than she liked. His eyes appeared slightly dilated, and they roved back and forth like he was deep in REM state, gripped by a dream or a nightmare.

He was burning up. She didn't have a thermometer, and obviously '92 Honda Civics didn't generally come equipped with them as standard features in the glove box. But if she had to guess, she'd say he was at one hundred and four degrees. At least.

That was a danger level. At that high, an adult could quickly become dehydrated, could undergo hallucinations, seizures. A few more degrees and brain damage could occur, if not death.

She got the car started and went in search of a hospital. They were in the middle of nowhere, though, a long stretch of road between towns on the I-15 between Barstow and Las Vegas. There wasn't much of anything–not so much as a city, let alone a hospital she could check her charge into.

Strange she should think of him that way. He had saved her time after time. But he had also gotten her into this, so–

No, you got yourself *into this, Serafina. Be fair.*

She had been the one to walk down that hall. No one made her do it. She had been the one to look in the room, to look after a patient. Her responsibility to that patient hadn't dissolved.

She was still a nurse.

She would have to ask for a raise.

During her musings that wandered between light hysteria and self-pity, the fog, and concern for the man who radiated a heat she could feel through her light scrubs, she almost missed the sign on the side of the highway that advised her of gas, food, and lodging–all available at the next exit.

She spun the wheel to the right, cutting off a semi-truck in the right lane. It should have been a welcome companion in this no-man's land, but now it was just a moving obstacle. It blared its horn at her and she heard the squeak of airbrakes as it shuddered to avoid turning the Honda into a flattened can on the two-lane highway.

She would have felt embarrassed, would have waved an apology under normal circumstances.

These weren't normal circumstances, though.

She pulled around the tight curve of the off ramp. The sign on the side gave a twenty-five mph speed limit. She drove forty-five, and wanted to go faster but she didn't think the Civic would have kept all four wheels on the ground.

The stop sign at the base of the ramp was completely ignored.

The "LODGING" part of the sign that turned her off the highway turned out to be a Motel 6 wannabe, the kind of place built forty years ago by some optimist who believed the area was ripe for development and who, when proven wrong, had abandoned all pretense of class or upkeep.

She left John in the car. He was mumbling something. She couldn't make much of it out, just an occasional "sir" and "are you sure?"

Serafina ran to the office. The fifty feet between car and office were fifty feet through an oven. They hadn't reached the Mojave Desert yet, but even here the temperatures were well into triple digits. She felt like the rubber on her tennis shoes was likely melting.

She wondered how fog could exist here, in this place in this heat at this time of day.

It's not possible.

None of this is.

There was no one in the office. Just an empty reception desk with a small black and white television behind it that showed nothing but static. Behind both stood an open door that she assumed led to a private office.

There was a Mr. Coffee on a rickety card table to one side of the office—both probably dating back to the Vietnam

War. What passed for a Continental breakfast at places like this.

A shiny bell sat on the desk. Serafina rang it.

"Yeah?" said a voice behind her. She had expected someone to come from the back office, so the voice coming up behind her surprised her so much she nearly screamed, but managed to jam the shout back into her throat before turning around.

The man behind her was grossly fat. Perhaps that was where the traditional Danish portion of the Continental breakfast had gone. For the last ten years.

Grossly fat, a few strands of hair clinging to the sides of his scalp. He was pasty white, which Serafina would have thought an impossibility based on the climate in this neck of the woods. He was holding a wilting King Size Snickers bar in one hand, a bag of Skittles in the other. He wore a goatee of melted chocolate and errant caramel strings.

His eyes roved up and down her frame without the slightest discretion or embarrassment. He licked his lips. His tongue was gray.

"Can I help you?" he said. He emphasized the word "help" and her skin crawled.

"You the manager?" she said. She tried not to let her face wrinkle in disgust, more because it was ingrained in her upbringing than because she wanted to avoid offending this guy.

He nodded.

"I need a room."

"Single or double?"

"Double." She emphasized the word harder than he had emphasized "help."

The guy's expression darkened a bit. "Ten bucks extra."

"Fine."

He moved around behind the front desk, passing by her closer than was necessary. He stank. The smell reminded her of some terminal patients at the hospital: blood and feces and the underlying scent of despair that accompanied the ones who had decided to die whether they had a chance or not.

"It's seventy-seven fifty per night, cash or credit is fine but I'll need two forms of identification either way."

Serafina nodded. She reached toward her waist. She had a pocket sewn into the inside of her pants where she always carried her driver's license and debit card–mostly in case she wanted to buy something at the hospital gift shop.

If they found us with traffic cams, how fast will my credit card get them here?

"You tryin' to hypnotize me or something?" said the pig-man. He licked his lips again.

Serafina realized she had been staring at him as she thought. Realized that was the last thing she wanted to be doing.

And realized there was no real option. She had to get John inside, and get him into a bath. Fast.

She handed over her credit card and license.

Maybe they're not watching.

Maybe whatever's causing all the weirdness is keeping them busy.

Maybe I'm going to win the Lottery and be elected Queen of Disneyland.

Piggy swiped the card. She expected it to be declined. Expected red lights to go off and sirens to shriek.

Neither happened. Piggy just gave her cards back to her along with a key attached to a huge plastic circle.

"I think room fifteen is free," he said, and she almost laughed. She suspected she had the run of the place, and probably would have for the last decade or so.

Then another thought struck her: how was she going to get John into the room? No way she could lift him: she hadn't even been able to keep him upright.

She looked at Piggy.

"Can I ask you for some help?" she said.

He leered at her. "Anything."

"My...." She hesitated. "My *fiancée* is sick. Really sick. He's got a bad fever and I need to get him in a bath. He's too big for me to move, though." She drew a breath and said words that were perhaps harder than any she'd spoken in her life. "Can you help me?"

Piggy looked behind him at the staticky television, as though drawing inspiration from the crappy reception. He looked back at her, a smile peeking out between streaks of chocolate. "Sure," he said.

Serafina ran back to the car. John was moaning louder. No words anymore, just a wrenching cry, like he was watching everything he loved go up in flame. Tears streamed down his cheeks.

He looked gaunt, as though he had lost weight in the few minutes she had been inside. Impossible. But when she put his head back on her lap, it felt lighter.

Impossible.

Piggy was walking along the side of the motel. He stopped a few doors down. She pulled the car over and hopped out.

He lumbered over to her. She made as if to grab John, but he waved her off. "I got him. You get the bath started."

And just like that, she felt bad for calling him Piggy in her mind. Felt like every thought she'd had about him was not a misjudgment, but merely a true judgment on *her*.

She ran to the door, unlocked the door, then hurried into the room. The place smelled like stale sweat and cigarettes masked by a cursory spritz of cleaning solutions. She didn't care, though. The place could smell like a hog rendering plant as long as it had a tub and cold running water.

The bathroom had both. It was barely big enough to hold the tub and the toilet–she could have peed while soaking her feet–but it did have what she needed.

She plugged the tub and began running the water. It came out too cool. She added warm water until it was tepid. Cold water was bad news for a high fever. It could cause shivering that actually raised the body's core temperature and brought more problems.

The tub was half full when she heard the huffing and puffing of a large man being hauled in by a huge one.

"You ready?" said the manager.

She nodded. "Ready enough."

She let the water keep running. There was a drain right in the middle of the bathroom, another hallmark of a classy place, so she wasn't worried about making a mess. Not that she would have cared much regardless.

She grabbed John's feet and together she and the manager got him into the too-small tub. Again she felt like he was much lighter than he should have been. Still too heavy for her to maneuver on her own, but too light to be the man she remembered.

John reacted instantly to the touch of the water. He screamed and thrashed. Serafina almost got a foot in the face.

"Jesus!" screamed the manager.

"Don't let him out!" hollered Serafina.

They wrestled John down. One of his fists caught the manager in the shoulder. "Ow!" he screamed, but he held him down just the same. He looked at Serafina and grinned a thin grin.

John settled down after another minute. He never opened his eyes. His head sunk down, but didn't fall below the level of the water. The tub just wasn't big enough for his whole body to fit inside. Which was great, since his trunk was what needed cooling right now.

The manager rocked back on his heels, then sat on the toilet. He looked at John. "Wow, he's really out. How long's he been like this?"

"Fifteen minutes? Longer?" She felt his head. Still hot, and the skin felt thin, stretched like parchment.

"So he might not come out of it."

"He'll come out of it."

"But he might not."

"He *will*. He's strong. He–"

A hand grabbed the back of her shirt. Yanked her back. She flew into the wall of the bathroom–a short trip, but one she traveled with enough force that the wind was knocked out of her. Before she realized what was going on, the manager was standing over her. His eyes blazed within the too-white mural of his face.

"So this is the fiancée?" he said. He licked his chocolate lips. "Not much to share a room with."

Serafina understood what was happening. Understood, but couldn't believe. "Are you insane?" she screamed.

She was on her back, staring up at the huge man, and now she scrambled backward out of the bathroom, moving away as fast as she could, her head and shoulders knocking into something. The queen bed.

The manager stepped toward her. She kicked at him. But he danced back, surprisingly agile for such a big man. That fact scared her.

"Someone will come," she said. More a hope–a prayer–than a conviction.

He laughed. She saw that gray tongue again. It glinted slightly and she realized for the first time that it wasn't *just* gray. It looked chapped.

Scaly.

She grew cold. Shivers ran through her body with abandon. Memories of men vomiting blood and half-changing to something no longer quite human.

It's happening to him, too.

"Someone will come," she whispered again.

"Are you kidding?" he said. Another laugh. A mad giggle. He started to unzip his pants. "Didn't you see the television? Every channel looks like that, chickadee. *Every channel!*" His pants fell to the floor and he kicked them away. Chocolate bars fell from the pockets, scattering behind him, across the bathroom floor.

"The world is ending." He held up his hands, a gesture that encapsulated the room, the motel, and the whole of creation. She saw chocolate smears on his palms.

For some reason that drove her fear to a whole new level. A touch of reality that kept her mind even from the mercy of convincing itself that this could be a bad dream or a descent into personal madness. "The world is ending, and the rules are all gone. I can eat, I can drink, and no one will make fun of me. I can finally do whatever I want!"

He licked his lips. The flickering tongue of a lizard.

"And I want to do *you*."

GAMES PEOPLE PLAY

From: POTUS <dpeters@secured.whitehouse.gov>
To: 'X' <xxx@secured.whitehouse.gov>
Sent: Friday, May 31 10:38 AM
Subject:

All the station and department heads are doing check-ins. So far it seems like we're at about 80%. No telling how long that will last.

From: X <xxx@xxx.xxx>
To: Dicky <dpeters@secured.whitehouse.gov>
Sent: Friday, May 31 10:38 AM
Subject:

I'm keeping my people on point, but circulate all our fugitives' descriptions to state, local, and federal law enforcement. We have to keep them from getting wherever it is they're going. But I might have some good news for you soon.

***

Melville was bored. Bored bored bored bored bored damn hell stupid bored.

"You ever been to Las Vegas?" They were traveling along the I-15, which Isaiah had chosen as the most logical route to follow based on the fact that their prey was going to head east and was going to want to hurry.

Or Melville *guessed* that was what the guy was thinking. His travelling companion hadn't said a single word to him the entire trip thus far, and after several hours it was getting old.

Melville thought about playing with his phone. He had a totally cool phone he had taken from one of his lovely corpses, filled with games and even a reading application that would let him look at just about any book on the planet. But the games never really excited him after he'd done some good killing. And though he *was* thrilled about the reading application–a good man was always well-read, after all–he had yet to actually use it.

Actual words in actual books always bored him. Just having them at his disposal was quite enough, thank you.

What was reading, after all, when you *lived* an adventure more exciting than any some novelist could come up with?

Besides, the combination of book ownership and life experience was certainly enough to qualify him as well-read. Certainly.

Still, if reading was out and games were a bore…what to do *now*?

"You gonna talk to me, Father?" he said.

Isaiah said nothing.

"We could be traveling a while. A little chit-chat could make it go faster. Unless you wanna get into a game of Slug Bug."

Still nothing.

Melville sighed. "You're mad at me, I get that. But really, what's the point? The old dude was *old*. He was gonna die soon anyway. And the retarded girl…." Another sigh. "What can you possibly see in something like that?" Then he understood, and slapped himself in the face. He hit himself hard, so Isaiah would know he was properly apologetic. He didn't really care that much about his mistake, but if they were going to work together it might be helpful to make nice. At least until he waxed the dude.

"I get it. You're screwing her. Makes more sense that you'd–"

"Shut *UP!*"

The scream was so forceful, so loud and–

(*powerful, frightening*)

–surprising in the car's confines that Melville actually screamed.

No, just a surprised shout. Like when a friend jumps out at you around the corner and you both laugh at it. Just good times. A little excitement.

And how I love *excitement.*

He turned the scream into a laugh and punched Isaiah in the shoulder. "Okay, not that. No diddling the dumbtard." He paused. "Wouldn't blame you if you were, though. She's kinda dishy."

Isaiah looked like he was going to scream, and Melville was tired–

(*and a little scared, Melville, buddy, admit it*)

–of that, so he held up a conciliatory hand. "No, don't freak out, Padre. I just want us to be friends. So tell you what. Let's play a game." He pulled out his phone. "It's time for me to check in."

He dialed. A voice answered. "Yes?"

Melville didn't know the voice. He never did, but he knew they were Mr. Dominic's people. He just *knew*.

In the final analysis, *everyone* was Mr. Dominic's. One way or another.

"Checking in."

"Are you unharmed?"

"Five by five."

"Excellent." The phone disconnected.

"Hey, would you stay on for a sec?" Of course the line stayed dead, but Melville never minded talking to dead things. It could be fun, it could be *exciting*, and in this case it promised to set up a game that would be both. "I need you ready for some orders." He paused as though listening to a curt, efficient response. Then: "Thanks."

He put the phone face-down on his lap. Turned to Isaiah. His fellow assassin had eyes forward, looking more robot than man. But Melville knew he was present and ready, one hundred and ten percent. Men like this–men like *them*–always were.

"Back to the game. I'm going to ask you some questions. Ready?"

Isaiah ignored him. Which was expected. Only instead of being boring, now it was so…so…*exciting*.

Melville had to suppress a giggle.

"Yeah, thought so. You're the strong silent type. Very sexy." Melville couldn't wait to get this guy into his place, eyes open and unseeing, body stiff and cold. Such excitement, such a life.

"Here are the rules. I'll ask the questions, like I said." He tapped the phone that still sat on his lap. "For every wrong answer, for every answer I don't like, for every lie, for every single time I think you're holding back, I'll have my people cut off one of your sexy little girl's fingers."

"You–" Isaiah's face grew red. Which was interesting to Melville, because he hadn't known that could even *happen* to black people. Before his death his dad had always said black people had no sense of shame. Maybe he'd been wrong.

Fun.

"Shhhhh...." He waved the phone. "If we run out of fingers, we start on toes. Then move slowly up her legs. We'll leave all the important pieces, of course, just in case we need them for, you know, later." He waggled his eyebrows lecherously. "Still, that's a lot of room for wrong answers. We should get where we're going before then."

Isaiah was quiet, but now it was a different kind of quiet. Melville liked it. Liked how the big man's shoulders slumped just a bit. Silence could be full of noise. The sound of defiance, the scream of terror crammed deep in a chest.

The invisible deflation of a spirit in defeat, of hope in retreat.

He smirked. Big men were just little men in big bodies. He saw that once on the social media he frequented. He liked social media. Memes and the quick blurbs there, he had found, contained the sum of all truth if you knew how to look for them. If you were smart.

Melville was *very* smart.

"First question...." He looked out the window. The fog that had followed them through the course of the trip was still out there. Creepy. Isaiah had turned on the headlights some time ago, which weirded Melville out. Who drove around the I-15 with headlights on in midmorning?

We do, today.

He looked back at the priest. He preferred to focus on things in his control: personal hygiene, weapons upkeep, who he would kill that minute or that day.

"Got it." He snapped his fingers as though to make a big show of figuring out what he was going to ask. He had known from the first, but this made it more fun. A bit of drama to increase the *excitement* of the game. "Who's the dummy? To you, I mean."

Isaiah clenched his teeth. Long silence.

Melville raised the phone to his ear.

"I'll answer," said the priest. Melville was delighted to hear a crackle in the big man's voice, the promise of tears to come. "Just...it's hard."

"Yeah," he said in a voice that he knew was friendly, even loving. The voice he reserved only for the bodies most special to him. "I knew it would be. Go ahead and let it out." He added a line he'd seen on an internet thread: "You're in a safe place."

That line did it. He knew it would. The guy was putty in his hands. They'd be friends for a long time. Maybe Isaiah would even smile when Melville killed him. That'd be cool.

Mr. Dominic would have been pleased.

"I killed her parents."

That surprised Melville. He knew the guy next to him was a bigwig hired gun. Beyond that he didn't know much—other than that he himself hadn't been first pick for this job, which irked him. He knew a lot of killers, though, and none of them had much affection for the children of people they killed.

"So they were targets and, what, you felt guilty afterward?"

Another silence. Melville didn't bother waving the phone, though. He knew the priest—if he *was* a priest, Melville was going to ask about that, too—would answer. Putty.

This was so cool.

Exciting.

"No. Not targets. I'd been a priest–"

"So you *are* a priest! For reals!" Melville laughed and clapped his hands with glee. "That's so cool!"

Isaiah was silent. This time Melville suspected the man was hoping they'd gotten off track. He shook his head. "Keep going. How'd you kill them?"

"I was messed up. A long time. Nicholas–"

"The old dude?"

Isaiah's teeth gritted again. Melville wondered if maybe he wouldn't smile so much when the end came, after all. "Yes. He got me out of...out of a bad life. And I followed him, all the way to the priesthood. Seven years after my ordination a girl came to confession. She confessed that she had unclean thoughts toward her father. I told her the usual things, be clean, gave her penance. Turned out she was being molested by him. She killed him, then killed herself."

Isaiah stopped. He licked his lips and looked stricken. "Go on," said Melville.

"I should have understood. I knew her, knew her voice even in the dark of the confessional. I should have understood, not what she was saying, but what she meant."

Melville sighed. This was kind of an okay story, but it was a bit off-subject. "How does this get us to the answer to my question?"

"I was upset. I went out that night and I fell off a wagon I'd been on for a decade. I drank. I got drunk. I hit a car."

Melville's eyes widened and he inhaled in sudden understanding. "The girl's parents?"

Isaiah nodded. "And the girl. The parents died. Not immediately. The girl would have seen them in the car, mangled and dying practically on top of her."

"And the girl herself?"

"The girl..." Isaiah clenched his jaw again. Melville resolved to get him the name of a good orthodontist. He could use one of those night-time braces for tooth-grinders.

Then he remembered he was going to kill him.

Ah, well, it's the thought that counts.

"Well," Isaiah finally said, "you saw her."

"What's wrong with her?"

"Brain damage. She was in and out of a series of comas for a year, when she finally came out she couldn't care for herself. Not vegetative, but nearly nonresponsive. She sees things, we think, but she can't talk, she can't dress or feed herself and can barely even move." He paused. "She likes cartoons. She likes going on walks. She likes to be read to."

"Ugh." Melville shuddered. The cartoons were okay, but it bothered him that a retard would like reading. Reading was for well-read men. "Then what?"

"What do you mean?"

"How did you end up killing people?"

"I had to pay her hospital bills."

Melville shook his head. "No, it doesn't work that way. You don't go from drunk driving to cutting people down for a living. There was something else. That's psychology, it's elementary really." He liked that last line. He heard it in a movie once.

Isaiah swerved slightly to avoid a dark shape in the road. It was large. Could have been a large coyote—did they have them out here?–or maybe something else. Melville thought he glimpsed a spiny back.

He didn't like that. That was *kind* of exciting, but mostly messed up.

"I was locked up."

"Ah," said Melville. "And jail screwed with your head, huh? You got diddled in the laundry room? Some Aryan Nation guy with swastikas tattooed on his ballsack turned you into his girlfriend and made you hate the universe, huh?"

Isaiah laughed bitterly. "I wish."

That was a surprise. "Not many people wish for that, my friend."

"We're. Not. *Friends*." Isaiah looked at him long enough that Melville worried they might crash. The highway was mostly long stretches of nothing, straightaways with only scrub on either side. Still, they were going over ninety in a dense fog, and flipping over sounded a bit *too* exciting.

"Okay, okay. Ease up. Eyes forward, man." Isaiah looked back at the road. The speedometer needle edged down to sixty. "So what happened in jail?"

"Nothing. I was out too quickly for anything to happen. I was charged with vehicular manslaughter and related charges. Open and shut, so the case came up fast. I pled guilty."

"How long did you serve?"

Another grim laugh. "I walked out the day of my trial. The judge liked priests, he liked *me*, and it turned out the girl's parents were scum."

"Scum?"

"Drug runners. Mid-level dealers the police had implicated in half a dozen murders. No one was going to miss them. So the judge actively looked for mistakes by the arresting officers and the lab techs who did my blood work. I was released on a technicality."

Melville shook his head. "Wait, you plead guilty and they just let you go?"

"Yeah."

Melville chuckled. Then he laughed. Then the laugh grew to the point that he doubled over in his seat.

"What's so funny?"

Melville couldn't answer for a moment. He wiped tears from his eyes. "Just...just I looked for so long, worked for so hard, for what someone just gave you on a silver platter."

"What are you talking about?" Isaiah spat the words. Melville didn't mind. He was in too good a mood. This was just too funny.

"I wished for the longest time that I could do anything I wanted. Anything at all. And for the longest time I couldn't. But you...you waltz along and kill people and maim little girls and the law bends itself to let you off." He dissolved into laughter again. "So...damn...*funny!*"

Isaiah didn't join him in laughter. But that was all right. Melville understood now that they were brothers, and brothers didn't always laugh at the same thing.

"You didn't go to jail. Then what?"

"I went a little nuts. I realized there was no justice. At least, none that I could count on."

"So?

"So I decided to provide some. I quit the priesthood. I didn't believe it was helping anyone, and I only ever had one other skill: hurting people."

"Now we're talking." Melville punched Isaiah on the shoulder again. Good buddies. Pals. He wouldn't say it out loud, because for some reason Isaiah got all nutso when he did, but he was really groovin' on their connection. "So you killed people?" He grinned as the final piece fell into place. "But only people who deserved it. Like a bitchin' avenging angel." He socked Isaiah on the shoulder once more. "You're freakin' Batman, brother! I'm gonna have to call you The Black Avenger."

Isaiah nodded, face taut in the dim illumination of dash lights and the headlights reflected off fog. "Yeah, that's me."

"And the money goes to take care of the reta–I mean, the girl." Another nod. "Don't hospitals usually get weird about strange men taking care of people?"

"Money takes care of a lot of things."

Melville looked carefully at the other man. Shook his head. "I'll give you this one because we're getting on so well. Don't leave stuff out or you can start calling the girl Stumpy."

Isaiah sighed. "I adopted her."

Melville's jaw dropped. "She's your *daughter*? How the hell'd you manage that?"

"Money takes care of a lot of things."

This time he believed his friend. He laughed. "This is awesome. You have led a really exciting life, man." He wiggled the phone. "One more question. You said you quit the priesthood, so why the priest outfit?"

Isaiah answered quickly, like he'd been waiting for this one. "Because once I represented God in this outfit. I'm not sure there is a God anymore, but I still represent what I wish there was of Him. I come to protect the good souls, and send the damned on to Hell."

He looked at Melville. "And I send them on as early as I can."

Melville suspected that was supposed to be a threat, but he just laughed and punched the priest again. This was so cool. Just awesome. *Exciting.*

His phone rang. Isaiah glared at him. "You said you had someone on the line."

"I lied. Folks like you and me do that sometimes." He picked up. Spoke to the new voice. Always a new voice. That was kinda exciting, in a boring way.

After a few short words he hung up. A grin stretched across his face so far he could feel it in his earlobes.

"What is it?" said Isaiah, aka The Black Avenger.

"We got 'em."

BALANCE OF JUSTICE

From: Director <KRSellers@dir.cia.gov>
To: FLASH LIST
CC: POTUS <dpeters@secured.whitehouse.gov>
Sent: Friday, May 31 10:42 AM
Subject: RDD/DefCon SitRep

FLASH ALERT:
At 10:39 hours, EST (14:39 UTC/GMT), an explosive device was detonated in Tehran. It is too early for definitive reports, but early analysis indicates it was likely an RDD (see Attachment A, info sheet 1, common radiological disbursement devices).

Based on the blast radius, it appears likely that the device was brought into the city via rail and detonated near the Tehran Station (see Attachment B, map 1). Explosive base was probably ANFO (see Attachment A, info sheet 2) or ANNM (see Attachment A, info sheet 3).

Winds are currently high, with unusual meteorological patterns rendering prediction as to radioactive fallout difficult. Analysts will provide information re projected casualties as it becomes available, but first area of impact likely confined to several square blocks (see Attachment B, map 2). Secondary area of impact has potential to encompass the entire city and possibly spread to surrounding areas (see *id.*)

Syrian forces began mobilizing immediately, though no formal or obvious targets have been apparent. IDF is involved in corresponding buildup, though Israel has already issued a statement denying culpability.

Analysts anticipate India and Pakistan will likely increase their military activities (see Attachment C, timelines A through F) in the wake of these events.

US forces in those operational theaters have already been put on full alert. Recommend force build-up.

NOTE: communications breakdown of some kind is in effect. Email and internet communications have not been affected, but broadcast media is intermittent, cell phone and encrypted SATphones are only partially functional. Analysis ongoing, further information as it becomes available.
END FLASH

***

Serafina couldn't breathe. Not just because of the crushing weight of the man on her chest, but because of the smell of sweat and madness shoving itself into her mouth and nose, ramming its way down her throat.

That and the terror.

She had never been this afraid.

It was a strange thing, to be so afraid of a single man in a night when many others had chased and tried to kill her, a night when forces hunted her that were so powerful and ruthless they were willing to destroy buildings, to kill hundreds to get to her and John.

But that had all been distant. Disconnected. The closest any of them had come was in John's room when this had all started, and in the elevator immediately after. Then she had been too unsure to understand what was happening. It all passed immediately, before the reality of her situation penetrated.

And after that? It was guns. Dispassionate, impersonal. She focused on the mechanisms more than the men. The triggers rather than the fingers pulling them.

This, though. A grunting, filthy creature trying to rut his way up her frame, and his body *everywhere* on her. Touching her with flesh so hot it burned her skin, so wet she felt like she was drowning in rank sweat.

She screamed. Screamed again. Screamed and it only seemed to thrill him.

"I can do whatever I want," he said, his voice coming out in heavy gasps. The exercise presented by an assault was too much for him. She hoped for a well-timed heart attack but knew it wouldn't happen.

He was on her, hundreds of drooping pounds pinning her. The concrete floor, poorly concealed below a thin carpet, ground into her back and burned her with cold where his body burned her with heat. Her neck was still cranked up against the frame of the bed and now she hoped not that the pig would suffer a heart attack but that she would have her neck broken. Preferable to the alternative.

Even if she didn't die, at least she wouldn't feel anything anymore. So preferable.

She was going to be raped.

There was nothing she could do.

She was five-five. Maybe one hundred and ten pounds when she came in from monsoon season.

The man on her was probably five-ten. Well over three hundred pounds.

She batted at him, but the sheer bulk of him settled over her and pinned her arms so wide that her strikes had no leverage and no strength. They made him laugh and then made him sigh like she was caressing him. It revolted her so much she almost stopped hitting him.

Don't give up.

He was fumbling under himself.

She didn't have long.

Think. Stop acting like a panicked fool and think.

She couldn't hit him. Her legs were pinned—one leg straight under him, the other sticking out from under him at an angle.

She still had her clothes on. But hospital scrubs weren't exactly high-security. No belts, just ties and elastic.

He was wheezing, wheezing. He licked her. The tongue rasped along her cheek and left a trail of slime.

She head butted him.

It wasn't much stronger than her punches had been, especially with her head already bent forward by the bed, but it struck him on the chin, and caught him with his tongue sticking out.

The man roared. His hand came out from under him and went to his face as blood streamed out of his mouth. He drew back a hammy fist and punched her in the face. The pain of the impact was twofold: she felt it first in her cheek and jaw, then in her neck as it folded forward even further. Electric shocks danced up and down her spine and she decided she didn't want a broken neck after all.

He pulled back his fist again. "I wasn't going to hurt you," he said. "Just wanted, just wanted…."

He blinked, his eyes glazed slightly. He looked up as though he was hearing something inaudible to Serafina. His tongue, gray and scaled and now streaming blood, stuck halfway out his mouth.

He looked at Serafina again and she was surprised to see fear in his eyes.

Why? Why is he scared?

He drew back for a moment. Far enough that she got one hand free. She hit him in the face. He didn't seem to notice the impact, even though she saw his lower jaw pop sideways and knew she must have dislocated it. He coughed and shook his head. The fear in his eyes doubled.

Blood came from deep within him. It dropped on her and she hit him again, fear mingling with disgust and fury.

She saw a man vomiting blood. Changing. Dying.

She felt the fat man's blood splattering over her skin, wondered if this was the same thing. Knew it was. Different symptoms, but the same underlying disease.

And wondered if it was contagious.

She hit him again. Again.

The attacks shook the fear from his eyes. He flopped back down on her. Tried to say something and screamed as the pain from his jaw washed over him.

"I'll kill you!" he screamed, though it came out "Ahll kchill oo" through his mangled mouth.

More blood came out of his mouth. She was coated in the stuff. He coughed harder.

He had small spines on his neck. Scales glistened on his cheeks.

"Kchill oo!"

She had nowhere to go. Felt one hand go around her neck, another tug at the waistband of her scrub pants. She tried to writhe her hips away.

Nowhere to go.

His fingers found the drawstring of her pants. Yanked it.

264

She tried to scream, but the hand at her throat clamped down and now everything was going black.

His body fell against her even harder. Her attacker must have been supporting himself to some extent. Now he was entirely resting on her, his weight crushing. Deadly.

The weight got heavier, heavier.

And then it plateaued.

And then it lightened.

The rapist rolled off her.

She looked up.

John.

He was holding the out-cold form of the rapist by the shirt, then tossed the man to the side like a rotten slab of beef.

John looked better. Wet, but his color was normal again, and he even looked less...*wasted* than he had only a few minutes before.

Serafina wanted to know what had just happened. What happened to John in the car, how he had gotten better so suddenly.

Then he reached down to her. Took her hand and helped her up. She was suddenly in his arms, strong arms so different from the flabby, sweaty things that had been grappling with her only moments before.

She held John and wept. The terror pounded through her and she let it. John's hands clasped behind her back and he held her so tightly she almost couldn't breathe. Again, the feeling so different than the suffocating assault she had just endured. This was not a prison, not an attack. It was the protection of an impervious cocoon. The world was gone for a moment. Only two people existed.

The sobs pounded at her, ran up and down her from feet to crown, exhausted her and ran through what little strength she had left. She let them come. Didn't fight them. Why do that? '

She was safe.

She had almost died.

He had saved her.

She had almost been raped.

He hadn't let it happen.

She had been alone.

But he had come for her.

The sobs petered out. She smelled something that made her gag. Something she suspected she wouldn't be able to smell again for the rest of her life.

"What?" he whispered.

"You smell like chocolate." She wanted to laugh. Strange first words after an attempted rape.

"I woke up in a bath with five empty chocolate bar wrappers." His concern for her was replaced for a split-second: he looked amused and confused at the same time. "Don't ask me why or how."

She pushed him away. "Well use the bath to wash your hands and face, and gargle."

"I didn't see any mouthwa–"

"Use the soap."

He looked to see if she was kidding. Saw she wasn't. Nodded and left the room. She heard running water. The sound of someone eating something nasty.

She looked at the motel manager. He was on his side where John had thrown him, blood on his face and a wet patch on the back of his scalp where she guessed John had cold cocked him.

She thought about kicking him repeatedly in the face. That might kill him. She thought that might be a good thing.

He had said the world was ending. If that was true, did that mean justice was now something everyone had to be responsible for on their own? Did she have a right to kill a man who had tried to rape her, and probably would have killed her as well?

She took a step toward him.

She was justified. There was no doubt.

That was enough.

She didn't want to kick him. She might twist or even break an ankle, and she couldn't afford that.

But there was a lamp on the table by the bed. And it would do the trick.

She picked it up.

"Onde está a minha filha?"

Where is my daughter?

The same voice she so often heard. A mother searching for a lost child.

Where is my daughter?

But this time she heard it differently. Not a question of location or even a demand that a wayward child be returned. Instead it meant "Where is the girl you have tried so hard to become? Where is the mercy I taught you?"

Serafina *was* justified. Justice alone would allow whatever retribution she saw fit to visit on the unconscious man before her.

But her mother had taught her that justice walked hand in hand with mercy.

She left the lamp where it was.

She kicked the rapist in the crotch. Three times, as hard as she could. He moaned and curled in on himself like a dying roach but didn't open his eyes.

Her mother might not approve of murder, but castrating a rapist was something she probably would have okayed.

John came out during the third kick. "Feel better?"

"Slightly."

"What happened?"

She moved to the bathroom and used the sink to clean the manager's blood off her face and hands and arms as best she could. "You just collapsed. Started running a severe fever. I had to get you in a bath." She looked at the unconscious mass of flesh on the floor in the other room. "This guy said he was going to help with that, but he had additional plans."

"I gathered. Sorry I wasn't around to help earlier."

"You were there when it mattered." She was still staring at the pig, her gaze fixating on the chocolate goatee. She snorted. "That's it."

"What's it?"

"I think I know what happened to you." Off John's questioning look, she said, "You got better from those gunshot wounds, from scratches and scrapes in the fights. Assuming for a second any of that's possible–even though we both know it really isn't–it must take a ridiculous amount of energy. Your body must metabolize like crazy to heal itself. In the hospital you were getting IVs, but nothing on the run so your body ran out of fuel in the car."

He thought, then nodded. "Think I woke up enough to get to the choc–"

"Don't say that word!"

"The, er, the candy bars?"

"Yeah," she said. "Maybe the bath cooled your fever enough for you to come to a bit. You saw the food and knew instinctively that you needed it. So you chomped it down and then came out here to...."

He didn't make her finish the sentence. "Makes sense. In a weird way."

"What about any of this *isn't* weird?"

"So I guess I should eat what's left on the floor."

"Yeah, if you want to gargle some more soap."

"Maybe I'll just put some in my pocket for later."

"That might be best."

He moved toward the bathroom door. Froze. "Did you pay cash? For the room?"

"I didn't have time or money for that."

He ran to the window at the front of the room. Heavy blackout blinds covered the panes, and he pulled one back. Just a crack, and Serafina wondered what he thought he was going to see through the fog.

Just a crack.

And more than enough for the lights to flash through. The one-side-to-another that marked a car passing by. On its way to the motel's front desk, no doubt.

She wondered what the odds were that this car—one of two vehicles in evidence since Los Angeles—was just a random traveler.

John snapped the curtain back in place. The motion was controlled. No panic. But the way he moved, the way he held his body, told her what she needed to know.

They had been found again.

FACES IN GLASS

From: POTUS <dpeters@secured.whitehouse.gov>
To: G Etheridge <getheridge@detail.secretservice.gov>
Sent: Friday, May 31 10:55 AM
Subject: Mrs. Peters

I've emailed several times and received no response.
Did you manage to get Mrs. Peters out of Washington?

From: G Etheridge <getheridge@detail.secretservice.gov>
To: POTUS <dpeters@secured.whitehouse.gov>
Sent: Friday, May 31 10:56 AM
Subject: RE: Mrs. Peters

Sorry. Weird things happening. Got her out but

***

Past. Present. Present. Past.
"Jesus loves me, this I know, for the bible tells me so...."
A black man who smiles, though his eyes are sad.

A woman with no face, skin peeled back from blood and bone. Also sad. For different reasons, for reasons that have to do with life lived and then lost before life itself was understood.

Men in white, women in white, some pushing tubes into her body, others taking them out.

People speaking to her about things that once mattered, though she does not remember what those things are or why they were ever important.

She sees them all, pushing past her quickly, a succession of faces that surround her.

A teacher she had.

A person she once knew, she thinks he gave her food, though whether he was a grocer or a relative or a stranger she cannot say.

So many things are blank, so many holes in her mind.

When she walks too close to the holes, she falls in. Sometimes she does not come out for long times–long pasts, long presents, long futures. The dark scares her. She has learned to stay away from those darknesses and the nothingtime they represent.

The nowplace she is in bounces. One of the men she is with curses as she falls into him.

The three men left–the ones that remain after they shot the fourth and pushed him out the door–are coughing. Two of them have blood coming from their mouths. The other has tried to hide his neck, as though he is ashamed of whatever flesh he has there.

She does not understand any of this. It frightens her. Not the lack of understanding, which is her always-friend, but the fact that she almost *does* understand. And the understanding brings a terror she has never experienced. Not just a dread for body, not even a fear for mind. This is worse, this is like the nothingtime, the darkness, has found a way outside her damaged thoughts and has somehow begun controlling the world of the Now.

That is too horrible to contemplate. For the nothingtime to exist throughout the world would not be pain, or even madness. It would be damnation.

Another bounce and once more she slides into the man beside her. He is damp. Perhaps sweat, perhaps blood. She has lain in blood before. She does not like it.

The man curses and pushes her away. She spins and hits the side window. Now she is staring outside. That is better than staring inside. She does not like these men, and does not like this place or this time.

The world outside is gray. Gray is fine, it is not the black nothingtime and it is not the bright red streaming down the face of the woman who sings or the brighter reds and blues of the lights that followed before she fell into the first black nothingtime.

Gray is fine.

The gray curls and twists outside the glass. Sometimes she sees faces in the misty place beyond her travels. She thinks it might be her own faces sometimes–the face she had before the first darkness, the larger and stranger face she wears now, and even the shining face she wears in her dreams of the tomorrow.

But soon she sees that none of the faces are hers. They are dark faces, ghost faces. Wraiths riding the edges of the mist, surfing the fog like ocean waves–

(I went to the ocean once)

(Mommy sold white powder to a man)

(Daddy shot him and took it back)

–and occasionally coming so close to the glass she feels they might reach through and touch her. She does not know if that would feel good or bad. She does not want to know. Something about the faces frightens her.

She cannot always tell now from then, past from present, present from future, here from there. But the faces seem to be a bit of all those things. All those things and more.

She wonders if she is finally dying.

"Jesus loves me, this I know ...."

The men next to her start moving, everyone starts yelling.

"Holy–"

"They said she wouldn't–"

"She's supposed to be gagged, how'd her gag come–?"

"Should we call Mr. Dominic or–?"

"Are you insane, what are we–?"

"*You* call–"

"And say what? What am I supposed–?"

The voices swirl around themselves like fog over glass. She does not understand why they are so upset. Unless they, too, can see the faces. But she does not think they can. At least, not yet. Though something inside her whispers that soon they will. Soon the faces will draw close, soon the mists will part.

Soon all will be revealed.

"Jesus loves me, this I know, for the bible tells me so...."

The voice that sings the song she has heard so many times in a life punctuated by so many darknesses sounds different.

"Jesus loves me, this I know, for the bible tells me so...."

She realizes why. And thinks this may be why the men are so upset. She does not understand their reaction. She is not upset. She feels like she might fly.

"Jesus loves me, this I know, for the bible tells me so...."

The voice is not that of the woman in the car. It is not that of the black man who reads to her.

It is her own.

She is speaking again.

She cannot move her body. She cannot even smile. But her voice sounds, clear and true. A song comes from lips long sealed.

She is still staring into the mist.

The faces are closer. She cannot see their features, but the fear she felt before is greater now.

"Jesus loves me, this I know, for the bible tells me so...."

The sound of her voice makes her braver. Not all-the-way brave, but strong enough. Strong enough to ignore the shouting of the men, strong enough to stare at the faces without terror, strong enough to keep from falling in the darktimes that she senses still lurking at all sides.

Most of all, she is strong enough to know something she has not known in a long time: this is Now. This is Present.

The woman with the bleeding face is Past. The black man with sad eyes: both Past and Present.

The shining dream she has had: Future.

Things have grown clear, if only for a moment.

"Jesus loves me, this I know, for the bible tells me so...."

The faces in the gray come closer.

The mists begin to part.

POST MORTEM

From: POTUS <dpeters@secured.whitehouse.gov>
To: 'X' <xxx@secured.whitehouse.gov>
Sent: Friday, May 31 10:57 AM
Subject: My wife

I need you to find her. Her seecurity detail isn't t communicating and I can't work on anyything els until I know she's safe. I cant think straight.

From: 'X' <xxx@secured.whitehouse.gov>
To: POTUS <dpeters@secured.whitehouse.gov>
Sent: Friday, May 31 10:57 AM
Subject: RE: My wife

I anticipated problems. She's with my people. Don't worry about it. Focus.

***

"There's no one back here."

Melville came out of the small room behind the reception area, looking right and left as though he might have missed something in the tiny front office.

Isaiah didn't look around. Unless the people they were after had the ability to hide under peeling linoleum floor tiles, this place was empty.

He kept his eyes forward, fixed on his new partner. Trying to keep himself under control. He was trembling, and hadn't stopped for some time. The tremors were small and, he hoped, not noticeable to anyone else, but he felt each individual shiver like its own earthquake weakening the structures of his mind.

He was reacting to a combination of factors. The fact that he had been up close to thirty-six hours. Seeing Idella Ferrell, a poor woman who had already suffered so much for so little reason, dragged out of a car after being ravaged and murdered. Losing Nicholas, man of God and friend and cribbage player extraordinaire. The unreal fog that had cloaked the world sometime after dawn. The fact that he was less his own master than he could remember being in years.

Mostly it was the violation he had endured. He had devoted himself to righting what he felt were otherwise unrightable wrongs–helping women who would never testify against abusive husbands, avenging dead children whose parents were negligent in states that just didn't care, destroying drug dealers whose tentacles pulled apart the foundations of entire neighborhoods–and he spent all the money he earned on Katherine, putting her in the best hospitals, securing the best help.

Still, most of the time he managed to avoid thinking of *why* he helped her. The facts were always there, of course, but he could push them underneath a layer of work, bury guilt beneath an opaque film of the love he had somehow created for his adoptive daughter.

Melville had torn apart his frail delusions, his fragile illusions. He had forced him to face reality, and reality was one of the few things that could crush Isaiah like a slug under a boot heel. Reality reminded him that, no matter what he did, he was still the most unjust of men. He was a killer, and no righting of other wrongs could ever put him in the black on life's ledger. Not just a sinner, but a man of evil. He had destroyed lives as a young man, then had merely *failed* to save them as a priest–not much of an improvement, simply destruction by omission instead of commission.

And then: a decade of intentional destruction. In service of an innocent, yes. To balance some wrongs, true.

But the acts still stained Isaiah's spirit. And talking about it with Melville was just a harsh reminder of how black a soul he had become.

Then there was Dominic. Isaiah still had no clue who the elegant man was, other than someone very powerful, very connected. But he had orchestrated all this, from the deaths of Idella Ferrell and Nicholas to the kidnapping of sweet Katherine. And the way he had done it–not the m.o., but the look in his eyes, the lack of any remorse–was a sure sign that this wasn't the first time he had practiced such tactics.

Isaiah no longer knew if he believed in God. And because of that he could no longer be sure of the reality of a Devil, either. But if pure evil had a face, it was sure to be aristocratic, elegant. Well-styled hair, graying at the temples, and eyes that smiled most when pain was present.

"We know they're here," said Melville. "Her card was tagged here, so they gotta be here."

Isaiah nodded. There had only been one car in the lot, an old Honda Civic, and they parked beside it. Isaiah always carried a few tools with him, among them a razor sharp knife he wore under his frock. He used it to slash the Honda's tires. Neither John nor Serafina would be going anywhere in that car. Nor did he think anyone could hotwire the sedan he and Melville had come in without a great deal of difficulty. It was too new and had too many failsafes built in against that sort of thing.

Melville raised his hand to ring the desk bell. Isaiah caught his wrist. "You want to alert everyone that we're here?" he said.

"They musta seen us drive in," said Melville. "Maybe we can get the manager."

"And maybe we can tell *them* exactly where we are and let the super soldier get the drop on us. Or is that your end strategy?" he said bitingly.

Melville's eyes narrowed. No punches on the shoulder or talk of being pals. He looked murderous. Isaiah far preferred that. The talk of being friends made his skin feel like it was curling off his flesh.

"What, then?" said the killer.

"The place is laid out in more or less a straight line," said Isaiah. "We just go down the rooms. Kick one door in at a time. One of us goes in each room to check it out while the other one stands guard to make sure they don't try to make a break for it."

Melville mulled it over. "Okay. You check the rooms, though. If one of us is getting jumped in the can, I don't want it to be me."

Isaiah rolled his eyes. He didn't say anything though, not with Katherine's life riding on his every move.

He would kill Melville eventually–kill them all–but for now he would be a good little doggy.

"Fine," he said.

The doors were arranged in a straight line heading north from the motel office. All of them were closed, with all the windows curtained. No movement. Both men watched for a moment.

John and Serafina were here. Isaiah could feel it. You got a sense after a while, a feeling when your quarry was near. A psychic scent that told you when a house was empty, as opposed to just empty *seeming*.

This place...the latter.

Isaiah was still holding his knife in one hand, and one of the Glock 34s he'd taken from the armaments in the back of the car in the other. Melville was holding the assault shotgun. No explosive rounds loaded in the mag, but even the buckshot he had chosen would kill anything within the confines of a motel room. Isaiah knew he would shoot first and ask questions later. Not only was that the intent of this mission, but Melville also clearly reveled in mayhem and bloodshed and pain.

Isaiah might actually get a bit cleaner on balance when he killed this man.

"Let's go," he said.

They went to the first room. Isaiah didn't bother knocking, he just kicked down the door. The door itself was fairly sturdy, solid core construction. But the lock looked like it was fashioned out of tin foil and shattered easily.

The door exploded inward. Slammed to ninety degrees and then crashed into a wall. Isaiah followed it immediately, leading with the gun. He didn't know if John was armed, but if he was this would be the most dangerous moment of entry: the doorway providing a perfect frame with himself in the center. The best hope would be a fast entry, a surprise attack.

Isaiah flew into the room. It was dim, though not much more so than the unreal twilight of the fog-ridden world outside. It was also empty. The closet, a shallow space big enough to hang a few shirts and not much else, hung open. The bathroom was directly to his side, door also open, shower curtain around the tub drawn aside so there was no way to hide anything within.

He walked to the bed. A twin. Looked behind it even though he knew nothing would be here. Unlikely that John and Serafina would choose a room with a single twin bed. Besides, the place felt empty.

He verified the space beyond the bed hid nothing but more of the ugly carpet that crawled through the rest of the room, checked to make sure the bed frame was set too low to allow anyone to hide beneath, then went back outside the room.

Melville was on the walkway. His back to the wall, he was looking back and forth, trying to keep an eye on the rooms where they were headed and also on the area beyond the main office.

The fog seemed thicker. Wisps pushed onto the walkway beside the motel, tendrils touching Melville's expensive shoes. He kept stepping away from them, though Isaiah couldn't tell if that was a conscious act or not.

"Empty," he said, jerking his chin at the room behind him. Melville nodded.

They went to the next room. Isaiah repeated the actions he had just taken. Nothing. He and Melville moved on.

The door to the third room was ajar.

Not completely. Not so much that either of them could have seen it from anywhere but directly in front of the door. The door was right against the inside of the jamb, the dead latch touching the inside line of the strike plate.

Melville stared at Isaiah. Isaiah moved his head toward the room, silently asking his partner/captor to come inside with him this time.

Melville's fingers gripped the assault rifle tighter. Answer enough.

Isaiah used the barrel of his gun to push the door open. It opened, but on hinges that squeaked noisily. He gritted his teeth as the sound tore holes in the silence he had hoped to drape around himself.

He leaned around the corner. Quick look.

A bed–queen, so it was the first one he had seen that was big enough to warrant two people. A bathroom at the far corner.

A fat man on the floor, blood dripping from his mouth. Pants loosened and hanging below a grotesquely oversized posterior.

Isaiah went in, fast and low. There was no one on the bed, and he suspected no one behind it, either.

The fat man groaned. The floor was wet beside him, the carpet sodden not just with blood but with water that trailed into the bathroom.

Isaiah followed the water. He glanced behind the bed. Nothing there, as expected.

The bathroom was a mess. The tub was full but water was splashed everywhere. The sink, the toilet, even the crappy drop ceiling had wet patches on it.

Other than the water, though, the bathroom was empty. Ugly–the only thing that looked in remotely good repair was the toilet lid, which was oddly heavy-duty and well-kept compared to the rest of the place–but empty.

Isaiah went back to the motel room. Melville had turned the fat man fully on his back. He was slapping him.

"Wake up," he said. "Wake up!"

The man groaned but didn't open his eyes. Melville resumed slapping him, harder and harder. Isaiah suspected that would only help him into deeper levels of insensibility.

He went back to the bathroom. There were a pair of plastic cups on the sink, each one wrapped in its own little plastic bag. He tore one open, filled it with water from the bath, then walked into the room and tossed it on the unconscious man's face.

Some hit Melville on the back of the head. Melville glared at him.

"Sorry," said Isaiah. He smiled as sincerely as he could.

"You sonof–"

The man on the floor sputtered and coughed. His eyes opened. He screamed. Blood poured from his throat. "Where'd she–?" His eyes roved over Isaiah and Melville, unfocused at first but gradually zeroing in on Isaiah's outfit.

"Father?" he said.

"We're looking for someone, son," said Isaiah. "A man and a woman."

The fat man looked supremely uncomfortable. "I...I don't...I haven't seen any woman."

Melville punched him in the chest. The fat man gasped. "Don't lie," said Melville. "Don't you know lying to a priest will get you sent to Hell?" He punched the man a second time.

"I don't–" began the man. Melville slammed his fist down a third time. Isaiah thought he heard a crack and wondered if the fat man's sternum had just fractured.

"Don't lie!" screamed Melville. The scream was high-pitched, dancing in and out of control.

"She was here! There was a woman here!" screamed the man. His thick arms went protectively over his chest, crossed like he was praying.

"Where is she now?" asked Isaiah.

"I don't know. She jumped me. Her and her fiancée. They just went nuts and–"

"I don't think that's what really happened." Isaiah stared pointedly at the man's still-lowered pants. "You're the manager?" The man nodded. "We'll ask you again. Where are they?"

"I don't know. They were here, but she–"

"Don't tell me she attacked you, or I'll have my associate beat your heart to a pulp," said Isaiah. The man's eyes widened. He looked at Melville, who was grinning like a dog with its face out the window of a speeding car. The manager moaned. "What happened?"

"I...I liked her."

Isaiah's lip curled. "So you attacked her." Not a question. The manager nodded anyway. "And then?"

"The fiancée hit me." He sniffled. Wiped some crusted blood from his nose and upper lip. "Sucker punched me. Coward."

"Where'd they go after that?" said Melville.

"I don't *know*!" screamed the manager. "I don't remember, I just...." He licked his lips.

Isaiah stepped back. The manager's tongue was gray. Scaly. And at the same time he saw spines erupt along the side of the man's neck.

Melville threw himself off the fat man with a shout. He had seen it, too.

Even though both of them were vaccinated against the terrible disease that John was carrying, it was still horrible to see it. More spiky growths shoved their way through the fat man's skin. He didn't seem to notice, but he saw the fear and disgust on their faces.

"What?" he said. "What's going on?"

Then he started to scream.

The scream was terrible. A high, wailing thing that was almost a song, a hymn whose verse and chorus were prayers to a god of fear. It grew louder and louder, higher and higher. Shearing away layers of rational thought from Isaiah's mind until he felt like joining the man in his screams.

The fat man wasn't afraid of him, either. Nor of Melville. He might have been a moment ago, but now it was something else. He had turned his head, and was staring past them. Still wailing, but ululating words danced through gaps in his screams. "Don't let it don't let it don't let it get me it's come it's finally come...."

Isaiah looked in the direction the manager was staring. Through the still-open door to the motel. He could see nothing. Only fog. Only the gray of the mist that now seemed like the only real thing left in a world gone mad.

"...don't let it come don't let it in–"

The shrieks died in a roar so loud it was like the first moments of creation. The roar was followed by a heavy splash, and Isaiah knew what he would see when he looked back.

The manager's head and neck were gone. There was only a red smear of gore that ran from the mottled stump at the ends of his collarbones all the way to the far wall. Dark black circles marked gunpowder burns, others circles on the floor marked spots where the shot had embedded.

"He could have told us something," said Isaiah.

Melville shook his head. "He couldn't tell us nothing."

"You didn't have to do that."

Melville laughed, and suddenly Isaiah recognized a similarity between this laugh and the scream of the manager. Both were sounds of men who looked into abysses too deep to fully understand, too dark to comprehend what beasts might hide within.

"I don't *have* to do anything," said the killer. He licked his lips, another eerie analogue to the fat man. "But I *get* to do a lot of things. Besides, he was creeping me out."

"Yeah," said Isaiah. He couldn't argue that point. He glanced at the open door. He almost expected to see something moving out there. Ghosts, specters come to drag him to where he belonged.

There was nothing. Swirls of fog.

Melville looked away from the headless corpse. "John and Serafina probably busted out of here a while before we got here." He sighed. "What a pain in the ass."

"Well, we–" Isaiah broke off. He strode into the bathroom.

"What is it?" said Melville.

"Maybe they didn't leave a while ago. Maybe they didn't leave at all."

"You think they're hiding in the toilet?" Melville smirked.

Isaiah ignored him. He looked around the bathroom again.

Water in the tub. Splashed everywhere. Even on the sink, on the closed lid of the toilet. The walls. Streaks on the cheap drop ceiling.

Isaiah looked at the toilet. The lid was even more out of place now that he was really paying attention. The rest of the bathroom was outfitted with cheap fixtures, things designed to break down after months at best.

The toilet lid, though, was heavy duty and well crafted. Not wood, which would have appeared so elegant as to be ridiculous, or the more likely thin plastic lids that tended to appear in places like this. Rather, it was a thick white slab of polystyrene. Most people wouldn't notice it, but Isaiah had grown up where *working* toilets were the most you could hope for.

This seat...it was too much. Discreet, meant to blend in. But still too much.

He stood on the toilet. The ceiling was low, and he couldn't even stand up all the way. He pushed on the acoustical ceiling tile right above his head. It went up easily. Isaiah moved it to the side and looked into the plenum above the drop ceiling.

The first thing Isaiah saw was exactly what he had expected to see. There was a small piece of wood nailed to one of the crossbars of the ceiling frame. Secured to that was a small plastic box, which had several leads running out of it. They disappeared into the darkness of the ceiling space.

Out of the other side of the box, a thin cable extended. It snaked about two feet along the ceiling tiles, then the end dipped down like a parasite burrowing into flesh.

Isaiah had seen these setups before; had used them, in fact. His were generally a bit more sophisticated, but the idea was the same. It was a fiber optic video camera. Someone, undoubtedly the manager, had rigged this room so that he could watch and listen to whatever happened in the bathroom.

Isaiah felt like scraping off the outer layers of his skin with a pumice stone. Maybe he'd have to thank Melville for wasting this guy. Justice had been done.

But he wasn't here just to observe the camera. He had suspected something would be up here—that was the most likely conclusion to be drawn from a toilet seat that would bear the weight of a grossly obese man. The manager had wanted to be able to get up here, and the fact that he wanted to do so without benefit of a ladder or other observable apparatus meant he was engaged in something illicit. The camera.

More important, though, was the fact that the ceiling was wet. And Isaiah knew now that it wasn't from the splashing. The walls weren't wet, an item he had glossed over when he first noticed the bathroom, but which his subconscious had tossed at him later. Unlikely that the walls had missed being wetted if the ceiling got doused.

So the water wasn't from the tub below.

It was from something above.

Isaiah had seen the bathroom and had figured out there was a space in the ceiling, room to put things that someone would want hidden.

Would John have seen those things, made those same conclusions?

Yes.

He reached into the ceiling space. Felt along the frame.

Wet.

They had been here. One or both of them wet for some reason, the water soaking through the acoustical tile and giving the impression that it had been splashed from below.

But where had they gone?

Just as he always carried a knife, Isaiah always had a small flashlight with him. He pulled it from his pocket and shined it into the crawlspace.

The void extended up and down the length of the motel. Cameras every few feet, cords snaking into the tiles and peering down through nearly invisible holes.

There was no sign of John or Serafina.

He swung his light away. Then swung it back.

One of the tiles–a tile over another room, probably just one or two rooms down–was missing.

He was about to drop down and tell Melville he had a bead on their prey when the other man's voice jammed into the darkness. "Batman! Get down here!"

Isaiah crouched and jumped off the toilet seat in one movement. Melville was standing outside the bathroom door. "What is it?"

Melville pointed with his shotgun. "Saw 'em. They're on foot!"

He ran out the door. Isaiah followed. He saw what Melville had seen: a pair of gray shapes in the mist, moving away but still visible.

"Car!" said Isaiah. They veered toward the sedan. "Keep an eye on them. We'll run 'em down!"

"Got it, Batman."

They hit the car running. Isaiah jammed the fob with his thumb, the sedan's lights flashed as it unlocked. Both men threw themselves in. "You see where they went?"

"Hard to in the fog, but I got the general direction. They're on foot and we're in the car, though, so we've got 'em." Melville smiled. He laughed, and sounded like a child who has just discovered the exquisite joys of yanking legs off insects. "Mr. Dominic is going to be thrilled."

"Yeah. Peachy."

Isaiah put the car in reverse. Pulled back.

Something felt wrong. He frowned. He cranked the wheel. It responded, but felt slushy. Slow. He put the car into drive, turned the wheel again, and floored the accelerator.

The wheels spun, but took far too long to gain traction. And when they did the car didn't leap forward as it usually did, but only gave a sickly lurch and then died.

Isaiah turned off the engine, then turned it on again. The ignition revved, but the engine didn't catch.

"What's going on?" screamed Melville.

Isaiah didn't answer. He got out of the car. Saw that he wasn't the only one who took precautions. Just as he had done to the Honda, someone had slashed all four of the sedan's tires. But that wouldn't have caused the engine to seize. He ran to the back.

Contrary to popular belief, it wasn't generally possible to stall a car by shoving a potato or a banana in the exhaust pipe: the exhaust pressure would just eject most obstructions. But if someone took the few moments necessary to completely seal the pipe with a few tight wraps of duct tape?

Isaiah jabbed his knife into the tape. The wheels were flat, but even driving on rims would be faster than running. He pulled the tape off, and found white strands attached to it.

Toilet paper.

They'd shoved toilet paper up the tail pipe. And who knew what else.

"We good?" said Melville.

"No," said Isaiah. He looked into the fog. He couldn't see anything. "We're not."

The car wouldn't start, they didn't have time to see if it would drive properly. Every second wasted was another ten or twenty feet between them and the people they needed to stop. Driving wasn't a worthwhile option anymore. The next part of the race would be on foot.

He was about to take off running when something caught his eye. The sedan hadn't gotten very far before hacking its way to a stop; they were only a few feet from the motel. Close enough to see the room they had just vacated.

Close enough to see the thing that slid through the doorway.

It was low-slung, ponderous. In the gloaming of the eddying mist Isaiah got the impression of a giant slug, searching for someplace to hide after an unseasonal shower. Wet, slick with slime, it rolled onto the concrete walkway that surrounded the motel, then off the side with a thud.

Now closer, Isaiah could see that what he had taken for slime was blood. The ripples of flesh were not the gelatinous tissue of a slug, but the fat-draped corpse of the man they had left behind.

The cadaver had bloated, impossibly swelling as though gases that would typically take days or weeks to accumulate within had done so in seconds.

The shoulders, barely discernible within the swollen mass, were flecked with patches of scales and spines.

The neck was ragged, a stump that ended in greasy patches of scabrous darkness.

The headless thing twisted, turning on squat legs and arms as though questing. Searching.

Isaiah realized he had stepped back. Ten feet, maybe twenty. Melville was next to him.

"What's going on?" he said.

Melville shook his head. "I don't...they didn't tell me about this."

"Is this the disease?"

"Must be."

"And we're safe?"

"Mr. Dominic said so."

The thing turned and twisted. Searching. Searching. A motion that was almost hypnotizing as waves danced along its length.

Isaiah remembered the manager, looking out the door–

(*"Don't let it don't let it don't let it get me it's come it's finally come"*)

–and wondered if the thing was searching for whatever had so terrified it only moments before. Looking for a way to run. Or–and for some reason this set Isaiah even more on edge–looking now to join it.

He turned a circle, suddenly feeling eyes on him, faces hidden in the blankets of fog on all sides.

"We should follow them before they get away," said Melville. His voice sounded dreamy. He was probably in shock. Isaiah thought he probably was, too.

"Yeah," he answered.

They began to run. Following the last course of their quarry. Isaiah tried to convince himself that it was because this was the only chance they had of turning back the tide of madness that had swollen over the face of the earth.

Because killing John was a greater impetus than the terror he felt at seeing a dead man roll out of a motel room.

But it was a lie. He was running from the undead thing in the mist. Just like he was running from his past, running from the truth. Running from the mist.

And from the huge shape that he tried to convince himself was imagination: the umbral form that lumbered toward the motel and the waiting undead as Isaiah and Melville fled into shadow.

UNCOVERED BY LIGHT

From: POTUS <dpeters@secured.whitehouse.gov>
To: Anton Koikov <jst14986@147265.2645.kremlin.ru>
Sent: Friday, May 31 11:14 AM
Subject: Proposal for Cooperative Action

Mr. President,

I presume that you are having the same telecom issues that we are. No one is sure why these are occurring, but when we know anything I will happily share our results with you.

I know that our countries and our administrations have had our differences, but we appear to be nearing a crisis. I would propose that you and I pool our resources to see if we can figure out exactly what is going on and how to stop it. Would you be amenable to this effort?

Yours sincerely,
Richard Peters

From: Anton Koikov <jst14986@147265.2645.kremlin.ru>
To: POTUS <dpeters@secured.whitehouse.gov>
Sent: Friday, May 31 11:18 AM
Subject: RE: Proposal etc.

Mr. Peters,

Thank you for your kind invitation. We are entirely capable of handling current events without assistance. We wish you best of luck with whatever issues you may be having and I look forward to seeing you at the environmental summit in August.

Please give my best to Mrs. Peters.

Cordially,
Anton Koikov
[dictated but not read]

From: POTUS <dpeters@secured.whitehouse.gov>
To: 'X' <xxx@secured.whitehouse.gov>
Sent: Friday, May 31 11:21 AM
Subject: Russia

Russian pres just told me to effectively screw myself. I thought you said you had people in Russia. Can we get some coordination going?

This thing has gone global. North Korea has effectively disappeared, and before sat coverage went offline most of Western Europe looked like it was mobilizing for WWIII. Africa has fallen to widespread bloodshed, last we heard (and last we heard was over an hour ago).

The fact that there are carriers in China implies that there might be others as well.

I thought you said your people came up with the original vaccine. How does China have carriers? What's going on? Did we originate this, or steal it?

Regardless, I don't think this is something we can handle from within our borders alone. We need to reach out, even to old enemies. This is a time to forget enmities and make friends. I need your help for that, just as I always have.

Just tell me what to do to solve this. Tell me.

From: X <xxx@xxx.xxx>
To: Dicky <dpeters@secured.whitehouse.gov>
Sent: Friday, May 31 11:21 AM

Subject: RE: Russia

I do have people in Russia. They are very busy, just as my people here are very busy. Trust me when I say that there's nothing you can do by reaching out. This has to be fixed here first.

There *are* other carriers, but the most virulent ones are the ones on U.S. soil. This is a terrifying situation, yes, but it also means that they are the ones who can most easily yield a solution if we can get our hands on them and perform some biological studies.

Further, their objective seems to be a common one: the carriers aren't scattering, they are moving toward a central location. This is another reason to contain yourself and your efforts to the confines of your own borders. It is true that no man is an island, but when cleaning dirty laundry you don't invite the neighbors over, either.

My people have the situation moving forward. I anticipate resolution within hours. Until then, whatever National Guard and other armed forces you have available, I would suggest mobilizing them and putting up whatever roadblocks you can at the following locations.

<mapattachment.jpg>

From: POTUS <dpeters@secured.whitehouse.gov>
To: 'X' <xxx@secured.whitehouse.gov>
Sent: Friday, May 31 11:35 AM
Subject: RE: RE: Russia

I sent out orders to the National Guard per your suggestions. I got no response. I honestly don't expect one. I'm just crossing my fingers at this point. There doesn't seem to be much left. Am I alone?

No, don't answer that. I know, I know.

You're here.

***

They ran, and ran, and ran.

Mist made everything dark, but at the same time it silvered the world, made all seem a land of faerie. Not fairies of the benevolent type, the subject of so many Disney platitudes and simple endings. No, the fairies hiding in this fog would be more devious, less well-disposed toward humanity.

Just as likely to kill as to bless.

John didn't look around. He faced only ahead, only east.

He didn't know how he could possibly still be headed that direction. There were no markers on the rough sand and rock that coated this land, the shroud of mist cloaked the sun in ash.

But he felt a pull. A tug that drew him on, something inside that whispered, "This is the way, here is the way."

It was a small voice, but real. Something he heard thudding through him as a steady beat that matched the pulse of his own blood, the rhythm of his footsteps, the breath in his lungs. Even through the terror he felt, the knowledge that there were men who would kill him and Serafina–or worse–he heard the voice. It was a comfort, and that surprised him.

The mission. It was all that was left, perhaps all there was in the world.

He still didn't know what it was, exactly. But he would move toward it.

Serafina was breathing hard beside him, trying her best to keep up. He slowed to match her pace. He was running well below his threshold, but he wasn't about to leave her. Not merely because she had saved his life as many times as he had saved hers. There was more. He felt that, too. The same voice that pulled him east told him also that she was more than an accidental part of this.

She had been a part of the mission. Part of what he had to accomplish from the very beginning.

She stumbled. Fell sprawling in the hardpacked dirt and inch-high scrubs that had managed to spear their ways through land too hard for life. It was a hard fall. She rolled to her back, gasping. Her arms were bloody, the knees of her scrub pants shredded. Her chin had a long laceration on it, and dirt and burs clung to her clothes.

She had always been beautiful. Now, wounded for her efforts, she was radiant.

"Go," she gasped. "You...gotta...finish...."

John knew then that she was hearing the voice. That whatever force pulled him along had managed to hook onto her as well.

She was part of this.

"Get...moving...."

She closed her eyes.

He growled. A strange sound, one of desperation and anger. The only reason he didn't bellow was that he knew the priest and the thin man were somewhere behind them. He had seen both at the window, getting out of the car, and almost rushed them.

Suicide. He could heal, but did that mean he could survive a direct hit by an assault shotgun? Not worth betting on.

He rifled through the unconscious manager's pockets, finding a screwdriver, some duct tape, a wad of used tissue. He grabbed it all, even the tissue, then looked for a way out.

There was no way. No back window, and the front door was hardly an option.

He heard a crash. The sound of a door being kicked in.

He looked in the bathroom, searching not for escape but for something more powerful than a screwdriver. Some weapon he could use.

He saw the toilet seat. Recognized it not as part of a plumbing fixture, but a stepladder.

Into the ceiling with Serafina as another crash sounded. Then across framing, through a dark crawlspace littered with the spy network of a rapist, a voyeur, an evil man.

They came out in another room. Unlocked the door. Ran.

John veered to their car. Saw immediately that it would be useless for flight. Saw as well that he would have no way of stealing the assassins' car in the time they had.

Still, maybe he could slow their hunters down a bit. He stabbed the screwdriver through the tires. He wrapped the duct tape around the exhaust pipe, grimacing at the sound of the adhesive unsticking, hoping no one heard it. He jammed the huge wad of used tissue into the tailpipe before sealing it off. Not that it would add anything concrete, but it felt good to do.

Then running.

They were in desert. The heat was heavy, more so when weighed down by the water trapped in the mist. His body dragged, and he knew that Serafina wouldn't be able to go on long.

They stayed on the road for a while, but John knew the others would follow them this way. It was the easiest and most obvious path, so had to be avoided. He drew Serafina off the road and into the desert.

They kept running. She slowed a bit with every footstep. He slowed with her.

And when she fell he yanked her to her feet.

She would not die here. Neither of them would.

"Get up," he growled. He almost felt angry at her. To come so far....

"No," she said, but didn't fight him when he stooped to put her arm around his neck. They took a few halting steps, then he knew that wouldn't work. Too slow.

He swept her into his arms and simply ran with her. Faster with a burden than most men were when running alone.

He hoped it would be fast enough.

He was stumbling now. Still fast, but the tiny bits of green and brown that passed for plants out here seemed to paw at his feet, to reach out and trip him.

East....

East....

East....

The rhythm moved him through the fog. Hypnotizing.

East....

East....

East....

He looked at Serafina. Her eyes were wide. Terrified. Her head pivoted back and forth, trying to take in everything at once.

John realized that he had fallen into some kind of a trance. No way to know how long he had run, how far. But he had disappeared from the world for a bit. Had found a dream state that was almost pleasant.

Memory?

(*The man. The man who gave me the mission. Telling us the sacrifice, but the importance. The pain, but the possible end.*)

Then it was gone.

Gone, and Serafina was terrified.

John focused on what she was seeing. The fog cloaked all. But it parted a bit here and there. Not enough for vision, but enough for implication and imagination.

Darkness was out there.

John kept running, but now he understood Serafina's terror. The mist churned, circles spinning around them like an unfelt wind was racing them through the silver-gray world.

And when the mist parted…the shapes.

They were huge, dark things. Two or three of them, far enough that he couldn't make out any kind of shape or form, only size and a sense of fearsome grace.

They were bigger than elephants. Easily twenty feet tall, at least that wide. They circled relentlessly, becoming now a bit darker as they closed in a bit, then lightening as they withdrew.

Worse, though, was the fact that John thought he saw others. Things beyond the things, shadows beyond the shadows. And though the nearby unknowns were huge, the farther ones…he got the sense they were enormous. The size of buildings, perhaps larger.

John ran, and the things circled them. Every once in a while darkness fell completely. Not sunset, not an eclipse, but a great shadow. One of the leviathans gliding in front of them, its great mass passing between them and the sun.

Then slight brightness as the monster continued its circuit, continued orbiting the fleeing couple.

John ran. He no longer felt the eastern pull. Now he was running because the things were herding them. He didn't know where.

The crunching that had accompanied his footsteps suddenly stopped. John stumbled and nearly fell as his foot hit an uprising, something even harder than the sunbaked hardpack. He managed to right himself, then almost fell again as his other foot landed on the smooth surface.

He was back on the road.

The things had led him back to the interstate.

What's going on?

He stopped, too shocked to move. The whole night and morning had been a rush of unreality. This was beyond unreality. This was a headlong pitch into madness, into the chaos *beyond* madness.

The shadows drew away. Disappeared.

A moment later, light lanced through the mist. John whipped around, Serafina still in his arms.

"Oh, no," she whispered.

Not one light. Two.

Headlights.

And John knew what it was. What it had to be.

The killers. Priest and cadaver. They had found another car.

What car? I slashed their car, and this one's coming too fast, too fast to be running on flat tires, too fast to run from.

Then the answer: *The manager's car.*

He could have hit himself for not thinking of that.

And in that moment, the car was upon them.

They were out of time.

BEARING GIFTS

From: POTUS <dpeters@secured.whitehouse.gov>
To: G8 (Group List)
Sent: Friday, May 31 12:19 PM
Subject: Check In

Ladies and Gentlemen,

Communications in this country are so sporadic as to be useless. Only the internet seems to have any functionality, and even that is limited to basic text functions, i.e., email.

It is no secret at this point to say that the world is in crisis. Before communications became compromised it was apparent that much of Africa had essentially imploded, and many of your own countries appeared in a state of such high alert as to be indistinguishable from war.

These are the facts as I understand them. Please understand they only came to my knowledge recently:

In the past few days the United States provided an experimental vaccine to a number of volunteers. This vaccine was intended to inoculate against most if not all forms of disease. The uses and potentials for this are obvious.

The results appeared hopeful at first. However, the vaccine apparently either mutated itself or caused mutations within the volunteers' bodies. They went insane and escaped.

The mutations apparently spawned a new disease. This disease is highly communicable. We do not know if transmission is solely via direct contact, or if it is also via indirect contact, droplet contact, airborne transmission, fecal-oral transmission, or vector-borne transmission. Early tests indicated *all* were likely.

We had–and still have–hopes of crafting a solution. We need to stop these men, however. Our intent is to terminate and study them intensely and quickly to create a biological counter to this new and deadly disease. Unfortunately, termination is extremely difficult. The same vaccine that was intended to provide their bodies with the tools to reject attack by disease has also provided their bodies with unusual levels of endurance, strength, and abilities to heal. I have been informed that it is likely that only complete destruction of the brain will result in final termination. After study, recommendation is that any remaining biological materials be incinerated.

Normally this would not be the type of information shared in an unencrypted email to a group of leaders, some of whom are viewed as hostile to one another. But at this point I view it more important that we save the world than that we guard our politics. I would also worry about accusations from others in this group that this administration has caused the current global crisis, but I have also been informed that most of your countries were running similar projects and at this point I honestly don't know who was the originator of this "vaccine" or who was the first nation to steal it.

To the end of salvaging what can be salvaged, both of our nations and of the world populace, I will be sending continual updates of progress capturing our subjects and/or any test results that yield beneficial progress in turning back the tide of this disaster. I would request that you consider doing the same.

I would also request that each of you please return this email, cc'ing to the entire list. Even if you have no intention of participating in the group effort this will at least inform us who is still alive and functioning.

Good luck, and God bless.

From: POTUS <dpeters@secured.whitehouse.gov>
To: G8 (Group List)
Sent: Friday, May 31 1:20 PM
Subject: Check In

Ladies and Gentlemen,

After an hour my request that you all check in to assure other members of the group of your continued functionality (and, indeed, existence), I have received a total of NO responses.

I repeat my entreaty. No message is necessary, a blank reply will suffice.

Yours sincerely,
Richard Peters

***

Serafina didn't know how long they had run. She felt like she could have taken to her feet again after a few minutes, but to be honest this was one of the first times she felt safe. Wrapped up in John's arms, held close to him. She could hear the beat of his heart, could feel the warmth of his breath on her neck.

He ran, and she felt better. No one could possibly find them, no one could catch them. There were no cameras here, there was nowhere to use a credit card. Just fog, the ground, the thud-thud-thud of his stride.

She finally admitted she was as rested as she ever would be. And still didn't say anything. Not because of selfishness, not because of some misguided notion of romance. She was guided by simple pragmatism.

John was still running. Running. Running.

Running.

His feet shredded the ground, pushing it away so fast that he left divots behind them, pushing it down so hard that she wondered if the earth was pushing a bit out of orbit with each step.

John had been holding her for Heaven only knew how long, and still he was running faster than she could sprint.

He held back for me.

She resolved to stay with him. And the only way to do that was to let him carry her. Sometimes that was the way of things: the only way to do your best was to put aside your pride and let others do the heavy lifting.

He carried her. She let him.

Then the things came. John seemed to have gone someplace far away. Maybe it was that "zone" that she understood long-distance runners got into. But she thought it was a farther place. He was almost smiling. She didn't want to draw him away from whatever happiness he might have found.

But the darkness grew. And *moved.*

She saw things lumbering about. Some big, some *bigger.*

Hit men. Rapists. Death by violence, death by strange sickness that not only killed but *changed.*

She had held it together, more or less, through most of it.

She almost lost it now. The rest was explainable. At least something she could rationalize.

There was no rationale for shadows big enough to be bulldozers, but silent and slinking like jungle cats on the prowl.

And less for the bigger ones. The juggernauts that moved without shaking the earth, the massive creatures that cast shadows so long they were their own midnight.

John came out of it. He saw them. He kept running. What else was there to do?

Then he tripped, almost fell...and the things were gone.

Still, any relief she might have felt dissipated so fast it was just the last wisp of a forgotten dream. Lights brightened. An engine revved.

The killers had come.

"Oh, no," she said. She looked at John and saw he knew it as well. He put her down and his hand darted into his pocket. He came out with the screwdriver he had taken from the manager's pocket. A pitiful weapon against what the killers had been packing this far.

Better than nothing. Better to fight than to give up. Always better.

(*"Onde está a minha filha?"*)

"She's here, Mom," said Serafina. "Your daughter's here. Not running anymore."

She fought the urge to move behind John. Held her ground beside him.

The vehicle that drove up was an SUV. An older model, but surprisingly well-maintained given what she had observed of the manager.

Yeah, it'll be nice to have my body tossed in the back of a clean car.

She shook her head at the strange thoughts that came along with death.

The driver side door opened. Someone got out. The headlights, beaming straight at them and reflected by the fog, cast weird shadows that kept Serafina from seeing anything but a general outline. It wasn't the thin man, she saw that instantly. So it had to be the priest.

For some reason that comforted her. She didn't know why, but she'd rather be killed by the priest.

The man spoke.

"Well, looky here, looky here."

Serafina's eyes jerked to John. He looked as surprised as she probably did. The voice was old, scratchy. Not the voice of either of the men who had been chasing them, surely. Nor any of the other agents, all of whom had been young to middle-age men.

"Yup," said the men as he continued toward them, "You're just where he said you'd be."

She felt John tense beside her. He dropped back half a step, his body lowering and the screwdriver jutting out like a knife.

The shadow stopped. Dark hands went up. "Wait, wait. Don't get the wrong idea, I'm just here to help."

"Who are you?" said John. "Who sent you?"

The man stepped forward. Finally close enough they could see him.

He was old, as she had expected. Dressed simply, in canvas pants and a blue cotton button-up that was clean and comely but unassuming.

"I'm just good ol' Jack Jones. Well, Jim Jones, actually, but I don't like to go by that. Still, I suppose I should be totally honest with you, given what's going on and all." He sighed as though what he'd just said had been an extreme trial. Then his back straightened. "But I don't drink Kool-Aid," he declared. And winked at Serafina.

Serafina didn't know what to do. She turned to John and saw that he was similarly confused.

"Who sent you?" he said again. She got the impression that he was repeating the last thing he said because his brain had shut down. If someone had whispered, "Monkey guts" to him right then, he probably would have said that instead.

Jack/Jim Jones chuckled, but his eyes grew suddenly sad. "Well, that's the question. And it's one I can't rightly answer. But I can say that I'm here to help."

That caused red flags to rise in Serafina's mind. So far no one they had encountered during their flight had been particularly helpful. Just murderous, lecherous, destructive.

But the flags went to half-mast almost immediately. Jack Jones (she decided to respect his wish not to be "Jim") was no assassin. And he couldn't be a government agent.

Could he still mean them harm? Yes. But....

But it didn't feel that way.

"What do you mean, you want to help us?" said Serafina.

Jack gestured at the SUV, its motor still idling. "Got some wheels for you." He winked at Serafina again. Not in a dirty-old-man way, but in fun. In joy. "No payment necessary, no strings attached."

John moved toward the SUV. He gave Jack a wide berth, and drew Serafina with him. She didn't mind, but she thought it less and less necessary. Jack was still smiling. Looking like he was considering another wink.

John looked into the SUV. Nothing inside other than a few cans of soda. He looked underneath. For what, she couldn't guess. Not tracking devices, certainly: if Jack was with the other team and had found them while they were on foot, they were well and truly screwed with or without GPS. Explosives?

Regardless, he grunted as though to say, "It's good."

Then he moved to the back. Another SUV was hitched to the back of this one. Same make and model. "What's this for?" he called out.

Jack came closer. Saw what John was looking at and rolled his eyes. "You don't think I'm just gonna stand out here and twiddle my thumbs when you zoom off, do you? That's crazy talk." He circled a finger around his ear to drive home the point.

John stared at the two vehicles, lost in thought.

Serafina looked at John. Then at Jack. The old man winked again. That did it.

"We can trust him," she said.

John stayed motionless for another moment. Then nodded. He moved to the tow hitch and released the trailing SUV, then got into the still-open driver side door of the lead vehicle.

Jack opened the front passenger door for Serafina. He even offered her his hand, and a little bow as she climbed in. She found the gestures charming. He was a remnant of an age when there were more wife beaters, more men who thought of women as below them. But also some who were mannered, some who were courteous. And some who, like this one, were deeply kind.

John thumbed the control to open Serafina's window. He looked at Jack. "Who said we'd be here?" he said.

Jack's eyes shut halfway. He shrugged. "Someone you know, but I can't tell you who."

John licked his lips. "Then," he said, and paused a long time. Jack didn't move, waiting patiently as though he knew what was coming. Serafina could guess. "Then do you know what my mission is? Who *I* am?"

Jack took a breath. Held it as though considering. Let it out.

He nodded. "But I can't tell you. Either of you. Any of it."

"Why?" Both Serafina and John asked the question at the same time. Serafina because the answers might explain what had happened to her world–to the world in general. John, she sensed, because the answer was rapidly becoming the difference between existence and oblivion.

Jack hesitated. Looking for words. He looked at Serafina. "I can't tell you because you wouldn't believe it." Then he switched his gaze to John. His eyes grew misty. "And I can't tell you, my friend, because it'd be more than you could bear. It'd destroy you."

The old man wiped his eyes, then held Serafina's shoulder for a moment, a gesture of friendship and encouragement.

"Get a move on," he said. "The tank's full, and it'll get you to Cedar City. Map's in the glove box. Don't stop for nothing–they'll be on you still."

He patted the side of the door and stepped back.

Serafina looked at him. She smiled.

John put the SUV into gear. They pulled away.

Serafina kept looking at Jim/Jack Jones until he had disappeared in the mist. She wondered if she would see him again. If *anyone* would.

She finally turned forward. Opened the glove box. A map was inside, and when she opened it there was a route outlined in yellow Hi-Liter.

The road glowed in the headlights, a gray strip in the larger gray of the mist. The shapes in the fog were no longer visible.

They drove. Lebanon, Kansas, was still ahead. The priest and the thin killer were still behind.

They had a long way to go.

BLIND LEADING BLIND

From: POTUS <dpeters@secured.whitehouse.gov>
To: Booker Randall <randall@lab18.cdc.gov>
Sent: Friday, May 31 1:19 PM
Subject: Crisis Analysis

What news?

From: Booker Randall <randall@lab18.cdc.gov>
To: POTUS <dpeters@secured.whitehouse.gov>
Sent: Friday, May 31 2:42 PM
Subject: RE: Crisis Analysis

Still nothing. Without a tissue sample we don't have much to work with. It's not normal procedure for me to work on a vaccine for a disease I've never heard of and had less to do with.

Even if I get a tissue sample, not sure what I can do here. All the other lab techs are dead. I have scales on my hand. That's outside what I was briefed on. Do you have any info?

From: POTUS <dpeters@secured.whitehouse.gov>
To: Booker Randall <randall@lab18.cdc.gov>
Sent: Friday, May 31 2:59 PM
Subject: RE: RE: Crisis Analysis

No, no info. Hopefully it's nothing. Please hold fast. You are doing important work and the country thanks you. Stay at your post and we'll beat this.

***

Walking was for suckers. This was one of the facts of life, one of the Great Truths. If God had intended people to walk, Melville figured, He wouldn't have invented cars. More important, Mr. Dominic had given them a series of cars, and that indicated they should *use* the things.

But instead Melville was walking. Scuffing up his Grafton Wingtips, which cost nearly a thousand dollars a pair, thinking how much he would like to kill John and Serafina, how very much he would like to get done with this job and return to normal life. Normal life was good. Out of this fog, this confusion.

He thought about calling for a new car. But he had no idea where they were. And besides, when he checked it, the cell showed no service. He didn't know if that was because they were in the middle of nowhere or if it was because of the fog.

"You have any idea where we are, Batman?" he said.

The priest just walked, silent as always. Melville decided to cut his tongue out before killing him. That way he'd have a damn good reason for not talking.

"I don't know why you don't want to chat. Not like we have anything else to do."

Still nothing. And the guy knew that there was no cell reception, so no making him play any little games right now. Melville supposed he could have threatened *future* reprisals, but somehow he doubted that would have much effect.

Bored.

Boring was the opposite of exciting.

That was some deep stuff right there. He would have to think on that sometime.

It got bright all of a sudden. Isaiah reacted first, which irritated Melville. Another deep thought: he was going to have to kill Isaiah when the big guy wasn't waiting for it. Which was what he usually did, but this time he suspected it would be necessity, not preference.

Melville's turn–a fraction of a second behind Isaiah, an eternity if you were drawing and firing–completed.

There was a car coming up behind them. No, an SUV. Melville's heart danced. Mr. Dominic had come through again. Forget the U.S., forget Russia, and China could bend over and screw itself–Mr. Dominic was the real and only superpower that existed.

Then Melville saw the vehicle more clearly. It was old and blocky. No smooth lines, no clean black paint. The engine chugged instead of purring. It was, in short, exactly the kind of vehicle Melville hated, and exactly the kind of thing Mr. Dominic *wouldn't* send.

Unless there's nothing else. Unless he had to.

Melville did his best to remain optimistic. Perhaps whatever was going on in the world, whatever mass catastrophe spawned by the disease he and Isaiah were trying to contain, perhaps it had also resulted in a colossal breakdown and the mass destruction of all late model vehicles. That would be acceptable. He would keep his fingers crossed.

The SUV pulled up and the last of Melville's hopes curdled. The man that got out was as disheveled and decrepit as the vehicle in which he arrived. No clean suit, no sharp creases, no expensive haircut. He sported boring khakis, a boring blue shirt that looked like he'd gotten it on layaway at Wal-Mart, and raggedy hair that had probably *never* seen a salon.

Melville determined to hate him on the spot.

The man walked toward them, and Isaiah had his gun trained on the old guy's head in a flash. Again, he reacted just a tad faster than Melville.

"Whoa," said the old man. "No reason to get antsy. I'm unarmed and I brought you some wheels." He jerked a thumb over his shoulder.

"Who are you?" said Isaiah.

"Jack Jones," said the man. "Well, Jim's my name. But I go by Jack, I'm sure you can understand." He winked at Isaiah and Melville realized this guy was some old faggot and his hatred pulsed brighter.

"Who sent you?" he demanded. His shotgun jabbed forward.

Maddeningly, the old coot seemed to take no notice of the weapon. Worse, he took no notice of *Melville*. He never even looked at him, just kept talking to Isaiah like they were the only two in the world.

"The road's only about five hundred feet that way," he said, pointing.

"That's impossible," growled Isaiah. "We've been walking for hours."

The man chuckled. Another wink. Faggot. "A lot of us tend to walk in circles when we can't see our way, I suppose." He shrugged. "Anyway, you can have this truck. There's a map inside."

"A map to where?" demanded Melville. Then, because the old asshole still wasn't looking at him, he slammed the side of the shotgun into his head.

The old man slumped. Fell to earth. Melville grinned.

His grin slid off his face when he saw the man slowly stand and saw *his* grin.

"I don't much like you, son," said the coot. Melville almost killed him right there, but the guy said, "But I've been told to help you on your way. To tell you where John and Serafina are going."

Melville didn't know how long he and Isaiah remained silent. But it finally dawned on him that the shotgun was pointed straight down. He had lost control of this conversation.

Melville, you never had control of it in the first place.

The voice that sounded wasn't his, it was Mr. Dominic's. He was deeply ashamed. Mostly because he knew it was true.

The old man bent over and put his hands on his knees, then craned his head up to look at Isaiah. "You're a big one, aren't you?" he said.

"Who sent you?" said Isaiah again.

The old man nodded. "No fair telling," he answered. "Didn't tell them, won't tell you." He straightened. "There's a map in the glove box that shows the route to Lebanon. Enough fuel in the tank to get to Cedar City. Drive straight and don't stop for anything or you'll never catch up to 'em."

"I don't understand." Isaiah looked so thoroughly confused that Melville almost enjoyed the moment. Only the presence of the old queer kept him from reveling in seeing the priest's bewilderment.

"No, I suppose you don't," said the old man. And then, before either Melville or Isaiah could react, he stepped forward and put a hand on the black man's shoulder. He looked deep into the eyes of the priest. "But you will soon."

At last Melville was the one to react first. He stepped forward and shoved the ancient queen. "Tell us what's going on, you...*homo.*"

The last word wasn't the one he wanted, but he was so angry at what was going on–the confusion, the lack of information, the lack of *control*–that it was all that came to mind.

The old man just stared at him. And then *winked*.

That was too much. Melville buried the end of the shotgun in the coot's stomach and pulled the trigger.

Even buried in aged flesh, the report was so loud Melville expected the fog to flee before it. It didn't. Instead it seemed to come closer as blood and meat exploded into the permanent twilight, darkening silver mist to full black before flinging away and disappearing in cloud.

The man fell forward. He clutched Melville. Agony writhed across his features, which was nice. But then he ruined it by talking. "You don't know what you're doing," he said in a hoarse whisper. "Nothing you do will change what's coming." He smiled, and the smile disconcerted Melville. Men whose guts have been blown out their backs should not smile.

He also realized that blood was probably all over his clothes. That angered him. He pulled the trigger again.

This time the gay flew away like a superhero in a comic, which was cool. He didn't go far, though, no up-up-and-away for him. Just up-straight-then-down-and-bounce.

He landed face up in the dirt. Blood poured from his nose, his lips. His stomach and chest were shredded so badly they were barely recognizable as human and Melville knew that the back would be worse.

The man gasped. A pitiful, wheezing last breath. Then he whispered, "Hey, Evie," and let out his breath and stared at nothing.

Melville grinned. That was *awesome*.

Isaiah spun to face Melville, and suddenly he was truly afraid. "Why'd you do that?" roared Isaiah.

Melville forgot completely about the shotgun in his hands. He fell back. "He bothered me," he said. His voice sounded afraid. That was impossible. He never sounded like that. *Never*.

"He *bothered* you?" Isaiah took another step, and his free hand formed a pincer that Melville knew was intended for his throat.

"Don't," he said. "They'll kill her. Cut her up and rape her and kill her if you do anything to me."

"How will they know?" snarled Isaiah. "You can't call, they can't call. Your phone doesn't work. For all we know *no* phones work."

Another step. One more and the big man would grab him, throttle him, kill him.

Melville's phone rang.

Isaiah stopped moving.

Melville pulled the phone from his pocket with a shaking hand. "Y-yes?" he said.

The voice that answered wasn't who he expected. Not just *a* voice. *The* voice. Mr. Dominic. And the moment he heard those elegant tones, Melville's fears fled. Buried deep inside where he didn't have to worry about them.

"Are you quite all right, Mr. Melville?"

Melville glared at Isaiah. "We ran into a few snags, Mr. Dominic, but we're back on track." He stared at Isaiah. "Right, Batman?"

Isaiah continued being the Strong Silent Type. Melville wondered if this was how he picked up chicks.

"I am gratified to hear it, Mr. Melville. Please continue with your work."

"Yes, sir." Melville smirked at Isaiah. "He'd like us to keep working together, wouldn't you know it?"

"I want to talk to her."

At first Melville didn't understand what the priest meant. Then he realized: "The retard?" Isaiah's hardening expression was answer enough. "She can't even understand you."

"You don't know that!" Isaiah roared, then calmed himself with visible effort. "I want to know she's alive."

"She can't even talk. How do you think we're going to prove it?"

"I actually have a solution to that, Mr. Melville," said Mr. Dominic. "Please put our friend on the line."

Melville looked at the phone as if he hadn't understood it, then shrugged and handed it to Isaiah. The big man took it, listened a moment. Melville heard something from the small speaker. Muffled and faraway, but it sounded like...singing?

Isaiah started crying. "Hang in there, baby," he said. "I love you." He handed the phone back to Melville, then turned to the still-idling SUV.

Melville put his cell to his ear. "What was that about?"

"Nothing much. Time is wasting. Please continue, and please keep me apprised."

"Will do, sir. Thank you for the vehicle."

"Vehicle?" Mr. Dominic actually sounded surprised. "I'm afraid you have me at a bit of a disadvantage. I'm not really sure what you are talking about."

Melville looked at the dead body. Blood pooled over the hardpack, unable to penetrate. He supposed it made sense: Mr. Dominic never would have sent anyone like *that*.

"Never mind, sir," he said. "I'll keep you in the loop."

"Very good."

The line cut off.

Melville walked to the dead man. He was still smiling that strange smile, which infuriated Melville. He kicked the corpse in the head. The neck cracked and the head went sideways, but the smile remained, so Melville stomped it–and the rest of the face–out of existence.

He went to the SUV and got in. Isaiah was at the wheel, a map unfolded. He was all but hidden behind it, and Melville got the feeling that was because he hadn't wanted to watch the destruction of the dead queer.

Melville liked that. He liked when people hid from his accomplishments. It was a tremendously exciting experience.

And, for that matter, just when everything had become excruciatingly boring, excitement had returned. In spades. He had gotten to kill someone, they had wheels again.

He had gotten to hear Mr. Dominic's voice.

"Where we going?" he said. He sounded so chipper. He thought he would sing show tunes as they drove. Maybe some Disney songs.

Isaiah folded the map. "Apparently we're going to Kansas."

"So you believe the queer?"

Isaiah didn't answer. The SUV bounced its way to first gear, and a moment later they were on the road, on the hunt.

Melville began with songs from *Aladdin*.

interlude:
POSSESSION

MUTED SONG

From: Director <KRSellers@dir.cia.gov>
To: FLASH LIST
CC: POTUS <dpeters@secured.whitehouse.gov>
Sent: Friday, May 31 4:18 PM
Subject: SitRep (FinalMsg)

Please see attached. Forgive the typos and brevity. No one around to fact check or edit.

<FinalELE.docx>

From: POTUS <dpeters@secured.whitehouse.gov>
To: Director <KRSellers@dir.cia.gov>
Sent: Friday, May 31 4:19 PM
Subject: RE: **SitRep (FinalMsg)**

What the hell does this mean?

From: Director <KRSellers@dir.cia.gov>
To: POTUS <dpeters@secured.whitehouse.gov>
Sent: Friday, May 31 4:20 PM
Subject: RE: RE: **SitRep (FinalMsg)**

What it says. Don't contact me again. I won't be here. Going home. If it's still there.

God forgive me for the things I've done. God forgive us all.

***

Alone in a tomb with the rotting bones of men newly dead.

This is the second time she has lain in a car, unmoving, trapped not by the metal coffin that surrounds her but by the closer confines of the coffin she herself has become.

This time there are no lights. No blue, no red. There is only mist.

She waits for the dark face with the sad eyes. The bloody nose. It does not appear.

She waits to see the face of the man, torn apart and single eye staring. It does not manifest.

She waits for the woman who stares and sings songs of love before dying as well. She does not come to her, and her song does not sound.

There is only her and the three men.

The driving ended abruptly, and now she is here. It ended because the men coughed. They coughed harder and harder. The car swerved when one of the ones in front lost control of his body. The car hit something and they all flew forward, trapped by seatbelts.

She did not move after that. Not even to sing, her new voice silenced by what happened next.

A man in front continued coughing. She heard something wet. Then the man next to her growled. A strange, alien sound. Feral. Maddened and maddening.

She could not turn her head. It had slumped forward, canted to the side so she saw only the jagged edges of glass that had once been a window, tinted and smoky like the uneven teeth of a witch or a troll.

She realized she was thinking. Clearer than she had in a long time. Still not sure of many things, but sure of this: she was afraid. So terribly afraid.

The growling grew louder. Shouts followed it. Then screams. Sounds of tearing, and she could not be sure if it was cloth or skin, thick upholstery or the thinner mass of flesh that made up the men in the car.

Something banged–

(*a gun, Mommy had a gun once and Daddy had many*)

–and light flashed through the broken body of the SUV.

Then silence.

Darkness.

Mist.

And now she waits.

She is afraid.

She sings.

"Jesus loves me, this I know, for the bible tells me so...."

The mist curls on her. Cool on her forehead, clinging to her like gossamer strands that caress then flee.

A shape appears. She hopes for the dark face, the sad eyes.

The mist parts. A face *does* appear, but no sad eyes shine, bright with half-hidden tears and regrets even less buried. No, these eyes are hooded, viperous...enraged.

It is the elegant man. The one who was in the car with her, whose presence exerted such power, caused such terror.

It still does. The fear she had felt alone is suddenly doubled, trebled. She wishes for the solitude of curling mist, the company of none but the dead.

The man stands outside the door. His fists balled at his sides, fingers curled in so tightly upon themselves it looks as though they are bloodless.

"Stop singing," he whispers.

She did not realize she had continued singing. She does not stop now. She cannot. There is a part of her that worries if she stops here, now, in the presence of this man, she will never regain the voice lost so long.

"Jesus loves me, this I know, for the bible tells me so...."

She does not know the rest of the song. Perhaps she has forgotten. Perhaps the woman with no face never sang more than that. Either way, she sings it over and over. The elegant man grows angrier and angrier. Face redder and redder until it nearly glows in the mist.

"Stop. SINGING. THAT. *SONG!*" He takes a step toward the broken SUV and the broken body within. She thinks he will tear the door off and tear her body out of its shell, then perhaps her soul from her body and her sanity from her mind.

What sanity she has, at least.

His hand reaches for the door. Fingers stop only inches away from metal. He looks even angrier. A wrath so pure that she cannot look at it. She closes her eyes, if only for a moment–and is surprised she can even do that. She never knew how to blink at her own command before.

Just an open and a close. The time a star takes to twinkle in a cloudless sky. But when she opens her eyes, another person has come from the mist, another member in this strange convocation of living and dead, mobile and motionless.

"Don't you dare!"

She cannot see a face or features, but she sees a hand stretching out, hears the voice of a woman, strong and unafraid and somehow wise.

The elegant man is stopped cold. He stares at the woman who has dared step between him and the thing he wants to have, the thing he wants to destroy.

"Get out of my way."

The woman crosses arms in front of her. She laughs. The laugh is joyous, a laugh that comes of many years well-lived. "Don't think so, old man. You got no backup here, no nothing here at all but you and me."

The elegant man snarls, somehow still seeming opulent, a red jewel flashing in reflected flame. Another step toward the woman.

In the car, she watches. She fears. The woman cannot stand before the elegant man. She believes that nothing can.

But the woman does not move. She stands firm. Arms crossed. She laughs again.

The tapered fingers of the elegant man hook into claws, the manicured nails seem talons as they move toward the woman's throat.

Then his visage changes. Gone is the rage.

He is wrath no longer. Now he is only fear. Head moving back and forth, then he turns a fast circle, looking around at things she cannot see. Perhaps the faces she thought she saw once upon a time, the things in the gray?

The elegant man coughs out a sound half whimper, half gasp. He spins one more time, ignoring the old woman, facing *her*, leaning toward her.

"I don't have time for you," he whispers, the sound a saw hacking through her last vestiges of courage.

"Jesus loves me, this I know, for the bible tells me so...."

"You'll sing again, but a different tune. You'll scream *my* songs."

"Go 'way, old man." The old woman's voice is a whisper. But another sound joins it. A yawning moan that makes the skin stretch and shrink at the same time. Different than the coughs and screams that came with the crash she just experienced, but related somehow. Perhaps not born of the same parents, but in the same neighborhood of a very bad place.

The moan comes again. And a roar this time. So loud she cannot hear her own newfound song.

The elegant man runs away. He disappears in the mist.

The old woman stands still, head slightly cocked as though listening to make sure the elegant man is truly gone. Then turns to look at the people in the car.

She sees the old woman's face. Black skin creased with wrinkles. Each line the tale of a day lived in laughter or tears, together a weathered book easily read by any who care to look. The old woman has been happy, the old woman has done right and done well. She is beautiful.

The old woman does something odd. She squats down, then rises again. "Haven't been able to do that in *decades*," she says with a laugh. "So used to bad hips I almost don't know what to do with myself." Another squat, another laugh. "Gotta run," she says. "Gotta find my man and then we got *mountains* to climb."

Then the old woman laughs and runs with the awkward grace of a foal and, like the elegant man, disappears into the mist.

The strange moan writhes through the air a moment later.

She is alone again.

Then not alone.

Darkness looms beside her. Something so big it blots out the mist, the last strains of light, the *world*.

She sees things writhing beside the door. Things that are flesh, but not. Things that are both separate and joined forever.

Each has eyes. Snakes joined at the base. They scream as one, the strange moan she heard.

Then the roar.

The thing moves. A huge eye looks at her. It is bigger than the bent window frame. Like the rest it is not a single thing, but a thing made of other things. Writhing, whining things that look like yellow maggots surrounding a dark hole to–

(*darknesses and nothingtime*)

–places unknown and perhaps unknowable.

The roar again. The SUV rocks with its force. And she hears it not only beside her, but behind and before. All around.

This thing is not alone.

She is not alone.

She blinks again, but this time there is no fear that overcomes this great beast. No salvation suddenly appears. The eye still glares when the twinkle-time of her eyes is over.

She is not alone. The beast is not alone. Something more powerful and so more fearful is astride the beast. A rider atop the darkness.

Something reaches through the window.

It touches her.

"Jesus loves me, this I know, for the bible tells me so...."

This will be her last song.

four:
ASYLUM

STRANGERS WE COME

From: POTUS <dpeters@secured.whitehouse.gov>
To: Anton Koikov <jst14986@147265.2645.kremlin.ru>
Sent: Friday, May 31 6:32 PM
Subject: RE: FW: RE: Proposal etc.

My Dearest Anton,

I appreciate your email of a few moments ago. But considering that I am in a bunker several hundred feet below ground, my options are a bit limited.

Also, given your attitude to my previous post and our personal relations in general, and especially given the present situation and its ever more likely outcome which likely means that this will be one of the final communications you and I must endure with each other, I'd like to take this opportunity to very cordially invite you to suck my big one and then go sodomize yourself on one of those ICBMs you are so ridiculously proud of.

Yours sincerely,
Richard Peters

PS Your Minister of Internal Affairs has been feeding us information for years.

***

Isaiah drove the long, lonely road and couldn't decide whether to rejoice or despair.

The world was dying, of that there was no doubt. The information given him in the envelope at the beginning of all this was definitely true. John had been a soldier, voluntarily infected with some sort of disease that had been intended to lead to world safety but instead maddened him beyond reason. Now he carried a virus that adapted nearly infinitely, that had a ninety-eight percent mortality rate, and that could be communicated and run its course in anything from minutes to a day. The only hope was to kill him, to retrieve his body, to bring it in for testing.

Isaiah had started this journey bent on saving Katherine, then following salvation with revenge–his usual practice and pattern. Those motivations remained, but there was also the larger reality that the deaths of millions–billions–might be in his hands.

What about this damn fog?

That was something he didn't understand. It was everywhere, as though the world itself was sweating out the last moments of humanity's existence. Sometimes thin enough that he could push the SUV up to ninety or ninety-five miles per hour, sometimes so thick the only way to make sure he didn't run off the road was to slow down and stick his head out the window so he could watch the highway lines running beside him.

He didn't know where it came from, and neither did Melville. He didn't have to ask the scumbag to know this–it was apparent from the way the gaunt man kept staring out the window, shaking his head and looking lost.

They passed through Las Vegas. It was dark. The fog had claimed it. The strip was black and unmoving, no illuminated fountains or world-renowned architecture attempting to gild the desert temple to hedonism, no frenetically flashing billboards inviting passersby to come inside and lose themselves and their money. Just quiet. Just dead.

Once past the strip Isaiah did spot one oasis of light. He turned off the freeway. Melville protested. Isaiah ignored him. He had to see what was left.

It was a hospital.

Isaiah veered into the parking lot.

The hospital was dimmer than it should have been: probably running on emergency generators. But bright enough for the windows to shine like the many eyes of a block-bodied monster half-hidden in the haze.

He pulled in close. There was no movement. A large sign, written with thick scrawls of black marker across a series of blue hospital sheets, stretched across the doors.

No Room

Underneath it, someone had placed another sign. A white sheet this time, a different color pen. Information that had been added later:

OnLY DEaD inSIDe

A crumpled form in a white coat lay at the bottom of the doors. His hand reaching toward the parking lot as though he had died turning the last cars away.

Isaiah honored the dead man's entreaty. He thought he glimpsed movement as he left, a quick flash of a white face in a window. But when he turned his head to look it was gone. Still, his skin prickled as he drove away, the creeping feeling that he was being watched.

Were there any alive?

Perhaps.

Yes. There had to be. The alternative would mean a barren world for Katherine.

If Katherine hasn't died in the outbreak as well.

"I want to talk to her," he said.

"Not how it works," said Melville. "I can call for support, but I don't call Mr. Dominic. He calls me."

Isaiah drove on.

The fuel indicator on the dashboard dipped slowly. Either the truck had the best mpg Isaiah had ever seen, an enormous gas tank, or some kind of magic was at work.

He thought of the bible story of the widow's oil. A woman who fed a prophet in a famine and as a reward was blessed that her small vessel of cooking oil and her tiny store of flour never ran out.

Only this is the story of the killer's gas.

He almost smiled. It had been a long time–years– since he had thought of a bible story. Longer since he had likened it to anything happening in his life. This version was hardly a good topic for a Sunday sermon, of course, but it still felt oddly comforting to return to the old stories.

They drove.

Through Mesquite, then St. George. He worried that they might lose their way; that the mist would obscure their path or make them miss turnoffs. But the line was a straight one after Las Vegas. Just miles of emptiness, swallowed by mist that silvered, then grayed, then darkened.

Night. Or perhaps only a dusk whose last light was blanketed by the fog. Either way, full dark surrounded them.

"How close are we?" he said. It was hard to speak: Melville had been quiet the last few hours and Isaiah preferred it that way, so opening the door to conversation was loathsome. But the fuel gauge was finally dropping to the "E" and he needed to know when they would hit Cedar City and could find gas.

Melville consulted the map the old man had given them in a place that seemed another part of a strangely disjointed dream. "Uh, looks like it should be any time now." He looked at the trip odometer Isaiah had zeroed out at the beginning of the expedition. Did a calculation in his head. "Aw, dammit."

"What?"

"I think...." He looked at the map again. "I think we might have passed it."

"What?!"

"Hey, don't blame me. Who uses frigging *maps* anymore? That old queer could at least have given us a GPS or something."

Isaiah rolled his eyes. "Well, if we don't find somewhere to get gas we'll be walking soon. And chances are no one is going to come along to pick us up again."

The prospect scared him. This stretch of road was lonely at the best of times. Now...they could die walking along its edges and waiting for another person to come by and save them. And that meant not only his own death, not only the death of everyone else, but—most important—that of Katherine.

Is this even worth it? Is there anything left to save?

Yes. There has to be.

The fog swirled in front of him. For a moment the headlights actually made some headway into the water droplets. A sign lit up.

GAS–FOOD–LODGING
NEXT RIGHT

"Thank you, God," said Melville. He wiped his brow. "That was close." He winked at Isaiah, like a good prank had just been played on him. "Good one, Batman."

Isaiah didn't answer. He took the turnoff. Signs led them to the location where they could find gas.

He turned into the lot. The SUV died suddenly as he did. A single cough, then nothing. Empty. Good timing for an empty tank, he supposed.

The mist parted, revealing the building that had been hidden.

Melville screamed and slammed his hand on the dash over and over again. "What the shit is *this*?"

Isaiah almost didn't notice. The sound of Melville's palm slapping the plastic dash had drawn his eye. But then he saw something else.

Melville's neck glistened.

Scales. The beginnings of spines.

"You got that shot, didn't you?" said Isaiah.

Melville didn't look away from the building ahead of them, the building that was most definitely *not* a gas station, though it was a building of a type just as familiar to Isaiah.

"Yeah, we both did, moron," said Melville. He looked at Isaiah and said through gnashed teeth, "What? Did you forget? Did you catch a case of retard from your girlfriend?"

He looked back at the building. The spines on his neck shifted.

"We both got the shots, we're both safe," he said.

"Yeah," said Isaiah. His mouth was dry.

God, it's been a while. And I don't deserve to ask for anything. It's okay that I'm going to die—I've been more or less dead for a long time. But let me finish this. Let me save what's left of the world.

Let me save Katherine.

"Well, let's see if there's any gas around," said Melville. He opened the door. "Let's go."

Isaiah nodded. "Yeah. Let's go."

EDGE OF REVELATION

From: POTUS <dpeters@secured.whitehouse.gov>
To: FLASH, CABINET, HOUSE, SENATE, JOINTCHIEFS, PRESSCONTACTS, NATGOVASS, DNC, RNC, MAJORDONORSGROUP, ...[42 more]
CC: FLASH, CABINET, HOUSE, SENATE, JOINTCHIEFS, PRESSCONTACTS, NATGOVASS, DNC, RNC, MAJORDONORSGROUP, ...[42 more]
Sent: Friday, May 31 7:58 PM
Subject: RING AROUND THE ROSIE

POCKET FULL OF POSIE ASHES ASHES WE ALL FALL DOWN ANYONE OUT THERE

From: X <xxx@xxx.xxx>
To: Dicky <dpeters@secured.whitehouse.gov>
Sent: Thursday, May 31 7:58 PM
Subject: RE: RING AROUND THE ROSIE

I will cut you off if you keep on doing this. You want to know what alone really feels like? Pull yourself together.

From: POTUS <dpeters@secured.whitehouse.gov>
To: 'X' <xxx@secured.whitehouse.gov>
Sent: Friday, May 31 7:59 PM
Subject: RE: RE: RING AROUND THE ROSIE

Look what I learned how to do!

(o)(o)

It's boobies!

***

"What now?"

The words were loud in the confines of the SUV. Louder still in John's head. They sounded like an accusation, though he knew Serafina didn't intend them that way. Still....

What now?

What do we do now?

Where have you taken me?

What now?

Where is this?

Where are we going to die?

"Maybe there are some gas pumps in back," he said. The words fell limp from his lips, born and dying in the same instant. Serafina nodded. Though what else *could* she do?

The engine sputtered. John pulled past the building the signs had led them to. Not a gas station as promised, but what looked like an abandoned church. The sign on the ornamental gate beside the door said Our Mother of Mercy.

John prayed the mercy was a good supply of unleaded.

The church was small, which was unsurprising in a part of the country where only ten percent of the population was Catholic–

(*and there I go again, random trivia popping into my head at random times*)

–just a brick building, squared with a belfry at the front corner. The cross at the top of the belfry had one of its arms missing. The church's windows were boarded over to protect against vandals, and the dark brick of the walls was darker in spots with water damage and perhaps the beginnings of a long final dissolution.

A small place, built humble and made humbler still by abandonment and time and the elements.

But as small as the building was, the trip around its side seemed to take forever. The SUV's engine sputtered, coughed. John made it to the back of the church, where a small building had been appended: likely the rectory where the priest at one time lived.

The fumes they had been running on ran dry. The engine stopped cycling. They coasted to a halt. The mist wrapped itself around them.

There were no pumps, no gas.

"I hope whoever did signs for this city got fired and tied on top an anthill with honey in his jockeys," said Serafina.

John laughed. The situation was dire, but she was refusing to stop wisecracking. Even black humor was humor. And where real laughter existed, fear could not.

Serafina laughed, too. Laughter is a benevolently contagious disease, and it brings lightness of spirit, an increase of resolve. Perhaps that is why it is so close to madness at times: because it brings hope where none could possibly exist.

"Let's check inside the church," said John.

"Yeah, maybe there's a car in there."

"We can hope."

"Or a plane."

"We can pray."

"Good place for it."

"True."

"Let's ask for a hot meal and a shower, too. And that the people following us all caught terminal syphilis."

"We shouldn't push our luck."

"If you're gonna go, go big."

He laughed again. Hope and perhaps a bit of madness keeping the darkness at bay.

They got out of the car and headed to the rectory.

John worried they'd have to force entry, which seemed not merely wrong but somehow indecent. The idea of slamming his way into a church, even an abandoned, decrepit one, didn't sit well with him.

He thought that was something from his past. For an instant he almost grabbed something solid. Something real. A moment from memory loomed, a shadow in the mists of his history.

The man who had given them the SUV spoke in his mind. *"And I can't tell you, my friend, because it'd be more than you could bear. It'd destroy you."*

In that instant, standing before the closed door of the church, John almost understood. Almost knew what the old man had been saying, what all this was leading to.

"John? What is it?"

The moment of near-revelation passed away. He realized he had stopped moving. Serafina was staring at him, concerned. "You okay?" she said.

He had to restrain a shout of frustration. Instead he bit his lip and then said, "Fine." It wasn't her fault. She didn't know what her words had caused to slip by. Hopefully the moment would come again.

"...it'd be more than you could bear. It'd destroy you."

Or maybe he was better off not knowing.

The door to the rectory was not only unlocked, it was ajar. There was a note taped to it. In simple handwriting it said, "If anyone comes here, please meet at the town hall.– Father Thomas."

John left the note on the door. Clearly the priest had come here when things started changing for the worst, believing that some in the community might gather at the church as a common point of reference, an old landmark or a once-refuge. He hoped the note had been read many times, and still would be would be many times more.

He went into the rectory. Serafina followed.

He fumbled around on the inside wall near the door, found a light switch, and flicked it upward. Nothing happened. Unsurprising, but he still felt sad for some reason. Like even when everything else had failed there should still be light at a church, if anywhere. And the fact that there was not meant that things were much worse than they knew.

He left the door open behind him as they entered so they would be able to use the wisps of illumination the mist permitted to pass through it; hopefully that would be enough to get by.

The priest's living quarters were nearly empty, and even in the darkness John could see that a layer of dust covered everything that remained. A single cross hung on the wall directly across from the front door: the first thing visitors would see and apparently left behind as a memory of blessing.

Serafina moved to the left, where a small kitchenette held a sink, an oven, a few cabinets. She started going through the cabinets, then looked under the sink.

John moved right. There was a dingy hutch and a desk that hadn't been removed when the church fell into disrepair because they were built into the wall. A part of the structure, so left to die with the rest.

Inspecting the front room took only a few seconds. Then there was another doorway to the side that led to a small bedroom. Nothing in it beyond the remains of a fire that some squatter had lit on the carpet. That made John mad. A place like this had once been the center of life for many. The fire seemed like the desecration of a corpse.

"Nothing," he said.

"There's still the church," said Serafina.

He nodded, trying to quell his discouragement. Not many Catholic churches carried spare gas in the nave, stashed unleaded under the altar or diesel in the narthex. But the alternative to looking inside was to simply sit and die in despair…or to venture blindly into the mist.

He didn't care for either of those alternatives.

They headed back into the main room. There was a doorway that John figured would lead to the sacristy, where the priest would have kept his vestments and the items he used for mass. That then would lead to the church proper.

Precisely in the center of the room, Serafina froze.

"What is it?" John said.

She held up a hand, a quick command to silence. John's own brain immediately shifted all attention to his ears. He heard the throb of his heartbeat, the low soughing of wind in the mist, the cavernous nothing-sound of a world growing empty and cold.

Then something else.

344

He looked at Serafina. Her eyes were so wide they glowed in the darkness.

He hadn't heard the first sound, whatever noise she had originally heard. But he heard the next: a thud. The metal-on-metal *chunk* of a car door. Then another.

Two doors.

Two people?

Serafina's face had paled to the point it nearly lit the room. She mouthed a word: "Them?"

John started to shrug, to shake his head. Neither gesture succeeded.

Two car doors.

Two.

What were the chances of any two other people being in this place, at this time?

A moment later, they heard crunching footsteps. A voice.

"We better damn well find somewhere with gas. We don't, then forget finding those two. And forget saving what's left of the world or your little bitch."

John started to shake.

...forget finding those two....

There could be no doubt. The men who had followed them had found them once more. And the voices sounded close enough that it was certain the killers would see him and Serafina if they tried to run out the door and escape in the mist.

Their place of possible respite had been converted to a cage.

Worse, perhaps, was the implication inherent in the other words.

...and forget saving what's left of the world....

345

…what's left of the world….

What did that mean? Again, John felt like he was at the threshold of understanding, a revelation that would not only tear away the veils of forgetfulness draped over his memories but would also…what?

Destroy me.

Suddenly he did not wish to know his past. Suddenly he feared it. Knew that if he understood who he was, he would never forgive himself. Would never recover.

He pushed away the threatening memories. Tamped them down in the deep places, the vasty depths of his heart.

Serafina saved him. He would have stood there and struggled with himself until they came for him, until they killed him. But she grabbed his hand. Yanked him away from the still-open door that led outside.

She pulled him toward the door that led to the sacristy. With the part of his mind not devoted to resisting what he knew, John hoped it was unlocked.

Together those two things occupied him completely.

That was why he tripped.

THINGS MADE FLESH

From: POTUS <dpeters@secured.whitehouse.gov>
To: 'X' <xxx@secured.whitehouse.gov>
Sent: Friday, May 31 8:13 PM
Subject: I'm sorry

Sorry sorry so so scared.
Didn't mean to say all that stuff. Its dark dwon here & Im having trouble thinking. The last of my detale just died and guess what? I realized I dont know how to leave! Place designed to be the most secure in the entire world, but it's nothing but a huge lead and concretecoffin now.

Can you find meee?

From: X <xxx@xxx.xxx>
To: Dicky <dpeters@secured.whitehouse.gov>
Sent: Thursday, May 31 8:13 PM
Subject: RE: I'm sorry

Of course. I always will. You'll have to wait a bit and be patient, but I'll come for you. I promise. We can still salvage this.

From: POTUS <dpeters@secured.whitehouse.gov>
To: 'X' <xxx@secured.whitehouse.gov>
Sent: Friday, May 31 8:14 PM
Subject: RE: RE: I'm sorry

Will try. I keep hearing things. Everyones dead, all the lights are out but the computer screen, but I keep hearing things moving and its scaring me.

***

There was nothing beside the church but more mist. Isaiah barely managed to care. When they got out of their dead vehicle Melville drew close to him and Isaiah immediately pulled away.

"What the hell, Batman?" he said. The man was such an egomaniac he couldn't conceive of a world–of a single moment–where he wasn't both the center of attention and the focus of all affection. Then, surly: "Whatever."

Isaiah didn't want to be anywhere near the scumbag. This was a truly evil human, and he had no desire to stain his soul further than it already had been. But more than that, he feared the spines rising up Melville's neck, the scales appearing in shining patches here and there under his chin and below his ears.

Then he realized being worried about catching the disease was ridiculous at this point. They'd been driving together in close quarters for hours. If he was going to catch it, he already had.

So maybe I'm immune. I can keep taking care of Katherine.

That gave him hope. Because implicit in the thought was not merely his survival, but hers. That was all that mattered.

They walked around the back of the church. A short trek, unsurprising given the humble aspect of the place. It was old, a bit rundown, but it reminded Isaiah of Nicholas' church, the place he thought of as his own first church, the place he had been rescued–if only for a time–from his sins and their consequences.

It was hard walking so close to a place that reminded him of his dead friend. Especially when that place was a church. The night before presenting himself for what would be his too-short incarceration he had gone to Nicholas' church and prayed that justice would be done. That was also the last time he had gone in a church.

Justice could not be found kneeling at pews or reading the Gospel from the pulpit. It could only be found in violence. In the destruction of the wicked. In righteous murder, and, eventually, in his own death.

Now he walked again beside a church, holiness on his right side and a man whose inner *and* outer forms epitomized corruption on his left. A tug-of-war that he knew he had already lost.

There was no gas at the back of the church. Just more mist. He thought he saw something in the darkness, a shape that might have been a car. Maybe they could siphon it?

"If I find the person who lied about the gas, I'll pull his eyes out and make him watch me feed them to his kids," rasped Melville.

Isaiah didn't point out the obvious problems with that threat. He did look at his companion/keeper, however. The growths on Melville's neck were larger. They had spread to his chin. And the man seemed...shorter. His tall, gaunt form had curled slightly, drawing down as though a weight had been tied to his neck.

"There's nothing here," said the other man.

"No," agreed Isaiah. "But maybe there's a car parked some–"

Something crashed inside the rectory.

Isaiah didn't bother looking at Melville before springing toward the closed door. It was them. John and Serafina. It had to be.

They could end this. Perhaps he could save the world. Katherine.

Melville was close behind him. But his gait sounded odd. Not the even *thump-thump-thump-thump* of a person running, it was more a *thump-THUD, thump-THUD*. Like something was wrong with one of the other man's legs.

Isaiah wondered what he might see if Melville were to roll up his pants legs.

Then he was through the door. It wasn't locked, wasn't even fully closed. It flew open under his hand and slammed back against the wall.

It was dark inside. Not much to see. A small room, nearly empty. A door to the side that would no doubt lead to a bedroom. Another door that would lead to the sacristy.

A cross on the wall ahead of him drew his attention. Isaiah had to resist the urge to genuflect. He shook himself.

Focus.

The sacristy door clicked as its lock engaged.

Isaiah realized he hadn't brought his gun with him but had left it in the SUV–a lapse brought about by the sight of Melville's infection. Melville didn't have his shotgun, either. Otherwise Isaiah was sure the other man would have just aimed and fired at the door to blast it open. Instead, Melville ran at it full-tilt. Hit it with his shoulder.

Bounced off.

Melville fell to the floor with a bone-shuddering thud and a screamed curse. Isaiah ignored both and knocked lightly on the door. The sound came back so muted as to be nearly inaudible. It wasn't some cheap door, but a thick security door to protect the sacristy.

The front door was nothing special. But this one had been chosen to withstand nearly anything but its keys. The priest of this place had valued himself less than the accoutrements of worship. Had seemed by this architectural choice to say, "Do what you will to *my* body, but leave the body of Christ alone."

It was exactly the kind of decision that Nicholas would have made. Isaiah smiled in spite of himself.

Melville leaped to his feet, moving to the front door. Isaiah tried to ignore the weird gait–

(*thump-THUD, thump-THUD*)

–just as he tried to ignore the fact that the other man was now bent nearly double. Spines poked through his hair.

"Where you going?" he said.

"To get the gun," said Melville. His voice sounded wrong. Jagged, like he was speaking through a mouthful of tacks. Broken glass and broken teeth.

"It won't work," said Isaiah. "The door's too thick, the knob is designed to–"

"How the hell else you suggest we get in then?" snarled Melville.

"I believe *I* can help with that."

The new voice made Isaiah start. He had been so intent on watching Melville's form, both curious to see his face and fearful of what he might see, that he hadn't noticed the newcomer who now stood at the open doorway to the rectory.

Melville's voice still sounded strange, rasping through a mouth whose structure was shifting. But there was no mistaking his joy. "Mr. Dominic!"

"Hello, Mr. Melville," said the man. He stood framed in the doorway, rimmed by mist, hands clasped like a particularly well-dressed monk about to take up residency here.

Isaiah gaped. "How did you–?"

Dominic shook his head slowly and *tsk-tsk*ed like a British Dame at tea. "Do you really think I would simply track your cars alone? With so much at stake?" He put his hand to his cheek, thumb extended to ear, pinky to mouth. "Mr. Melville's phone lets me know where you are at all times." He looked around the interior of the sacristy. "Rather filthy in here." He turned on his heel. Walked away. "Follow me, please."

Melville loped after his master. Isaiah followed as well. "Where are we going?" he said.

Dominic didn't answer, just walked silently through the mist, with Melville padding along behind him on legs that seemed to curve in all the wrong places. The man's knees had relocated to a point a full six inches lower, and a strange outcropping that reminded Isaiah of the jutting tarsals of a dog now strained at the confines of the killer's pants.

Melville's form drooped lower and lower, his back arching more and more. Finally he simply dropped to all fours. The back of his jacket split open. Spines and scales slashed through the fabric.

Melville had always been a monster, but at least before his monstrousness had been internal. Now it was apparent for all to see.

Dominic looked back at Isaiah sadly. "See what's happening? See what we have to stop?"

Melville laughed. If sanity had ever been within his grasp, it had flown far beyond the man's fingerless reach.

They walked perhaps a hundred feet. Far enough that the church became nothing but a shadow behind them. Isaiah looked back. "We won't see it if they run," he said.

"They won't," answered Dominic. "They're cowering in the middle of the church, probably praying for something to save them." He sounded thoroughly disgusted.

Another shadow appeared in front of them. Smaller than a building, small enough that they were right on it before Isaiah realized what it was. A truck. Sturdy, rough around the edges. A workhorse of a vehicle.

"I found it when I came in," said Dominic. Melville sat on his haunches and stared up at the impeccably-dressed man. He licked his lips, and Isaiah saw that he seemed to have far too many teeth; that many snarled their way not only between his lips but *through* them, piercing mouth and cheek alike.

What's happening? How can this be possible? How can we stop it?

"How *did* you get here?" said Isaiah.

"Same as you. I drove," said Dominic. He gestured into the mist. "I ran out of gas a few miles back, then walked toward Mr. Melville's signal." He patted Melville's head absently. "I hoped I'd find you, as I was in a bit of a bind, to be honest." A rueful smile. Then he said, "Regardless, this truck affords us the opportunity to take them unawares."

"How so?"

"Isn't it obvious?" said Dominic. "You drive it through the side of the church. Even if you don't kill them when you crash through, you come out shooting." He drew a finger across his neck. "Then we get in the truck and take the bodies to the nearest CDC and," he continued, looking sadly at Melville, "we hope for the best."

"CDC's in Georgia," said Isaiah.

Dominic sighed. "Yes, but Hill Air Force Base and Wendover Air Force Base are less than three hours away. Both have emergency biohazard lab facilities onsite with the capabilities to begin analyses, as well as hardline communications with CDC Atlanta so they can begin testing until a CDC team arrives. They've already been briefed and are waiting on us, in fact." He showed his teeth, a too-wide grin that Isaiah thought eerily like Melville's post-transformation rictus.

Dominic gestured to the truck. "I've laid out all the pieces, Isaiah. And this is where you take over, I believe."

Isaiah looked at the truck. Then behind him, where the church hid in the darkness. He shook his head. "No," he said.

Dominic looked startled. "You're refusing to work with us? You know what will happen–?"

"No, I'm just not going to bash through the side of a church for you."

Dominic looked at him, his eyes narrowed to thin black lines. "You've got religion, eh?"

Isaiah shrugged. Maybe it was that. Maybe it was that this place looked like Nicholas' old church, or that he felt more and more like he was working with truly evil people–even if what they were hoping to do was, in the end result, something good. Maybe it was simply the weight of his own sins finally pulling the wool away from his eyes.

No matter. He wasn't going to destroy a church to find the people inside. People who had definitely caused the spread of death and disease, but who weren't going to do any more of that while they were alone in a house of God.

"We'll wait for them to come out. Melville waits for them on one side, I wait on the other. We take them down when they come out."

"I don't think Mr. Melville will like that," said Dominic. "I'm not even sure he's *capable* of that, to be perfectly frank."

"Then you watch," said Isaiah.

Dominic's eyes remained slitted. But the rest of his face changed. He no longer looked irritated. He looked dangerous. "I don't do that kind of thing, Isaiah. It's not what I'm here for. It's what *you're* here for."

Isaiah knew at this moment he was definitely facing the most dangerous person he had ever met. Forget the drug dealers, the abusers, the killers–even himself. He got the feeling that Dominic could murder him in the next second and even if he knew it was coming he would never be able to stop it.

His bladder clenched. He nearly wet himself. His legs started to tremble and the words of the Our Father started running through his head–a prayer he hadn't thought of in years.

Dominic's face suddenly relaxed. "Fine. You just wait until they come out."

Isaiah nearly collapsed with relief. "Okay," he managed. "Okay, good."

He turned away, as much so that Dominic wouldn't see the naked fear he suspected was still on his face as to return to the church.

"Isaiah?"

He didn't turn back. "Yeah?"

"You won't have to wait long, though. They're going to come out soon. And they'll be screaming."

Dominic whispered something.

A form tore past Isaiah. Running on all fours, a transformation complete. No longer human, but not merely an animal, either. Isaiah caught an impression of a wolfish snout, the dark eyes of a shark. Spines along crested ridges that rode the length of a strangely curved back. Muscles that were stringy and powerful.

He ran after the thing that had once been Melville.

Saw it spring to the wall of the church. Run straight up the side, clinging like a huge insect. It ran to the nearest boarded window. Dug a clawed hand into the wood. Pulled it apart with a single yank, a movement so powerful that the entire sheet of plywood splintered.

Then the thing crashed through the window beyond and disappeared inside the church.

Isaiah watched. The mist surrounded him, and he knew the world was over. It no longer mattered what he did, because no matter what, the things of nightmare were real and madness had been made flesh.

THE MIGHTY HAVE FALLEN

From: POTUS <dpeters@secured.whitehouse.gov>
To: 'X' <xxx@secured.whitehouse.gov>
Sent: Friday, May 31 8:22 PM
Subject: Things of Great Interest

I've been going over old emails between you and me. They all have one thing in common. Guess what it is! Guess guess.

From: X <xxx@xxx.xxx>
To: Dicky <dpeters@secured.whitehouse.gov>
Sent: Friday, May 31 8:22 PM
Subject: RE: Things of Great Interest

No. What are you talking about? Is this more of your gibberish?

From: POTUS <dpeters@secured.whitehouse.gov>
To: 'X' <xxx@secured.whitehouse.gov>

Sent: Friday, May 31 8:23 PM
Subject: RE: RE: Things of Great Interest

Ha! You didn't guess, but you DID it.
I'm really starting to wonder about you, you know.Myabe I'll take my ball and go home.

***

Serafina had never felt like this in a church. Her mother–

(*"Onde está a minha filha?"*)

–had taken her every week, often two or three times a week, until she ran away. Serafina hated it then, resented the standing, the kneeling, the sitting, the standing, the ups, the downs, the confessions, the everything about it. She came to love it, at first in memory of her mother, then for its own sake.

But through it all she had never felt afraid. Her mother had always insisted she go to church because it was "a place of refuge." A sanctuary. Serafina had never really considered those words before. Now, rushing from side to side with John, looking for another way out, looking for something to use or a way to escape, she did.

A place of refuge.

A sanctuary.

Such kindnesses. Such words of safety.

But when you really thought about them, they carried implicit horrors. Because when you thought about it, what they really meant was that you were surrounded on all sides by danger, and this was your only place of asylum, your last defense.

The church might be safe, but all else was a deluge of death and darkness and despair.

And they couldn't stay here forever. Even if they had supplies for a millennium, she suspected that the storm was going to batter its way in very soon.

There were no doors but the one they had come through and the four in the narthex at the front of the church, going outside. Those four were sealed. Not just the locks, but chains triple-wrapped around the stile crash bars, heavy padlocks securing them together like slaves in a sinking galley.

The rest of the space–the nave, the chancel, the apse– was empty. Not even the pews remained; all had been removed. There was only blank concrete and a few small strips of carpet along the edges, pinned down under moldings that had once been ornate, lovely, but were now chipped and warped.

The rounded ceiling bounced the sound of their footsteps back at them, mocking their attempts at escape or defense.

"Anything over there?" said John. He was on the other side of the nave, looking for the same thing she was: anything that would help them, anything at all. Finding the same thing she was: nothing that could help them, nothing at all.

"No!" She looked at the windows. Most were surprisingly intact. Stained glass scenes from the Old and New Testaments that could barely be made out in the dark void of the church. Men walking through split seas, other men crucified. Terror and triumph, all shadowed by the boards that covered them from behind.

And no way out.

The board closest to her separated from the window. The glass showed an angel stopping Abraham from slaying his son Isaac at the command of God, and the darkness of the scene brightened slightly as the wood shattered. Then the window shattered as well as something threw itself into the church.

Serafina's arms went over her head. Barbs of glass slashed them and she screamed as her blood flowed.

Another scream came as the thing landed in front of her.

She didn't know what it was. She had no words for what it *could* be. It was on all fours, like a dog, and like a dog it had legs that seemed to bend backward at the knees– an optical illusion caused by bony growths at the backs of its feet. But it was entirely un-canine in genesis, that was certain. No dog had spines like this thing did, or a waist so thin that chest and hips were barely connected, so thin that lengths of intestine snaked not hidden deep within, but clearly visible barely beneath the surface of the skin.

Its teeth jabbed through cheek and lip and chin. Its skin sloughed off in ragged sheets to reveal scales that looked rough enough to rasp the skin from anything it embraced.

The thing growled at her. Took a step toward her. It hunched its back legs, readying to leap. She realized that not all of the ragged stuff falling from it was skin. Some was cloth. The remains of a suit.

And she knew: this was one of the killers.

The cloth wasn't black. So it wasn't the priest, it was the other man. The thin man.

Where the priest was, she didn't know. But the thin man was *here*. Still thin, but no longer a man. No longer a man, but still hungering for her death.

The creature jumped at her.

She fell back with a scream. The pain of glass slivering her arms fled from her awareness. Her head slammed down on bare concrete, her legs curled up to her abdomen, a fetal position that was her last and only refuge.

The thing fell on her. Teeth grinding together inches in front of her. She had managed to get her knees into the thing's gut–one of the only places on its body not covered by spikes–and now pushed it away with all her might. Her right thumb jammed its way into the soft spot at the back of its mouth, in the place where upper and lower jaws came together. Her left went to its right eye and pressed.

Something popped under her left thumb. The thing writhed and a horrible sound came from inside it. But it didn't stop pushing down on her. The teeth came closer. The ones that stuck out at angles were so close she could see the slicks of spittle that coated them.

Then something slammed the thing to the side. The beast tipped and rolled off her, and Serafina saw that John had plowed into the creature. Heedless of the bony quills that stood along its length, he had used his own body to knock the thing off her.

Now they stood across from one another, staring at each other. John was bleeding up and down the length of his body. His shirt and pants a bloody wreck.

Several of the thing's quills were shattered. One eye was a black ruin. Serafina had to resist an urge to wipe her hands on her pants.

John gestured for her to get behind him. Before she could, the thing snarled and jumped at her again. John intercepted it in midair, the two of them crashing to the floor and then tumbling along the ground in a spray of rage and blood. Something cracked along the way, and the thing bellowed.

The rolling bodies separated, and Serafina saw that John had broken its forearm. It limped back on three legs. Its muzzle wrinkled and it growled, but the growl was half-whimper.

John didn't make a sound. His hands were out, ready to fight and kill. But he looked sad. Serafina tried to remember if he always looked like that when he fought. Had he worn that look of sorrow each time he had to attack someone, to take a life? She thought perhaps he had.

And even if he hadn't, she knew suddenly that it was how he felt. This wasn't anything he wanted. All he *did* want was to continue on his way, to reach his destination. And there....

What?

She still didn't know. But she trusted. She knew John, and knew that whatever he wanted would have to be a good thing.

The creature kept retreating. It tripped. John took advantage of the opening. He leaped forward, his own leg sweeping low to knock the thing's other limbs out from under it.

The monster wasn't there.

It jumped back. Going to two legs suddenly, standing as a man once again. And the wound to its front leg didn't seem to be as bad as it had made out, either, because then it leaped forward and grabbed John in its arms, a strong grip that John couldn't break.

The thing snarled, a noise that turned into the hysterical cackle of a hyena.

It leaned down and tore John's throat out.

Blood sprayed toward the ceiling of the dead church. Serafina screamed.

The monster laughed that rat-a-tat laugh, a carrion eater that has lucked into the greatest kill of its life. John gave a series of jerks, danced a shallow dance that grew ever shallower as the blood pumped out of him.

The monster laughed.

The dance slowed.

Ended.

The monster let go of John's body.

As John fell, the thing dropped to all fours again and turned to Serafina.

She was no longer screaming. She was too shocked and frightened to scream. Sound did not belong here, for fear had chased all but death from this place.

The monster licked its face with a tongue that was long and black and forked and covered in glinting scales.

It leaped at her.

The world fell down.

A RISEN BEAST

From: POTUS <dpeters@secured.whitehouse.gov>
To: 'X' <xxx@secured.whitehouse.gov>
Sent: Friday, May 31 8:25 PM
Subject: My Balls

I got your last email. I changed the subject line, though, because this one is funn ier. No, Im not REALLY going to take my ball and go home. WHere would I GO? SHeesh. I'm still your guy! You know that. You and me, through and through to the end!

I do think its funny how you haven't figured out what all our emails have in common. Kindof an oversight on your part.

I found all the Secret Service guns, even in the dark. I'm playing Jenga with them..

***

Isaiah watched Melville–the thing that Melville had turned into–tear the board off the window, then watched it crash through stained glass and into the darkness beyond.

He heard screams. Growls. Some sick noise that was half laugh, half bark. More screams.

A moment of silence.

The silence was short in duration, but long in effect. In the eternity of that short second, he wished he could take back his decision not to go into the church. Regardless of the fact that it reminded him of Nicholas, regardless of the idea that it could be hallowed ground–something Isaiah was suddenly unsure whether he believed in or not–

anything would be preferable to letting someone fall to a creature like the Melville-thing.

He stepped forward. No longer intending to stop John and Serafina, no longer intending *anything*. Just knowing that whatever Melville was doing, it was wrong. It was something that should not be, and so something that had to be stopped.

Isaiah had devoted his life to penance and to justice. To turning what should not be into what no longer was. But here he was, actively participating in something that his soul knew was an atrocity.

Should John and Serafina die? Perhaps.

But not like this. Never like this.

Another step forward.

"Whatever you're thinking, I advise you to think again," said Dominic.

Isaiah turned. The man still stood beside him, still looked perfectly-groomed, perfectly-attired. Someone who would be more at home on the cover of *GQ* than out in an otherworldly mist on a mission of murder. Except for his eyes. Those definitely belonged in places of death.

"This has to be done, Isaiah," said the older man.

"Not like this."

"By any means necessary."

There was another scream. A last, piteous scream.

Isaiah turned back to the church, and took one last step. No longer knowing what he was going to do: follow his heart or follow Dominic's orders.

The church was but darkness in the mist.

A greater darkness suddenly appeared.

The mist whirled as something the size of a mountain appeared. It should have come with thunder and earthquakes. But there was no tumult accompanying it. Only a breathless silence as it moved.

Isaiah got the impression of legs. Perhaps as many as twelve, each of them moving in perfect harmony, ordered by a single brain though surely the creature had to be too large for one mind to control. Each leg stretched hundreds of feet into the sky, disappearing into the fog-clad night, and each was dozens of feet in diameter. They landed softly, so softly that each step was barely noticeable, and that only if you were watching for them.

Isaiah could not see a body. Whatever thing connected the legs was too far above him to see, too high to fathom.

The legs were covered with blinking lights. Tiny pins of illumination that glimmered and glittered with a brightness that did not warm. They looked like the eyes of predators, reflecting a fire lit by frightened campers in the desert.

Isaiah sensed he wasn't far wrong in that thought. They were eyes. Though of what he couldn't guess, and what they saw he didn't care to contemplate.

Dominic gasped. Isaiah couldn't tell if the sound was rage or ecstasy.

The front leg of the creature came down on the church. No second footfall. None was needed. One moment the church stood where it had likely stood for fifty years and more, the next there lay a pile of rubble in a roughly square pattern around a huge leg-thing that rose into the nothing above.

Isaiah stared at the leg for a moment. The thing was ringed on the bottom by claws that looked like nothing more than fleshless bones. Above them: the winking lights, which he now saw were seated at the end of corded things that twined in and around themselves. Some kind of writhing vines, almost serpentine.

The leg lifted. The monstrous thing in the mist stepped away. Three huge strides and it was lost to sight in the fog.

Isaiah and Dominic stood in silence for a moment. Then Dominic said, "Well?"

"Well what?"

"Go check it out."

Isaiah glared at the other man. "Are you serious?"

"The stakes haven't changed. The world is still at issue." Dominic removed a cell phone. "As is the fate of a little girl."

A horrible feeling swept over Isaiah. "Call her."

"Of course." Dominic didn't seem at all dismayed, either by the request or by the fact that a leviathan had just pounded a church to pieces. He dialed his phone, then said, "Is she there? Put her on." He pressed a button and the cell switched to speaker mode.

Katherine's voice wafted out. "*Jesus loves me, this I know....*"

Isaiah felt a horrible mix of emotions. Happiness, sadness. Brightness, darkness. The lift of hope, the dragging certainty that all was lost.

He didn't know what to do.

He remembered a line of poetry he had learned in the seminary, a bit of *Paradise Lost* that had stuck with him as clearly and strongly as any scripture:

> *Familiar the fierce heat; and, void of pain,*
> *This horror will grow mild, this darkness light....*

Was that where he was? Had he followed the coaxings of Belial, growing so comfortable with where he was that he failed to recognize it as Hell? So used to inaction that now he could not move, could not change the world in which he found himself?

A bit of wall, still clinging together, gave up the fight and fell to nothing but brick and dust and shattered mortar. The sound moved Isaiah. It pulled something in his heart.

"*...for the bible tells me so....*"

The sound of Katherine's voice was so innocent. So pure and *good*. It was the sound of everything he had always wanted to be, had always hoped to save in himself.

"I'm coming, sweetie," he said, and hoped she heard him. She liked to watch cartoons, she liked to be read to. Perhaps she liked his voice. Perhaps she knew his words.

Dominic switched off the phone.

Isaiah went to the church. To what was left of it. The titan in the darkness had pulverized it so it lay nearly flat. Isaiah doubted he would be able to make out much more than bricks and wood and perhaps some bits of metal.

He was wrong. He found a body almost immediately. Twisted and wrecked and dead beyond doubt.

A few hours or even minutes ago, Isaiah would have rejoiced to see Melville this way. He had been a blight, a disgrace to life. Those facts were still true, but Isaiah was no longer thrilled at the death of the sociopath-become-beast. He stared at the body–smashed to scales and spines and blood and bone–and felt only a distant sadness. One more person gone in a night that had seen so much life stolen away.

He looked for the others. He figured that John and Serafina would be nearby Melville's body. The sounds he had heard before the huge monster had appeared must have been them, reacting to the surprise entry of the killer in their midst. So they should be right next to the dead man/once-man.

But they were not.

Isaiah picked over the remains of the church, walking gingerly over the debris. He didn't know if he walked carefully to avoid turning an ankle, because he didn't want to step on John or Serafina, or simply out of respect for what this place had once been.

He heard a moan.

Ran to it.

A hand stuck out from under a pile of pulverized brick. He scooped away dust and wood and bits of nothing that had once held the prayers of a people. His black frock grew gray with the powder of once-holy places.

Serafina was beneath it all. Blood ran from her nostrils, a deep gash at her forehead bled copiously. Scratches and scrapes ran the length of her arms, but they looked superficial.

Other than that she seemed surprisingly unmarked.

He looked at her. Her eyes fluttered open as he did. She sat up. No spinal injuries, apparently.

He grabbed her arms. She struggled. He put her in an arm lock. Firm, but careful not to harm her, careful as could be. "Let go of me!" she screamed.

"Sorry, can't," he said.

"John!" she screamed. "John, run!" But she was crying as she shouted. And Isaiah knew.

"He's dead, isn't he?" he said. A sudden sadness swelled inside him.

Serafina didn't answer. She fell to her knees. He didn't let go of her, wary of a trick but knowing it was no such thing.

John was dead.

"What happened to him?" he asked. He expected no answer. He received none. She glanced toward where he had found Melville's body. Answer enough.

"Bring her out," shouted Dominic. The man was standing outside the ring of debris, clearly worried about messing up his shoes. Isaiah counted to ten internally. He did this to calm himself. He also did it to irritate Dominic.

"Did you hear me, Isaiah?" Dominic screamed. He sounded beyond irritated. Sounded *pissed*. Which was good.

Isaiah got Serafina to her feet. Didn't force her, just helped her. She let him, moving like a stringless marionette in his arms. Whispering something under her breath.

"Pai Nosso, que estás no céu, santificado seja o Teu Nome, Venha o Teu Reino, Seja feita a Tua Vontade...."

They navigated the debris field of the church as she whispered, and the rhythms of her words captivated Isaiah. They sounded somewhat like Spanish, but not. The words...*slid*, was the description his mind came up with. The language shushed and slanted away from Spanish, though clearly Latinate in origin. Not Italian. Portuguese?

"Would you shut her *up*?" spat Dominic.

Isaiah realized that Dominic still hadn't moved, that they were standing in front of him, that Serafina hadn't even acknowledged his presence. She just kept on whispering, over and over.

"Pai Nosso, que estás no céu...."

Isaiah looked at Dominic. Rage blazed in the older man's eyes, a wrath he'd seen before and that was growing ever closer to the surface. Was this a symptom of the disease that had taken so much of the earth? Was Dominic not immune?

He suspected that must be the case. Dominic was changing. What his final form would be...that remained to be seen.

Isaiah turned to Serafina. He lifted a hand to her forehead. She flinched away, but relaxed slightly when he wiped some of the dust from her face.

He had seen her before, both in photographs and in person. But this was the first time he had seen her like this, close-up and not in flight. She was a beautiful person, even under the dust and blood. And it wasn't just beauty of body, either. He could tell it was a beauty like Katherine's: a beauty of soul. Not innocence; Serafina possessed a different kind of loveliness. But something good, praiseworthy. The kind of beauty that, in another life, Isaiah would have protected.

"...*santificado seja o Teu Nome, Venha o Teu Reino ....*"

"*SHUT HER UP!*"

Isaiah stared at Dominic. The man's hands were no longer clasped, they were fisted at his sides. His face was white, bright spots of red highlighting his cheeks.

Isaiah waited a second. A long time in this dark place. Then he turned to the beautiful woman. "Serafina. I need you to stop that. Just for a few minutes."

She kept talking, kept up what he sensed to be her prayer. Isaiah felt a dangerous build-up behind him. Wondered what Dominic would do if Serafina defied him, and didn't want to find out.

"Please," he whispered. He put his big hands on her shoulders. "There's a lot going on that you don't know about. My daughter's life is at risk, and I need your help."

He hadn't intended to say that. He meant to ask her again, to plead with her. No one knew about Katherine–no one but Dominic.

And though he had told others that he had adopted Katherine, he had never in his life called her that.

"*My daughter.*"

He almost smiled.

Serafina quieted.

"So is the life of one you love worth the deaths of so many others?" she said.

He shook his head. "It's not just–"

"We're not here for a summit meeting," broke in Dominic. "Kill her."

Isaiah spun on the man. "What's the point of–?"

"The same reasons apply. We need her body. We need the information her biology can supply."

Serafina looked like she was about to run. Isaiah put a hand on her shoulder. He tried to make it look like he was restraining her, but at the same time he squeezed lightly, as though telling her, "Wait, wait, trust, have faith."

He didn't know why he hoped she would understand or listen to the gesture. But she didn't flee.

"What if John's gone?" he said.

"She said he's dead," said Dominic.

"But you and I both know that guy's tough to kill," answered Isaiah. "What if she's wrong?"

"You didn't find him anywhere in the rubble," said Dominic. "He was crushed by that freak that came out of nowhere."

"Maybe," said Isaiah with a nod. Serafina looked like she was going to say something. He squeezed her shoulder again and she was silent. "Or maybe he got up and walked away. And if that's the case, then wouldn't it be helpful to have her as a bargaining chip? Maybe we could use her to get him to turn himself in voluntarily."

Dominic sighed. "And where do you suggest we go, to find him, Isaiah?"

"Lebanon. Kansas."

Serafina looked startled when Isaiah said that. Dominic noticed. "Why there?" he said.

Isaiah was at a loss for a moment. What could he tell Dominic? "Because an old guy met us in the fog and gave us a car with a pre-marked map to Lebanon"? Truthfully, Isaiah didn't really know why he wanted to go there, other than it was the place that popped in his head and was as good a one as any given that he mostly just wanted a chance to get Serafina away from here.

The beautiful woman at his side spoke. Her voice did not quaver, she spoke without fear. She said words that Isaiah knew were true, and he suspected that this was a woman who rarely if ever lied.

"We should go to Lebanon because that's where John was going. That's where we'll still find him if he's still alive."

Dominic stared at her, clearly shocked that she would provide this information.

Then he threw back his head and laughed into the night.

CHANCE ENCOUNTERS

From: X <xxx@xxx.xxx>
To: Dicky <dpeters@secured.whitehouse.gov>
Sent: Thursday, May 29 8:59 PM
Subject: Your Balls

As much as I despise this kind of humor, it might actually be apropos in this situation.

Get out your football and get ready to throw it. LAT. 39°50' LONG. -98°35'

I'll let you know the time.

From: POTUS <dpeters@secured.whitehouse.gov>
To: 'X' <xxx@secured.whitehouse.gov>
Sent: Friday, May 31 8:59 PM
Subject: My Balls

In the words of that great American philosopher Homer Simpson: WOOHOO!

Also, I just did that thing that I always say you do that you say you don't know what you do even though I told you you do it every time. Hint hint.

PS The toilet stopped working. Also, I would like a pizza but Im not sure Dominos will deliver down here so can you get someone to bring me a triple meatlovers asap? Signed, The Commander In Hungry.

***

The men who had been trying to kill her and John had found them both.

One of them had turned into some kind of monster and ripped John's throat out.

The other, the man clothed as a priest, had found her after the church blew apart for some reason she still didn't understand, and now seemed like he was trying to *save* her.

And this other man? She had never seen him before, and disliked him instantly. From his perfect clothes to the mirror-polished shoes on his feet to the hair that looked like it cost more to cut than she made in a month, she hated everything about him with a fervor that nearly shocked her.

He was so put together that he was an offense. Everyone in the world wanted to "have it all together," but the simple reality was that no one did. This was a world where people bounced checks, or had friends die, or left their flies open at dinner parties, or simply had to pick their noses from time to time. No one was perfect, because no*thing* was perfect. It was a fallen world, and the people in it matched that actuality.

But this man...he seemed like he had devoted his existence to proving that he *was* perfect. The exception in all things. And of course that couldn't be possible, so he would have to settle for appearances. To look this good he would have to spend every waking moment grooming, preening.

This was a man, she knew instinctively and instantly, who embodied the old saw about beauty being only skin deep.

He *was* beautiful. Stately, elegant, with a face that would have sent any used car lot owner scrambling for the new hire forms. He could probably sell snow to penguins.

And he wanted to kill her. Wanted to, but the killer dressed as a priest–Isaiah–had convinced him not to. For the moment, at least, though she had no doubt this perfect-looking man would murder her the second they had verified John's death.

John's death.

That was the thing that was strangest of all. She had seen his throat yanked out, had seen the blood pulse out and then slow and stop. She had seen him fall, then had seen the thing slam through the roof and right onto her friend.

Whatever that thing had been, it had been huge. Whatever it had been, it had landed on John.

Whatever it had been, it had killed him.

John was dead.

Hard to kill?

Yes.

Impossible to kill?

Nothing was. Not in a fallen world.

The priest had said they should go to Kansas to find John if he was still alive. She didn't know if he believed it was actually a possibility or not. But *she* knew it wasn't.

John was dead.

"Well, then," said the too-perfect man, "let's proceed posthaste, shall we?"

He gestured into the fog behind them. Serafina didn't see anything back there, but Isaiah started her walking, his hand firmly but not uncomfortably pushing her in the direction of the nothing-world behind the remains of the church.

After a while she saw something. It darkened and she worried it might be related to whatever it was that had destroyed the church and crushed whatever remained of the best man she had ever known.

It was just a truck.

"Are the keys inside?" said Isaiah as they walked. She almost asked, "How should I know?" but the other man answered.

"I believe so, yes."

Isaiah walked Serafina around to the passenger side and opened the door for her. A strange date, she thought, escorted to my death by a priest.

She wondered, madly, if she would get a corsage.

And she got in the truck. No struggle, no complaint. Not only because she didn't know where else she could run, but because she felt a strange sense of necessity in that moment. A conviction that what was happening now was happening because it must, and no other alternative was possible.

She looked at Isaiah, too. He had sad eyes. Sad and deep and kind. Real in a way that the too-perfect man's eyes could never hope to be. A man who had experienced life in all its vagaries, the caprices of a world designed not to coddle humanity but to prove its capacity to endure.

He smiled at her. The smile was sad as well. "You inside?" he asked, another strangely gallant gesture that belonged to a different era. She nodded and he closed the door.

Isaiah walked around the front of the truck, then got in. He closed his door.

"What about me?" said the other man as Isaiah started the truck.

The killer/protector grinned. His eyes were still sad, but rage and defiance also flickered in them. "You're a resourceful guy, Dominic. You'll find a way there. I'll see you in Kansas."

He pulled away before the too-perfect man could say anything. The tires spun a bit as the truck yanked itself across gravel, not fully gaining traction for a few dozen feet. Serafina looked at her sideview mirror and saw the other man, Dominic, standing in a cloud of gray that was half mist and half dust. He disappeared in both.

Isaiah bounced across the unpaved area behind the church. He was driving blind as far as she could see, but within a few hundred feet the tires thumped onto a road. He followed it to an onramp, then picked up speed as he turned onto a freeway. A sign flashed by that said I-15.

"You know the way?"

He nodded. "Someone gave me a map."

"Who?"

"Guy named Jones."

She jerked her head toward Isaiah. Could it be the same Jones? The same old man who had appeared out of nowhere and given her and John their SUV? Who had given them directions to Cedar City?

Did that mean they had all been guided to a point where they would meet? That someone had *wanted* all this to happen?

No. That's impossible. He couldn't know we'd run out of gas then, or that Isaiah and the other men would come along.

He knew that we would be where he met us in the first place.

Still, it's too crazy.

Is it? Look around.

It would be a miracle.

Sometimes miracles happen.

("Onde está a minha filha?")

"What was that?"

"What was what?"

"You said something." The priest shrugged as if embarrassed, as if he had been caught listening to her outside her window, spying on her as she dressed. "Something in another language. It was pretty."

She looked out the side window. The headlights reflected to the mist, and that in turn reflected to the glass. She saw her face. Only it wasn't hers, it was her mother's, looking for her through time.

"It was something my mom said. A long time ago."

"It was pretty," he said again.

They drove in silence.

They drove for a long time.

interlude:
POWERS

ALONE IN THE DARK

From: POTUS <dpeters@secured.whitehouse.gov>
To: 'X' <xxx@secured.whitehouse.gov>
Sent: Saturday, June 1 10:02 AM
Subject: When is the game?

I've got the football ready, but I don't know when were playing. also I don't know if we can play without the full team since they have the codes.

Captain Peters
MVP of The Final Game at the End of the WORLD!
(and the crowd GOes WIldD)

***

Richard Peters knew it had been over a day in the bunker, but time was still hazy.

Sometimes he thought the men were talking to him. Other times he thought his wife was with him. She usually screamed at him about Patricia, and that was when he knew she was dead, too, because his wife had never known about Patricia. He was certain of it. Two things he had learned from his previous indiscretions: the importance of public penance and the greater importance of private precautions. After the last girl he had completely cut off his wife's detail from his own, had agreed to her demands that they sleep in separate bedrooms, had all but divided their lives into two distinct entities.

So when she appeared and bitched him out not only about Tristi and Jennifer and Dawn and a few others but

381

also about *Patricia*, he knew she was dead. And that pissed him off because he'd asked Gill–*ordered* the man–to keep Mrs. Peters safe.

If you couldn't trust the head of your own service detail, what was the world coming to? Plus, that meant he was going to have to fire the guy. And since Gill was very likely dead along with his wife, it was going to be especially difficult to do that. He didn't know if the Senate was in charge of firing dead people or if that was an Executive Branch thing.

He'd have to ask counsel. Lawyers knew everything.

He looked at the light. The one light. The computer light. It was his only friend, the only person that didn't yell at him here in the loud bunker where the dead did nothing but scream.

"You know you could have stopped this."

That was General Lawniczak. He never yelled like the others did, but he also hadn't shut up since he blew his head off an hour after he started coughing. Blood dripped over his forehead. Down his bulbous nose, over his lips.

"You know you could have stopped this."

"Shut up."

"You could have."

Peters turned back to the computer. This was the real problem. Not the screaming, but the fact that he was supposed to play a game and he didn't have the codes. He was in the dark.

And then there was light.

He blinked, blinded for a moment by the sudden illumination. Then his vision cleared and he saw that, with the light, the dead had lain down and stopped their shouting, their accusations.

He started to cry with relief.

When he stopped he realized that someone was with him. Well, not with him, but watching him.

To get into the bunker you had to take an elevator. Hundreds of feet straight down through earth, rock, concrete, lead. Then into a corridor, also steel and lead. Then through a security checkpoint manned by a pair of Marines who had guns and no sense of humor. Retinal scans and then you were into a big box that–theoretically– could resist a direct hit by a five-megaton nuke.

There was only one way to see what was outside, and that was through a viewscreen next to the door. The door itself was sealed, and could only be opened by the retinal scans and codes of three of the men in the box. Since there was only one living person still in said box, the man didn't know how he was going to get out.

But he wasn't thinking that far ahead. Just to the game. For which he also needed those damn codes.

The viewscreen lit up. And Peters rejoiced, because he saw someone who was neither coughing nor wounded.

Nice shoes, nice suit. Nice smile.

"Dominic!" he shouted.

The man on the viewscreen smiled at the camera.

"Hello, Dicky."

If anyone else had called him this, Peters would have been upset. And, in truth, it did upset him a little that Dominic took this liberty. But only a little.

"Get me out of here, Dominic!"

"I can't, Dicky." Dominic shrugged.

"Then what am I supposed to do?" he wailed. "I'm hungry and alone and people keep yelling at me and it's *dark* in here!"

"I'm truly sorry, my boy. Truly I am. But you do know what you're supposed to do."

"Play the game?" said Peters. And suddenly, though it had been all he wanted only moments before, now he was afraid of it.

"That's right, Dicky." Dominic smiled. That perfect smile that had gained him entrance Peters' life in the first place. That had given him access, and that had gained him the man's trust.

He had gotten so much from Dominic. Information, money, power.

But what had he given?

"You know there are only two computers that work in here?" he said. "How does that happen?"

Dominic spread his hands, fingers wide. "I move in mysterious ways, my wonders to behold, Dicky. That's enough for you to know. Are you ready to play?"

"I can't play," he whispered. "I don't have the codes."

"Don't worry about that," said Dominic. He waved his hand. In the viewscreen, where there was no blood and no dead laying in clotted blood or, worse, screaming accusations that were horrible and true. Everything looked fine. Right. Hunky-dory. "I can give you the codes."

"But...I don't really think I want to play."

"Oh, Dicky," said Dominic. And suddenly the other man's eyes changed. Grew smoky and dark and deep. The man knew there were worse things than being in a box with the angry dead. "It's too late for that. You owe me."

Peters nodded.

There was nothing else he could do.

Not really.

The game would go on. Though not for long.

five:
THIS DARKNESS
LIGHT

CRUEL MERCIES

From: POTUS <dpeters@secured.whitehouse.gov>
To: FLASH, CABINET, HOUSE, SENATE, JOINTCHIEFS, PRESSCONTACTS, NATGOVASS, DNC, RNC, MAJORDONORSGROUP, ...[42 more]
Sent: Saturday, June 1 12:18 PM
Subject: Big game at my pplace!

Kay guys theres a big game at myplace be there or be square.

Time: 3:14 pm sharp–???
Pllace: You know the place
BYOB

RSVP, please. If anyone actually does the game might be called off.

***

The mist was a constant companion, but it no longer seemed strange or frightening to Isaiah. Instead it seemed like the only way life *could* be. Just a confused trip on a road you could barely see, with traveling companions you had not near enough time to know, and going somewhere you understood not at all.

Wherever they were going, he hoped he would see Katherine there. He doubted, but hoped.

This, my son, is faith. To doubt, to fear, and still to continue.

Nicholas' voice sounded in his head, and the ghostly words were a comfort. A day ago they would have pierced Isaiah, reminded him of all he had lost. Now...the loss was still there, but he also felt a measure of joy at the knowledge that Nicholas had never given up on him. That even to the end, the old man's eyes had smiled.

Nicholas was good.

Katherine was good.

He sensed this woman beside him was good.

Perhaps there were others.

Perhaps life was a thing worth living for many, even for most.

Perhaps his self-imposed penance had been something neither needed nor deserved.

The mist parted when they needed it to. They saw the turns onto the I-70, the US-24. When gas was low they turned off the freeways and there was always a car somewhere nearby. Always full of gas, always with a key in the ignition or ashtray or center console.

Serafina never tried to fight, never tried to run.

In one of the cars they found peanut butter and jelly sandwiches and a six-pack of Pepsi. They ate together. Serafina insisted on offering a prayer over the food. "Bless us Oh Lord, and these thy gifts, which we are about to receive, from thy bounty, through Christ, Our Lord. Amen."

Isaiah drove. He did not say amen, but he listened, and did not break the bread until she had finished.

They drove all night. Neither slept. Isaiah did not grow tired. He felt renewed.

Eventually Serafina asked about his outfit. He told her. Not about why he was hunting her, but about Katherine. What he had done to her, and what he had done for her since then.

He told her that Dominic and his men had her hostage, and required his servitude. He did not tell Serafina about the disease John carried, about her own part in this tragic play. That, he suspected, would come later.

He called Katherine "his daughter" again. It felt good.

Serafina said she would like to meet his daughter.

Isaiah said that he thought Katherine would like that. He meant it.

"She has beautiful blue eyes," he said. "She used to, at least. Now one's blue, one's...not so blue."

A leaden silence fell upon the car. He turned to Serafina. "You okay?" She laughed and he realized the ridiculousness of the question given their circumstances. "I'm not going to let anything happen to you if I can help it," he said, trying to sound as reassuring as possible. "I don't like Dominic any more than you do."

"I know," she said. "Just that I think...I think I *know* Katherine."

Isaiah almost drove them off the road. "What?"

"Does she have red hair? Skin so white you can almost see through it?"

Isaiah's gaze jerked to Serafina. He nodded. "How did you–?"

"I didn't put it together until you mentioned her eyes." She shrugged. "I'm a nurse in an ICU. I see a lot of patients, a lot of sad cases. But I should have remembered her." She was quiet for a long time before she looked at Isaiah. He sensed her gaze, settling on him as closely and thoroughly as the mist around them. He finally looked at her. She was smiling, a strange smile, a sad smile.

"She was my first patient," said Serafina. "I was barely able to put in an IV, and there was a staffing shortage and a scheduling screwup so I ended up wandering around in the ER. First thing I know a gurney slams through the door and there's this little girl, car accident, critical condition."

She fell silent. Isaiah couldn't speak. He wanted to, wanted to tell Serafina to be quiet, to spare him the agony of reliving that night. But he couldn't. Whatever momentary lightness of spirit he had enjoyed, whatever feeling that he no longer deserved to suffer, disappeared.

"She was beautiful. Even through the blood, the injuries. So lovely."

He had ended a girl's life. He had changed her forever.

"She was talking. When she came in."

Isaiah didn't want to know. But Serafina continued. No mercy for him. "She was singing. That 'Jesus Loves Me' song. Then she stopped. She said she was missing her favorite cartoon."

Isaiah felt a hand on his arm. He looked over. "Stop the car," said Serafina.

He did.

She took his hands in hers. "She said this, Isaiah. She said, 'The sad man saved me. They would have killed me, but he saved me from them. He took me and saved me and prayed for me and I know he'll stay with me forever.'"

Isaiah started to shake. He couldn't stop.

The words were cruel. Cutting. Hard.

And in them he found, at last, mercy.

TRAVELING COMPANIONS

From: POTUS <dpeters@secured.whitehouse.gov>
To: FLASH, CABINET, HOUSE, SENATE, JOINTCHIEFS, PRESSCONTACTS, NATGOVASS, DNC, RNC, MAJORDONORSGROUP, ...[42 more]
Sent: Saturday, June 1 1:18 PM
Subject: Big game at my pplace!

I waited and no one RSVPd. I cant do an evite because the internet doesnt work here so I cant do an evite. So your not evited. But if you want to come you still can. GAMES ON!

***

"Why have you been chasing us?"

They were almost there, and she had waited this long on purpose. Isaiah was different than she had expected. Not a rabid killer, but a man of great sadness, and one with great purpose in his life–even though at least some of that purpose appeared to be a mystery to him.

He looked at her out of the corner of his eyes. "My daughter," he said. "I already told you that–"

She shook her head. "You wouldn't do that. You wouldn't go so far to hurt so many if it was just her."

He sighed. "They said that John was some kind of soldier. That he was given a vaccine that would essentially protect him from all disease. Instead it mutated and drove him insane. He became a carrier of a deadly disease that would wipe out mankind of he wasn't stopped."

She snorted. "That's ridiculous."

"Is it?" Isaiah gestured, a whirling motion that took in everything around them. "You saw what happened to Melville–that other guy who came after you. And I've seen a lot of other people get sick, too. Some just died. Others...."

He left the sentence hanging. Didn't have to finish. They both heard the unsaid word: *changed.*

She snorted again. "No disease could cause this fog. Those weird creatures out there. And John was not insane. He had a problem with his memory, but he was about the sanest person I've ever met."

"What was wrong with his memory?"

"He couldn't remember things."

Isaiah shook his head. "Well he sure remembered enough to keep ahead of me. And not many people know enough to do that."

Serafina laughed. "Yeah, it was strange. He remembered things when they needed remembering, but then they left. He didn't know anything about who he was or what he was doing."

"So why head to Kansas?"

"He had a mission." She shrugged. "He never told me what it was, but I got the impression it was important."

"But you said he didn't remember things. Did he even know what his mission was?"

Another shrug. "I trusted him." She glared at Isaiah. "And he wasn't insane."

Isaiah thought for a while. "I believe you. Definitely more than I believe Dominic."

"So what are you going to do?"

"Same as before: go to Lebanon."

"What are you going to do there?" For a moment she felt afraid.

He patted her leg. If just about anyone else had done that she would have felt uncomfortable, invaded. But with him it was reassuring. "Nothing to you. Promise." He held up three fingers. "Scout's honor." Then he grew serious. "But we need to figure out how to stop whatever's going on. We have to find answers." And his face grew grimmer still. "And I have to find Katherine."

She nodded.

And something smashed down in the road ahead of them. A tower of darkness. A huge column coated in blinking pinlights that hung on the ends of writhing stalks.

Isaiah screamed a wordless curse. Spun the steering wheel to the side. The car fishtailed wildly.

The thing disappeared, fast as it had appeared. Nothing behind to show it had ever been there, not even a vortex to mark its movement in the mist.

"What was that?" screamed Serafina.

Isaiah didn't answer until the car stopped swerving all over the road. "I think it was the same thing that flattened the church," he said.

"No." She shook her head. "I saw that. It was maybe fifty feet wide. That thing looked like it was *hundreds* of feet across."

Isaiah didn't answer. Serafina suddenly wished her mother was there again. There like the day she had come to find a wayward daughter, had come to a crack house to rescue a girl who had run away and been shot in the back for doing so.

But she did *save me. Always there, like my guardian angel, my angel of mercy.*

Serafina had no mother to rescue her from these monsters. No one to swoop in and save her. John was gone. Darkness surrounded them.

It was just her and a man who had been trying to kill her.

And then *not* just them.

"You seeing this?"

She nodded. Didn't know if Isaiah saw the response or not. It didn't matter.

The mist was blinking. Flashes, innumerable as all the stars of the firmament, surrounded them on all sides. They twinkled and winked. They also moved, not only turning on and off but shifting left and right, forward and back, up and down.

The mist dimmed, silver to gray. Lights all around, but the shadows somehow grew stronger. The mist had brightened slightly as night had given way to day–if either could be said to exist in this new world clad eternally in fog. Now it darkened again and Serafina knew that the huge pillar she had seen in front of the car had been joined by others just like it. The writhing vines with lights at their ends that coated those towering things were all around them.

The legs walked around the car. Serafina and Isaiah were dwarfed by beings so large they had no basis for comparison. Not bigger than whales or dinosaurs or even mountains, they simply *were*, and that was all that could be said of them.

She suddenly felt that these creatures were not held to the earth by gravity. No, it was the earth that was held to them. If they left the world would spin into darkness and be lost. Or perhaps that had already happened and these creatures were simply along for the final ride.

Isaiah kept driving. What else was he to do? Serafina would have done the same in his shoes.

Answers were near. These things were accompanying them—or hounding them—to the end of the journey.

The rhythm of the car changed.

They were getting off the freeway.

"We're here," said Isaiah.

WHERE ALL ROADS LEAD

LOCAL DATE/TIME: 0601.1445
AUTH: POTUS 474653565GREEN
AUTH: CHIEF1 658989465RED
AUTH: CHIEF3 986465843RED
TargCoord: 38.8951N77.0367W
TargTime: 1914GMT
FINAL AUTH
CONTINUE?
y
ARE YOU SURE (this cannot be revoked)?
y

***

The first thing that greeted Isaiah after he left the freeway was the sign at the side of the road:

LEBANON, KANSAS
POP. 214

The sheet of metal hung askew, a single bolt keeping it from fluttering to the weeds below the support posts. The support posts themselves were wood, and Isaiah could see that someone had written something on them. He stopped the car. Just for a moment—he suspected that stopping long would not be tolerated by the massive things surrounding them, the creatures that were somehow clothed in light while at the same time shrouded in darkness—but long enough to see what was written on the wood: "*WEVE ALL GONE*" on one and "*GOD B WITH YOU*" on the other.

395

"That's not good," said Serafina.

Isaiah nodded. They drove into the town.

There was only one street. A few houses and shops on either side. A church. A city hall.

As they passed through, the dark/light things crushed down on either side of the car. Muted thunderclaps sounded as otherworldly flesh fell to earth.

The buildings were crushed. The small town in Kansas that had once held few people and now held none was trampled to dust. A ghost town that became a nothing.

Isaiah slowed the car. Was he supposed to stop here?

No. One of the monstrous things crashed down behind the car. For the first time the impact was so hard it rocked the world, slamming the car forward. Isaiah got the picture. He drove forward.

The street continued for a few miles, heading north and then veering sharply west.

Isaiah glanced at Serafina. She shrugged and shook her head. Her hand reached for his. Fingers clasped.

The road continued for nearly two miles in the darkness. Then a figure loomed. A man standing beside a sign. For some reason the sign could be seen first. The man was dark, a shadow in shadow.

The sign said, "The GEOGRAPHIC CENTER of the UNITED STATES," followed by latitude and longitude. Isaiah also saw a small building nearby. It looked like a tiny church. Just a twenty by twenty building with a cross atop it. Someplace for people to rest and meditate and pray.

The shadows around the figure drew back like folds of a cloak as Isaiah pulled up beside the sign. The man leaned down and gestured for Isaiah to roll down his window.

"Hello, Isaiah," said Dominic. He shifted his gaze to Serafina. Winked. The wink wasn't aimed at Isaiah but it still made him feel dirty. "Hello, my dear."

For some reason Isaiah wasn't in the least surprised to see that Dominic was here, or that he had somehow arrived before them.

"I've done what you asked," Isaiah said. "John's dead, Serafina's here." He squeezed her hand. Hoped she would know that he still intended to protect her.

But he had to know.

"Where's Katherine?" he asked. And his voice choked.

Dominic shrugged. "Who knows?" he said. "I lost track of her almost immediately." He looked up at the sky as though searching for answers in stars that could not be seen. "I can keep track of most people, but a few fall into my blind spots."

Isaiah swallowed a knot that tried to claw its way up his throat. His control threatened to crack in a way it hadn't for years.

"But...I heard her. I heard her. I *know* it was her." He looked at Serafina. She appeared stricken, though she had only seen Katherine years ago and knew her not at all. "She sang to me," he whispered.

Dominic leaned in close. Almost through the open window. His mouth gaped and a pure song came out. "*Jesus love me, this I know....*" The voice wasn't his. Not the perfectly-enunciated baritone of a man of power. It was the lisping sound of a child. The halting tones of innocence.

He smiled at Isaiah's confusion. Spoke again, and his voice changed once more. "I can speak with many voices, Isaiah," he said in a woman's voice. And Isaiah recognized it as one of those he had heard on the phone, one of those he had spoken to in order to ask for cars, ammunition.

"Many voices, indeed," said Dominic. And this time the voice Isaiah heard was the most terrifying and terrible. This time it was his own.

Isaiah resisted the urge to shrink back. "What are you?" he said. But he feared he knew. "You're the Dev–"

Dominic shook his head and waved. "No, no, nothing so grand, my boy." He looked up again. Dark towers draped in flashing lights moved around them. They were ringed in now. Trapped. "Things have certainly gotten interesting these last few hours, haven't they?"

The thundering monsters came to rest. Solid walls of flesh that joined at the edges and became mountains that went up forever. It was just Dominic, Serafina, Isaiah, the small chapel, and the sign that marked the center of a country that had ceased to exist.

And then the light.

RESTORATIONS

From: POTUS <dpeters@secured.whitehouse.gov>
To: 'X' <xxx@secured.whitehouse.gov>
Sent: Saturday, June 1 3:12 PM
Subject: Last Message

I know where I am. I figured out who you are, and that helped. It made it obvious.

Do you know how I finally figured it out? It wasn't the things you shouldn't know or the deals you helped me make or how good you still look after all these years. It wasn't even the fact that I've had access to a single line of communication–these emails–even when everything else has shut down, and so could talk to you if needed.

It was the times.

I looked through all our archived communications. And even though all your personal information is encrypted and impossible to trace (a trick that always had my security people chewing the walls in frustration), there is one thing that you left alone: the time stamp.

In all the years we've been communicating like this, all the hundreds and thousands of emails, you always answered immediately. Not quickly, *instantly*. If you deigned to reply, it came back within the same minute. It didn't matter if it was one line or ten pages, the response was always that fast.

I never noticed that. Perhaps I never wanted to notice it.

I feel better. More aware of what has happened, and what my part has been. Though I suspect this sanity and awareness are simply provided so that I can better suffer at your hands. That seems to be your style.

I suspect you will not respond to this email. Because I've already done my work and served my purposes for you. But I wanted you to know that I figured you out. I figured out that I was nothing to you. You used me, the way I hoped to use you, and joke's on me for that.

Joke's on us all.

***

The light seemed to come from everywhere and nowhere at once. It blanketed Serafina just as completely as the mist had ever done, but with a far greater power. She closed her eyes and still saw it, white and pink sheets of brightness that caused fires to erupt in her mind.

She suddenly remembered John, saving her.

Herself, saving John.

All the people she had ever watched over in the hospital, especially the ones who died.

The look on her mother's face as she died outside the crack house. The smile.

The fires died. The light dimmed.

She opened her eyes.

Isaiah was staring. "Katherine!" he screamed. Then he threw his door open and tried to get out of the car so fast his limbs tangled up in one another and he ended up sprawled in the dirt at Dominic's feet. The man danced back and laughed.

Isaiah didn't seem to notice. He only noticed the girl who had come from–where?–and was now standing in front of the car.

Katherine.

Serafina knew it was her. Would have known even without Isaiah's reaction. The red hair, that skin so white. Even in a child they had been stunning, and now in a teenager they were more so. And the eyes…so blue.

Both blue.

That was wrong.

Serafina felt herself getting out of the car as well, watching as Isaiah stumbled toward his daughter. Dominic's laughter danced around them with malicious glee.

The eyes were both blue. Both clear. The clouding Serafina remembered was gone, as was the dreadful dip she had seen in the side of the girl's head. Katherine was whole and strong, and *standing*. Even if her brain and spine had been capable, her muscles shouldn't have been up to that.

But she was tall, straight. Dressed in blue jeans and a white shirt, unadorned but looking for all the world like a…a…. Serafina's mind rejected word after word before coming up with the only two that fit.

Queen.

Angel.

Isaiah stopped in front of her. He didn't touch his daughter. Serafina ached for him as she realized he wouldn't; that even now he still held himself responsible for every ill she had suffered. Even now he had not forgiven.

Katherine just looked at her adoptive father. Dominic's laughter grew louder, more jagged, and Serafina had the feeling that this was the moment they had all come for. This was the moment the world hinged upon.

The laughter spiked. Serafina wanted to punch the man in the face.

Isaiah fell to his knees in front of his daughter. He sobbed.

Say something, Isaiah. Say something!

She couldn't speak. The world was utterly still. The only sound was Dominic's cackling, an obscenity thrusting itself into what should be a holy moment.

Isaiah reached out a hand. His head was bowed. "Forgive me," he whispered.

Dominic's laughter stopped. Just ceased like he was a toy whose batteries had been yanked out.

Katherine shook her head. "I never will."

Isaiah sobbed again. Serafina felt her heart drop. She also realized something was behind her. A new presence. But she couldn't look.

Dominic began laughing again.

Katherine took her father's hand. "Only you can forgive yourself. I never will, because you haven't done anything that needs forgiving. You have none of my forgiveness, only my love."

The presence behind Serafina moved. She felt a hand on her shoulder. "Go to them," said a voice she knew. She did. Turning her head as she went to make sure she hadn't been mistaken.

John moved to stand beside Dominic. The older man's laughter ended. Slower this time, not a sudden cease but a slow ebbing to nothing. The end of Dominic's laughter was not dramatic or powerful, just weak and wheezing.

"You never should have done this," said John. "You never should have tried to stop what had to be done."

Dominic snarled. "Nothing *has* to be done. That's your side's line, not mine." He stepped back from John, mouth curled in disgust.

Serafina saw Isaiah looking from one man to the other. "I don't know what's happening," he murmured. Serafina could sympathize.

"Leave," said John. A single word, quietly stated, but it felt like a lightning strike. A shattering instant of power, and all of it focused on Dominic.

The man wilted. He seemed to *fade* from Serafina's sight.

Then his outlines firmed. "I figured out what you want for them," he said. "Do you think I'm *stupid*? But I've made plans. Plans and backup plans and backup plans for my backup plans." He grinned and made a show of looking at his watch, then winked at Serafina. It made her feel like roaches were crawling over her eyes. "You know what time it is in Washington, D.C.? It's the end of the world, and we're at ground zero, baby. I'm taking you out–taking you all out. *NOW*."

Dominic looked up at the sky.

And nothing happened.

FROM DARKNESS LIGHT

From: POTUS <dpeters@secured.whitehouse.gov>
To: 'X' <xxx@secured.whitehouse.gov>
Sent: Saturday, June 1 3:14 PM
Subject: (REAL) Last Message

Forgot to mention: I didn't set the nukes for Kansas. I set them for here. Figured it'd be a better way to go than sitting with a bunch of dead men and ghosts.

So…joke's on you, Dominic. I'll see you soon.

***

Isaiah watched it all, and it jumbled together in a mix that made no sense at all.

Katherine: alive and well and *whole*.

John: also alive, and apparently he knew Dominic and was not afraid of him.

Dominic: throwing a fit like a spoiled toddler who has been banned from the world's biggest candy store.

The only thing he felt he understood was Serafina. She had rushed to his side, held his arm. She was, like Katherine, good. She was flesh and blood and the goodness of humanity. Something that he could hold onto not just for support but for hope.

John laughed. Unlike Dominic's laugh, this one was a deep belly laugh that seemed to part the mists and allow more of that sourceless brightness among them.

"I think it's time for you to leave," he said.

"I don't *want* to," Dominic yowled.

Isaiah strode forward. Gripped by sudden anger. "You heard the man," he said. He reached for Dominic's shoulder, intent not just on removing the man, but killing him.

He had sworn to do it, after all. And where justice was concerned, he had always been a man of his word.

His fingers came down on Dominic's expensive suit. Closed. And grabbed...

...nothing.

Isaiah looked at his hand, a fist that had nothing but air in its grasp. He reached for Dominic again, and again when he clutched at the man, he came up empty.

Dominic laughed again. Not the harsh laughter of before, but a mad, jittery giggle. Isaiah thought of a child he had once saved, one whose father had beaten and raped him with dreadful regularity. The boy had sometimes laughed like this.

So had the father.

Dominic danced. His clothes, so immaculate, so perfect, were suddenly dusty and dark. "You can't catch me," he said.

"No, they can't," said John. He looked at Isaiah. "Go back to your family," he said. When Isaiah hesitated, he added, "Please."

Isaiah nodded, and was already holding Katherine in one arm and Serafina under the other before he realized what John had said.

Your family.

John stared at Dominic. He raised his right hand. Brought it down.

Darkness fell. Fast and full, a velvet curtain cut from blackest night. The everywhere light that had illuminated the fog was gone, as were the millions of blinking lights on the monstrous things all around them.

Beside Isaiah, Serafina screamed in surprise and terror.

Katherine was silent. She squeezed his hand. He didn't think it was fear, but rather that she was trying to give him courage. He was thankful.

The light returned.

John still stood nearby, but where Dominic had been there was only a dark-stained patch on the ground.

The fog remained, but it was growing brighter. Thinner. Light–real light, natural light–seemed to be pushing through.

"Who are you?" said Serafina.

John didn't answer for a while. Then he walked toward them. "Every once in a while things grow so good and so bad that it's better to start over. I was sent to do that."

"So you weren't a soldier?" said Isaiah. It was as much statement as question. John surprised him.

"Oh, I am a soldier. Dominic told the truth about that. He and others like him always tell as much truth as they can–it's easier to lie with half-truths."

"But why couldn't you tell me this before?" said Serafina. "Why did you pretend not to know?"

"I wasn't pretending," said John. "Before I and the others like me came here we gave away our memories for a time."

"Why?"

"Because if we knew what we were doing it would have been too hard. We loved you all too much to do what had to be done." He swallowed, and his eyes were suddenly grave, the eyes of someone who not only knew sorrow but knew he had caused it. "I didn't know what I was here for, but I knew I had to get to this place at this time. Part of that was to bring you all here, and bring you together. But part of it was because I really did carry–and was spreading–a disease meant to end the world."

"I don't understand," said Isaiah. "Was this because of a vaccine that went wrong, or–?"

"No. There was never a vaccine. That was a story invented by very bad people at the service of evil masters to try and stop me and the others like me. We came as destroyers. That was always the intent. To destroy most, and spare only those who were most worthy to start anew. Those who hunted us just ended up helping as they forced us to run from place to place." A sad smile touched his face. "Foolish to hunt what can't be killed."

Isaiah reeled with the implications of that remark. He would have demanded more, but Serafina said, "But you bled. You almost died. Several times."

John shook his head. "There is a difference between a feint and a loss. Things had to happen: you both had to come together. You both had to learn some things. Katherine had to be found and saved. Everything we did and everything we suffered–including my injuries–was in service of that."

"So there was no control," said Isaiah. He was surprised how bitter he felt. "We were just puppets."

"Hardly. Puppets just dance. They don't feel the strings, they don't feel joy or pain. You were more trees. Cut occasionally, pruned into a direction meant to grant you more light and better growth and longer life. Does the tree give up its growth when cared for? No. Does the student give up his agency when given homework that will bend him to a test and then to later knowledge? Never. You both had to change, and the path was laid out for you. But the decisions were always yours, as they will continue to be in the life you make together."

Serafina gasped. Her hand flew to her mouth and she looked at Isaiah with an expression of fear and wonder. John touched her cheek. "*Onde está a minha filha?*" he said. Isaiah didn't understand the words, but he felt Serafina start trembling. More so when John continued, "*Ela espera por você ainda.*" Then she was weeping as he finished, "You have always been a good daughter. She loves you."

"I know," said Serafina.

John turned to Isaiah. "You hold at your side a woman born of an act of mercy, who then became a woman of mercy herself," he said, gesturing to Serafina. "A woman who has devoted herself to caring for those who cannot care for themselves." His gaze grew piercing. "You don't have that quality, do you?"

"No," said Isaiah. Shame burned his cheeks.

"But you do understand justice. Mercy and justice are good things to have together. They balance one another." John put a hand on Serafina's shoulder, another on Isaiah's. "Take care of Katherine. She's special."

The fog continued to clear. Blue sky appeared. A day like any other. But new.

"How many others are left?" said Isaiah.

John's shoulders sagged a bit. "Not many. My brothers claimed the souls of the wicked, twined them together so they became great beasts that they chained and now we will drive to the abyss, to places from which they can never again escape." Then he straightened, and managed a smile. "But there are a few left. The good remain, immune to the disease we brought, unafraid of the future they face."

"Some of the good died," said Isaiah, thinking of Jim/Jack Jones, thinking of the young gang member who died dragging children from a collapsing building.

"Everyone does, eventually," said John. "But life is one part, death another. Just steps in a process, and neither one the last or even the most important." He winked. "Nicholas would tell you the same, and will again, I suspect."

He opened the door to the chapel. Stepped inside.

"Wait!" said Serafina. John stopped. Waiting. "Are we safe? I mean...Dominic...."

John shook his head. "There are girls and boys like Katherine, children so good and pure they are the hope of a new world. Children upon whom we place the great responsibility of a world born free of evil. They're everywhere, on every continent, just as there were people like me in every part of the world...and people like the ones who tried to stop us."

John knelt before Katherine. "The children are strong. They've all been through great tragedy and survived and been unbroken in spirit or heart. But we give them to you. To people who will nurture...and who will protect. Because Dominic–though that's not his real name, as I'm sure you know by now–is never completely gone. We cast him out, but he and his master are sly serpents, crafty and cunning. They always find their way back in." Another smile. "Still, we manage. We always do."

Another step and he was fully inside the tiny chapel. Isaiah saw that there were only a few pews inside. A cross. John started to swing the door shut.

"Hold on!" shouted Isaiah.

John rolled his eyes as though annoyed, but his smile hadn't faded. "Yes, Isaiah?"

"Dominic wasn't that guy's real name. What's yours?"

John's grin widened. "You'll have to ask me again next time you see me. We can chat over a game of cribbage– I know a guy who's looking for people to play with."

He shut the door.

No one moved to open it. Isaiah knew there would be nothing inside if they did.

The last of the mist blew away. It left traces of moisture in the air, that clean smell that comes after a rainfall that drags away the smog and dirt that lays like a subtle blanket over everything.

Katherine looked up with eyes that were both bluer than any sky. He would watch her and protect her until she was old enough for those eyes to watch over him.

The world had ended.

The world was beginning.

Life and death were just steps, after all. And neither of them the most important ones in the process.

The new family got in the truck. It started without complaint and they drove away. Looking for others, the good who were left and who would help them start again, and do better.

Isaiah drove. Serafina navigated. Justice driving them forward, mercy deciding the course to take.

And sheltered between justice and mercy: innocence, the little child who would be the balance of both. Who would grow in a world where life was important, and so was death...but where neither was all, or even the most important thing.

Isaiah put his arm around the girls. There was love in the car. And with that love there was hope, and joy, and a new world of unlimited possibility.

"What's cribbage?" said Katherine, her voice still small and so lovely that it wrung great laughs from Isaiah.

"I'll show you," he said. More laughter as he drove, turning onto a freeway and knowing that wherever they went they would find what they needed. "I'll teach you both and we can all play together."

"Promise?"

"Promise."

He laughed again. So did Katherine. Serafina joined in. They drove and laughed, and when at last they stopped laughing the smiles remained, and never fully left their faces.

Justice.

Mercy.

Innocence.

And together: joy.

A REQUEST FROM THE AUTHOR:

If you loved this book, **I would really appreciate a short review on the page where you bought the book**. Ebook retailers factor reviews into account when deciding which books to push, so a review by you will ABSOLUTELY make a difference to this book, and help other people find it.

And that matters, since that's how I keep writing and (more important) take care of my family. So please drop a quick review – even "Book good. Me like words in book. More words!" is fine and dandy, if that's what's in your heart.

And thanks again!

*

HOW TO GET YOUR FREE BOOK:

As promised, here's a goodie for you: sign up for Michaelbrent's newsletter and you'll get a free book (or maybe more!) with nothing ever to do or buy. Just go to http://eepurl.com/VHuvX to sign up for your freebie, and you're good to go!

*

FOR WRITERS:

Michaelbrent has helped hundreds of people write, publish, and market their books through articles, audio, video, and online courses. For his online courses, check out http://michaelbrentcollings.thinkific.com

*

ABOUT THE AUTHOR

Michaelbrent is an internationally-bestselling author, produced screenwriter, and member of the Writers

Guild of America, but his greatest jobs are being a husband and father. See a complete list of Michaelbrent's books at writteninsomnia.com.

*

FOLLOW MICHAELBRENT
Twitter: twitter.com/mbcollings
Facebook: facebook.com/MichaelbrentCollings

NOVELS BY MICHAELBRENT COLLINGS

PREDATORS
THE DARKLIGHTS
THE LONGEST CON
THE HOUSE THAT DEATH BUILT
THE DEEP
TWISTED
THIS DARKNESS LIGHT
CRIME SEEN
STRANGERS
DARKBOUND
BLOOD RELATIONS:
    A GOOD MORMON GIRL MYSTERY
THE HAUNTED
APPARITION
THE LOON
MR. GRAY (aka THE MERIDIANS)
RUN
RISING FEARS

THE COLONY SAGA:
THE COLONY: GENESIS (THE COLONY, Vol. 1)
THE COLONY: RENEGADES (THE COLONY, Vol. 2)
THE COLONY: DESCENT (THE COLONY, VOL. 3)
THE COLONY: VELOCITY (THE COLONY, VOL. 4)
THE COLONY: SHIFT (THE COLONY, VOL. 5)
THE COLONY: BURIED (THE COLONY, VOL. 6)
THE COLONY: RECKONING (THE COLONY, VOL. 7)
THE COLONY OMNIBUS
THE COLONY OMNIBUS II
THE COMPLETE COLONY SAGA BOX SET

YOUNG ADULT AND
MIDDLE GRADE FICTION:

THE SWORD CHRONICLES
THE SWORD CHRONICLES: CHILD OF THE EMPIRE
THE SWORD CHRONICLES: CHILD OF SORROWS
THE SWORD CHRONICLES: CHILD OF ASH

THE RIDEALONG
PETER & WENDY: A TALE OF THE LOST
    (aka HOOKED: A TRUE FAERIE TALE)
KILLING TIME

THE BILLY SAGA:
BILLY: MESSENGER OF POWERS (BOOK 1)
BILLY: SEEKER OF POWERS (BOOK 2)
BILLY: DESTROYER OF POWERS (BOOK 3)
THE COMPLETE BILLY SAGA (BOOKS 1-3)

PRAISE FOR THE WORK OF
MICHAELBRENT COLLINGS

"Epic fantasy meets superheroes, with lots of action and great characters.... Collings is a great storyteller." - Larry Correia, New York Times bestselling author of *Monster Hunter International* and *Son of the Black Sword*

"... intense... one slice of action after another... a great book and what looks to be an interesting start of a series that could be amazing." - Game Industry News

"Collings is so proficient at what he does, he crooks his finger to get you inside his world and before you know it, you are along for the ride. You don't even see it coming; he is that good." – *Only Five Star Book Reviews*

"What a ride.... This is one you will not be able to put down and one you will remember for a long time to come. Very highly recommended." – *Midwest Book Review*

"I would be remiss if I didn't say he's done it again. Twists and turns, and an out-come that will leave one saying, 'I so did not see that coming.'" – *Audiobook Reviewer*

"His prose is brilliant, his writing is visceral and violent, dark and enthralling." – *InD'Tale Magazine*

"I literally found my heart racing as I zoomed through each chapter to get to the next page." – *Media Mikes*

Copyright © 2019 by Michaelbrent Collings
All rights reserved.
No part of this book may be reproduced or transmitted in any form or by any means, electronic or mechanical, including photocopying, recording, or by any information storage and retrieval system, without written permission from the author. For information send request to info@michaelbrentcollings.com.
NOTE: This is a work of fiction. Names, characters, places, and incidents either are the product of the author's imagination or are used fictitiously, and any resemblance to actual persons, living or dead, business establishments, events, or locales is entirely coincidental. The scanning, uploading, and distribution of this book via the internet or via any other means without the permission of the author is illegal and punishable by law. Please purchase only authorized electronic editions, and do not participate in or encourage electronic piracy of copyrighted materials. Your support of the author's rights is appreciated.
Cover image element by Justin Hamilton from Pexels and Vladimir Melnikov and vladibulgakov under license by Shutterstock.
Cover design by Michaelbrent Collings.
website: http://www.michaelbrentcollings.com
email: info@michaelbrentcollings.com

For more information on Michaelbrent's books, including specials and sales; and for info about signings, appearances, and media,
check out his webpage,
Like his Facebook fanpage
or
Follow him on Twitter.

Made in the USA
Middletown, DE
19 December 2019

81460764R10255